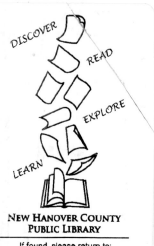

the Crimson Skew

BOOKS BY S. E. GROVE

MAPMAKERS
The Glass Sentence
The Golden Specific
The Crimson Skew

the Crimson Skew

MAPMAKERS

BOOK THREE

S. E. Grove

VIKING

VIKING

An imprint of Penguin Random House LLC

375 Hudson Street

New York, New York 10014

First published in the United States of America by Viking,
an imprint of Penguin Random House LLC, 2016

LIBRARY OF CONGRESS CATALOGING-IN-PUBLICATION DATA IS AVAILABLE
ISBN: 9780670785049

Printed in the USA

1   3   5   7   9   10   8   6   4   2

Designed by Jim Hoover   Set in Albertina MT Std

For Rowan

At that time I had three children who went with me on foot, one who rode on horse back, and one whom I carried on my back.

Our corn was good that year; a part of which we had gathered and secured for winter.

In one or two days after the skirmish at Connissius lake, Sullivan and his army arrived at Genesee river, where they destroyed every article of the food kind that they could lay their hands on. A part of the corn they burnt, and threw the remainder in the river. They burnt our houses, killed what few cattle and horses they could find, destroyed our fruit trees, and left nothing but the bare soil and timber. But the Indians had eloped and were not to be found.

Having crossed and recrossed the river, and finished the work of destruction, the army marched off to the east. Our Indians saw them move off, but suspecting that it was Sullivan's intention to watch our return, and then to take us by surprize, resolved that the main body of our tribe should hunt where we then were, till Sullivan had gone so far that there would be no danger of his returning to molest us.

This being agreed to, we hunted continually till the Indians concluded that there could be no risk in our once more taking possession of our lands. Accordingly we all returned; but what were our feelings when we found that there was not a mouthful of any kind of sustenance left, not even enough to keep a child one day from perishing without hunger.

The weather by this time had become cold and stormy; and as we were destitute of houses and food too, I immediately resolved to take my children and look out for myself, without delay.

—Dehgewärnis (Mary Jemison of the Seneca), 1779

Contents

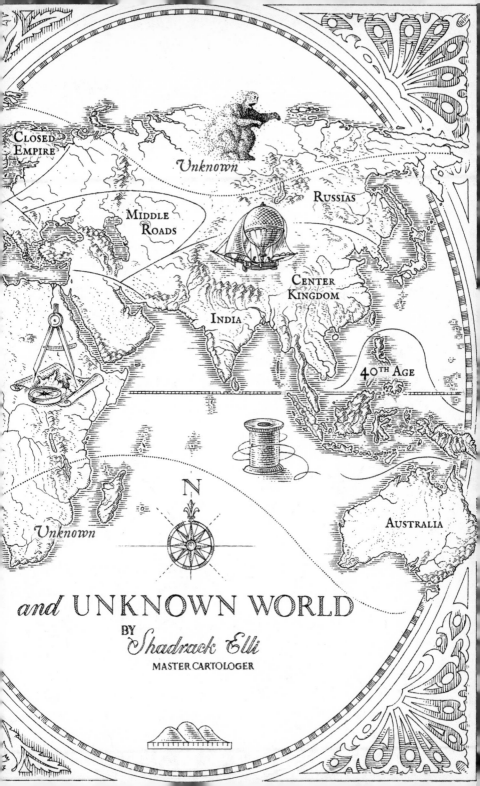

CLOSED
EMPIRE

Unknown

RUSSIAS

MIDDLE
ROADS

CENTER
KINGDOM

INDIA

40TH AGE

Unknown

N

AUSTRALIA

and UNKNOWN WORLD

BY *Shadrack Elli*

MASTER CARTOLOGER

NEW *Occident*

Indian
Territories

The Baldlands

N

e

BY
Shadrack Elli
MASTER CARTOLOGER

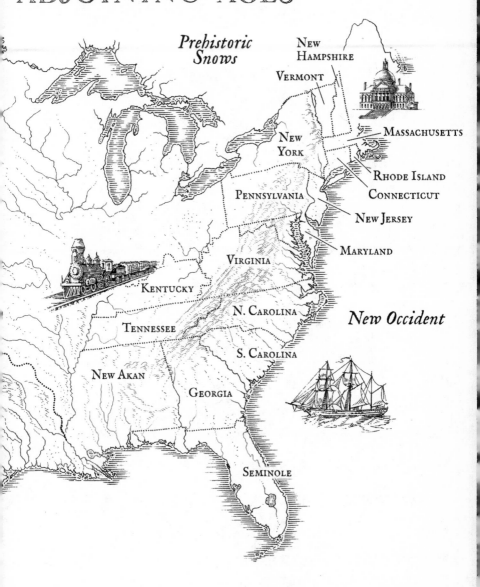

and ITS ADJOINING AGES

Prehistoric Snows

New Hampshire

Vermont

New York

Massachusetts

Rhode Island
Connecticut
New Jersey

Pennsylvania

Maryland

Virginia

Kentucky

N. Carolina

New Occident

Tennessee

S. Carolina

New Akan

Georgia

Seminole

THE EERIE SEA
AND ITS ENVIRONS

EERIE

Indian
Territories

N

SALT LICK

You will understand that our priority was to prevent the advance of the Glacine Age and save our own skins—I could not indulge my inquisitive nature as I usually do. So what did we learn? We knew that Blanca, the Lachrima who had held me captive, relied upon Nihilismian recruits to do her work. We knew that Blanca altered their minds and took many of their memories with the hourglass device, a horror I had seen at work firsthand. We knew that the Sandmen, as she called them, were loyal to her, and I suspected that they were drawn to her in the first place because they perceived in her grand vision for the world a way to return to the Age of Verity. They imagined, as she did, that the consequences of the Great Disruption could somehow be reversed. But our questions outnumbered and still outnumber our answers. How did she find and recruit Sandmen? What Ages did they come from? And, most vitally, what would they do now that Blanca was gone? Would they retreat and disappear from sight? Or would they reemerge to pursue some greater, perhaps even more terrible purpose?

—From Shadrack Elli's private reports to Prime Minister Cyril Bligh

Prologue

July 23, 1892

Dear Shadrack,

The foul weather in the Territories has continued. The heavy clouds, motionless and low, seem now to be a permanent fixture. I cannot remember when we last saw the sun. But now things have taken a turn for the worse. Something has happened this day that I have never seen before and that cannot be explained. I scarcely trust myself to describe it. Let me tell you how it happened.

I awoke in the middle of the night to a commotion at my door. A woman I know from the nearby town of Pear Tree stood there. Esther had a look about her that I have seen only once before, on the face of a man who fled and outran a forest fire: grief, disbelief, and confusion swirled in her eyes. She seemed unsure of whether she was among the living or the dead. "Casper?" she whispered. "Is it you?"

I told her it was. I did not understand the tale she related to me, and it had to be repeated many times. Even when I finally understood her words, I still could not make sense of them.

She said it had started in the evening, a while still before sunset, for there was yet light enough to see. She had been taking the children's clothing down from the drying line when she saw a red vapor spilling over the stone wall of her garden. Wondering what it was, she watched the strange substance approach until it rose and swelled, immersing her and the clothesline, obscuring even her house from view. For a time she stood, waiting anxiously. She realized the vapor smelled sweet, like a flower. Then the smell changed. It grew foul—like rotting meat.

She heard a distant scream, and the sound filled her with panic. Fighting through the fog, she burst into the house. She found the crimson vapor clogging every room and passageway, and the panic rose to terror. Calling for her children, she made her way through the house half-blind. Then she saw the intruders: three giant rats as large as full-grown men, their black eyes cruel, their yellowed teeth sharp. Seizing a knife from the kitchen, she chased them through the house, fearing what they would do or had done to her children. The rats closeted themselves in the pantry and hissed at her through the door.

She could not find her children anywhere.

She called for them with growing desperation, finally stumbling outside. Then she realized that her own cries were being echoed by others everywhere, in every house of Pear Tree. The entire town blazed with panic. Something tugged at her mind, some uncertainty, but she could not place it. She knew only that something was not right.

It is the fog, she finally realized. I am confused, and it began with the fog.

She found her way along the road, though the sounds on either side were terrifying. When she finally made her way out of Pear Tree, darkness had fallen. She could tell that she had left the fog behind, because her mind began to clear. Looking back upon the town, she could see nothing in the settled darkness, but she heard ceaseless screams and shouts. The impulse to turn back and seek her children warred with the impulse to seek help elsewhere. Uncertainly, still confused by what she had seen, she came here and woke me in the dead of night.

I assembled all the council and within the hour we were on the road to Pear Tree. We arrived just as the gray day was dawning, putrid and damp as every day has been all this month. The crimson fog had passed, but it had left its mark in more ways than one. A thin sediment of the purest red coated every surface: the stone wall surrounding Pear Tree, the leaves of every tree, the roof of every house, the surface of every path and road. As we made our way slowly into the silent town, we saw what else the fog had left behind: the human wreckage.

The first thing we saw was a man sitting on his front step, holding a woman's laced boot. When we spoke to him, he ignored us entirely. I approached and asked if he was hurt. Finally he turned his eyes to me and held up the boot, saying, "Wolves don't wear shoes." He seemed stunned by his own statement. We could gain nothing more from him.

Some of the houses and barns had been burned with their occupants. The smell was unbearable. Many houses that stood intact had doors ominously ajar, and I caught glimpses of broken furniture, torn curtains, shattered windows.

I will not describe it further, Shadrack, for it is too horrible, but I believe in those few hours half the lives of Pear Tree were lost.

We returned to Esther's home. She was shocked, of course—shocked into silence and shaking beside me as we walked. "There is something," she said, her voice breaking, as we neared her house. "There is something I do not understand."

"There is much that I do not understand," I said.

"How," she went on, as if I had not spoken, "how were the rats able to barricade the door to the pantry?"

I confess that I did not take her meaning. It seemed a pointless question in the midst of such a catastrophe. No doubt the truth had begun to dawn on her before I saw even the faintest glimmer of it. But when we reached her house I understood. Hurrying, anxious with her sudden doubt, she rushed in and made her way to the pantry door. She knocked upon it urgently. "Open the door," she sobbed. "Open the door, I beg you."

There was a scuffle, and we heard heavy things shifted aside one by one. The door opened a crack and Esther's three children peered out at us, their eyes wide with fear.

It is a distortion, Shadrack, a skewed perception that changes the reality before you into something dreadful. The survivors who could assemble their thoughts described to us different visions—all terrifying. There were no intruders, no monsters. The fog caused the people of Pear Tree to turn upon themselves.

If this is done by human hand, it is the cruelest act I have yet to see. If it is done by nature, it is no less frightening. I ask you: What is this? Is it part and parcel of the weather that plagues us, or is it something unrelated? Has it happened only in Pear Tree, or elsewhere, too? Please—tell me what you know.

(This will be given to Entwhistle, as you asked. Instruct me if I should do otherwise in future.)

Yours,
Casper Bearing

PART I

Clouds

1
HISPANIOLA

—1892, August 2: 7-Hour 20—

Though the United Indies makes a legal distinction between merchants and pirates, safeguarding the privileges of the one while prosecuting (on occasion) the crimes of the other, in practice they are almost indistinguishable. Both hold property in the Indies— sometimes lavish property. Both exert considerable influence on the Indies' government. Both enjoy access to the seas and trade with foreign Ages. Indeed, it is, for the outsider, difficult to see where merchants end and pirates begin.

—From Shadrack Elli's History of the New World

SOPHIA AWOKE TO the sound of a woman singing. The voice was low and languid and sweet, as if the singer had all the time in the world; it sang of mermaids and silvery stars and moonbeams shining on the sea. It took Sophia a moment to remember where she was: Calixta and Burton Morris's estate on Hispaniola.

With a sigh of contentment, Sophia stretched against the soft sheets. She lay in bed with her eyes closed, listening to Calixta singing in the neighboring room as she brushed her hair and dressed. Suddenly the song was interrupted by a shout of dismay and a thump, as if from a booted foot striking a trunk. *"Where are my tortoiseshell combs?"* Calixta wailed.

Sophia opened her eyes and smiled. Splinters of light were pushing their way into the dark room. As the protests next door became fervent curses, she got out of bed and opened the tall wooden shutters, revealing a small balcony. The sunlight of Hispaniola was blinding. Sophia shielded her eyes until they adjusted, and then she caught her breath with delight at the sight before her: the grounds of the estate and, beyond the grounds, the shining ocean. Marble steps led down to a long lawn bordered by bougainvillea, jasmine, and birds-of-paradise. A straight path paved in white stone cut through the lawn to the beach. The *Swan*, anchored at the private dock, bobbed serenely on the sparkling waters.

"Sophia!" Calixta called. Sophia reluctantly made her way back into the bedroom, where Calixta stood holding what appeared to be a billowing curtain in a shocking shade of fuchsia. "Look what I found," she declared triumphantly. "This will fit you perfectly!"

"What is it?" Sophia asked dubiously.

"Only the finest silk New Orleans has to offer," Calixta exclaimed. "Try it on."

"Now?"

"It's midmorning, you lazy thing! We have plans to make and people to see, and I insist you be well dressed for it."

"Very well," Sophia replied agreeably. *Of course Calixta already has plans made,* she said to herself, *and of course she already has outfits chosen for everyone as part of those plans.* Sophia had found on the voyage from Seville, across the Atlantic, that it was almost always better to let the pirate captain have her way.

She slipped out of her nightgown and let Calixta help her into the silk dress, which was indeed beautiful. Sophia examined herself skeptically in the tall standing mirror beside the bed. "I look like a little girl impersonating the famous pirate Calixta Morris. And I can barely breathe." She reached for the shoulder strap. "I'm taking it off."

Calixta laughed. "No, you're not! We'll do your hair properly and get you stockings and shoes. A little powder and orange-flower water. That's all." She gave Sophia a quick kiss on the cheek. "And you're not a little girl anymore, sweetheart." She turned to the doorway. "Yes, Millie?"

A maid wearing a black-and-white uniform stood in the doorway. "Will you want breakfast here or downstairs, Captain Morris?"

"Have the others woken?"

"They are all downstairs, Captain, except for your brother."

"Still snoring soundly, no doubt," Calixta muttered. "We'll join the others downstairs, Millie—thank you."

Millie left the room with a brief nod.

"Let me just get my things," Sophia said, moving to gather her satchel.

Calixta stopped her, taking her hand. "You're safe here, Sophia," she said. "Our home is yours, and you have nothing to fear. We won't have to bolt at a moment's notice. You can leave your things in your bedroom."

Sophia pressed Calixta's hand. "I know. Thank you. Let me find my watch."

Damask curtains, gilded mirrors, and delicate furniture upholstered in cream and blue: Calixta's hand lay behind the effortless luxury. Sophia's pack, satchel, books, and clothes—gray and worn from two Atlantic crossings and a perilous journey through the Papal States—made a dirty pile that seemed to have no place in the sumptuous room. "Got it!" She tucked the watch into a hidden pocket of the fuchsia dress.

"Down we go, then," Calixta said. Not to be outdone by the fuchsia, she was wearing a lemon-colored silk with gold trim. She trailed a hand along the polished banister as they descended the wide marble steps to the main floor.

Their travel companions were in the comfortable breakfast room. Sitting side by side on a white couch beside the windows, Errol Forsyth, a falconer from the Closed Empire, and Goldenrod, an Eerie from the edges of the Prehistoric Snows, looked out at the ocean with rather dazed expressions. Sophia thought to herself, not without amusement, that they seemed just as out of place in the gilded mansion as she felt in the fuchsia dress. Goldenrod sat stiffly, her pale-green hands folded in her lap, her long hair wild and windblown. She looked like a tuft of grass on a plate of porcelain. Errol, his clothes even more worn than Sophia's, rubbed the scruff of his chin, pondering the view. Seneca, Errol's falcon, blinked unhappily from his perch on the archer's shoulder.

At least Richard Wren, the Australian sea captain, seemed at ease. He stood in a wide stance before the windows, happily munching a piece of toast as he took in the view.

"I trust you all slept well?" Calixta asked, gliding toward the table, where fruit and pastries, butter and jam, coffee and sugar awaited.

"I can't remember the last time I slept so well," Wren exclaimed, saluting her appreciatively with his toast. "The most soothing sound of the waves, the softest pillows, the most comfortable bed. Calixta, I am afraid that once this search concludes, you will find me at your doorstep, an uninvited but eager guest."

"You are most welcome," Calixta replied, pleased.

"Thank you for your hospitality," Goldenrod said, rising from the couch. "It is wonderful to be at last on land and in safe circumstances. You and your brother have given us the safest of safe havens."

Sophia had wondered, when she saw the *Swan* in the port of Seville, how Goldenrod and Errol would take to the pirates. Calixta and Burr were flashy and boisterous, while Errol and Goldenrod were grave and quiet. But to her surprise, after only a few hours, the four seemed fast friends. Their common bond with Sophia paved the way, and then, as they conversed, each pair discovered in the other the quality they most valued: loyalty. From there, it was easy for Errol and Goldenrod to find amusement in what they perceived as the pirates' frivolities, and it was easy for the pirates to pardon what they perceived as Errol and Goldenrod's incorrigible gloominess. The *Swan's* pirate matron, Grandmother Pearl, who watched the unexpected friendship emerging among them over the course of their monthlong voyage, affectionately dubbed them "the four winds." And Wren was like an ocean current among these four winds: warm and good-natured in temperament, he adapted to his circumstances. He could be loud and rowdy, and he could be grave and quiet.

"Agreed," Errol said. "We should not stay more than a day—"

"I insist you stay a week." It was true that two of the four winds blew much more forcefully than the others, directing them and anyone around them with merciless, if friendly, force of will. "I am only too glad that we can offer you safety," Calixta continued, spooning brown sugar into her coffee, "when there seems to be so little of it to spare."

A month's worth of newspapers had been waiting for them the previous evening. Despite their weariness, the travelers had snatched them up, reading and exclaiming while Millie and the other servants answered the volley of questions about the embargo declared by the United Indies, the secession of New Akan and the Indian Territories, the acquittal of Minister Shadrack Elli in the murder of Prime Minister Bligh, and the declaration of war by the new prime minister, Gordon Broadgirdle. "What does the morning paper say?" Calixta asked.

"This thing they are calling 'the Anvil' appears to be making life difficult throughout New Occident," Wren said.

"'The Anvil'? Sounds like the name of a tavern I'd rather avoid," she replied breezily, seizing a slice of pineapple.

Wren gave the pirate a wry look. "It's an anvil cloud. A heavy cloud that precedes a storm."

The previous night, Sophia had taken a pile of newspapers

upstairs and pored over them before falling asleep. Though the political events dominated the news, the growing prominence of what the newspapers called "the Anvil" had intrigued her. "But they're using it to describe any number of things," she put in. "Weather disruptions that have been happening all month. Sinkholes, storms, flash floods, even earthquakes."

"'A second sinkhole in Charleston,'" Wren read from the paper he had picked up, "'consumed Billings's crossroads to the west of the city, and noxious fumes were reported emerging from the sinkhole the following evening.'" He paused. "And on the coast off Upper Massachusetts, the anvil clouds obstructed a lighthouse, causing two shipwrecks." He shook his head. "New Occident seems to be experiencing very strange weather."

"It's very worrying," Goldenrod said, her green brow furrowed. "So many unusual patterns at once cannot be coincidental."

"Yes," Calixta murmured. "Bad weather. Always annoying. Any *important* news?" she asked meaningly.

Wren glanced at the paper again. "Skirmishes in the Indian Territories, but they are described in only the most general terms."

"I very much doubt the veracity of these reports," Goldenrod said.

"Naturally," Calixta agreed. "One wonders about the reliability of the sources, and I have no doubt that Broadgirdle is doing his best to shape what we do and don't know. Where is my useless brother?" she asked pleasantly, and considered a slice of cake drizzled with honey. "We have plans to make."

"I am here," said a groggy voice from the doorway. Burr's handsome face was still heavy with sleep as he staggered into the room. "I heard a rumor that somewhere in this fantastically overstaffed mansion one could procure a hot cup of coffee. Is it true?"

"Oh, poor thing. You were expecting it to appear at your elbow when you woke up?"

"I was, rather," Burr grumbled, pouring coffee into a porcelain cup. "But you have trained everyone who works here to think of it as *their* mansion, and they are wonderfully independent thinkers, so apparently what I expect counts for very little."

"You will feel better after the coffee, my dear neglected brother." Calixta pushed a plate toward him. "Have some cake. We need to find a way to get in touch with Shadrack, and we need to decide on our entry point to New Occident, since all the ports are closed to us."

"New Orleans, surely," Wren said, sitting down at the table beside her.

"If the *Swan* can take us to New Orleans, Errol and I can take Sophia north through the Indian Territories," suggested Goldenrod.

"Is that not too much of a detour for you?" Much as Sophia wanted their assistance, she was well aware of how every day prevented Errol from searching for his brother. Indeed, she was well aware of how every member of the company was there because of her, accepting risk and inconvenience on her behalf.

"We go as far as you do, miting," Errol assured her. "Until we see you safely back in Boston with your uncle."

"There is no safety to be had in Broadgirdle's Boston," Burr commented dourly.

"The Ausentinian map says we are to part ways," Sophia said carefully, voicing the concern that most troubled her. "I know we have discussed this before—"

"You put too much stock in the divinatory power of those little riddles, sweetheart." Calixta patted her hand.

"However much the Ausentinian maps may prove true in retrospect, we cannot plan to separate because they predict that we will separate," said Errol.

"He is right, Sophia," Goldenrod agreed.

"But they are not little riddles," Sophia insisted. They had gone over this many times on the Atlantic crossing. "Everything the maps have said has come true. And I am not saying we should plan to separate. What I am saying is that we should use the map to anticipate what might happen and plan carefully."

Burr suddenly looked much more awake. "Speaking of divinatory power," he said, "that's how we should get word to Shadrack: Maxine!"

"Who is Maxine?" Wren and Sophia asked at the same time.

"Yes, Maxine," Calixta murmured. "That is actually a good idea."

Burr sat back with a satisfied air. "Of course it is. I am only surprised you admit it." He turned to Sophia. "Maxine Bisset. In New Orleans. We have known her for years—utterly reliable. A bit of a fortune-teller, which is why my sister turns up her nose, but she also runs the best correspondence—"

There was a shout from the other end of the mansion. Everyone at the breakfast table fell silent and waited, listening; they heard the anxious clatter of running feet, and then Millie's voice calling, "Captain Morris! Captain Morris!"

Calixta stood up just as Millie reached the room, breathless. "What has happened?"

"Tomás has seen horsemen," she panted, "coming this way along the road."

"And what of it?"

"He was out repairing the gate. And brought this." She handed Calixta a long, thin sheet of paper, looking rather the worse for wear from exposure to the elements. "They have been posted everywhere the last two weeks. But we thought nothing of it until now." The group gathered around Calixta, who swore under her breath.

A fair drawing of Richard Wren occupied the center of the flyer. Around it were written the terms:

**Reward: 2000 pieces silver
for the capture and conveyance
to authorities in Tortuga
of outlaw Richard Wren**

"Why did you not tell me of this last night?" Calixta demanded.

"I'm sorry, Captain Morris." Millie wrung her hands. "We didn't think. I only heard you call him 'Richard,' and it didn't occur to me—"

"How many horsemen?"

"At least thirty, Tomás said."

"Too many," Calixta said quietly.

"It is the League." Wren's face had gone ashen as he realized the Australian forces from which he had fled were so closely in pursuit. "They must be searching for me everywhere on the Atlantic, for they have no way of knowing I am here." Everyone looked at him in silence. "The safest thing would be for me to turn myself in."

"Absolutely not!" cried Calixta.

"Two thousand pieces of silver are terribly tempting," Burr conceded, "and they would jingle most cheerfully in a little wooden trunk, devised especially for silver pieces, which we could shake now and then to remind ourselves—"

"Burr," Calixta cut in, rolling her eyes.

"Only jesting!" Burr smiled. "Of course we cannot give you up—absurd. But we must leave, and soon." He pointed at the tall windows. "I can see them cresting the hill, and they will be here in minutes. Though the staff are disconcertingly adept with sword and dagger, I think my sister would prefer to keep such confrontations out of the house. Very bad for the upholstery."

Calixta gave him a smile full of warmth. "You can be so thoughtful, Burr." Then she put her hands on her hips. "To the *Swan*, then."

"To the *Swan*!" her brother agreed. "Friends, you have three minutes to pack."

There was a moment's pause, and then everyone raced from the room.

2
PULIO'S PERFUMERY

—*1892, August 2: 8-Hour 11*—

New Orleans was a divided city during the rebellion of New Akan. The rebellion's organizers met and recruited in New Orleans, but its opponents were a powerful majority. It is a wonder that more of the city was not destroyed in the rebellion itself. It was spared for two reasons: first, the rebellion's intentional focus on plantations and estates; second, the opponents' decision to flee the city at the first sign of violent unrest. New Orleans was left in the hands of the rebels, and in the wake of the revolt it has become the seat of independent New Akan.

—From Shadrack Elli's History of New Occident

SOPHIA FELT GRATEFUL, as she counted the seconds aloud to keep track of them, that her shabby belongings were still piled at the foot of her bed where she had left them the night before. With no time at all to change out of the extravagant fuchsia dress, she pulled on her boots, stuffed her clothes into her pack and her books into her satchel, and threw each over a shoulder. She dashed out of the peaceful little bedroom, peaceful no longer, and rushed down the stairs to the breakfast room.

Burr had miraculously found time to exchange his silk morning robe for the trousers, white shirt, boots, and sword belt that he usually wore. Wren carried his rucksack, Goldenrod carried next to nothing, and Errol promptly reached for Sophia's pack when she entered the room. "Let me take that, miting," he said.

"Calixta!" Burr shouted.

"Coming, coming," came the unconcerned reply.

"She will be trying to stuff every gown she has into a trunk," Burr grumbled. "Dearest," he shouted up the stairs, "why don't you leave everything here and buy some new things in New Orleans?"

The sound of drawers being frenziedly opened and shut suddenly stopped. Calixta appeared at the head of the stairs wearing her same lemon-colored dress and an elaborate sword belt. "An inspired suggestion," she said.

"I'm glad you think so. And," Burr added, "since our front door, which I am rather fond of, will be smashed to pieces at any moment if we do not leave, could I suggest we depart immediately?"

As Calixta pattered quickly down the stairs, Burr led the group to the rear of the house. Seneca clung to Errol's shoulder. The glass doors stood open, and the five hurried down the marble steps, along the white stone path, and across the lawn.

"Millie has already alerted the crew," Calixta said to her brother, keeping pace. "They will be lifting the anchor as we speak."

Sophia did not turn to see the horsemen as they reached the mansion, but she heard them shouting when they spotted their quarry. The horses' hooves pounded the lawn, and Sophia strained against the long, billowing dress, feeling it rip at the seams as she pushed herself to run faster. The pirates, Wren, and Goldenrod had already reached the dock. As the crew shouted encouragement, she raced after them and ran up the gangplank. Errol followed her with a leap, and the plank was hauled aboard in a single motion. A sudden jolt carried them away as the sails caught the wind. Some of the horsemen had reached the dock; they reined in violently, the horses wheeling perilously at the edge. More than one man drew his pistol, but every one held his weapon in the air.

"Why don't they shoot?" Sophia asked, gasping for breath.

"They cannot sink the *Swan* with mere pistols," Errol replied, only slightly less winded. "And they know we have cannon." Seneca cried overhead and circled toward them, landing with a flutter on Errol's arm.

Sophia sank to the deck with a groan. "I was so glad to be rid of the seasickness," she said. "And here we are again."

"I know, miting. I know." Errol briefly rested a hand on her shoulder. "But it will be a short journey. And then you will be back on dry land for good. Try to lose track of time a little. We will be there before you realize it."

THEY HAD ALREADY known that Richard Wren was a fugitive. What they did not know was the lengths to which the League of Encephalon Ages would go in order to find him. Wren had once been a vital member of the League, believing in its mission to protect early Ages from the destructive knowledge of future Ages. Now he was forced to flee from the very organization he had once served.

On the first night of their long Atlantic journey, Wren had explained how he found himself in such a predicament. They were gathered in Calixta's cabin—Burr idling with a deck of cards, Calixta cleaning her pistol, Errol mending his cape, and Goldenrod listening along with Sophia. Despite her unrelenting seasickness, Sophia was mesmerized.

"As you've read in your mother's diary," Wren began, indicating the pages that he had copied for Sophia, "I met Minna and Bronson in February of 1881. I left them safe and sound in Seville, and then I returned with the *Roost* to Australia. Soon after our arrival, my crew and I were arrested." He gave a wry smile. "There were many charges, but they all pertained to how I had broken the law in assisting your parents. The watch I gave them was the greatest breach. I soon found myself serving a very long prison sentence. Ten years, to be exact. Most of my crew were let off, fortunately."

"How did they know—how could they know—about any of it?" asked Sophia.

Wren waved his hand dismissively. "The League has ways of knowing these things—many things. Sometimes it seems they know all things."

"An informer?" Calixta's pistol lay disassembled before her on a canvas cloth, and she looked up at Wren with a shrewd look as she polished the handle.

"My crew are beyond reproach," he said. "No—it is nothing like what you can imagine. Let me put it briefly so you can understand what I am up against." He enumerated the points on his fingers. "Each Age has its reigning wisdom. For the Papal States, which we leave behind, it is religion. It organizes and directs all forms of knowledge. In New Occident, where your uncle's mapmaking is so prized, Sophia, it is science. Before the Disruption, the ruling wisdom in Australia, too, was science. But once we joined with future Ages, we were caught in their sway, and the future Ages are dominated by the Ars—the arts."

His listeners waited. The cards in Burr's hands rasped and rustled as he shuffled them from one hand to another. When he spoke, his voice was perplexed. "As in . . . painting? And music?"

"Those are certainly artistic forms." Burr gestured around the cabin, filled with paintings of Hispaniola that Calixta had acquired and curated with care. A girl splitting coconuts hung by the door; a battle at sea dominated the wall above a rack of rolled maps; and a breaking storm at sunset hung across from it. Each brought a spot of lightness to the dark wood walls. "And they have more power than people generally recognize. Each of these canvases is transporting in a way that you may not immediately realize. It is why Calixta liked them in the first place, no doubt—each had an undeniable influence."

Calixta looked up from her work. "Of course they do."

Wren gave her a nod. "I'm glad you agree. But it is the impulse of the Ars—the intuitive, interpretive, imaginative faculties, the 'Three Eyes,' as they are called—that really lie at their foundation. They can be channeled into painting and music, theater and sculpture, as they are in your Ages, but they can also be channeled into reading and understanding and shaping the world itself. Human minds. Cities. Societies. Landscapes."

"I don't understand," Errol said flatly. The cape he was holding lay in his lap, his mending forgotten.

"It is almost unimaginable unless you have seen what the Ars can do, just as the world seen through a microscope is unimaginable unless you have seen what one can do."

"What is a microscope?" Errol asked.

Wren smiled. "I am making this too complicated. Errol, how would you communicate the purpose of the True Cross to someone who had never heard of it? Sophia, how would you explain the workings of modern medicine? The Ars are like this: a system of meaning and thought with so many centuries behind it that you must be fully immersed to understand it. And being fully immersed, you have trouble explaining the assumptions—they seem obvious to you. You understand them without knowing how."

"Is this the secret that the League is keeping?" Sophia asked. "The Ars?" She did not entirely understand Wren's explanation, either, but she understood his saying that the Ars might be incomprehensible from a distance. Memory maps were like that—impossible to imagine until one had immersed oneself in the memories. Perhaps the Ars were similar: an entire world springing into being, a world that could not be described, only experienced.

"No, no." Wren shook his head. "That—that I will tell you

another time. I merely mention the Ars so you understand how I was accused and sentenced so easily. While I was out on the ocean they knew nothing, but once I returned and was in their hands . . . everything was revealed to them. I did not even know that your parents had called me with the watch, Sophia, because I was serving my sentence already. By the time I found out—when I was released, only a few months ago—it was far too late. Still, I felt keenly my promise to help them and my failure in keeping it. I communicated with Cassia—Remorse—in New Occident, and we made a plan. Your extraction was not originally what we intended, Goldenrod, but when we learned of your circumstances, Cassia improvised."

"But if they punished you before for helping my parents," Sophia said, "surely they would not let you help me now."

Wren looked down at his hands. "You are quite right. I can never return to Australia. I left knowing I would be a fugitive for the rest of my days."

Sophia looked at him wide-eyed, shocked at how much this near-stranger had lost for the sake of her and her parents. She thought of the pins that had dotted Shadrack's map in the underground map room—the pins tracking possible sightings of Minna and Bronson after their disappearance. *To think,* she realized, *that each of those pins could be someone like Richard Wren. Someone not just catching a glimpse of Minna and Bronson, but helping them—at great cost.*

"And will the League give pursuit?" asked Calixta.

"Perhaps. But I suspect they have more important matters to attend to. I am a very small fish in their ocean. Most likely they will cast a rather loose net, hoping it will catch me some time. I have done everything possible to ensure they will not."

IT SEEMED NOW that Wren had been very wrong. Or perhaps, Sophia reasoned, two thousand pieces of silver were a loose net for the League: they advertised a reward and waited for the pirates and smugglers and merchants of the Indies to do their work for them. But it did not seem that they had decided to forget about Richard Wren—not yet.

On the four-day journey to New Orleans, Wren set out to change his appearance. Since the flyer had showed him long-haired and bearded, he shaved his face and head. After that, Calixta painted his face, arms, and hands with a lasting ink, drawing the elaborate swirls and patterned lines typical of the Indies tattoos.

The *Swan* approached the harbor at midday, and its passengers had their first glimpse of the weather that had plagued New Occident for weeks. A bank of yellowish clouds lay piled like cotton batting to the edges of the horizon. "I have never seen clouds of that kind," Goldenrod murmured.

"What makes them yellow?" asked Sophia.

Goldenrod shook her head. "I do not know. Perhaps dust?" She frowned. "They seem so still." The clouds hung low and heavy over the docks; even with the breeze from the ocean, the air felt packed and stale.

Calixta's enthusiasm was not dampened by the foul weather. As soon as they had dropped anchor, she left the *Swan* in the hands of the skeleton crew that had manned it and hurried to secure two coaches. "Before we go to Maxine's," Calixta announced, "I must purchase a few things in the shops."

Burr groaned.

"It was your idea!" Calixta protested.

"I only said that to persuade you to leave."

"Well, it was very sound advice, and I intend to take it. Sophia rides with me."

"I don't need anything." Sophia had changed back into her worn travel clothes at the first possible moment, and she had no desire to find herself trapped once more in an elaborate silk cocoon, no matter how fashionable it might be.

Calixta eyed Sophia's footwear meaningfully. "What about new boots?"

Sophia looked down. One of the laces was torn and knotted in several places. The heels were worn down by half-moons. "Well," she admitted, "maybe new boots wouldn't be bad. If we're going to be traveling north for so long."

"Excellent!" Calixta bustled Sophia into the waiting coach and waved merrily to the others. "We'll see you at Maxine's in a couple of hours. Maybe a little more," she amended.

Burr rolled his eyes. "Before nightfall, Calixta. Do try."

Calixta settled into her seat, tapping the roof lightly. "Henri's boot shop on Rue Royale, please, driver," she called.

As the coach jostled forward, Calixta pressed Sophia's knee. "You must be thinking of the last time we were here. With Theo."

Sophia nodded. "Yes. It seems so long ago." She looked

out the window at the retreating harbor, remembering how she had lost track of time trying to find the pirates' ship. She recalled the sudden appearance of Burr, the mad scramble to climb the gangplank, the Sandmen in pursuit, and Theo taking aim at a barrel of molasses. The last thought brought a smile to her face.

"You'll be back in Boston soon, sweetheart," Calixta said. "And won't Theo be envious when he learns of all your adventures!"

Sophia's smile grew wistful. "I think he will be. Especially that I've spent so much time with you and Burr."

Calixta laughed. "Poor thing. I'm sure he's bored to pieces these days. Now," she said, with a businesslike air, "apart from boots for you, we both need to get some new hats, petticoats, at least a pair of dresses, slippers for the evening, stockings, small clothes, not to mention a brush, hairpins, soap . . . what else?"

"That seems quite enough."

"Ah!" Calixta exclaimed. "Stop here, driver!" She tapped the roof. "Perfume, of course."

As soon as they came to a halt, she pulled Sophia from the coach. "I really don't think—" Sophia started.

"Please, don't question me when it comes to purchases. It isn't wise." Calixta looked up at the driver. "Wait here."

They were on the outskirts of the city center, and a long street lined with shops stretched before them. A millinery stood open across the way, and a pair of ladies carrying parasols looked in the window, admiring the hats. Next door, a girl in a white apron swept the steps of a pastry shop. Sophia glanced up at the sign over the doorway through which Calixta was leading her: VINCENT PULIO'S FINE FRAGRANCES.

Scents of orange blossom and almond, musk and cinnamon, gardenia and rose wafted through the air. Calixta headed toward the counter while Sophia looked around her. Delicate tables dotted the room like little islands, laden with glass bottles. The walls were lined with shelves, where heavy jars labeled *Magnolia* and *Honeysuckle* and *Meadow* stood side by side. A portly man with a carefully groomed mustache stood behind the glass counter, wiping the ornate atomizers in his display case with a white cloth.

"Vincent!" Calixta greeted him.

"Ah!" The portly man looked up, startled. "Captain Morris." He glanced at the doorway and then at the back of the shop, where another customer was testing a row of perfumes.

"You seem disappointed to see me, Vincent," Calixta observed, narrowing her eyes suspiciously. "What ails you?"

"Me?" Vincent replied nervously. "Nothing. Nothing at all."

Calixta laughed. "I've known you for seven years, Vincent. What is it?"

"Calixta Cleopatra Morris," came a low voice from the back of the store. Sophia turned to see the customer who had been examining bottles now facing Calixta, his sword drawn. He had long, curly hair, which he wore tied back with a length of frayed leather. His black boots, shined to perfection, were poised to spring. "I will not call you *captain*, Calixta," he hissed, "for you do not deserve the title."

"O'Malley," Calixta said coolly. "It is wonderful to see you, as well. What flea has bitten you that you greet me with a drawn sword? Not advisable under any circumstances, even if this were one of those rare days that happened to find you sober."

"You know quite well," O'Malley said levelly, taking a step toward her.

Calixta slowly removed her lace gloves and tucked them into the bosom of her dress, all the while eyeing O'Malley with disdain. "Truly, I am at a loss. The last time I saw you, we were dining aboard the *Swan*, drinking Burr's best rum. If we've run into one another since then and memory fails, do remind me."

"This has nothing to do with you and me," O'Malley said, his mouth twisting as if he had tasted something rancid. "This has to do with what you did to the *Eurydice*. I only learned of it yesterday, but all of New Orleans is aghast at your crime. Such cruelty cannot stand unanswered."

Calixta rested her hand on the hilt of her sword. Her face had lost all traces of amusement. "I commend you on your righteous indignation, O'Malley, but you will have to enlighten me as to its cause. I have not seen the *Eurydice* in more than three years. What is it I am supposed to have done to it?"

"Despicable," O'Malley said, raising his sword. "I never thought you capable of it. You capture the ship, accept their surrender, leave the entire crew to drown—and then deny any knowledge of the atrocity? You have no place at the helm of a ship! I am delighted to be the one who will ensure you never sail again."

Calixta drew her sword in a single motion and held O'Malley at bay. Her eyes were angry slits. "Every word you have spoken is a lie. I will gladly defend my honor and the *Swan's*, but let us do so in the street. Your clumsy blows are bound to break every one of Vincent's bottles, and I have no wish to pay for thousands of dollars of spilled perfume when I will already have to foot the bill for your funeral."

"Gladly." O'Malley smiled. "In the street there are sure to be others who will be delighted to see the demise of the once esteemed Captain Morris."

There was a sudden movement Sophia could not follow, and the blades flashed and rang between them. Sophia let out an inadvertent gasp.

"Sophia," Calixta said quietly, without looking away from O'Malley. She stepped backward toward the shop's doorway.

"Yes?"

"Do you remember the name of the person we came to see?"

"I do."

"I want you to get into the coach and ask the driver to take you there. He will know the address."

Sophia took a deep breath and steeled herself. "No."

Calixta scowled. "Do as I say."

"I will not leave you here." She glanced through the windows. There were already curious onlookers staring in at the duel. The sound of running feet promised more. "People are coming. If what he says is true, I cannot leave you here."

"This is very unhelpful, Sophia," Calixta said, her eyes still trained on O'Malley.

"I'm sorry. But I'm not leaving."

Calixta's blade dove forward, and suddenly O'Malley's shirt hung open. Behind the counter, Vincent let out a yelp and ducked, disappearing from view. O'Malley lunged, his sword slashing viciously, and one of the tables nearest him toppled to the floor with a piercing crash. Calixta threw her sword upward, embedding it in the ceiling, and then hurtled forward, throwing her shoulder into O'Malley's stomach. He was caught off guard. Still clinging to his sword, he fell backward and struggled to rise, but Calixta had drawn a short dagger from her belt. "Sorry, Finn," she said quietly. She drew the dagger across the back of his ankles: first one, then the other. O'Malley gasped in pain.

"They will heal," she said, rising quickly. "But you will not walk for a pair of weeks." She tossed her head and looked down at him. "It saddens me that you would believe such a rumor. You know me better."

She plucked her sword from where it dangled from the ceiling and sheathed it, then took Sophia by the hand. "Come with me, my insubordinate friend."

The crowd outside Vincent's had grown considerably, and it gave Calixta a wide berth as she fled from the shop. "Into the coach," Calixta ordered Sophia abruptly. "Drive," she said to the coachman. "I'll give you the address once you've turned the corner. Make sure no one follows us, and I'll double the fare."

3

THE ARMOR

—1892, August 2: 17-Hour 00—

The Indian Territories are of an Age with New Occident—
that is to say, no boundary was formed between them by the Great
Disruption. But the political boundary between them was and is
formidable. It is a frontier of knowledge as well; historians in New
Occident are not as well acquainted as they should be with the
peoples of the Territories. We know their history of the last two
hundred years, because we were a part of it. But what do we know
of the remote past? What do we know of their origins? Very little.

—From Shadrack Elli's History of the New World

THE PORTION OF Pennsylvania where Theo's company was sta-
tioned had no roads to speak of: only overgrown deer trails and
a seemingly endless supply of thorny brush. Theo and the others on the work crew had been given the task of transforming
those overgrown trails into wide, clear roads that troops could
march along unimpeded. Then the dank humidity had begun,
with the yellow clouds that made the air heavy and even the
slightest movement taxing. The vegetation seemed to thrive in
it, unfurling luxuriantly so that weeds cut one day reappeared
the next. The work was grueling, and it was made no easier by

the prospect of what those roads would be used for. They were clearing the way for the army of New Occident, heading west to bring the rebellious Indian Territories to heel.

The scarce free moments Theo had were spent on tasks that under normal circumstances would have seemed trivial: eating, bathing, and washing his clothes. At times he felt too tired to eat, but he forced down the food, knowing his muscles would punish him later with terrible cramps if he did not. Somehow he had been able to get through the work and the tasks alike by suspending his thoughts, feeling almost nothing.

That is, he had been able to do so until the last few days. He had received another letter from Shadrack, full of reassurances and news about life in Boston. Shadrack wrote very little about his work in the ministry, avoiding all mention of Gordon Broadgirdle. The prime minister was a loathsome subject for both of them. He had framed Shadrack for murder; he had engineered a war with the west; and he had cast Theo, who knew all about the man's sordid past, into the very center of that war. Broadgirdle was present in the letter—in every letter between them—as a great, odious omission. Shadrack reported that Sophia's whereabouts were still unknown, but he was sure she would return home, and he hoped that the war would soon end and they would all be reunited.

Reading the letter, Theo was suddenly aware of a dull ache deep inside himself. His entire body slowed and his muscles rebelled. All the chores that had previously been tiring but manageable—even the simplest ones, like cleaning his boots—became detestable and almost impossible. He did not want to be there, in the wilderness, surrounded by his former cell mates, clearing paths so that hundreds of boots could march west. It had always seemed pointless, but now it seemed starkly wrong. *What am I doing here?* Theo wondered.

He had hoped Shadrack's letter might reveal some careful hints about a plan to end the war—Shadrack was the War Cartologer, after all, and he was not without power in Broadgirdle's government. Alternately, Theo had hoped that Shadrack would have a plan to extract him from his company. At the very least, Theo had hoped for some news of Sophia. Knowing she was safely back in Boston would have been some comfort as he headed into danger. But Shadrack offered none of this.

Theo's company was only days from the border of the Indian Territories. Soon they would venture past the border and, no doubt, into battle.

And so Theo was sitting on his cot, wondering what he could possibly write to Shadrack, when his tentmate, a man everyone called Casanova, made his way into the candlelit space and rolled onto his cotton bedding. Casanova understood Theo's mood at a glance. He lay down quietly on his cot, giving the younger man time to say the first word.

Casanova, like all the rest of the men in Theo's company, had once been an inmate of the Boston prisons. Theo had, in fact, met him on his own first day there. The volunteers and recruits, who formed a separate battalion, called the prisoners' corps "blocks," a derisive reference to their recent incarceration. In reality, the time in prison made Theo's company the better prepared for war. The volunteers were inexperienced young men—children, practically; the prisoners were men of all ages who had known their share of misfortune and what it meant to be subject to another man's will. They did not all conform well to either condition, but their experience made them more cautious and generally more patient toward the indignities of soldiering.

Casanova was a special case. Tall, with broad shoulders and a thick neck, he had the aspect of a boxer. He had been a handsome man, once. But in some event or accident that he never discussed, one side of his face and head had been burned. Theo had seen him washing, and knew that the scar disfiguring Casanova's scalp and face extended down across his chest and back: a mottled, pocked, rippled thing. Theo had his own scars, years of accumulated lines and gashes, on his iron-boned right hand. There was something different, Theo felt, about people who wore the damage of the past on their skin. The scar gave Casanova such a terrifying appearance that he maintained a fearsome reputation without any effort. Yet he was anything but terrifying: quietly observant, good-humored, and as kind to Theo as an older brother.

At least once a day, sometimes more, either Theo or someone else needled Casanova for the story of the scar. And every time he brushed them off, prompting them to invent ever more outlandish explanations: a favorite book and a burning tent; a chicken, a rooftop, and a pot of tea; a blind old lady, a pipe, and a box of matches. Casanova laughed indulgently at each one and said nothing.

To explain his quiet nature, his preference for books over rowdy company, he professed to be a great coward. Some men treated their weapons with exaggerated fondness, as if holding family heirlooms; Casanova could barely stand to touch his sword and rifle, which he tossed under his cot at night like a pair of old brooms. He scowled whenever anyone boasted of victory in a knife fight. He rolled his eyes at the sight of men who, after training all day, threw fists at one another over some imagined insult. Casanova preferred to read in his tent. But Theo noticed that despite the constant claims to cowardice, no one ever goaded Casanova or threw insults—let alone fists— in his direction. No doubt, Theo surmised, his height and build and fearsome scar protected him, despite his peaceable nature.

Casanova waited, now, locking his hands behind his damp hair—he had just washed away the August dust in the nearby stream—and regarded the yellow canvas of the tent ceiling.

Finally Theo sighed. "Cas, I don't know what to say to Shadrack."

Casanova continued to stare at the ceiling. "Why is that?"

"There's no news about Sophia. There's no news about the war. And everything here . . . Well, you know. What can I possibly say?"

Now Casanova looked at him, one side of his face a handsome smile, the other side a puckered and twisted knot. "You don't have to tell him that. Tell him unimportant things—he'll never know the difference."

"But what?"

"Tell him how Lumps fell yesterday, certain as he was he

could lift the branch off the road by himself, and ended up sitting waist-high in mud."

Theo chuckled at the memory.

"Tell him how it took almost an hour for Lumps to wash the mud out of his clothes, and he had to stand naked in the river to do it. If you have the stomach for it, you might even describe what Lumps looked like naked."

Theo laughed.

"And you can mention how often you think of him and Sophia," Casanova added gently, now that he had gotten Theo to laugh. "And how much you wish this war would end."

Taking a deep breath, Theo nodded. "All right. I'll do that." He ran a hand through his dusty hair and tiredly put the paper aside. "I'll write it tomorrow morning."

Casanova watched the younger man for a moment. "I saw something interesting today."

Theo looked up sharply, recognizing the shift in tone.

"The supply caravan that arrived yesterday. I managed to look inside."

Theo waited.

"I thought the amount of food might give a sense of where we're going—how long we're meant to march. But there was no food in the wagon. There were crates with armor."

"Armor?" Theo echoed, curious.

"Glass shields for the eyes, set in a leather mask."

"Like goggles?"

"Look for yourself." Casanova sat up, reached under his cot, and pulled out a confusion of leather straps and buckles.

"I'm starting to guess how you landed in prison, Cas," Theo commented amiably.

Casanova eased the leather hood over his head and faced Theo. "How does it fit?" he asked, his voice muffled.

Theo frowned. "Hard to say. Well enough, if you wish to look like a giant fly." Green lenses, bulbous and oblong, were set in at an angle, giving the mask a saddened aspect. Leather stitching ran down the center, and a pear-shaped screen of stiff cloth covered the mouth and nose. At the neck, a strap and buckle hung loose. "Can you see?"

"I can, but everything is distorted." Casanova took one bulging lens in each hand and, with some effort, snapped them upward. "They have hinges—a little tight." His brown eyes blinked expressionlessly through the mask. "There's something in the fabric here—a smell like charcoal."

Theo grimaced. "Better take it off."

After he did, Casanova said, "I hope Merret doesn't mean to make us wear those. Hot as an oven in there."

"Why would we have to wear them? I guess they're protection, but protection from what?"

Casanova stuffed the mask under his cot and lay back with a sigh. "We'll know soon enough. Merret has us arriving in the Indian Territories in three days."

There was a silence. Casanova again contemplated the low canvas ceiling, where the candle flame threw moving shadows. Theo stretched out on his cot and reached to snuff the light. But for once, he did not fall asleep immediately, and his thoughts ran haltingly, as if through a maze.

4

FIVE LETTERS

—*1892, August 2: 8-Hour 31*—

Newsprint, letters, even a painting: these things we call "dreck" can be from the past or future, but a past or future lost through the Great Disruption. They can sometimes offer surprising revelations. A piece of dreck from 1832 served as a warning: it cautioned New Occident to consider what conditions might serve as a foundation for war. For decades afterward, the threat of warfare hung over the hemisphere like a storm cloud, but the threat was always averted. The wars before the Disruption had cost enough bloodshed, and the rebellion of New Akan had demonstrated what misery was possible when the Age turned against itself.

—From Shadrack Elli's History of New Occident

PRIME MINISTER GORDON Broadgirdle had clearly expended significant resources and no small amount of energy on his War Room. Lavish and excessively comfortable, it seemed to suggest that war was a cozy business—even a luxurious business—to be enjoyed from the confines of a cozy and luxurious chamber.

Shadrack hated it.

Everything about it turned his stomach. The room looked out in the direction of the Public Garden, its wide windows curtained with ochre velvet. Pin-striped wallpaper, dark blue and white, was interrupted by portraits of pre-Disruption politicians. Shadrack felt dizzy whenever he looked at it. Heavy armchairs upholstered in tan leather waited obediently around a polished oval table. In the humid air that even Broadgirdle's expenditures could not avoid, everything was faintly damp; with some distaste, Shadrack marked a whiff of mildew. He suspected it came from the over-thick carpet, dark blue to match the pinstripes, which muffled even Broadgirdle's heavy tread when he strode into the room.

And stride he did, every morning at eight-hour, thirty. Broadgirdle met with his war cabinet each day at this time, and he clearly enjoyed the meetings as much as he enjoyed his sumptuous War Room.

"Good morning, gentlemen!" He beamed, pulling out a chair beside Rupert Middles, the recently appointed Minister of State and the architect of the "Patriot Plan," the parliamentary bill that had closed the borders to foreigners. Middles, with his outsized mustache and fat fingers, sat across from Salvatore Piedmont, the Minister of Defense.

"Good morning, Prime Minister!" Piedmont replied, harrumphing with energy. "A fine day to plan a war!" Shadrack groaned silently; he said the same thing every morning.

Salvatore Piedmont was a military man who had seen better days. His father had been a general in the first years after the Disruption, when slave rebellions in the south led to the formation of New Akan. Piedmont had inherited from his father a dislike for rebellion and a trenchant certainty that New Occident's armed forces could solve any problem, great or small. Over the course of his long life, he had seen those beloved armed forces marginalized as New Occident remained at peace with its neighbors. Now, well into his eighties, he was delighted that they were finally in the spotlight. Broadgirdle, for his part, seemed not to mind that the head of the Armed Forces was a rather weak-witted octogenarian. It made it all the easier to have his way.

"Good morning," Middles agreed, sitting up in his chair. He had still not overcome the sense of importance that came with being appointed Minister of State, and whenever Broadgirdle was present, he set his face into a stern mask, as if determined to embody the air of gravity and solemnity required for his position.

"Good morning," Shadrack said wearily.

Broadgirdle flashed him a serpentine smile, pleased as ever to see Shadrack's dispirited exhaustion. "We have a great deal to discuss today. I have reports from Griggs and June."

"What does June say, then?" Piedmont rumbled happily. "A fine soldier. A very fine soldier, Erik June."

Shadrack suppressed the desire to roll his eyes.

"He and Griggs both report considerable obstacles to their progress," Broadgirdle said.

"*What?*" cried Piedmont.

Middles frowned worriedly. "More sinkholes?"

"Indeed, gentlemen. More sinkholes." Broadgirdle sat back and watched them levelly, as if awaiting an explanation.

The first sinkhole had appeared in early July. Overnight, an entire city block in the western portion of Boston had disappeared into a gaping hole whose black depths seemed endless. There were no survivors.

The second had opened two days later, this time southwest of the city. Fewer lives were lost, for the area was less densely settled, but it was just as confounding. In total, seven such sinkholes had appeared within a day's ride of Boston, and now more were appearing where the New Occident troops were meant to march. Shadrack had heard no shortage of desperate theories—the poor construction of roads, improper drainage, unprecedented volcanic activity—as well as more informed scientific debate, but as yet no one had been able to suggest a convincing explanation.

"It is a considerable problem," Broadgirdle said, looking meaningly at Shadrack, as if he were responsible. "The troops are following maps made by the war cartologer, and that war cartologer is not accounting for sinkholes."

"Well," Shadrack said dryly, "the sinkholes don't always appear where I ask them to."

Broadgirdle raised an eyebrow, unfazed by the sarcasm. "There should be alternate directions for each route."

Shadrack was about to protest that this would create a logistical nightmare, but he was interrupted.

"Excuse me, Prime Minister," a woman's voice said. Cassandra Pierce, Broadgirdle's new assistant, had materialized at his elbow. She handed him a piece of paper. "I thought you would want to see this before it's published. It will be in this evening's *Boston Post*. I understand it's already gone to press."

As Broadgirdle silently read, Shadrack could see the effect of the text on his countenance: first surprise, then anger, then a concerted effort at composure, and, finally, a settling disdain. "Who wrote this?" he asked coolly.

"The editors," replied Pierce.

"May I?" Shadrack asked.

Broadgirdle handed it over with a sneer. "I'm not entirely surprised no one is willing to sign a name to such a piece."

Shadrack scanned the beginning of the editorial:

END THE WESTERN WAR

The editors appeal to the Prime Minister and Parliament to reconsider the costly and fruitless war with our neighbors. At the root of this war is Parliament's border policy, which is so intolerant to foreigners. This policy has provoked New Akan and the Indian Territories to secede; it has provoked the United Indies to declare an embargo. As a result, New Occident finds itself isolated and friendless where it was once at the center of the hemisphere's trade.

What do we gain by such policies? What do we gain from expansion to the west? Is the acquisition of Baldlands territory truly more valuable than the thousands of dollars in weekly trade with the United Indies? Is it more valuable than peace with the Territories? Is it more valuable than the port of New Orleans? We think not.

Shadrack had to stop himself from nodding his agreement at every line. *Finally!* he thought. *Someone is writing reason. I hope the reading public comes to its senses.*

"Outrageous!" Piedmont declared, his voice trembling. Shadrack looked up to find that the Minsters of Defense and State were both reading over his shoulder. "'What do we gain?' An absurd question that could only come from a civilian."

"I notice that the editors don't mention how the border policy has kept them safe for so many months," Middles sniffed. He shook his head. "Another reminder that our system of purchasing parliament seats is invaluable. Can you imagine if such rabble had a voice in government?"

"Regardless," Broadgirdle observed, "many of the rabble do read. And since this piece is already in press, I think it expedient to write a reply." His voice was calm, and it was apparent that he had already devised a solution to the problem.

"A reply!" Piedmont exclaimed. "Surely this does not even merit a reply."

"I think it does. And who better to write it than our Minister of Relations with Foreign Ages?"

Shadrack yanked his eyes up from the editorial. "I . . ." he began. "I am not sure I'm the right person for it."

A smile began on Broadgirdle's face, and Shadrack felt the widening grin like a vicious bite. It reminded him of everything that the man had done to compel him into his present predicament. Broadgirdle had learned that the two foreigners living in Shadrack's home, Theodore Constantine Thackary and Mrs. Sissal Clay, were using falsified citizenship papers, and had threatened to deport them; he had somehow discovered Sophia's entry to the Nihilismian Archive under false pretenses, and had said he would inform the archive so that they could press charges. Every member of his household was at the prime minister's mercy. Every one of them would be lost if Shadrack did not do as Broadgirdle asked.

The desperation Shadrack felt was no less for being familiar. He had no choice but to labor as War Cartologer for a war he detested. He had no choice but to support policies that he considered discriminatory, injurious, and rash. He had no choice now but to write a scathing reply to the editorial, despite the fact that he agreed with every word of it.

—August 3, 16-Hour 40—

"READ THE LAST part again, Shadrack," Miles ordered, scowling, "from arriving in Pear Tree."

Shadrack looked around his kitchen table at the others, who nodded their agreement. The kitchen of 34 East Ending Street, with its disordered piles of maps, its mismatched dishes, and its fragrant peach cobbler, could not have been more different from Broadgirdle's War Room. And the plotters who met twice a week in the kitchen could not have been more different from the Prime Minister's war cabinet—but they were just as determined in their objective.

Miles Countryman, explorer and adventurer, was Shadrack's oldest friend in New Occident. He was also the most argumentative person in Boston. He fought with Shadrack about everything from the pitfalls of politics to the size of a proper meal. Mrs. Sissal Clay, the housekeeper who resided on the top floor, was a widow from Nochtland, and since arriving at East Ending she had not argued with Shadrack even once. She almost never traveled.

The last two plotters were so dissimilar that they made Miles and Mrs. Clay seem like two peas in a pod. Nettie Grey was the very respectable daughter of Inspector Roscoe Grey, and Winston Pendle—Winnie for short—was the very disreputable son of an asylum inmate. Though Winnie was rather cleaner of late than was his custom, since he was now living with Miles instead of on the street, he had a persistent unruliness that no amount of clean clothes could repair. He perched crookedly on his seat while Nettie sat with perfect posture. He tousled his hair as he pondered Shadrack's news, making a tangled nest of it, while Nettie's hair was plaited beautifully. He chewed thoughtfully on a pencil, leaving it mangled, while Nettie remained calm and still.

What the plotters all had in common, different as they were in their ages, backgrounds, and tendencies, was a loyalty to the residents of 34 East Ending Street—present or absent—and an invincible loathing for Prime Minister Gordon Broadgirdle.

On the day Theo had been conscripted and sent to war, he had extracted a promise from Winnie that he would look after things in Boston while Theo was gone. Winnie took the promise seriously. The following day, he had made his proposal to Shadrack. The five of them would work together to bring Prime Minister Gordon Broadgirdle to justice. They would make him pay for the murder of Cyril Bligh, the missing Eerie he had taken prisoner would be found, and upon his imprisonment the senseless war with the west would end.

Shadrack had agreed, partly because he could see in the dirty little boy's fierce eyes that he would go after Broadgirdle with or without him, and he rather thought Winnie's chances were better if he had assistance.

Their progress was discouraging, to say the least. No new evidence had emerged to implicate Broadgirdle in Bligh's murder. Not even the slightest clue—beyond a memory map found by Theo—pointed to the Eerie's whereabouts. The five of them were unable to learn more about Wilkie Graves, the man Broadgirdle had been before bursting onto the political scene in Boston. While the plotters plotted in vain, Broadgirdle's war was in full swing.

And, it seemed on August third, things were getting worse.

Shadrack's friend Pip Entwhistle had arrived early that morning with correspondence from the Indian Territories: a letter from his friend Casper Bearing and four others like it. The plotters listened in silence as Shadrack read aloud one horrible story after another. The effects of the crimson fog were everywhere catastrophic; its source was a complete mystery. When he was done, Shadrack stood up and rested his forehead against the kitchen cupboard in despair.

For some time, no one said anything.

"Flowers and rotting meat. What *is* this blasted fog?" Miles finally demanded, pounding a fist on the kitchen table. The empty plates with their spoons and the dish of peach cobbler rattled in alarm.

Shadrack straightened. "I have no idea, Miles. I've never heard anything like it. But I reported it to Broadgirdle."

"To *Broadgirdle?*" Miles cried. "Why tell that villain?"

"Think, Miles—all of those soldiers heading into the Territories." At the other man's frown, Shadrack continued. "Whether you like my decision or not, it does not matter. Broadgirdle already knew of it. He might be a villain, but he is not wholly incompetent."

"We wish he were," Miles growled. "And what does he mean to do about it?"

"He is sending the troops protective clothing."

"Fat lot of good that will do."

Mrs. Clay had been brought to tears by the account of the children locked in the pantry. She looked down at her half-full teacup and uneaten cobbler. "May the Fates help us," she said now. "Perhaps it is some kind of ill wind—like the weirwinds that are so much more common in the Baldlands than here." Her voice grew agitated. "Perhaps they are moving east!"

"It sounds manmade to me," Miles countered. "Too convenient that it has struck in four towns and all of them towns in the Indian Territories."

"What if there is a new Age," Mrs. Clay said, even more agitated, "like the Glacine Age to the south, and this fog is what emerges from it? Recall that the soil in the Glacine Age is poisonous. Why not an Age with poisonous *air*?"

"Nonsense. Then why does it always strike at dawn and in localized areas?"

Mrs. Clay pondered for a moment. "Oh!" she exclaimed. "It could be a *creature* from a different Age—a monster of some kind that breathes these poisonous fumes."

Winnie waved his chewed pencil for attention. "What are we going to do about Theo?" he asked, interrupting the debate.

"Exactly," Nettie said, shooting Winnie a glance. "We have to warn him somehow."

"We have only a few days," Shadrack replied, "before Theo enters the Indian Territories. I presume from what Broadgirdle has said that most troops will have the protective clothing before crossing the border."

"That's not enough," said Nettie.

"I don't trust anything Broadsy sends," Winnie said at the same time.

"We need to do more," Shadrack agreed. "I can warn him in a letter, but without knowing who or what causes this fog, I cannot advise him how to prevent its effects. But I have an idea for how to minimize the likelihood of an encounter for Theo's company." He unrolled a paper map that showed a detailed portion of western Pennsylvania and lower New York. "All of the attacks that I have heard of have taken place in towns—usually midsized towns. I might be wrong, but perhaps more isolated places are safer. This is a copy of the map I sent today to

Theo's company, plotting their movements west. You can see here"—he pointed to a clump of trees—"that I described the easiest path as one cutting through this sparse forest. What this map fails to show," Shadrack continued with a smile, "is that this route will lead into a deep ravine, which it could take days to emerge from."

"So getting Theo stuck in a ravine is the solution?" Winnie asked skeptically.

Shadrack looked deflated. "It keeps him away from the nearby towns where the crimson fog might appear."

"I think it's a good idea," Nettie reassured him.

"It's only a short-term solution," Shadrack admitted, sitting down heavily. "The long-term solution is to bring Theo home. And to find the source of this fog. And to end the war." He put his head in his hands.

"We need to get a closer look at the fog," Miles said. He pushed back his chair and stood. "And we need a scientist capable of studying it."

Shadrack lifted his head and looked wearily at Miles. "A scientist? What are you suggesting?"

"I think you should send the best explorer you know and the best natural scientists you know to discover what is afoot. In other words," he said, grinning fiercely, "I go west. And you write to Veressa and Martin Metl."

"Oh, yes!" Mrs. Clay exclaimed, her eyes lighting up at the mention of the famed Nochtland cartologer and her botanist father. "They will certainly help us."

Shadrack considered in silence, his eyes lighting with faint hope. It had not occurred to him to ask for the Metls' expertise. "Martin and Veressa. Why did I not think of them?"

"Because you are overworking your brain, which is already of limited capacity, and you forget too easily about your friends. As I well know," Miles added, looking more pleased than offended.

Shadrack's shoulders lifted. "It *might* work, if you are willing—"

"Of course it will work. I know everyone who has written to you, and I know where to find them. Martin knows more than anyone about strange substances. And Veressa knows how to keep her father from going overboard with dangerous experiments."

Shadrack smiled wryly. "She does not, however, know how to prevent you from going overboard."

Miles beamed, delighted with his plan. "All the better. I can be ready to leave in an hour. Tell them to meet me near the town of Pear Tree."

5

MAXINE'S DOVECOTE

—1892, August 6: 12-Hour 09—

The Mark of Iron and Mark of the Vine are rarely seen in New Occident, but in the Baldlands they are common. Nevertheless, even in the Baldlands they are not entirely understood. Where do they come from? What do they mean? What can they do? To these, we should add the question of how widely the Marks are found. For example, we have not fully explored how the Marks manifest in animal species. How many animals have the Marks? Why do some animals have them and not others? Can learning about animals with the Marks help us understand their purpose?

—From Sophia Tims's Reflections on a Journey to the Eerie Sea

SOPHIA AND CALIXTA arrived at Maxine Bisset's door only minutes after Burr, Goldenrod, and Errol. "I knew you would come at once," she said. "Get in off the street."

"I must ride to the harbor and warn the crew," Calixta said.

Maxine shook her head. "Too late. My rider has just returned. The *Swan* was spotted and had to pull anchor or risk being torn to pieces. It is long gone."

Calixta stared at her, aghast.

"Come in, child!" Maxine insisted. "This is no place to discuss these things."

Silent for once, Calixta paid the coachman and followed Sophia through the doorway. "You must be Sophia," Maxine said warmly, taking her hand and pressing it.

"Sophia Tims. Nice to meet you."

"And you." The fortune-teller smiled. "Don't let the circumstances alarm you. I hope you will feel at home here—I am delighted you've come." She was a woman of some fifty years, her springy brown hair streaked with gray, threaded with beads, and piled into a soft and ornate mound atop her round face. Her complexion was like Sophia's; her smile appeared easily and often; her hands had the sturdiness that comes from long years at a stove or a washboard. Her eyes twinkled with kindness, intelligence, and something else—perhaps a nostalgia she had tried to mask with cheerfulness, or a curiosity about the dark corners of the human soul.

Sophia liked her instantly. "Thank you. What is this all about?"

"We will discuss it in due time," Maxine reassured her, leading her down the corridor and glancing back at Calixta, who followed them. "The long and short of it is this: someone has spread a nasty rumor about the Morrises. The lie is intended to provoke them, and it is difficult to ignore."

It was, Sophia reflected, a well-calculated lie—sure to tarnish their name, but impossible for them to address while in hiding. "A man named Finn O'Malley just attacked Calixta in a shop." The pirate did not say a word.

"I'm not surprised. They are in grave danger," Maxine said soberly. "You are safe here, but we must plan very carefully."

The open corridor they walked along bordered a patio lush with plants. Brightly colored birds perched at the edge of a stone fountain. Dark rooms with shuttered windows led off the corridor, the air coming from them cool and damp. "We are gathered in the dining room," Maxine explained, "because it has the largest table. And," she added, "because Burr has a terrible weakness for my cook's pastries." She gave Sophia a broad wink. "You will soon discover why."

Burr, Wren, Errol, and Goldenrod were assembled in the dining room. Half a dozen tiered plates filled with tiny cakes and pastries were arranged on the long dining table. Above it, a massive chandelier hung ponderously, its pendants winking in the occasional sunlight from the patio. The room was both luxurious and worn, as if some things about it had been used so much they had become too dear to part with. A set of dining chairs in perfect condition lined one wall, but many of the seats at the table were faded armchairs with mismatched upholstery. Maxine settled into one of these comfortably and gestured for her guests to do the same. "Please, my friends. Don't offend Celia. Start with the pastries. Tea and coffee will be here at any moment."

"Are you all right?" Burr asked Calixta, his voice serious.

Calixta put her arms around him. "I'm perfectly fine, thank you. But I'm worried about the *Swan*."

"They have orders to return to Hispaniola should anything like this occur," her brother reminded her. "They will be fine."

"And you will be perfectly fine, too." Maxine passed Sophia a small plate with a pink piece of cake.

"This is not what we had planned," Calixta said, taking a seat beside Maxine.

"And what, exactly, was it that you had planned? What brings you all here? I have divined some of it, but not all."

Calixta glanced at Sophia. "They are all here to help me," Sophia said ruefully, "and I am so sorry for the incredible complications it has caused for everyone."

"Nonsense," Burr said, sounding more like himself. "Wren you cannot pity, for his entire existence is a complication. And you know quite well how Calixta and I enjoy complications. Enjoy? No—such a pallid word. Love. *Adore*. They fill us with delight. What are complications but unsolicited fun? Errol and Goldenrod . . ." He reached to fill his plate with pastries, and at the same time he gave the pair a skeptical look. "Well, you can see that they do not know the meaning of fun. Complications or no, it is all the same to them."

Sophia smiled despite herself as she ate the pink pastry. Errol and Goldenrod, well accustomed to Burr's sense of humor by now, blithely ignored the comment. "No complication is too great, miting," Errol said, "as you well know."

"And I am grateful for it," Sophia replied. "As you see," she continued to Maxine, "fun-loving or otherwise, they are all here to help me. I am looking for my parents, who went missing eleven years ago. Wren met them as they were sailing to Seville, and then they disappeared. We've learned now that while in the Papal States"—she paused, looking down at her lap—"they were transformed."

Maxine eyed her keenly, that other quality beyond the

intelligence and kindness bubbling to the surface. "What do you mean, transformed?"

"They became Lachrima." Avoiding Maxine's eyes, Sophia reached into her skirt pocket and drew out a roll of paper. "In the Papal States, we traveled to a place known as Ausentinia—a place that gives travelers maps to anything and everything they have lost." Maxine's gaze sharpened even more. "Along with a purse full of garnets, I was given a map to find my parents. And they"—she indicated Errol and Goldenrod, Wren, Calixta and Burr—"have all been helping me follow it."

"Is that the map?" Maxine asked, pointing to the roll of paper.

"Yes."

"Can I see it?"

Sophia handed it across. Her eyes wide with excitement, Maxine read the map aloud.

> *"Missing but not lost, absent but not gone, unseen but not unheard. Find us while we still draw breath.*
>
> *"Leave my last words in the Castle of Verity; they will reach you by another route. When you return to the City of Privation, the man who keeps time by two clocks and follows a third will wait for you. Take the offered sail, and do not regret those you leave behind, for the falconer and the hand that blooms will go with you. Though the route may be long, they will lead you to the ones who weather time. A pair of pistols and a sword will prove fair company.*

"Set your sights on the frozen sea. In the City of Stolen Senses, you will lose your companions. Remember that though in your brief life you have met Grief, confronting it alone, you have not yet met Fear. It dwells in the west, a companion on every path, a presence in every doorway.

"You will meet the wanderer who is sweet and bitter, and you will travel together, your fates bound on each step of the journey. Trust this companion, though the trust would seem misplaced. You will travel to the Forest of Truces, where the silent bell rings and the dormant seed grows. From then on, the map you follow must be your own. Find it in the lines you have drawn, the paths made by your past. The old one remembers more than anyone."

Maxine turned it over and brushed her fingers over the illustrated map—the nebulous lines that led from the City of Privation to the Frozen Sea, the City of Stolen Senses, and the Forest of Truces. "Beautiful," she sighed.

"Beautiful perhaps, but damned difficult to follow," Burr said pleasantly. He followed the statement with four pastries, eaten in quick succession.

"This is a divining map," Maxine declared, ignoring him.

"We have found," Goldenrod put in, "that the map is difficult to interpret but invariably accurate. Most of what is described in the first two paragraphs has already taken place. I am the hand that blooms; Errol is the falconer. Calixta and Burr are the sword and the pair of pistols, naturally. And we have taken our direction from its line about the frozen sea, which we understand to be the Eerie Sea."

"Oh!" Calixta exclaimed. She reached out for Sophia's hand. "Now I see why you wouldn't leave me at Victor's. I'm sorry—I'd forgotten."

"*In the City of Stolen Senses, you will lose your companions,*" Sophia repeated. "Yes," she said, her brow furrowed with worry. "It is bound to happen. But if there were some way to anticipate it, we might, well . . . not avoid it, but make the same meaning less awful. Where is the City of Stolen Senses? Could we figure out where it is? If we could, would we be able to do something so that *losing* is just 'losing track' and not—not something worse?"

Maxine considered this. "So you believe it is possible to fulfill the meaning of the map in various ways, and that you can *choose* how to fulfill the meaning."

"Exactly," Sophia said, grateful that Maxine—unlike her travel companions, whom she had been trying to persuade for weeks—understood this so quickly.

"It is an astounding piece of divination," the woman said, returning the map to Sophia. "And my own view on such things is like yours—prophecies are loose, not rigid. They can be remarkably protean, so that a single prediction may fit many circumstances. Perhaps Calixta and Burr have told you that I am something of a diviner myself?"

Calixta's face was a picture of politeness as she put her teacup down. "We did, Maxine dear, but really we are here for the pigeons." She hurried on: "Sophia's uncle is Shadrack Elli, the cartologer. He has had no news of her since she sailed for the Papal States. We wish to send him word that Sophia is safe, in our care, and that she is heading north."

Maxine nodded. "Of course, I see. So we must send a pigeon to Boston."

"And ideally, we would ask him to send a reply to a location farther north. How far in that direction does your network extend?"

Maxine waved her hand dismissively. "As far as you like. My pigeons fly to the Eerie Sea, to the western coast, and to the new border of the Glacine Age to the south."

"Perhaps," Goldenrod ventured, "I might suggest we aim for Salt Lick."

"One of my depots is in Salt Lick," Maxine replied, "so that would work quite well. Would you like to see the pigeons?" she asked Sophia.

Sophia pushed her empty plate to one side. "Very much. I had heard pigeons could carry messages, but I have never seen any who do."

"You may be disappointed," Maxine said with a smile. "They look just like ordinary pigeons. But their feats of stamina are quite extraordinary. And they are remarkable in another way, too. These are iron pigeons."

"Pigeons made of iron? How do they fly?" Sophia wondered.

Maxine rose from the table. "Pigeons with the Mark of Iron."

"Oh!" Sophia exclaimed.

"Come with me to the dovecote, and we'll dispatch your message to Shadrack right away."

"Could I come as well?" Goldenrod asked.

Seneca shifted on Errol's shoulder, dancing from one clawed foot to the other. "Oh, no, my friend," Errol said to him firmly. "You and I are staying here."

Maxine led them toward the kitchen—a long room with several worktables and multiple ovens, where the cook and two assistants were toiling in the aftermath of the afternoon pastry production—and then out into a second garden patio. Beneath the heavy yellow clouds, insects buzzed in slow circles while a hummingbird dipped and darted. Herbs grew in dense clusters at the edges of the garden: lavender and thyme, sage and mint.

A stone walkway wove through the herbs to an ornate iron stair. The narrow grillwork steps led to a low-ceilinged room, musty and close with the murmuring of pigeons. A long window with no glass or screen looked out onto the patio and, beyond it, the city of New Orleans. The pigeons were free to fly in and out. Nestled in narrow wooden shelves lined with straw, they fluttered and shifted, eyeing Maxine and the visitors dispassionately.

"Here we are," she said, "with the most well-traveled pigeons in the western world."

Goldenrod knelt by one of the shelves and extended her pale-green fingers toward the pigeons who warbled happily, inching toward her.

"I see you have a way with them," Maxine said approvingly.

Goldenrod beamed up at her. "They seem very happy here."

Sophia noted Maxine's startled reaction with a smile. Calixta and Burr were so flamboyant, so extravagantly beautiful, that they filled the room and dazzled onlookers wherever they were. Beside them, Errol and Goldenrod seemed like dusty little sparrows in the company of peacocks. But the two had a radiance of their own, and Maxine was seeing it now.

"I hope they are," she replied. "We try to take good care of them." She opened a cupboard in the wall and took out a slip of paper, a pen, and a small piece of Goodyear rubber. "What shall we say to your uncle, then, Sophia?"

"How many words do we have?"

"Tell me your message, and I'll abbreviate."

"Let him know that I'm safe with Calixta and Burr and here in New Orleans. We are heading north to Salt Lick and hope to be there . . ." She looked questioningly at Goldenrod.

"The train would be fastest. But Calixta and Burr might be recognized. We shall have to see. Two days would be the soonest. Ten days at the latest, if we cannot take the train."

"I have already thought of a solution for Calixta and Burr," Maxine said, looking pleased with herself, "so do not worry on that account. I will let him know the time frame." She wrote quickly on the slip of paper, rolled it expertly within the rubber, and wound a string tightly around the bundle. "Now," she said, turning to the pigeons. "Where is Marcel? He is my most reliable courier, and he will brave his way through this horrid air we've had of late." She petted the pigeons gently with the tips of her fingers, pushing one or another aside. "Marcel, little heart, where are you hiding? Ah!" she exclaimed, drawing a gray pigeon toward her. He was cupped in the palm of her hand, his feet between her fingers. "Here you are, my brave bird." She kissed the top of his head and slipped the little roll of rubber into a slender tube attached to his leg. Murmuring quietly to Marcel, she went to the open window and then let him go, releasing him into the air. The bank of yellow clouds that blanketed the city rumbled ominously, but Marcel flew steadily and swiftly northeast, staying low to avoid them.

She watched him depart, smiling with pride. "There he goes."

"Will he be all right with the storm?" Sophia asked anxiously.

"I doubt there will be a storm," Maxine said, gesturing to a weather glass that hung just inside the broad window. "These clouds roll and rumble and the pressure rises and falls, but for weeks we have not had a drop of rain. It is passing strange. Still, my pigeons have had no difficulties with it." Turning to tidy and close the writing cupboard, she said, "The Mark of Iron is what guides them. You can tell an ordinary pigeon where to go, and it would understand you, but it wouldn't know how to get there. But pigeons with the Mark can locate anyone, anywhere. In a busy city, in a crowded courtyard, on a remote island. It is all the same to them."

"But how do they do it?" Sophia asked. "How does the Mark of Iron make a difference?"

"It guides them like a compass, my dear!"

"Oh!" Sophia said, understanding dawning.

"In this case, we have depots, so Marcel's task is easier. He will fly to the depot in Greensboro, where my colleague Elmer will transfer his message to another pigeon and send it to Boston. When it arrives there, Percy, the head of the Boston depot, will take down the message and send it to Shadrack by regular messenger. The whole thing will take a little over a day and a half."

"Thank you so much, Maxine," Sophia said gratefully.

"I would imagine that for many people these days yours is the only correspondence that crosses the lines of battle," Goldenrod remarked.

"Indeed," Maxine said, looking out at the city. "All regular mail has ground to a halt. To be a human courier is very dangerous these days. But I am sure Marcel will have no problem. Now," she added, heading back to the stairs, "let us return to the dining room, and I will tell you my idea for how Burr and Calixta might travel safely out of New Orleans." There was a wicked gleam in her eye. "It is an excellent idea, and I think no one is going to like it."

6

MOREL AND VIOLETS

—1892, August 6: 13-Hour 07—

Moreover, researchers (such as Veressa Metl) have suggested that the Marks should be thought of as a spectrum. My observations of the Elodeans, known as the Eerie in New Occident, indicate that they bear more of the Mark of the Vine than people in the southern Baldlands. Could it also be that the spectrum, as Metl describes it, corresponds to geography? And could it be, then, that there is also a spectrum for the Mark of Iron, resulting in some places with people and animals more "marked" than others?

—From Sophia Tims's Reflections on a Journey to the Eerie Sea

"RAIDERS?" CALIXTA EXCLAIMED. "Have you seen what raiders wear? Their clothes are invariably in tatters. Not one knows the meaning of 'clean hair.' And I have yet to see a raider who understands the fundamentals of footwear fashion."

"I knew you would hate the idea," Maxine said, looking rather pleased. "It's precisely because you *do* hate it and because everyone knows you would never be caught *dead* wearing ragged clothes that dressing as a raider would be ideal. No one would suspect you of wearing such a disguise."

Calixta scowled. Burr, Wren, Errol, and Goldenrod were absorbing the proposal with rather more success.

"These raiders," Errol asked, "parts of their body are made of iron?"

"In the Baldlands," Goldenrod explained, "people like me are said to have the Mark of the Vine—for the parts of me that resemble a plant. So there are also people who, instead of plant, have parts made of metal. Often iron. And many of them are raiders."

"Not all of them," Sophia put in. "My friend Theo isn't a raider, but he has bones in one hand made of iron. I like your idea," she told Maxine.

"Wren is unrecognizable with his tattoos," Calixta pointed out. "Why don't we all disguise ourselves in the same way?"

"A band of tattooed smugglers from the Indies would draw attention on a train in the Territories," Maxine said. "But raiders are so common there that no one would spare you a glance."

"You and Burr could stay here," Sophia offered. "I know the *Swan* has sailed, but you don't have to go north. That wasn't part of the plan."

"Of course we will go north with you," Calixta grumbled. "I certainly won't stay cooped up like one of Maxine's pigeons while all of you are merrily rolling into a war zone."

"The other concern," Wren said, "is that the League may have devised additional traps for us. I had not anticipated that they would set a reward for me, much less spread rumors about you and Burr. I am afraid they are proving far more intent on my recapture than I had expected. This being so, they might well have set further obstacles in our path."

"It's decided, then," Burr said, clapping his hands. "We travel north as raiders. Maxine, what do you have for us by way of disguises?"

She smiled, not a little smugly. "I have everything you might possibly want—and more."

They began the transformation in a long room on the ground floor. In the center were tables stacked with boxes, burlap bags, and hay, and the walls were lined with shelves and wardrobes. All manner of strange objects filled them: a plaster statue of a winged horse; the wooden head of a cruelly grinning bearded giant; a stuffed beaver with beady glass eyes. Sophia shuddered inadvertently. "Maxine's house is a smuggler's treasure chest," Burr said, smiling reassuringly. "Sneaking a few pirates out of New Orleans is nothing compared to what she's already done."

"I appreciate the compliment, but I believe," Maxine said, opening one of the wardrobes, "my feats will never match those of my great-grandmother, who smuggled slaves out of New Orleans."

Sophia's eyes opened wide. "She did?"

"Two hundred and seventy-three of them, over the course of her lifetime. She smuggled all of them to freedom in the north and west, long before the revolt and the formation of New Akan. I come from a long line of smugglers," she said proudly.

Burr helped her pull several crates from the wardrobe; they tinkled tellingly as he set them on one of the tables.

"Ugh, the *bells*," Calixta complained. "I had forgotten that in addition to being unwashed and unfashionable, we also have to jangle about like human tambourines."

"Stop your protests," Burr scolded. "It is most unseemly for a pirate who has built a sizable fortune out of almost nothing and sailed to half a dozen Ages, all the while cheerfully breaking hearts in every port as if they were made of the flimsiest glass. And leaving me, often enough, to pick up the crushed and rather sharp pieces," he added wryly. "I issue you a challenge: Is it possible to be a comely raider? I propose that it is impossible. Even you, dear sister, cannot transform the raider into an alluring creature."

Calixta narrowed her eyes. "Very well. I accept your challenge. I submit to you that I will be the most irresistible raider ever to jingle-jangle a worn boot through the Territories."

"Bravo!" cried her brother. "Bravely put!"

Wren and Errol exchanged a brief smile.

"There are silver teeth here!" Sophia exclaimed, drawing open a small wooden box lined with velvet.

"Several sets, my dear," Maxine said. "You will have no trouble at all disappearing into your costumes."

THE AFTERNOON WAS spent assembling their disguises, and the early evening was spent enjoying more of Celia's cooking. Sophia almost forgot that, beyond the walls of Maxine's house, a suspicious city—and the League—was waiting for them.

She was reminded of it as the evening drew to a close and the travelers rose to find their beds. Maxine approached with a gleam in her eye. "Sophia, dear, would you like me to tell your fortune?"

"Oh, you'll frighten her out of her senses, Maxine," Burr objected, before Sophia could reply.

"Nonsense," Calixta protested. "Sophia frightens less easily than most pirates in the Indies."

"You must not remember the first time Maxine told your fortune. You were so pale I thought you would faint. All the sun in Hispaniola would not have—"

"Ridiculous!" Calixta exclaimed. "Me? Frightened of fortune-telling? Besides, Sophia is well used to mysterious prognostications, thanks to those nonsensical Ausentinian maps."

Goldenrod and Errol looked meaningly at Sophia, and she gave them a slight smile. Unchecked, the pirates would make every decision for everyone. "I wouldn't mind having my fortune told, Maxine," Sophia said. "Though I don't believe in the Fates."

"This has nothing to do with the Fates," Maxine told her. "It's a much older power—you shall see."

"I'll be awake, Sophia," Goldenrod said gently. "Whenever you are done."

Sophia gave her a nod of thanks as Maxine led her out of the drawing room and toward the back of the house, near the kitchen. There, in a room that Sophia had not yet seen, Maxine began to light candles in the darkness. Slowly, the contours of the space appeared: a round table of smooth, white marble stood at the center of the room. Tall candles encircled the table, leaving only a narrow passage in and out. Dark drapes covered all the windows. An armoire—tall, of pale wood with scroll-work—stood closed, hunkering in the corner of the room.

"Wait here for me a little while, Sophia," Maxine said, disappearing by another door that led in the direction of the kitchen.

As she stood by the table, Sophia listened to the sounds of the house. It had been a long time since she had been alone, and in silence. She heard Calixta and Burr still bantering somewhere down the corridor. She heard the quiet noises of Maxine in the kitchen, opening and closing cabinets. In the background, she heard the murmuring of the pigeons in the dovecote. And beyond all of this, she heard the distant noises of the city: cries and calls; the clatter of hooves on cobblestone; a sudden muffled burst of laughter. There was something else, too—a remote roar or rumble, like the wind or the ocean.

Sophia closed her eyes. She lost track of time as she stood there, trying to place the strange sound. It was the clouds, she realized: the yellow clouds that sat upon the city and refused to yield rain. Even inside Maxine's house, buttressed by the thick walls, the air felt dank, heavy, and somehow foreboding. *Why?* Sophia wondered. With her eyes closed, she explored the question, listening to the distant rumble as if trying to hear words within it.

A nearer sound disturbed her thoughts, and Sophia opened her eyes, startled, to see Maxine returning. The first thing she noticed was that her eyes had adjusted to the darkness, and more of the room was revealed. The walls were covered with dark drawings: lines and spirals and faces that seemed to describe a specific shape, only to alter and become something different. *It's a tattooed room,* she thought, *like Wren's arms.*

Maxine was holding a silver pitcher and a platter. She wore

a black veil that covered her entire person, leaving only her hands free. Placing the pitcher on the table, she gestured to the armoire in the corner of the room. She opened its doors, revealing a darkened interior of shelves filled with objects. Sophia approached the armoire and peered into its depths, trying to make out its contents. "Choose as many as you'd like," Maxine said, her voice slightly muffled by her veil. She held the platter before her, waiting.

There were four shelves, all of them piled high. Sophia wanted to protest that she could not see, but she realized that perhaps this was partly the point. A pale shape like a moon at the back of the middle shelf drew her eye, and she took it out. It was a circle of wood, smooth and flat, that seemed cut horizontally from a tree. She placed it on the platter Maxine was holding. Something on the lower shelf winked in the candlelight, and Sophia reached for it: a silver chain.

Her eyes had gotten used to the deeper darkness, and she saw more clearly what the armoire contained. It looked like wreckage: the contents of an abandoned attic; the dregs of a shipwreck; the bits and pieces at the bottom of an old trunk. And yet, here and there some things intrigued her. She picked them up and set them one by one on the platter: a broken piece of glass, a horseshoe, a smooth brown shape that might have been wood or amber, a white shell, a velvet ribbon, an old key, and the porcelain arm of a doll.

Without meeting Sophia's eye, Maxine walked back to the table. Slowly, she placed the objects from the platter on the table, creating a perimeter. Making her way back to where Sophia stood, she put the empty plate aside, then reached beneath the veil and produced a pair of silver scissors. Sophia flinched as the fortune-teller's veiled figure leaned toward her. Without a word, Maxine cut a strand of hair from Sophia's head and dropped it into the silver pitcher.

"Morel for honesty, violets for sight. Truth in tresses and payment in blood." She stabbed her forefinger quickly against the scissors, letting a slow drop of blood fall into the pitcher. She tucked the scissors away, then swirled the pitcher high over her head. Drawing it down toward the table, Maxine had to pull as if tugging it out of the hands of some invisible being. The pitcher jolted slightly as it came free. Sophia heard Maxine let out her breath.

Then Maxine emptied its contents onto the table.

Sophia gasped. The liquid was viscous and dark, almost black against the marble. Instead of pooling where Maxine poured it, the substance spread outward, stopping just at the edges of the table. A thick trunk channeled across the surface and then fanned out into branches, which split into even thinner branches. The pitcher poured far more than it seemed to contain, and when the last drop had fallen, a black shape like a tree filled the white stone. The branches reached out toward the objects Maxine had placed at the perimeter, making it seem as if each was a piece of unusual fruit on this most unusual tree.

"Ah, here we are," Maxine whispered, walking around the

table appraisingly, admiring each branch of the black tree. "Yes, yes—I can see," she continued, following the dark limbs with a pointing fingertip as if reading a text spread across the table. "I would never have thought . . ." she trailed off. "Astonishing. Not impossible, but astonishing." Again, she circled the table slowly, commenting under her breath until she had reached Sophia at the roots of the tree.

Without removing the veil, she looked up and finally seemed to meet Sophia's eyes. "Your fortune lies told before you," she said quietly. "Not one fortune, but several. The objects at the edges are all pieces of a life you may live. Some will prove meaningless. Others will prove essential. Just as the tree suggests many fortunes, so the objects pertain to many possible lives.

"The main trunk of the tree is unavoidable—the path you will certainly take. But the branches are all uncertain. You might take this one," she gestured, "or that one," she pointed to another. "These possible paths are so numerous that it would take a lifetime—your lifetime—to describe them. I will describe only those that are most dangerous, most probable, or most important."

Sophia did not speak. She waited, an unexpected tenseness coiled in her stomach. The Fates no longer meant anything to her, and she had stopped believing that the world was ordered by some greater power. Yet she found herself watching Maxine's movements with hopefulness and dread, as if this would actually determine her fortune.

"This is one path you might take," Maxine said, indicating the lowest branch of the tree. It ended at the horseshoe. "It is a dangerous path. Along it, you seek vengeance for a friend you have loved. The vengeance takes you into darkness, into a world of terrible deeds. By the end of this path, some of those deeds are your own."

Sophia nodded wordlessly as Maxine looked to her for acknowledgment.

"This path is less likely, but you will find it alluring," she went on, pointing to a higher branch that led to the broken piece of glass. "It is the path of knowledge. Along it, you will become the greatest cartologer of the known world. Your uncle's mantle will pass to you. But along with knowledge comes peril. This form of knowledge, while pure in itself, attracts the attention of those who would misuse it. You find yourself a fugitive, an exile, and your knowledge becomes a great burden."

Again, she looked up at Sophia, who nodded once more. The knot in her stomach was tightening. Were none of these possible futures happy ones?

"Now, this path," Maxine continued, gesturing to the path that ended in the velvet ribbon, "is safer. It is the path of prosperity. There is happiness, though there is less knowledge. Your cartology fades into the background, and your life becomes firmly anchored in the material world. Exploration and profit. Treasure and adventure. This path holds only trivial dangers and many pleasures. But I see a vein of discontent pulsing through the pleasure: a sense of being dissatisfied. Be forewarned—this path will bring you happiness, but it may not bring you fulfillment.

"And then there is this path," Maxine concluded, waving her arm over a broad branch that led to the tree ring and the small, brown shape. "I am mystified by this path, for parts of it are obscured to me. It seems dangerous, but I cannot tell you what the dangers are. It seems fulfilling, but I cannot describe the forms of fulfillment. What I see is a pattern: losses followed by discoveries; grief followed by intense joy; bewilderment followed by a font of certain knowledge. This is a complex path."

"How will I know?" Sophia finally asked. "How will I know which path I am on? And do I have a choice?"

"There are choices everywhere," Maxine replied, waving her arm over the table. "They begin here. Which path of these do you wish to take? I will tell you how to find it."

Vengeance, knowledge, prosperity, or uncertainty. Sophia could see, even with such brief descriptions, that all but the first path had both good and bad things about them. Knowledge was important, Sophia reflected, but it would count for very little if she had to spend her life running from others who sought it. Prosperity was pleasurable, but she had already seen what a life of prosperity looked like: Miles, Calixta, and Burr had followed that path. There was a certain carelessness to their lives that Sophia found appealing but somehow . . . deflating.

"I would follow the last path," Sophia said aloud. "Though there are uncertainties, the pattern you describe is one I think I could live with. One I think I would like. I am used to loss and

I am used to finding things in the wake of that loss. This seems the right path for me."

Maxine nodded gravely, almost bowing as she let her head fall forward. As she rose, she took the tree ring and the brown shape in her hands. "Then let me tell you how to find this path. There are three things to remember—three crucial junctures. One will happen very soon. The other two will not happen for quite some time. Are you ready to hear them?"

Sophia swallowed. "Yes."

"First. When you see the knight and the dragon, you must think only of your own safety. Your instinct is to stay. You must flee."

"A knight and a dragon?"

"That is what I see—I can only imagine that they are symbols."

"How will I recognize them?"

Maxine smiled under the veil. "You will recognize them. Second, you will learn something that causes you to doubt the honesty of someone you love. When this happens, you will be wise to look beyond reason for your judgment."

"What do you mean, beyond reason?"

"Reason and rationality alone cannot decide this for you. Listen to the part of you that judges the world on feeling."

"Very well."

"Third. Something will change the ground beneath your feet. What was natural will become unnatural. Dust will change to water. Water will change to dust. You will feel fear.

You must overcome this fear—your accumulated knowledge has the answer."

"So I must ignore my instincts, my reason, and my feelings in succession," Sophia said, disheartened.

Maxine's voice was steady and encouraging. "It is not a matter of ignoring them, but of knowing when to trust which part of yourself. In the first case, put your instinct aside and trust the virtue of self-preservation. In the second case, put your reason aside and trust the virtue of affection. In the third case, put your feelings aside and trust the virtue of knowledge. You have all these things—instinct, reason, sentiment, and knowledge. This telling of your fortune only counsels you when to heed each."

Sophia nodded slowly. "I understand."

"Take these," Maxine said, holding out the tree ring and the brown shape. "They hold the keys to your path. They are first steps to launch you upon it."

Sophia took the two objects and looked at them in the half darkness, mystified.

Maxine smiled reassuringly. "And now you may help me extinguish the candles. The fortune-telling is done."

SOPHIA RETURNED TO her room feeling unsettled. She had accepted Maxine's offer thinking that it would be amusing—like having one's cards read at a fair. But Maxine had seemed so solemn, her vision of the future so true, that Sophia found herself shaken.

The little bedroom was lit with lamps. Dark violet curtains

had been drawn shut, and the bed with its violet-trimmed bedding had been turned down. Sophia placed the two objects Maxine had given her on a spindly little table by the side of the bed and stared at them in the flickering light of the flame lamp.

There was a light knock on her door. "Come in," Sophia called. She knew already that it would be Goldenrod, and she turned expectantly.

Goldenrod made her way in quietly, shutting the door behind her. "You are upset," she said, coming to stand by Sophia. She wore an embroidered nightdress that fell to her bare green feet—clearly borrowed from Maxine's closet.

"I didn't know the fortune-telling would feel so . . . real."

"Perhaps a little like the Ausentinian maps," Goldenrod suggested. "Truthful but confusing at the same time."

"Yes," Sophia agreed. "Exactly like that."

"All attempts to describe the future have such an effect. They have the ring of truth because they seem possible, but they are unclear because nothing of the future is known with precision. What are these?"

"Maxine gave them to me. She says they are objects with meaning for the path I have chosen. But I don't know what they mean."

Goldenrod took them up one at a time, examining them silently before placing them back on the small table. "From a tree and an élan."

"An élan? What is that?"

"It is also known as an elk, or moose. Both these objects hold memories."

Sophia started. "Memories? What do you mean?"

"These rings each correspond to a year of the tree's growth. The most recent year is here, by the bark. And this," she said, picking up the brown shape, "is a piece of élan antler. Males drop their antlers each year."

"Moose antler," Sophia said wonderingly. "But how can they hold memories?"

"Memory maps, the kind you know, are made by people using other objects as their vehicles. These maps here are less complex, more intuitive. They were made by this tree"—she indicated the circle of wood—"and this moose."

Sophia took this in. "And you can read them because you could speak with them while they were living."

"It is likely the moose is still living," Goldenrod corrected her, "since this antler looks quite fresh—it may be from last year or the year before. Yes—just as I would communicate with them in the present, I can read their memories of the past. But it is not entirely beyond you, Sophia. These may be the perfect way to begin."

"Begin what?"

"Begin to understand the world as an Elodean does."

"But I am not Eerie—Elodean. I can't do what you do."

Goldenrod smiled. She put down the antler and reached out, clasping Sophia's hands in her own green ones. "You will remember what I told you in the Papal States—how the Weatherers read more deeply than we do, heal more expansively than the rest of us."

"I remember."

"It has always struck me that the quality that sets the Weatherers apart is also that which sets you apart. They weather time—this is what gives them their name. It is a different way of describing what you do: to wander, timeless."

Sophia's breath caught in her throat. "Really?"

"Yes. It is true that you are not Elodean, but I think our form of knowledge is not restricted to our blood. I think it can be taught—and learned. It might be easier to begin with something inert, like this bark and this bone. For you, it will resemble map reading."

Sophia felt a sudden thrill rising in her chest. "If you think it's possible—of course! Of course I want to learn. How do I begin?"

Goldenrod squeezed her hands. "We will begin tomorrow. Before then, if you like, spend time with these two sets of memories. Discover everything you can by examining them with all your senses. Then you will tell me what you find."

Sophia nodded.

Goldenrod considered her closely. "Do you feel less anxious about your fortune?"

"Yes." She looked up at the Eerie, her kind face inches from her own. Impulsively, she threw her arms around her friend's neck. "Thank you." Goldenrod could not know that apart from relieving her anxiety, she was giving Sophia what she had wanted for so many months: a way to keep learning, a way to keep reading the world through maps.

7

THE LESSON

—*1892, August 4: 5-Hour 15*—

In fact, we know almost as little about the Territories themselves—the landscape and its elements—as we know about the inhabitants. Cartologers have neglected the Territories for decades, and recurring conflict makes an expansive survey project unlikely. The maps included here (see pages 57–62) are drawn from the observations of New Occident explorers (this author included) and the expertise of locals. Contrasting one source with the other, it is evident that local knowledge reaches far beyond what outsiders can observe.

—From Shadrack Elli's History of New Occident

MAJOR MERRET HAD been raised in a military family. Both he and his father had attended the military academy in Virginia. His grandfather had fought against the rebellion that had earned New Akan its statehood. And now Merret was battling New Akan himself, more than ninety years later and in far more dangerous circumstances: that state had allied with the vast Indian Territories, a polity of unpredictable strength and resources.

Major Merret was inclined to think little of that strength

and those resources, because in general he thought little of people outside of New Occident. In fact, he thought little of people beyond southern Virginia, his home turf. But he was also a cautious man, and though he might privately think the Indian Territories a dusty wasteland and New Akan a damp one, each populated by ragtag bands of cowards, he would professionally treat them as formidable enemies. For this reason, it infuriated him that he had to face the enemy with his own band of what he knew were ragtag cowards: the "blocks"—former inmates of the prison system who hardly knew the proper handling of a weapon, and whose experience of fighting had been motivated by greed, or viciousness, or bumbling self-defense. Merret brooded over the speculation that he had done something—he could not fathom what—to displease his superiors, and it had landed him in charge of this collection of loafers and scoundrels.

Major Merret's contempt was no secret. In fact, it became more and more evident by the day, so that on the morning of August fourth, when his troops found themselves nearing the edge of New Occident and thereby on the very threshold of enemy lines, it fell upon them like burning walls that had smoldered slowly for hours.

Despite his attempts to teach them discipline, Major Merret realized, the blocks had learned nothing. He said as much to them now, as they stood before him, awkward and disheveled in their uneven rows. Days of humid weather had tried what little discipline he had been able to instill in them. The heavy, yellow clouds that sat motionless overhead made the air rancid. Occasional rumbles brought no rain, only heavier humidity, and the troops were not coping with it well. Their clothes were rumpled. Hardly anyone had slept peacefully, and more than one fight had broken out the night before. Instead of orderly, obedient faces, Merret saw men that were unkempt, under-slept, and on edge. The sight filled him with furious despair.

His voice carried and he spoke with control. "I have wasted weeks attempting to pound into your imbecilic skulls that in a few days you may be fighting for your lives against people who actually *chose* to fight in this war. And because you are too rock-headed to understand this, you fight with each other instead of preparing to fight the battle that awaits you." He looked at the two men who stood beside him, the culprits who had most recently provoked his outrage and who now faced the entire company. One of them, MacWilliams, looked bored. His massive hands rested at his sides, his knuckles red from where he had hit the other man. Trembling, his blackened eye trained on the ground, Collins could hardly stand up straight; he seemed on the verge of collapse. Merret considered them judiciously and decided to make an example of them: the bully and the weakling. They both had their uses.

"If it were up to me," Major Merret snarled, "I would gladly send you across that border to meet your incompetent deaths. But, unfortunately, I have a job to do, and you are the inade-quate tools with which I must do it." He turned sharply to Col-lins, the trembling soldier. "Are you afraid of what awaits you in the Indian Territories, Collins?"

Collins startled. He gave Merret a fearful sidelong glance. He had no idea what answer the major wanted.

"Answer me, Collins," barked Major Merret.

Collins drew himself up and clenched his jaw in what he hoped was an impression of staunchness. He did his best to stop trembling, balling his thin fingers into fists and locking his narrow knees. At home, in Philadelphia, Collins was a printer, and he had been thrown in prison for publishing a satirical cartoon of Gordon Broadgirdle. Before being incarcerated, the most violent altercation Collins had ever experienced was an amicable dispute with his brother over the cost of a new printing press. He had no place in the Western War, and he knew it. "No, sir?" he lied.

"And are you afraid of MacWilliams?"

Collins swallowed, baffled once again. "I can try not to be, sir," he said.

"And are you afraid of me, Collins?"

Collins took a deep breath. He had thought that his answers were somehow, miraculously proving correct, but now he feared that he was being led into a trap, and he could not imagine how to get out of it because he had no idea what the trap even was. He decided to be truthful, because he had already tried lying. "Yes, sir," he said. Suddenly, so suddenly that he had no idea how it had happened, Collins found himself sprawled on the ground with the damp earth inches from his face, and he realized that there was something holding him down.

Major Merret looked with concealed satisfaction at the surprised faces of his company. Even MacWilliams was a little startled. With his boot planted firmly on Collins's back, the major pressed down—hard. "You are not nearly afraid enough, Collins," he said, his voice steely. "Let me tell you why. The Indians might kill you. And MacWilliams might give you a black eye every morning for the next month. But they can't do what I can. They can't destroy your self-respect, making you wish you'd never survived that prison in Philadelphia."

Collins coughed. He tried to lift his head just a little, but the boot pressed down harder.

Merret waited, allowing the company to absorb Collins's humiliation. MacWilliams, he noticed, had exchanged his boredom for smugness. "They can't make you eat dirt the way I can," Merret finally said. He looked down at the pitifully thin man. Collins's uniform was ripped, no doubt from the altercation with MacWilliams. The skin of his hands was pinched, as if worn to the bone. Merret felt a shudder of disgust. "Eat dirt, soldier," he said, saying each word clearly.

He heard a murmur moving through the company, and he pointedly ignored it. "I said, Collins, *eat dirt*." He pressed his boot down and waited.

Slowly, hesitantly, Collins turned his face toward the ground. The boot let up slightly. Then he opened his mouth and took a small mouthful of dirt between his teeth. The boot pressed down again.

"I said *eat* dirt," Merret said. "Swallow it." He looked at MacWilliams; the smugness had been replaced by an air of discomfort. Merret felt Collins's ribs rise underneath his boot.

"Again," he said. Then he lifted his boot so that Collins could once again turn his face to the ground.

Theo stood in the second row, watching Merret's lesson in discipline. He felt as sick to his stomach as if he, too, were eating the soil. Beside him, Casanova radiated rage. All of them did. But Theo could sense something else, along with the rage: fear. It was like being in a dark cave, where the smell of damp hung all around, and then the smell of something rotten slithered out from within it: part and parcel of the damp, one made by the other, until the scent of mold overpowered the damp and they became an indistinguishable whole. Theo couldn't tell if the fear was in him, too, or if it just filled the air so thickly that he was surrounded by it. He watched as Merret forced Collins to eat mouthful after mouthful of earth. And in the midst of that lesson in fear, Theo felt something unexpected: a wish to defend Collins, no matter what the cost. For a moment, the wish felt good, like a flare of clean, bright fire in the dank cave.

"Well, MacWilliams?" Major Merret asked, into the still silence.

MacWilliams was looking at him now with open hatred. His boredom-turned-smugness-turned-discomfort had crystalized into something else.

"Are you going to do anything about it?" the major prodded, his tone insolent. "Do you have the decency and common sense to help a fellow soldier being made to eat dirt? A soldier who might well be you next time? Or don't you?" He stared at

MacWilliams, a sneering smile on his face. Then he lifted his boot and stepped back.

Collins coughed. A moment later he began retching. MacWilliams, with a final look of loathing at Merret, crouched down and gently helped Collins to his knees. He kept his hand on the man's back as Collins vomited.

Theo's brief flare of good feeling evaporated. Instead, he felt a cold repellence at how Merret had manipulated MacWilliams—and the entire company. He had intentionally brought about the anger, the fear, and finally the wish to defend Collins.

Merret's lesson had succeeded. They would not fight one another again. They had a common enemy now.

As the major gave them leave to begin breaking camp, and the soldiers dispersed, fleeing as quickly as possible, Theo stood rooted to the spot. The clouds overhead rumbled, and Theo wiped sweat from his forehead with the sleeve of his uniform. "Hey," Casanova said, putting his hand on Theo's shoulder. "Come on." Theo didn't respond. "I know. Merret is a brute. But there's nothing we can do about it."

Theo blinked and turned to look at Casanova. "He's not a brute. He's a clown. That's what this company needs to see."

Casanova shook his head. "What do you mean?"

"He's a joke. What we have to do is laugh at him. If we can laugh at him, we won't be afraid of him."

Casanova's good eye narrowed. "I don't know what you're planning, Theo, but don't plan it. Just let it pass." He pulled Theo back to their tent, a worried look on his scarred face.

8

BARK AND BONE

—*1892, August 6: 19-Hour 36*—

I have come to the conclusion that there is a fine line between observing the present and predicting what might happen in the future. They seem distinct, but could it not be that through one lies the other? I have seen how a saturated understanding of the surrounding circumstances can be so complete, so all-encompassing, that the supposed future is not so much an unknown element to be imagined or guessed, but a direct and indeed obvious result of the present.

—From Sophia Tims's Reflections on a Journey to the Eerie Sea

SOPHIA KNEW SHE needed to sleep, since they planned to leave Maxine's house before dawn. But Goldenrod's words—that she, Sophia, might be like an Eerie—excited her so much that she sat on the edge of her bed, eagerly studying the two objects Maxine had given her. *Just for a little while,* she told herself, *and then I'll go to bed.*

The flat disc of tree trunk was almost perfectly circular. It had been cut cleanly—so cleanly that the rings stood out crisply from one another, all slightly different shades of light brown. Sophia ran her finger along them, thinking that the tree's memories might be felt by touch, just as on an ordinary memory map. But no memories woke in her mind.

She scrutinized the outer edge. A thin, crusty layer of bark had protected the tree. *I don't even know what kind of tree this is,* she realized. Reaching into her satchel, she pulled out her notebook and pencils and turned to a clean page. She drew a careful sketch of Maxine's tree, including the paths she had not taken, and she added the instructions the fortune-teller had given her at the end: the three crossroads. Then she drew the two objects and listed her questions:

> *Questions about Maxine's maps.*
>   *1. What kind of tree?*
>   *2. What was used to cut it down?*
>   *3. Who cut it down?*
>   *4. Does how it was cut / who cut it matter to the map?*
>   *5. Was the map made by cutting? After cutting? During life of the tree?*

Sophia tapped the pencil lightly against her chin. Then she added,

>   *6. Do these maps sleep and wake like other memory maps?*
>   *7. If so, what would wake a tree map?*

She stared at the ring once more, her thoughts wandering to different possibilities. Water? Sunlight? Soil? She dipped her finger into the glass of water on the spindly table and allowed several drops to fall onto the tree ring. Nothing happened. "I can't try sunlight or soil until tomorrow," she murmured aloud.

On the next clean page in her notebook, she wrote:

> *Observations about the tree and antler.*
> *Tree: smooth to touch apart from bark.*

She pulled it close and sniffed it. *Smells as though it might be pine?*

Then she realized what she had not yet done: count the tree's rings. Running her finger from the outer edge to the middle, she counted forty-three. *43 rings, so the tree was 43 years old when it was cut down.*

Next, though she felt silly doing it, she held the tree ring up to her ear. *No sound,* she wrote.

After a moment's hesitation, she touched the tip of her tongue to the bark. *Tastes like wood. Obviously.*

Though she pored over the cross section for some time more, she could add nothing else to her observations. Putting it aside with a sigh, she took up the piece of antler.

Antler, she wrote. *Smooth to the touch, except for where it broke off from the rest of the antler: jagged and fractured like bone. Dark brown, almost like wood.*

She applied her other senses to it tentatively. *Tastes like nothing. Sounds like nothing. Smells like old coats.*

She shifted back to her page of questions.

1. *Why was the antler piece broken off from the rest?*
2. *Did it break before or after the moose shed antlers for the winter?*
3. *How are memories put into an antler?*
4. *If this is a sleeping map, what would wake the memories?*

Stumped, Sophia stared off into the distance, considering. She found herself imagining—out of pure speculation, since she had never seen a living moose—what the days of a moose might be like in the wild. Presumably this moose would graze for food and look for water. He might walk long distances. Would there be other moose nearby? Would there be people? Or did moose live in solitude? She imagined green, hilly landscapes and cool pine forests and warm ponds with mud at the bottom.

Resting her head on her pillow, she stared at the ceiling. She pictured a slow meandering path through a green field. At the far end of it was a forest. Insects buzzed in endless circles over the tall grass, and birds dipped through the air in pursuit.

The dark curtains shifted gently with a sudden breeze, and the dank air from outside stole into the room. A quiet rumble sounded from the gathered clouds above the city. The antler lay cradled in Sophia's palm, and her fingers closed over it reflexively. Her breathing slowed. Soon, she was asleep.

And the dreams began.

It was raining. She walked heavily along a track through the woods, and she saw the world from an elevated vantage point. Aspen, willow, and spruce grew all around her. She knew them well—each was as familiar and specific as a friend. Their branches brushed her sides gently, the cool water on the leaves soothing her skin. A clearing stood in the distance, and she felt a sense of exhausted relief, knowing home was nearby. As they reached it—she knew without knowing how that someone else was present—the rain stopped, and a thick mist swirled all around them. From out of the mist, a low bermed house appeared. Beside it was a lean-to made of logs. A short spout poured water from the house's gutters into a stone bowl inside the lean-to. "We're here, Nosh," a low voice said in her ear.

The dream shifted to another scene. She was standing at the top of a hill. A boy stood beside her, squinting into the distance. They were above a valley where a grove of trees grew alone. Something about the trees struck her as incomprehensibly beautiful. *These are not for eating*, she thought wryly. She felt drawn to them, but something much greater—some powerful impulse that spoke directly to her heart—told her to stay away. The boy beside her turned his face toward her. "What do you think, Nosh?" He looked puzzled. He was Eerie, with close-cut hair and skin that turned green as it reached his scalp. Under black eyebrows, his eyes were dark, the expression in them pensive. She felt a throb of protective affection for him as he gazed at her searchingly. "Why can't we go closer?" he asked, echoing her thoughts. The boy put his hand loosely on her shoulder and absentmindedly ran his fingers back and forth over her neck.

As they stood watching, a distant figure appeared at the crest of a hill on the far side of the valley. Sophia felt the boy beside her tense with interest. As the figure wound its way downhill, it came into closer view, and a faint cry reached them. "A Wailing," the boy gasped. Sophia's eye was drawn by movement to her left. Another figure had appeared between the hills to the south; this one moved more quickly, as if pulled forward by a string. Its cries were low sobs that echoed on the wind. She grunted to alert the boy. "You're right," he whispered. "Two Wailings." Both figures converged on the grove of trees and disappeared among them. There was a sudden silence.

The dream drifted once more, and she found herself running: running hard in the darkness. She could smell fire. Her heart was pounding. The trees that had brushed her sides so lovingly during the day scratched and tore at her now. She felt the unbridled panic in her chest outpacing her, as if it were a separate thing that was running before her, faster and faster. "We're safe, we're safe," she heard someone say. But they were only words, and they seemed to mean nothing. What were words when she had a panic to chase? There it was, light as anything, streaking through the dark woods like a pale malevolent spirit, always out of reach.

Sophia woke with a start, her own heart pounding. The antler rolled out of her palm. She pressed her hand to her heart and took deep breaths of air, air untouched by smoke. The dreams had seemed so real that it took some time for her to realize where and who she was. *There's no fire,* she repeated to herself reassuringly. *There's no fire, and I'm safe.* The flame lamp was still lit, and she rolled toward the spindly table to look at her watch. It was almost three-hour. She would have to rise soon to be on time for the train. With a sigh, she rolled back onto her pillow.

Then she remembered the antler. Searching for it among the sheets, she took up the rough object and looked at it critically. *Were those memories of yours or dreams of mine?* she asked the antler silently. Putting it carefully on the table, she closed her eyes and tried to take what rest she could before Maxine knocked on her door.

9

WREN'S VOICE

—1892, August 7: 3-Hour 51—

The obstacle in most cases is time. But imagine circumstances in which time was not an obstacle. Imagine watching the progress of a snail along a garden path. Watching the snail wind its slow way toward the cabbage leaf, you are in no doubt as to the future—it is obvious. Just as the snail's fate is obvious when you see the gardener approaching with a bucket of salt. How is it not the same with us? Could it not be that astonishing prognostications of the future are, more correctly, quite un-astonishing observations of the present made with wisdom and ample time?

—From Sophia Tims's Reflections on a Journey to the Eerie Sea

MAXINE BUNDLED THE travelers into a six-person coach in the early hours before dawn. Already wearing their disguises, they would board the earliest train to Salt Lick, which left New Orleans Station at four-hour, twelve.

She murmured quick words of encouragement and embraced each of them as they stepped up into the coach. "You look very convincing, my dear," she said to Sophia.

"It's dark out," Sophia replied with a wry smile.

"You *sound* convincing," Maxine countered. The tiny bells on Sophia's cape tinkled quietly as she wedged herself in between

Goldenrod and Errol. Calixta, Wren, and Burr sat across from them. "Be safe," the fortune-teller quietly said, and shut the open door. Calixta knocked on the roof. The horses stepped forward and the coach began rolling over the cobblestones.

The coach was pitch dark, but Sophia had seen her fellow travelers in the light and warmth of Maxine's kitchen. To her surprise, they did make convincing raiders. The ragged clothes lined with brass bells changed everyone's appearance. Goldenrod's mask was a bundle of silver chains covering the upper half of her face. Only her eyes were visible. On her hands were leather gloves dotted with tiny steel studs. Her hair was beaded with bright bells no larger than a fingernail. Errol, curious despite himself, had fitted one of the sets of metal teeth into his mouth and laughed at his own reflection. "Asr wrong ash I jont haf to chalk," he managed.

"I'll do the talking," Calixta assured him. She wore a costume similar to Goldenrod's, but upon her head was a crown with tall, sharp points that seemed half ornament, half weapon. Her heavy necklace was made of long, cylindrical bells that chimed with her every movement. The footwear, which she had modified herself—finding none of Maxine's footwear suitable—was high leather boots with steel caps. "Do I win your bet?" she had asked Burr, delighted.

He and Wren had dressed almost identically, with threadbare capes over heavy, studded vests. Their trousers had rows of bells along the outer seams. Sophia held her cape, also lined with tiny bells, folded in her lap. She had kept her own clothes—they seemed threadbare enough—and opted only for gloves, a cape, and a sturdy pair of boots trimmed with steel studs. She wore a simpler version of Goldenrod's mask: three silver chains draped delicately across her face, meeting at a single silver bead on her forehead. She found the thin chains strangely reassuring against her skin; insubstantial as they were, they made her feel protected. *That's probably why raiders wear so much metal,* she reflected, looking out through the open coach window at the dark streets of New Orleans.

The train station lay a short distance from Maxine's house. They had ridden in silence for some few minutes when the coach ground to a halt. "This isn't the station," Calixta muttered. "Driver?" she called through the open window. There was no response. Calixta was reaching for the door handle when a stranger's voice cut through the darkness.

"Richard Wren. This is Bruce Davies, agent number six-one-one. Exit the coach alone. I have orders to return you to Sydney immediately."

The travelers in the coach froze.

Calixta leaned toward the open window. "There is no Richard Wren here. We are raiders from Copper Hill headed north to Salt Lick. You have been misinformed."

"We are rarely misinformed, Captain Morris," came the dry reply. "I not only know the occupants of the coach, I know all of your movements for the past twenty hours. We did not approach you at the home of Maxine Bisset for reasons of our own, but we could easily be having this conversation there." He cleared his throat. "Agent Wren?"

After several seconds, Wren leaned forward toward the open window.

"Agent Davies, I will exit the coach and accompany you to Sydney on one condition."

There was a pause. "You are not in a negotiating position, Wren. I have four other agents with me."

Wren hesitated. "Blast his four agents," Calixta whispered fiercely. "You can't go with him. We'll get rid of them and go on to the train."

"I must," Wren said. "You don't understand. We would almost certainly all be killed." He leaned toward the window. "Agent Davies, this could be a costly engagement for you if my companions and I resist. I will go with you quietly if you promise that my friends will be allowed to continue undisturbed. The League will leave them alone. Always."

"Look, agent," came the reply, "you know the process as well as any of us." There was a pause. "The best I can offer is that we won't take them in now. But I can't make any promises for the long term."

There was another pause. In the sudden quiet, Burr leaned forward and addressed his sister. "Do you remember when we tried to capture Felix to take him back to Havana? What a day that was," he ended wistfully.

Calixta chuckled, apparently not finding this unexpected recollection out of place. "How could I forget? It's the way we met Peaches."

"It was a well-played hand."

"It was indeed. A little underhanded, but well-played."

"Do you mind?" Wren snapped. "I'm trying to decide what to do."

"Wren?" the voice from the street prompted.

Wren shifted to the front of his seat. "Very well," he said heavily.

Before he could move, Burr, who was closest to the door, flung it open and jumped from the coach in a single bound. He slammed the coach door behind him. "Ride on," he shouted to the driver, and the coach jolted abruptly into motion.

Wren stared, aghast. *"Wait!"* he cried, rising from his seat.

Calixta covered his mouth with her gloved hand and pushed him back. "Oh, no, you don't."

He made a muffled complaint from behind the glove and began trying to throw Calixta off.

Perched on Errol's shoulder, Seneca fluttered his wings in agitation.

"What good will it do now, Richard?" Calixta argued, pushing him roughly.

"I can't let him—" Wren leaped for the door.

Seneca burst into movement, flapping anxiously, his wide wings brushing the ceiling of the coach. In a rapid movement that Sophia did not entirely catch, Calixta took out her pistol and knocked Wren firmly on the head. Seneca screeched and jumped onto Goldenrod's shoulder.

Wren slumped backward. Sophia gasped.

"What have you done?" Errol asked Calixta. Struggling

against the coach's rapid movement, he switched seats and tried to pull Wren upright.

"Oh, I was only saving him from a certain death," Calixta said calmly.

"By knocking him unconscious?"

"Yes. Precisely."

"And what if you are sending Burr to certain death instead?" Errol, who was not quite as tall as Wren, finally succeeded in righting the Australian, who now lolled against his shoulder.

Goldenrod held Seneca on her forearm and whispered to him earnestly, soothing the falcon in a strange language.

"Burr knows what he's doing," Calixta replied complacently.

There was a silence.

Sophia could not see them, but she could sense Goldenrod and Errol sending their thoughts across to one another, wondering what to do.

"Are you sure this is wise, Calixta?" Goldenrod finally asked. "We know little of the League and its ways. Perhaps we should return."

"And take Sophia back into danger?" Calixta asked archly.

"Yes," Sophia said, finally finding her voice. She had been too shocked until now to speak. "We should go back and help Burr."

"No," Errol and Goldenrod said at the same time.

Sophia could almost hear Calixta smiling. "Trust me," the pirate said. "Burr has this well in hand. But I will need help carrying Wren to the train."

Errol did not reply.

"Burr's stratagem will be all for naught if we leave him in the coach," Calixta pointed out.

"Very well," the archer agreed reluctantly. "Though I cannot pretend to like this."

"It would not have been my first choice, either," Calixta admitted as they slowed to a stop. "But we could not hand Wren over, and this is the best possible course." The lights of the station illuminated the coach. Calixta smiled brightly, as if she had not just seen her brother disappear into the night with hostile strangers wielding unknown powers. "We have just enough time to board the train. Come along!"

10

THE REPRISAL

—1892, August 7: 10-Hour 19—

Many of the roads connecting the states of New Occident to the Territories are no more than footpaths—trails followed by messengers and peddlers. There are a handful of wider roads—originally post roads—appropriate for wagon travel: one west out of Pennsylvania, two out of Virginia, one each out of North and South Carolina, and two out of Georgia. For the most part these are safe, and leisure travelers, should they wish to follow them, would encounter few surprises. Inns every few miles, left over from the establishment of the postal routes, offer sustenance and shelter.

—From Shadrack Elli's History of New Occident

MAJOR MERRET'S COMPANY passed into the Indian Territories on August seventh. None could tell where Pennsylvania ended and the Territories began, for the woods and hills looked much the same and the farms had long since dwindled. The craggy hills, barren in wide patches, allowed for easy passage; Theo and the rest of the trail crew had little work as the march progressed west. Every article they carried seemed heavier in the humid air: the canvas cots reeked of mildew and the Goodyear-lined packs were slick with moisture. At ten-hour, they stopped with relief to take the midday meal.

Major Merret always ate in a tent, however brief their rest stop. A five-poled canvas affair, it could fit a small dining table that doubled as a desk, and it crouched amid the seated company like a spider at the center of its web. While Major Merret rested and the company stretched or slept on their packs, the cook prepared a meal of beans and onions.

The major had his own cook, who traveled with the supply wagon and protected the store of special foods packed and carried all the way from Virginia. Fortunately for the company men, the major's cook, Private Betts, was eminently corruptible, and for the right price could find clever ways of trimming off a hunk of choice ham or a link of sausage. Private Betts disliked the major as vehemently as did the rest of the company, but he knew the advantages of his position and kept his dislike well hidden behind an obsequious exterior. As a result, the major trusted Betts. To the extent that the major liked anyone, it could even be said that the major liked Betts.

So the company was particularly surprised when, in the middle of shoveling beans and onions into their hungry stomachs, they saw the major storming out of his tent, shouting for Private Betts. "Where is he?!" Major Merret shouted. "Where is that man?"

The company went silent. All eating ceased: spoons froze in the air, all eyes fixed on their commander, and no one moved. The major was fuming. His napkin, still tucked into the collar of his shirt, fluttered in a sudden breeze and flapped up to cover his face. The major yanked the napkin away and glared.

"I believe he went to find water for washing, sir," one of the men said.

"Find him and bring him to me," the major shouted. He turned on his heel and strode back into his tent, shaking the very poles with the vigor of his entrance.

The company resumed its meal. Slowly at first and then more quickly, like a marble rolling downhill, word of what had caused the major's anger traveled outward. There was a hiccup of hesitant laughter. And then another. The sound rippled through the company, a genuine wave of laughter, to where Theo and Casanova sat side by side, eating their lunch with the other soldiers. Word had not yet reached them of what had happened to the major, but Theo smiled, enjoying the eruptions of mirth all around him.

And then it arrived. The man sitting next to Casanova leaned toward them, chuckling. "You'll never believe what happened. Someone went and put dirt in the major's lunch! Ate a few mouthfuls before he even noticed."

Theo's smiled broadened, but Casanova, with a worried glance at Theo, frowned. "Someone? It wasn't Betts?"

The soldier shook his head. "Betts denies it. Says he left the fire for a minute and anyone might have done it." As he finished his words, they saw Major Merret emerging once more from his tent. He called them to attention, and with a clattering of spoons and bowls, and the thud of packs hitting the ground, the men hurried into rows. Within seconds, they stood before the major for a lesson in discipline, as they had three days earlier—with one difference. Now there was a current of laughter moving through them. It was not a joyous laughter, but a triumphant one: less delight than vindictive glee. It bubbled up at the sight of the major, red-faced, pacing back and forth in front of them, barely able to contain himself. Every man was imagining the moment when the major had taken a bite and chewed, then stopped, wondering at the strange texture, and then suddenly understood, with a jolt, that he had been made to eat dirt. The thought was contagious, irresistible.

"I want all of you to know," the major began, without pre-amble, "exactly what will happen to this company if no one takes responsibility for this." Betts, confused and shocked, stood at the flap of the tent. The major paused, creating one of the long silences that worked so effectively to cultivate fear during his discipline lessons.

Unfortunately for the major, his ponderous silence was cut short. Only a few seconds after issuing his threat so that it hung over the company like a cloud, a voice called out from the second row. "I take responsibility."

The major jerked his head to see who had spoken.

"I take responsibility," repeated the voice.

"State your name and step forward," the major barked.

Theo stepped out from the second row and walked to stand before the company. "Theodore Constantine Thackary," he said, refusing to add his title. Somehow, Theo managed to make his stance at attention look careless. He stared straight ahead, as if the major did not exist, and the ghost of a smile lingered on his face.

The major glared at him.

"Private MacWilliams," he said, turning toward the enormous man who had been the subject of the disciplinary lesson on August fourth.

"Yes, sir," the soldier replied, stepping forward.

"Bring the spare harness from the back of the wagon."

MacWilliams hesitated. "The harness for the mules?"

"Yes."

Theo stood calmly, waiting for MacWilliams to return. The major was silent. The air of suspense began to thicken. MacWilliams walked as hurriedly as his girth would allow, returning with the heavy wooden yoke used to harness the mule when one animal rather than two hauled the wagon.

"Place the harness on Private Thackary," the major said coolly.

Once again, MacWilliams hesitated. "How do you mean, sir?"

"Place the yoke on his neck."

Theo turned, unbidden, to MacWilliams. "I won't kick like a mule, I promise," he said, smiling.

There was a flutter of uneasy laughter from the company.

"Be silent," the major said. "MacWilliams," he said sternly.

MacWilliams, prodded into action, walked up to Theo and gingerly placed the heavy wooden yoke on his neck. "I'm sorry," he whispered.

Theo turned his head as much as he was able. "S'alright. Least I'm not pulling your weight around with this thing."

MacWilliams looked at the boy with surprise and gave a faint smile. Then, his work complete, he stood back. Theo could not raise his head to face the company. He knew it would be only a matter of minutes before the weight of the yoke became unbearable. In the silence that Merret allowed to grow, interrupted only by the footfalls as he paced back and forth, Theo imagined how he must look to the men before him: bowed, penitent, shamed. They could not see his face, so they could not know that he wasn't ashamed in the least. He was glad—glad to have paid Merret back in kind and glad to have drawn out of him this retribution that made the man look petty and vindictive.

Theo waited, looking down out of the corner of his eye, until the major had turned away from him. Then Theo shuffled his feet—with a hop back and a little kick: a pair of breezy dance steps. There was a familiar, low chuckle from somewhere in the company. Casanova was probably furious, but he could still be counted on to know what Theo was thinking. Around Casanova, there was more stifled laughter. The major came to a halt and turned. Theo felt content; his purpose had been accomplished. He had wanted to show the company that Merret could be made light of, and now they had seen it.

"Enough," the major said, his voice thunderous. Somehow, though, it sounded less imposing than usual: more like an imitation of fury than fury itself. "We march west. As of this morning, we are in enemy territory and will be prepared for attack at all times. You will wear the issued headgear. And Thackary," he added, turning to Theo, "will travel with the mules."

—10-Hour 40—

CASANOVA WATCHED AS Theo was chained to the wagon. The rest of the company drifted away to break camp. Major Merret was already heading toward his tent, and Casanova, after a thoughtful pause, strode after him. He had never before been inside. When given permission to enter, he was surprised by how comfortable it was. Topping the cot was what looked like a real mattress and bedding, and a fine tufted carpet covered the coarse tent flooring. The major sat at his small writing desk, penning the last correspondence he would send before the company moved into the Indian Territories.

"What is it, Private Lakeside?" he asked, without looking up.

"I have come to make a request, Major," Casanova said. He knew the major responded best to humility, if not outright self-abasement, and he trained his eyes on the floor and clasped his hands behind his back.

The major finally looked up at him. "Members of this company are not in the habit of requesting favors from their superiors."

"I realize that, sir."

The major paused. "Well, what is it?"

"I wish to speak with you about Theodore—Private Thackary." Casanova paused, but the major said nothing. "He is just a child, sir," Casanova continued. "He is only sixteen. He may be headstrong and impudent, but he does not have the physical strength that others do." He paused. "I understand the punishment you ordered must be borne. But I would ask that you allow me to bear it in his stead."

The major was silent. Casanova glanced up and saw Merret looking at him with a mixture of displeasure and curiosity. Finally he turned to his desk, folded and sealed his correspondence, and stood up. He walked past Casanova to the flap of his tent and leaned out. "Post this before we leave," he said, handing it to the guard outside. Then he walked back and faced Casanova. He crossed his arms and studied the large man with the disfiguring scars. Then he smiled, and his words were light and sharp, like little shards of glass. "You're both Indians, aren't you?"

Casanova kept his eyes carefully on the ground. "Yes. I'm Indian. From near Six Nations City. Theo is from the southwestern Baldlands."

Merret sighed. "Assorted as a peddler's wares," he said with faint disgust, more to himself than to Casanova. Then his tone grew sharp once more. "Word around the company has it, Private Lakeside, that you are a great coward. Is this true?"

Casanova looked down at the major's polished boots. "Yes, sir. It is."

"So I can expect that in our first battle you will take cover in the nearest tree, cowering and fearing for your life."

Casanova stared at the ground. "In my experience, sir," he said quietly, "there are no battles. Only massacres." He paused. "And whom would you call a hero in a massacre? Violence is not easily directed or contained, and it makes cowards of all men."

"Are you suggesting I am unable to command my company?"

"Even the most brilliant commander cannot keep a guiding hand over the actions of others. Violence is its own thing. It defies control of even the Fates." Casanova took a deep breath. He realized he had lost his humble tone all too quickly. The major was an expert at provocation. "Will you consider my request regarding Private Thackary, sir?"

Major Merret looked at Casanova with repugnance, as if discovering a rat in the bedding of his cot. "No, Private Lakeside, you may not carry the harness for Thackary. But if you are so eager to shoulder an extra burden, you may carry Thackary's pack along with yours as we march west." He turned away. "You are dismissed."

PART II
Fog

11

SENECA'S EAR

—1892, August 7: 4-Hour 48—

New Occident does not speak and smile and cry like you or me, but perhaps we should nevertheless consider what our world would look like from the vantage point of an Age. Might we not learn something about ourselves (and the Age) by considering this vantage point? I do not wish to echo the old sentiment that we are insignificant before the majesty of nature, for I do not think we are insignificant. On the contrary, perhaps if we were to consider that vantage point, we would realize, instead, that it is vital to be aware of our significance: that our actions and our sentiments have an effect on the Age around us.

—From Sophia Tims's Reflections on a Journey to the Eerie Sea

SOPHIA COULD HEAR Calixta and Wren arguing in the neighboring compartment. Wren, who had never before lost his temper in their presence, was shouting at the top of his lungs. "Do you think they will be deterred when they find themselves in possession of the wrong man? No! They will just keep hounding us as we travel north, putting all of you in danger!"

Calixta remained completely unfazed. "You underestimate Burr," she told Wren yet again—she had been saying as much for the last fifteen minutes. "Calm yourself. The Morrises do not give up their own, and you are one of ours. Burr has this well in hand."

"Listen to you!" Wren raged. "'One of ours'? I am *not* a hapless urchin who made his way onto the *Swan* to beg for scraps. I have made decisions that must be answered for by me and me alone! The two of you are far too used to having your own way. Goldenrod, Errol, and I—not to mention Sophia!—have indulged your domineering tendencies because they are mostly harmless and often amusing. But this time you've gone too far!"

"None of our crew are 'hapless urchins.' Well," Calixta amended, "unless you count me and Burr. Orphans, and all that. But hardly hapless."

"You're missing the point. You can't make this kind of decision for others. You *cannot*. I'm going to get off at the next station and return to New Orleans."

"If you do that, you will ruin everything Burr has done for you up to now."

There was a pause. Wren's energy was clearly flagging. "I could probably think my way out of this," he groaned, evidently in pain, "if you hadn't bashed in my skull."

"That wasn't my fault!" Calixta countered cheerfully.

Wren did not reply. A palpable exasperation hung in the silence. "I'm through with this conversation," he finally said. Sophia heard the compartment door being thrown open.

"Don't go too far," Calixta called as Wren's unsteady footsteps sounded in the corridor.

"I'm only looking for Errol," he grumbled, "so I can talk to someone with more than a shred of common sense. No need to knock me out again."

Sophia sat at the edge of her seat, her hands clasped anxiously. She searched Goldenrod's face for reassurance. But Goldenrod was staring out through the window, her expression distant and preoccupied. "This doesn't feel right," Sophia said.

"No—it does not," Goldenrod murmured, without taking her eyes from the landscape beyond the window.

"What is it?" Sophia asked, realizing that Goldenrod was referring to something else. Outside, the dank yellow clouds hung low, seeming almost to brush the treetops. "The clouds?"

Instead of answering, the Eerie threw open the window and leaned out as they slowed in anticipation of a passing train. She let the wind rush over her face, her eyes fixed on the middle distance, her expression intent and listening.

Goldenrod drew her head back inside just as Errol and Wren appeared at the compartment door. "Goldenrod," Wren said as they stepped into the compartment, "I've consulted with Errol, and he agrees—"

"It's not speaking, Richard," Goldenrod said, in agitation.

Wren stopped, his mouth open, the sudden shock draining him of color. "What do you mean?" His voice was barely audible.

"There's nothing." She swallowed hard. "There wasn't in New Orleans, either, but I thought it was because we were in the city."

Wren dropped onto the seat beside Sophia.

"Can you explain?" Errol shut the compartment door behind him.

"Yes," Goldenrod said, taking his hand. Sophia felt more unsettled by this than anything she had seen yet. She was used to the affectionate gestures between them, but now Goldenrod was taking Errol's hand for comfort and strength. Her own was trembling. "I have told Errol and Sophia of the old ones," she explained to Wren. "It was necessary, to follow Sophia's Ausentinian map."

He nodded, still in shock.

"As you know," Goldenrod said to Sophia and Errol, "Richard and I met many years ago, when he was traveling near the Eerie Sea."

"Yes, you said you were on an expedition there," Sophia said to Wren.

"He was," Goldenrod answered for him. "An expedition to persuade us, the Elodeans, to join the League of Encephalon Ages."

Errol raised his eyebrows. "Then Elodeans are of the future?"

"Our origin is disputed," Goldenrod said. "But the year of one's Age alone is not what warrants membership in the League. Many pockets of the Baldlands are from the future, and the League has no interest in them. It was interested in us because we have part of the knowledge that the League protects."

Sophia felt her pulse quicken. This was it. They would finally learn the secret that the League was concealing. Time and again, Wren had avoided speaking of it, but now, it seemed, the moment had at last arrived. "What is it?" she whispered.

"It has to do with the old ones," Wren said hoarsely, "as Goldenrod calls them. The Climes. In the Encephalon Ages . . ." He paused. For a moment he stared at his hands. Then he looked at Goldenrod. "I don't know how to explain."

"Let me," she said quietly. "The Encephalon Ages know what we Elodeans know—that Ages are sentient."

"You told us," Sophia replied eagerly. "And that people such as the Eerie might even be able to persuade them to do things— like the weirwinds."

"That is one consequence," Goldenrod assented. "But it is more complicated. Elodeans hold this knowledge as a kind of intuitive faculty. But in the Encephalon Ages, the ability to speak with and ultimately influence the old ones emerged as a form of defense."

"Defense against what?" Errol asked.

"A defense against their influence upon us."

Sophia caught her breath. "They influ—but how?"

"It is not malicious," Goldenrod said earnestly, as if responding to an accusation that she was used to hearing. "The old ones are never manipulative or malicious. It is simply not in their nature. And they cannot direct our actions outright. They only guide and suggest. You have both undoubtedly felt it—you experience it constantly. You simply do not recognize it for what it is." She leaned forward, her hand still clasping Errol's, her expression passionate. "Consider arriving at the edge of a forest and feeling a sense of foreboding that you cannot place. Or when you see a fork in the road and something irresistible suggests you go in one direction. Or when you feel compelled to climb to the next hill, even though you have done more than enough walking."

"Only in the wilderness, then," Errol said.

Goldenrod shook her head. "The same would be true in a village or town. Although the denser the concentration of beings, the less powerfully we hear the old one's voice. In cities, it can be near impossible. But surely you have walked by some dwelling and thought to yourself, 'I never want to cross that threshold.' The intuitive sense of dread or delight, the inspired pursuit of certain paths and roads, the certainty that we sometimes carry about where we are headed—these are all the influences of the old ones."

"I have certainly felt such inclinations," agreed Errol.

"So have I," Sophia said. "I thought it was . . . instinct."

"It is, in a way," Goldenrod replied. "The old ones never influence us in ways counter to our nature, our will."

"But nevertheless," Wren broke in, his voice aggrieved, "in the Encephalon Ages, this influence was feared. And arts—the Ars—were developed to speak back. To keep the Climes from shaping our actions—and more, to shape them in return. It should never have happened that way, and it is a terrible way to live."

Sophia could not make sense of any of it. "Why? What is it like?"

Wren shook his head. "How to explain?" he said helplessly. "Consider this—the Encephalon Ages can never be reached by those from other Ages, because they control the old ones so closely. Every approaching ship will encounter a storm. Every expedition will be lost in a blizzard. And in the Encephalon Ages, these manipulations abound for other purposes, not only for protection—every human intention for good or evil that you can imagine finds expression in the manipulation of the Climes."

Sophia tried to imagine a world of human actions on such a scale.

"But this is not all," Goldenrod said. "As I learned from Wren only weeks ago, as we sailed to Hispaniola . . ." She took a deep breath. "The League's secrets are deeper than I had imagined."

"In the early years after the Disruption," Wren continued, his face still pale, "those who sought to control the Climes would gladly have stretched their reach to pre-Encephalon Ages who were ignorant of this knowledge. Until—" He looked at Goldenrod.

"One of the old ones stopped speaking."

"It stopped doing anything," Wren said. "It was still there— but only in body, and not in soul. It was a shell. A corpse."

Sophia gasped. "The Climes can *die*?"

"Perhaps. We do not know. For all their advanced arts, the Encephalon Ages do not understand what happened. They only observe it. Whatever sense of spirit was in the Clime no longer existed. It was inert, without consciousness. Every living thing upon it withered and died. And so the League was formed," he concluded, "out of the realization that, if human beings had only partial knowledge, the old ones might be irreparably damaged."

"But then," Sophia said, remembering what had begun the conversation, "is that happening here?"

Goldenrod and Wren looked at one another. "I don't know," she said. "When I encountered the Dark Age in the heart of the Papal States, I was baffled by a Clime that seemed to have no consciousness. But I did not know then what I know now. And moreover, this is different. I've never . . ."

"Tell us what you perceived," Errol prompted.

"I have been listening since we arrived at the harbor, and I could hear nothing. I assumed it was because of New Orleans—such a crowded place. Full of so much human life. But now, away from the city, I should be able to hear. And there is only . . . silence."

Sophia's mind reeled at the possible implications. "Has this ever happened before in New Occident?"

Goldenrod shook her head. "Never. Remember, this old one is known to me—it is my home. I have spoken to it since I was born. It has never met me with silence." She turned away, hiding her expression, to look out the window.

The others followed her gaze. The open, unvaried landscape of northern New Akan seemed flattened by the ever-present anvil clouds. There was a slow, rolling movement within them, accompanied by a shifting patch of darkness, as if a giant serpent were tunneling through.

"What does Seneca say?" Errol asked, breaking the silence.

Goldenrod abruptly straightened, her eyes lit with hope. "I have not asked him!"

Without another word, Errol rose to retrieve Seneca, whom he had left hooded in the neighboring compartment. The three travelers waited, and moments later Errol returned with the falcon. Seneca peered at them unhappily, but perched on Goldenrod's arm without complaint.

Goldenrod murmured quietly to the falcon, who made no sound but shifted his head back and forth, as if considering a question. Errol, Wren, and Sophia watched expectantly. Suddenly, Goldenrod's face cleared. "Seneca can hear it."

Wren let out a sigh of relief. "What does it say?"

"Nothing. It does not speak, but Seneca can sense something. A knot of fear, deep in its heart. The silence is intentional."

"But surely that does not bode well?" wondered Errol.

"Much better than the alternative," Wren said.

"It is deeply concerning." Goldenrod stroked Seneca's smooth feathers. "I cannot imagine what would provoke such fear that the old one would refuse to speak. But I agree with Wren—better silent than senseless."

"Is this fear about something in particular?" Sophia asked.

"It is about a place. Seneca cannot say where—somewhere in the distant north."

"This changes matters," Wren said, sitting back with a frown. "I had made up my mind to return to New Orleans, but now I am not sure."

"What is it you suspect?" Errol asked.

Wren and Goldenrod exchanged a glance. "We cannot rule out the possibility," Wren said, "that this is an interference. That it is caused by someone from the Encephalon Ages."

"It would make sense," Goldenrod said pensively. "The strange weather. The silence. The localized fear."

"How would someone cause this?" Sophia asked.

"It is the entire purpose of the League," Wren said quietly, "to protect pre-Encephalon Ages from the kind of manipulations I described to you. To protect not only people, but the Clime itself.

"It may be that here, in New Occident, the League has failed."

12

TREE-EATER

—1892, August 7: 17-Hour 20—

Having pondered the oral traditions of the Elodeans (Eerie) and the lore of the Erie, with whom they are often confused, I am now in a position to say definitively that the two are not connected—at least, they have been separate peoples for the last several hundred years. The Erie are one of many peoples who lived in the vicinity of the northern lakes well before the Disruption. The Elodeans (Eerie) are from a remote future Age on the western coast of this hemisphere. They did not travel east to find the Erie, as is sometimes suggested, for they had no particular reason to seek them out. Rather, they traveled east to escape a catastrophic natural disaster that occurred in their region soon after the Disruption.

—From Sophia Tims's Reflections on a Journey to the Eerie Sea

THE LONG DAY was spent in speculation, but nothing new could be learned while speeding northward through the Indian Territories. The travelers could only conjecture. With a sense of foreboding, they watched the darkening clouds, listened to their rumbling whenever the train paused, and felt the air thicken with humidity and the faint scent of sulfur.

At sunset, Wren and Errol withdrew to the neighboring compartment, leaving Goldenrod and Sophia alone. Calixta had remained closeted for most of the day in her own compartment—sulking, worrying, or plotting: Sophia could not be sure.

Now, as the darkness overtook them and the flame lamps burned low, Sophia asked the question that had filled her mind since that morning. "I don't understand how people in the Encephalon Ages influence the Climes. I cannot picture it. What does it look like?"

Goldenrod leaned back. "I have never been to an Encephalon Age. I have no wish to see such a place."

"But you have some idea of what it's like?"

"I do," Goldenrod said. "The Elodeans are conscious of the danger—we are well aware of how the world would be distorted if we chose to abuse our intuitions. The arts Wren speaks of are familiar to us—we simply do not cultivate them as they were cultivated in the Encephalon Ages." A flash of pain and what seemed like guilt crossed her face. "I know of only one instance in which some among us tried. It did not end well. Those Elodeans were cast out; they live as exiles now, removed to a place where they can do no harm."

"But what is the harm? Wren only spoke of keeping outsiders away."

Goldenrod unlaced her studded boots with evident relief and drew her feet up onto the bunk bed. "I will tell you a story that the Elodeans tell to children—a story about the danger of these arts." Sophia curled up in anticipation on the opposite bunk as Goldenrod idly tapped the bells sewn onto her skirt. "It is a story from the far west, the place we come from, and it is about a wise man—a great wise man who was beloved and revered by his people. He was known for his cures and his knowledge of the elements and even his occasional ability to foretell future happenings.

"One day, a man who laid stone went out to the field where he was building a wall between a farm and the great Red Woods. The Red Woods are trees so tall that twenty people standing at their base holding hands are too few to encircle the trunk."

This was something else Sophia found hard to imagine. "Are they real?"

"Very real—I saw them myself on a journey to the western coast. I stood at the base of one and looked up so far into the treetops that the branches blurred and disappeared into the clouds."

"Amazing," Sophia breathed.

"They are wondrous trees, and they make wondrous forests, full of great clearings like vast chambers and soft pathways padded with their fallen needles. Such forests are formidable, with all manner of creatures, and so the stonemason had been hired to build a wall between the forest and the farm, to keep the pastures safe. But when he arrived at the field that morning, he saw that a whole tract of the forest nearest him had vanished. He stared in shock; the entire landscape had changed. Stepping forward, he saw the base of the many Red Woods still there—only the trunks and tops were gone. But the trees had not been cut cleanly. They were mauled and broken. The stonemason could see at once that this was not the work of men.

"He told the farmer what had happened, and word of this strange occurrence spread. The next day, more of the forest had been destroyed, and the next day even more. Well, you may imagine that this confounded them, so the people gathered and sought out their wise man, taking him to the field. He studied the ruined forest for a long time, a ponderous look upon his face. He walked among the savaged trunks, examining the remains of the trees. In his mind, the wise man knew that this happening lay beyond his knowledge. He had no notion of what had destroyed the trees. But a wise man, he reasoned, could not admit to ignorance. His people counted on him for an answer. He had grown so accustomed to their adulation and respect that he could not bear the disappointment that might result if he admitted to ignorance. And so the wise man decided to invent an answer.

"He told the people that he knew well what had destroyed the forest. It was a dangerous demon called 'Tree-Eater.' The demon emerged only once every hundred years, but when it did emerge, there was nothing that could be done. It would ravage the forest until it had eaten its fill, and then it would return to its cave, sated, for another hundred years.

"Naturally, the people were terrified. They responded as the wise man had hoped. Staying safely in their homes at night, they dared not emerge for fear of encountering the demon; and each morning more trees were gone, just as the wise man had predicted. The Tree-Eater had not yet eaten its fill.

"There was, however, one problem. A girl in the village—a

girl no older than you are now—who was called Bumblebee, believed the wise man just as everyone else did, but she also believed that it must be possible to stop the demon from eating any more of the Red Woods. Bumblebee was not satisfied with the wise man's advice to simply let the Tree-Eater eat its fill. She inundated the wise man with questions: What did the demon look like? Why did he eat trees? Did he eat every kind of tree? Could they offer him some other food to appease him? If not, could they lead him to a poison tree and end his destruction for good? The wise man answered her questions with elaborate explanations. The demon was a giant made of stone, and he ate only Red Woods, for only those could fill him. He had eyes of liquid gold and antlers upon his head that he used to tear the trees to pieces. 'There is nothing you or I can do,' the wise man said. 'Trust me.' Each time Bumblebee arrived to demand more answers, the wise man felt a growing guilt that gnawed at his heart: his lies could not be taken back. He was deceiving Bumblebee and the entire village. What if the force that had destroyed the trees was not content to destroy trees, but then destroyed the village, too? Though the wise man worried, his lies continued.

"And then the wise man's fears were realized—albeit not as he had predicted. The villagers woke him in the middle of the night, pounding on his door. Bumblebee had gone to the edge of the woods in the middle of the night to confront the Tree-Eater—and now the demon had her in its grasp! The wise man, frantic and baffled, went with them. As he ran, a single question resounded in his mind: How could the Tree-Eater have Bumblebee in his grasp when the Tree-Eater did not even exist?

"When they arrived at the edge of the woods, the wise man stared in horror at the sight that confronted him. It was the Tree-Eater. As dark as smoke, as tall as a mountain, as hard as stone, the Tree-Eater towered over the Red Woods with his great antlered head and his long teeth; he dove down, over and over, breaking each tree with his antlers and then chewing it to pieces. He held Bumblebee in one of his stony, clawed hands. When the wise man approached, the Tree-Eater stopped. He crouched down, crushing the trees around him with his weight. As he leaned his massive head forward, the villagers cowered. The wise man, more out of shock than courage, stood his ground. The Tree-Eater stared at him with wide, golden eyes.

"'What do you want of us?' the wise man managed to ask. 'Give us Bumblebee and you can eat all the trees you want.'

"The Tree-Eater stared at him a moment longer, and then, with a voice like the crashing of the ocean, it said, 'You tell me what I want, wise man. You made me.'

"The wise man felt a coldness pass over him. And he realized that, however unbelievable, the demon's words were true. He had made the Tree-Eater: imagined him, described him, and given him life.

"The wise man stared back at the demon, feeling both awe and fear. For a moment, he wondered at the power he had to shape the world, and the prospect of shaping it further shone as brightly as the demon's golden eyes. But then he thought of Bumblebee, and he realized how the shaping of the world had a cost. There were people who believed him and trusted him, and what he made of the world mattered to them.

"'You want your own forest, Tree-Eater,' the wise man said. 'You will give Bumblebee back to us. You will travel to the ocean and make an island there, crouched against the ocean floor, and the Red Woods you have eaten will spring from your stony shoulders, keeping you company for the rest of your days. This is what you want, Tree-Eater.'

"The demon looked at him for a moment longer, and then, with a great sigh that blew from his jagged mouth like a hurricane, he reached forward and placed Bumblebee on the ground. He rose, lifting his head up into the cloudless sky, and headed west to the ocean."

Sophia sat in silence next to Goldenrod, imagining the great demon stalking away into the distance. She could picture his dark silhouette against the starry sky. "Bumblebee was very brave," she finally said.

"Bumblebee is a seeker of truth, and the wise man is the soul of invention," Goldenrod said. "There are many lessons in the story, but I have always marveled at how both the seeker of truth and the soul of invention are powerful, each in their own right."

"But how could the trees have been destroyed before the wise man had invented Tree-Eater? Did something else destroy them?"

Goldenrod smiled. "What do you think?"

Sophia pondered. "I think it could be that the wise man had already imagined something like Tree-Eater, before even speaking of it, and the monster he imagined came to find him."

"That would be a grave lesson indeed."

"Do demons like Tree-Eater really exist? Is that what people in the Encephalon Ages do?"

"The story is meant to show the power of the imagination, for both good and evil. I cannot say if creatures like Tree-Eater truly exist. But you heard what Wren said—every intention finds its expression."

Sophia drew her knees up and wrapped her arms around them. "I have imagined terrible things sometimes," she said quietly. "I am glad I don't have that power."

"You may have more of it than you realize. When you learn further about Elodean ways, you will see how some of your intuitions already lean in this direction."

Sophia had found no opportunity to tell Goldenrod what had happened after they had spoken of the two tokens Maxine had given her, and now, as the train rattled on in the dark night, she saw her chance. "Last night I looked at the antler and the tree for a long time, just as you said. I wrote down all my questions and my observations. And then I fell asleep holding the antler. I had dreams that were so real, they felt like memories. Were they really memories?"

Goldenrod's eyes were bright. "What did you dream?"

"I dreamed of walking through a forest and reaching a

house deep in the woods. A boy spoke in my ear, saying that we were home. Then in a different dream, the boy and I looked down into a valley with a cluster of trees. And then in the last dream, we ran from a forest fire. I was afraid of the fire, and the fear seemed to be a thing outside of myself that ran through the woods ahead of us."

Goldenrod nodded. "Animals see fear as a living being—an entity—while we do not. Those were memories."

Sophia smiled, elated. "So these maps are read while sleeping?"

"It is a way to begin—the sleeping mind is most open to these kinds of memories. What did the house look like?"

"The house in the woods?"

"Yes—the house the boy said was home."

"It was set in a mound, so that part of the house was a hill. There were two windows and an arched door. And next to the house was an open space with a roof. There was a barrel collecting rainwater and a stack of firewood."

Goldenrod smiled. "I believe you have met Bittersweet."

"The moose is named Bittersweet?" Sophia asked, confused.

"No—the boy. Young man now. He lives in such a house, and though I have not been to that corner of the forest for more than two years, it sounds as though it has not changed much."

"Then he is Elodean?"

"He is Elodean. And it is telling that this token Maxine gave you pertains to him."

"Why?"

Goldenrod sighed. "He is the fourth Weatherer. Of those four Eerie healers, he is the only one who did not disappear in Boston. It was his family I went in search of early this year."

—18-Hour 30—

GOLDENROD FELL SILENT, and Sophia knew that she was reflecting upon her failed attempt to save the Eerie in Boston. It visibly gnawed at her conscience, and no doubt she felt anxious, having finally returned to New Occident, to learn what she could about the fate of those missing friends. Sophia's own conscience gnawed at her—she was well aware of how her own search was delaying Goldenrod's own—as she prepared herself for sleep.

Sophia removed the remaining pieces of her raider costume so that she was wearing only her cotton shift. She undid her braids and put the leather ties inside her skirt pocket, then tucked her clothes into the compartment beside her bunk. Placing the wheel of tree trunk beside her pillow, she rested her fingers on its coarse surface. Gently, she tapped the pine face. *It's like a clock,* she thought to herself as her eyes closed. *A clock of the past that has stopped telling time.* The long day that had begun before dawn caught up with her quickly, and she was asleep in minutes.

The dream was unlike any she had ever had. It was late winter. A heavy snow was falling. She was aware of the other trees around her; they were perfectly still as the snow fell, but their thoughts coursed through their cold limbs, into the soil and the damp air. And these were not the only thoughts she sensed: tranquil or urgent, lazy or quick, contented or hungry, the impulses of living things nearby filled her consciousness so that they transformed the stillness into a scene of humming activity.

This went on for hours. In some ways, nothing happened. The snow continued to fall. It accumulated on her branches, a comforting weight that covered her like a kind of blanket. The weak sunlight gave out slowly as the afternoon waned. Steadily, the temperature began to drop. There was no visible movement as far as she could tell. And yet, in other ways, the dream was full of busyness as the dense cluster of living things near her watched and felt and hungered and slept and woke.

The dream ended abruptly and shifted. Now it was midsummer. The landscape had altered entirely. Instead of standing surrounded by other trees, she stood at the edge of a field. She knew that the trees that had stood there before were gone, and she felt their absence without grief, but with a constant, unremitting awareness. Tall grass, heavy with flowers, grew now where those trees had grown, and a house made of those very trees stood not far away. Beyond it were more houses, and where they gathered in the greatest number rose a bell tower.

The air was thick with bees and other insects. She felt the same sense of busyness around her, hearing the bees and the flies and the trees and the grass and the nodding flowers among them, but now another activity overlaid this, like a trumpet sounding in an orchestra. Two girls ran toward her through the tall grass, one chasing the other, and their laughter rang through the warm summer air. One of them reached her trunk, touched it, and then embraced her, still laughing, her soft arms warm and poignantly fragile. She felt a pang of tenderness for this breakable creature. "I won!" the girl cried.

In her sleep, Sophia pulled away from the wheel of tree trunk, drawing her fingers under the thin blanket. She sighed, and the dream ended.

13

Two Pigeon Posts

—*1892, August 8: 18-Hour 00*—

In some of these inns you can still find, discarded in a stable or an unused room, the leather trunks used to transport the mail along the major post roads. Now the riders forego the trunks—and the wagons required to carry them. They travel lighter, with saddle bags, and the steady stream of messengers ensures that these smaller deliveries will be sufficient. The post is delivered four times a day within the city of Boston and twice a day in its environs. Each of the inns I have described on the major post roads sees a messenger pass by three times each day: they leave Boston in the dark of night, late in the morning, and late in the afternoon.

—From *Shadrack Elli's* History of New Occident

IN THE HUMID summer evening, by the bright light of three flame lamps, Shadrack was committing treason. He was creating two maps that looked nearly identical. Both showed the projected route for New Occident troops marching through Kentucky. One showed the troops following a path that led through a low valley. The other showed the troops following the same route, but instead of taking them through the valley, it led them to camp on the banks of a river. Apart from this, there was one other important difference between the two maps, a difference almost any eye would miss: the one with the valley bore a small insignia—three hills atop a slender ruler—while the other did not.

It was through such calculated inaccuracies and the deliberate "loss" of maps into enemy hands that Shadrack managed to foil Fen Carver, the leader of the Indian Territories' troops, arranging for there to be as little bloodshed as possible. Some days he drew and copied as few as ten; most days he drafted more than twenty. Shadrack's pen slipped, and he paused. He sat back in his chair and put the pen down. The exhaustion he felt had been building for weeks. Pressing his fingertips to his temples, he closed his eyes.

In the silence that followed, he heard a sound that he could not place. Then he realized what it was: the quiet flutter of snow.

Snow, he thought, with an unfolding sense of ease. *If it's heavy, I might work from home in the morning.* Then something shifted, and he realized what his exhaustion had at first obscured. *But it is early August!*

Shadrack hastened through the silent house and opened the front door. The night sky seemed bright and faintly yellow, as it would be during a snowfall. Downy white flakes were falling all along the street, coating the roofs and the leafy branches. *Snow,* Shadrack thought, astonished. *It really is snowing in August. And it isn't even cold.* The brick walkway to 34 East Ending Street was already hidden. Then he put his hand out, allowing the flakes to gather on his palm. He gasped. *Not snow,* he realized.

It was ash. *Ash.*

Shadrack's first thought was a fire: a great fire, since only a conflagration of massive proportions would cause so much ash to fall on the city. And yet there was no smell of burning in the air. Looking up, perplexed, Shadrack watched the thick clouds overhead drift and part momentarily. The waxing moon shone through, and the falling ash paused. "Unbelievable," he murmured. "It's actually coming from the clouds." He stared as the clouds gathered, obscuring the moon once more, and the ash resumed falling.

In the silence, there was a shuffling sound. Shadrack saw a messenger with a cap coming down the street, kicking the ash aside as if it were a mere inconvenience instead of an ominous wonder. The messenger saw Shadrack at the door and raised his cap, turning into the walkway of 34 East Ending Street. "Good evening," he said.

"I'd say a strange evening," Shadrack replied.

"It's falling all over the city," the boy said matter-of-factly, turning on the step to survey the street. "The Common is already under an inch of it."

"Have you heard any speculation as to the cause?"

The messenger looked at Shadrack. "None at all," he said, seemingly unworried. "Well, plenty of speculation, but none that makes an ounce of sense. I heard one man say it was a volcano."

"But there are no volcanoes anywhere in this Age," Shadrack protested.

The boy shrugged. "Like I said. None that make sense. Message for Shadrack Elli," he added, holding up a piece of paper.

"A message," Shadrack said, recalled to the moment. "I am Shadrack Elli."

The boy handed the paper over and settled his cap back on his head. "I'll wait for a reply."

Shadrack opened the sheet of paper and read four lines of blue writing:

> *Safe with Calixta and Burr in New Orleans*
> *Heading north to Salt Lick*
> *Will be there between ninth and nineteenth*
> *Love, Sophia*

Shadrack stared at the letters on the page, the ashfall forgotten. "How did this arrive?" he demanded.

"By pigeon post, sir. Maxine's Iron Pigeon Post of New Orleans. Message came through Greensboro."

"Iron pigeon post? What does that mean?"

"Mark of Iron, sir. Guides them to any destination."

"Iron pigeons." Shadrack shook his head. "Incredible." He scanned the message again. "She is traveling through the Territories," he said to himself, aghast. Then he addressed the messenger. "Can I send a reply to Salt Lick?"

"There's a depot there. So, yes—makes it easier. You can send a message to Salt Lick. It has lodgings and everything. Run by Prudence Seltz. It's one of the nicer depots. Not as nice as Boston's, of course."

"Come in," Shadrack said, opening his door. "I will write the note. How long will this take to reach Salt Lick?" he asked, hurrying along the corridor to his study.

"If the bird leaves within the hour, it can arrive in Salt Lick by midmorning," the boy assured him. "It's seven hundred and thirty-four miles."

"Even in this weather?" Shadrack hurriedly took pen and paper from his desk.

"They've flown through worse."

Shadrack wondered what was worse than an inexplicable storm of falling ash. "Is there a limit to how much I can write?"

"Just don't write a novel, sir," the boy replied with a smile.

Shadrack quickly wrote:

> *Relieved you are safe. Wait in Salt Lick depot for Miles.*
> *He will arrive in—*

He looked up at the boy. "Can I send something to Pear Tree?"

"Charleston in Virginia would be the closest depot. I'd advise sending it direct. A little extra cost, but the pigeon will deliver straight to your recipient."

"How long would it take to send a message there?"

"It will arrive around the same time, tomorrow morning, but it's a little unpredictable if your recipient isn't expecting the pigeon. Might be they figure it out right away or might be they don't. Tomorrow night, if you're lucky."

"That's still much faster than I could manage," Shadrack

observed. "Can I send a second message to Pear Tree?"

"Absolutely, sir."

Making a rapid calculation of how long it would take Miles to reach Salt Lick from Pear Tree, he continued: *three days.* He paused.

> *In case Miles does not arrive, the following are friends nearby: Casper Bearing and Adler Fox in Salt Lick, Sarah Smoke Longfellow in Oakring, Muir Purling in Echo Falls, and Tuppence Silver in East Boyden Township.*

He paused again and looked up, wondering how he could possibly warn Sophia about the dangers of the crimson fog. With a sharp, worried exhalation he finished his message.

> *If you see any red fog, take cover <u>alone</u> at whatever cost. <u>The fog is lethal!</u>*
> *All my love, Shadrack*

On a separate sheet of paper, he wrote to Miles:

> *Sophia is heading to Salt Lick from New Orleans, due to arrive between 9th and 19th. Meet her there at the pigeon depot run by Prudence Seltz. I fear for her safety.*

He read the notes over and then handed them to the boy. "How far does your network extend?"

"All over New Occident and the Territories," he said proudly.

"I am astonished I did not know of it."

"It's for smugglers, sir," the boy answered matter-of-factly. "You wouldn't have."

"In any case, I'm very grateful."

"Very happy to be of service, sir."

Shadrack thought to himself that for a smugglers' correspondence system, it was surprisingly professional and courteous. Having paid for the outgoing messages, he saw the boy to the door. The sky had cleared, and the ground was covered with almost an inch of gray-white ash. More people were emerging from their houses now, and there were even two boys down the street playing, catching it in fistfuls and throwing it at each other.

Though the ash was a surprising and inexplicable distraction, Shadrack forced himself to return to his study. Pacing the worn carpet, he reflected yet again how effectively and cruelly Broadgirdle had bound him to Boston. His place now was in the Indian Territories, where Theo and Miles and Sophia were all converging west of Pennsylvania. They were in danger, and he was here, all but manacled to his desk. There was nothing he could do.

But—yes, there is, he thought, taking up the wooden ruler that held the memories of three Eerie, trapped belowground in a windowless chamber. *I can end this war if I can prove what Broadgirdle has done. I have to find the Weatherers.*

He had examined the ruler countless times. In fact, he had read it so often that it had become predictable; when he immersed himself in the recollections of the terrified Eerie, the terror no longer touched him. He anticipated the indifference of the Sandman, the dread of the bound girl, the sense of weariness and deflation and grief that the maker of the map had experienced. The challenge now was to see anything new in something that had become so familiar. But Shadrack knew better than anyone that memories were rich and changeable, and even stored memories took on a different aspect when revisited.

He let his mind drift in the memories of the Weatherer. First, he saw the girl and the old man slumped in their chairs. Then he saw the girl recoiling from the fire, her hands bursting with red blooms as her terror peaked. Then he saw the coffins and the tools and the fearful gaze of the old man. The one moment that never lost its power for Shadrack was this: the way the old man looked at him, sending grief and love and despair across the room like a current. He flinched every time. And because he flinched, he did not feel the memory fully.

This evening, tired and stunned as he was, he arrived at the moment unguarded and did not brace himself. The memory hit him with all its force, and he felt an agony of helplessness as the man's eyes met his own. *Father,* he thought, in the back of his mind. It was the first time this had occurred to him. He forced himself to stay in that terrible moment, as the man's fear and desperate love poured from his eyes.

Then Shadrack sensed it: a smell. It drifted by only for the briefest moment, sweet and heavy, like the scent of a flower. In its wake was another smell: sickly, like rotting meat. Then it was gone.

14

THE YOKE

—1892, August 7: 12-Hour 34—

The Six Nations of the Iroquois expanded after the Disruption, spreading south and west until they encountered the Miami and the Shawnee. In the early decades of the nineteenth century, the government of New Occident was too occupied with the rebellion in New Akan to the south, the disintegrated relationship with Europe across the Atlantic, and the new relationship with the United Indies. And so the Six Nations grew in wealth and power, establishing a close-knit cluster of nations that straddled the boundary between New Occident and the Indian Territories. Indeed, the Six Nations in many ways behaved as if the boundary did not exist.

—From Shadrack Elli's History of New Occident

BY THE END of the first hour, Casanova was sure Theo's neck would be permanently bent at a ninety-degree angle to his chest. By the end of the second hour he could see that Theo was beginning to stumble.

When the major rode to the front of the column, Casanova slipped away and hurried forward, sidling up to his friend. "Let me," he said, his voice muffled by the leather hood, and lifted the yoke.

"Ugh—thanks, Cas," Theo said. He could not turn his head, but he did manage a smile. His face was coated with sweat and dust. "I think," he said, between gasps, "I got the better deal. Those helmets must be murder."

"Don't talk," Casanova said, shaking his head. "Save your breath." But Theo was right. Even with the glass eyepieces snapped upward, the helmet made a bubble of heat around Casanova's head; he was sweating so profusely that the leather was soaked through. Nevertheless, the entire company wore their helmets; they made a swarm of hooded flies, trudging along the road. Even the major was wearing his, and Casanova thought Theo would be in danger without one. As he looked at his friend critically, he saw with dismay that Theo's neck was bleeding freely where the yoke had rubbed the skin away.

"Hey," Theo said hoarsely.

"What is it?"

"I thought of something that would help."

Casanova continued to hold the yoke away from Theo's neck. "Yes—tell me. What else can I do?"

Theo rotated his head as far as he could. He grinned. "Could you tell me the story of your scar?"

"Theo!" Casanova burst out, exasperated. "You're impossible. This is not *funny.*"

Theo laughed. Then, quietly, he added, "I think it is."

Casanova shook his head, half-furious, half-relieved that Theo was still able to make jokes. "I said *don't talk,* you maddening idiot." Craning with effort to the men marching behind them, he looked for help. The troops were nearly unrecognizable in their masks. He raised his free hand, hoping one of their friends from the work crew would see. Immediately, one of the larger men broke away from the ranks and joined them. Without a word, he took one side of the yoke. Casanova realized, with faint surprise, that it was MacWilliams.

"Collins will whistle if the major is coming back," MacWilliams said.

"Thank you," Casanova said, feeling a rush of gratitude.

MacWilliams nodded.

With one man to hold each side of the yoke, Theo could comfortably walk upright. He let out a breath of relief.

Casanova reached for the water bottle at his hip and gave it to Theo, who lifted it over the yoke and took a long drink. "Thanks," he whispered, handing it back.

"I'm going to put a cloth on your neck," Casanova said, taking out his handkerchief, "in case Merret comes back and we have to let it drop."

He grimaced at how it stuck instantly to the bloody skin. He could not see how Theo would survive this day. The boy had scored a minor victory, poking fun at the major and making his lesson in discipline another occasion for jest, but the lesson was not yet over. The real lesson, Casanova feared, would begin when Theo collapsed from exhaustion and fell to the ground, only to be dragged along by the wagon and the harness. He could only hope that the major would remain at the front for as long as possible so he and MacWilliams could carry the yoke.

Their luck held for another hour. They descended from the

hills out of Pennsylvania, and the terrain grew flatter. The broad road they walked, clearly the principal throughway from east to west, was bordered by trees, which gave them a brief respite from the worst of the summer sun. Casanova wondered, not for the first time, what danger could make the cumbersome helmets they wore worthwhile. The pouring sweat obstructed his vision, and the rustling leather made it difficult to hear. What threat rendered such impairment an advantage?

Casanova marched onward, the two packs he carried digging into his shoulders with each step. A low warble, like the cry of a mourning dove, reached him distantly. Casanova ignored it. The cry came again, more urgently. "That's Collins," MacWilliams said quickly. "We have to get back."

"I'll stay here," Casanova said. "I don't care what Merret says."

"You'll care when he makes the boy carry the yoke for a second day as punishment," MacWilliams replied. Then he slipped away.

Cursing silently, Casanova lowered the yoke as gently as possible. "I'm sorry, my friend," he said. "This is going to hurt."

"Not your fault." Theo gave a faint smile, then gasped as the full weight of the yoke pressed against his neck.

"I'm sorry," Casanova repeated. His handkerchief was not nearly enough protection.

"Go," Theo whispered.

Casanova dropped back. Through the eyeholes of his helmet, he could see that he had been just in time. Merret was riding back alongside the troops.

One advantage of the helmets, Casanova thought, was that Merret could hardly tell one man from the other, and he would not realize that Casanova was in the wrong place. The major rode past, the hoofbeats fading as he continued to the rear of the column.

Casanova's relief was short-lived. Ahead of him, Theo tripped on an unseen stone in the road and launched forward, tipping perilously with the heavy yoke. He threw a hand up to seize the wagon, but his legs had not yet caught up. Casanova watched with alarm. As he watched Theo's feet, wondering if this would be the moment when they would tangle up and give out at last, Casanova noticed a flash of brown to his left: a shape in the trees.

His first thought was that it must be a deer, and he was turning back to help Theo, no matter the cost, when the first long arrow flew past his line of vision and buried itself in the wooden bed of the wagon. There was a keening squeal of panic from one of the mules, and the man marching beside him suddenly crumpled, crying out in pain. Casanova observed with shock the arrow embedded in the man's arm. It had happened in less than a second.

In the next moment, everything changed. As if conjured from thin air, men with high buckskin boots and bare arms were taking aim from the edge of the road. All of them wore kerchiefs—gray and brown and dull green—to cover their noses and mouths. They were only a few feet away; at that range, they would not miss. They stood almost shoulder to shoulder, their arms moving like the limbs of a hundred swimmers, pulling arrows, drawing back on the bowstrings, and releasing.

Abruptly the mules of Theo's wagon bolted, terrified, and the wagon charged forward. With sudden clarity, Casanova watched the chain that hung slack from Theo's yoke. He knew that at any moment the chain would pull at the harness and Theo would be forced to the ground. Theo tried to lift his feet, but he was too slow. The chain straightened and snapped taut, and the harness yanked Theo's neck like a collar. He fell. The mules took off, and a cloud of dust sprang up behind the wagon as Theo was dragged along the road.

15

THE COWARD

—1892, August 7: 12-Hour 46—

It is not unheard of for some people of the Six Nations to settle in New Occident proper. Some come and go as merchants, others take advantage of what the cities of the eastern seaboard have to offer. But the majority stay comfortably within the area settled by the Six Nations. Salt Lick, to the west of Pennsylvania, offers everything one might wish for in a city other than a seaport. In fact, if there is migration between New Occident and Six Nations, it tends to flow from the former to the latter.

—From Shadrack Elli's *History of New Occident*

THE ARROWS WHISTLED as they flew through the air and struck the unprepared company. In the distance, Major Merret shouted instructions. "Theo," Casanova shouted, over the thudding of arrows and the groans of falling men.

He realized that if he did not reach Theo in the next few seconds, the boy would be crushed under the wagon's wheels. With a grunt, he dropped their packs, losing all his protection against the arrows, and burst into a run. He jumped over a fallen man and dove forward, head down, toward the vanishing wagon.

Merret's lessons had accomplished their intention, for the company was fighting with more discipline than Casanova would have imagined. Turning to face the trees on either side, the troops fired on their attackers. Casanova ran between them, in the wake of the wagon that had charged through. The troops' only insubordination was in their use of equipment; almost to a man, they had thrown off the unwieldy masks that made it impossible to see or hear clearly. Casanova did not stop to remove his. Theo was being tossed beside the wagon like a fallen kite dragged by the wind.

"Whoa!" Casanova shouted. "Whoa!" It was no use—the mules could not hear him, or if they did, their terror was too great. Tucking his head down, Casanova ran with all his might.

Suddenly the mules hesitated, impeded or startled by something in their way. Casanova reached Theo, passed him, and then flailed at the mule nearest him, attempting to grasp the reins. He missed, and grabbed again. Then he had it. Pulling fiercely, he wrenched the mules to a halt. But it was only momentary: he knew that at any second they would take off once more. He spun back to where Theo lay on the ground and rapidly unhooked the harness from the chain. Casanova lifted Theo and then, using all his strength, heaved him upward into the covered bed of the wagon.

Theo was unconscious, and an arrow jutted from his shoulder. "No, no, no, no," Casanova said under his breath. Putting his fingers against Theo's wrist, he felt a weak pulse. "Wake up, Theo," Casanova urged. He unfastened the harness as quickly as he could. As he tossed it aside, the mules bolted and the wagon hurtled forward once again. Casanova crouched in the wagon's bed.

He could not think what to do next. Then he realized there was no hope of saving Theo while staying with the company. They would be killed—at best, captured. He threw himself toward the opening at the front of the wagon bed and crawled up to the empty seat. As he fumbled for the reins, he saw that they had already left the scene of their attack behind. He tore off his helmet with relief and threw it into the back.

Driving the mules as fast as he dared, he took them north for another ten minutes and then led the wagon off the path and tied the agitated mules to a tree. One, he could see, was badly injured. It had continued running out of sheer panic, but it had lost a great deal of blood. Casanova shook his head and hurried to the wagon. Theo's injury needed attention first; then he would see to the mule.

Theo had not yet woken, which was a relief, given what Casanova had to do next. He ripped the shoulder seam of Theo's shirt, exposing the embedded arrow in his left upper arm. He needed a way to remove the arrow as cleanly as possible.

The wagon that had carried them to safety turned out to hold the major's private supply store. Fine food and linens surrounded them. Casanova opened a cask of water and found a clean napkin, which he soaked in the water. He wiped his hands with the napkin and then, holding the wound open with his fingers, prepared himself to pull the arrow out. To his surprise, the wooden shaft came loose with ease. Then he cursed quietly, realizing that the arrowhead had remained buried in Theo's shoulder. "Why couldn't they have hit your iron hand, Theo?" Casanova asked aloud. He tossed the shaft aside and carefully reached his fingers into the wound. The arrowhead was there, but his blunt fingers could not grasp it. "I need tweezers. Or tongs."

He found neither. But he did find two silver forks, and using these like pincers, he managed, over several long minutes, to pry the arrowhead out of Theo's shoulder. He examined the offending piece of weaponry after dousing it with water, and his worst fear was realized. The arrowhead was stone, and fragments of it had been chipped off. No doubt these were still lodged in Theo's shoulder. Casanova resisted the urge to hurl the arrowhead into the dirt. He needed to save it so that the pattern of missing pieces was discernible. And he needed a medic—a proper medic.

Casanova searched the wagon for alcohol, and washed Theo's shoulder with it, using a clean napkin. The boy had still not woken, and it unsettled him deeply. "Hang on, Theo," he said as he propped him up with the major's comfortable blankets. "We've got a journey ahead of us, and you must stay alive until we reach our destination. You hear me?"

Theo, his face strangely calm, made no reply.

16
SALT LICK STATION

—*1892, August 9: 4-Hour 11*—

Salt Lick is a good example. We can see by the very number and nature of institutions created there that New Occident is surprisingly ignorant of life beyond the borders. Consider that until this year, maps of Salt Lick did not even show the major railway line (apparently built eight years ago) reaching westward out of Salt Lick into the Baldlands. The only known railway ran north to south. How could this go unremarked? It demonstrates, once again, how poorly we are kept up to date on the developments of our nearest neighbors.

—From Sophia Tims's Reflections on a Journey to the Eerie Sea

THE PASSENGERS ABOARD the train to Salt Lick watched the ash fall. All through the second day of the journey and into the evening, it had fallen—at first sparsely, so that it was mistaken for apple blossoms out of season, and then thickly, so that it swirled and eddied around the train. The flat fields on either side of the tracks made a gray sea to the horizon. Even as the sun set, the sky remained light and faintly yellow, like a fading bruise.

The dining car was quiet, apart from the occasional murmured speculation. All of the passengers seemed to agree that the ashy precipitation boded ill. Goldenrod watched the mottled clouds with a worried expression. Errol, Wren, and Sophia sat beside her in a braced silence.

"It's a punishment from the Indians," a woman's voice suddenly declared shrilly. She was young, with a high buttoned collar and nervous hands. "They've sent a storm of ash to wipe us out!"

"Don't be absurd," another woman retorted, looking sternly through her spectacles. "Indians have no such power. And how is a storm of ash supposed to wipe us out?"

"There must be a great fire," said a middle-aged man. "A fire burning all the plains to the west—a fire so vast, the winds are carrying the ashes east."

"Then how do you explain the fact that when the clouds clear, the ash stops?" the spectacled woman demanded.

"What's your explanation, then?" countered the man.

"I have no explanation," she said firmly. "And anyone who claims to is fooling himself."

There was a silence. Then, finally, Goldenrod turned away from the window.

"What is it?" Errol asked in an undertone.

"I cannot hear the Clime," she replied, her voice strained. "But I hear the trees."

"What do they tell you?" Wren prompted.

"The ash does not trouble them. What troubles them are the men."

"The men?" Sophia asked.

Goldenrod turned back to the dark glass. "Thousands of feet, marching east. Men scorching fields, men cutting trees to clear roads."

"Is that where the ash comes from?" wondered Sophia.

"Perhaps. I cannot tell. The fires leave blackened earth and pillars of smoke. They send people fleeing, like ants whose hill has been crushed underfoot."

"The New Occident troops," Wren said.

"Both sides," Goldenrod corrected. "Miami, Shawnee, and Cherokee to the south. All the Six Nations to the north. There is such a movement of feet, and the footsteps leave poison in their wake."

"What does that mean?" Sophia asked, eyes wide.

"I do not know," Goldenrod said. She sighed deeply and pressed her forehead against the glass. Errol rested a gentle hand on her shoulder.

Sophia could see the agony on Goldenrod's face—Goldenrod, who was always so calm and untroubled. And she could see the worry in Errol's shoulders; he leaned toward Goldenrod as if hoping to shield her with his presence. But there could be no protection from the unrest of the Clime. It was all around them. With an inaudible sigh, Sophia rose. She wanted time to think things through.

Making her way back to the compartment she was sharing with Goldenrod, she pulled herself up into her bunk. She took out her notebook and set down the happenings of the last twenty hours, taking special care to draw the falling ash and Goldenrod's story of Tree-Eater. As she outlined the remnants of her dream from the previous night, she pondered what Goldenrod had observed about the trees, and how the footsteps of men troubled them.

If trees can remember, she thought to herself, sketching the insects that had appeared with jeweled precision in her dream, *then of course they can sense what is happening now all around them. They do not simply watch—they observe, they interpret. Perhaps they even like and dislike.* She looked up, struck by a thought. *Or are there stronger feelings? Do the trees love and hate like we do? Do they condemn some actions and praise others? Do they have wishes and wants that act upon the world? How would those wishes and wants appear?* Sophia shook her head, perplexed at her own questions.

Goldenrod had still not come, and it was growing late. Sophia put away her notebook and pencils and prepared herself for bed. Carefully, so that it would not slip too easily from her grasp, she placed the antler in her open palm. Then she settled back, pulled the blankets around her, and prepared herself for sleep. The train rattled pleasantly in the background, and it was almost possible to forget that, beyond the tracks, the land was covered with ash.

There was only one dream this time—a brief, disturbing dream that was more of a nightmare. It began and ended at the edge of a charred forest, where the boy sat on the ground and wept into his hands. She leaned her head down toward him and tried, with an aching sense of pity, to offer consolation. She tapped his head with her nose and sent him love with her thoughts, but it did no good. He wept as if his heart would break. When she woke from the dream, she could not fall back asleep.

THE TRAIN ARRIVED on time, almost exactly forty hours after departing the station in New Orleans. The fields alongside the track were green in the gray light of dawn; the falling ash had not reached Salt Lick. The trees nodded gently, seemingly untroubled, as the train slowed its pace, rolling into the station.

If she had not read the antler map during her sleep, she would not have realized that the builder was someone she knew. The company name—*Blanc Railroad*—had struck her from the first. But only when she saw the station in Salt Lick, with the sound of the boy's weeping still ringing in her ears, did she realize that this was the very line Shadrack had traveled along the summer before. The rail line was the one planned and built by Blanca. It felt at once ominous and familiar.

The station was magnificent. White marble supported a vaulted roof of shining steel. The many tracks bustled with activity, much of it freight. Carved into the marble above the station entrance for each track was a tilted hourglass.

Sophia gathered her belongings and adjusted the chains of her thin mask. All of them were still dressed fully in their costumes. The crisis of the moment—the Clime's silence and the falling ash—had taken precedence over Wren's pursuers, and he had promptly made peace with Calixta. As they left their compartments, he warned them yet again that the League might be waiting. "If we are approached," he cautioned, with a meaning glance at Calixta, "you will allow me to conduct the conversation."

"Talk all you like," she agreed, with a sly smile. "And I'll do everything else."

Wren shook his head but did not take the bait. Instead, he walked at the head of their short procession and stepped onto the platform. Sophia and the others followed him.

There had been no falling ash outside the station, and within it, there was no sign that the Territories were at war. Men and women of all ages, although fewer families than Sophia would have expected, made their way through the station's great hall. In peacetime, the route continued into New Occident through upper New York, but now the train service stopped before the border and backtracked, making the long return trip to New Orleans. Salt Lick was one of the last stations on the line. The ticket counters were open, as were the stalls selling food and supplies.

"Oh, we must buy breakfast," Calixta exclaimed. "They have bacon sandwiches."

"Calixta," Wren said warningly. "We go straight to the pigeon depot, as agreed."

"Very well," Calixta pouted, after a moment's indecision. "But you will regret missing the bacon sandwiches."

"I think I will survive without them," Wren replied dryly.

Sophia was dazzled by the station itself and the people who walked through it. At the very center of the great hall stood a towering statue of a veiled woman holding a torch aloft. Passengers and vendors made their way around the base of the statue. Circling her colossal head was an endlessly moving constellation of orbs that Sophia realized were spherical clocks. They emerged from the beams of the vaulted ceiling along their tracks, whirling and dipping.

Not a single person appeared to be from New Occident. Many were raiders from the Baldlands, with silver bells and armor similar to those worn by Sophia and her companions. However, as she saw by the clothes of most of the passersby— suede in tan or black, beaded cotton, long capes like the one Goldenrod usually wore, tall laced boots that reached their knees—the majority of the travelers were from the Territories.

Wren was leading them to a set of double doors that stood open only a few steps away. Beyond them, the city of Salt Lick was beginning to wake to another summer morning. A bell tolled to announce a train departure, and then the sound of running footsteps rang through the station. Sophia did not turn, assuming passengers were rushing to catch the departing train. Then she heard a voice cut through the noise of the crowd: "Richard Wren!" She froze. Calixta, Goldenrod, Errol, and Wren turned.

They stood at the foot of the statue: a dozen agents of the Encephalon League, all of them in long cloaks of a peculiar color—smoky gray, with patches of soot, as if they had been dragged through a dirty chimney. Like Wren, they were tall, men and women alike. Standing before them was Burton Morris, a rueful expression on his face. His hands were tied before him.

The agent who had her hand on Burr's shoulder called Wren's name again. "Richard Wren. Come forward, and Morris will not be harmed."

"Don't move, Richard," Calixta said icily. "Let me handle this."

People in the station had begun to take notice. Skirting the agents, they glanced with curiosity or concern at Burr's bound hands. Some of them stopped to watch. One man, a raider, assessed the situation and drew his pistol. "In need of an extra hand, friends?" he asked Wren and Calixta, then grinned menacingly at the agents.

His question caught the ear of many around him. Raiders in the station were drawn toward them like metal filings to a magnet. Within seconds, Sophia found that there were a dozen raiders at her back, all with their weapons drawn, their metal gear clinking and clanking in anticipation.

The agent's expression hardened. "An escalation is not to your advantage, Wren," she said.

Wren shook his head. "This is not my doing," he protested.

"This is entirely your doing," she replied.

The threatening silence hung in the air between them. Sophia could feel Wren's resolve withering. At any moment, he would step forward, giving himself up to the League. They would never see him again, Sophia thought, panicked. What would the League do to him? Surely his crimes this time were even worse? Would he survive?

A hush filled the station, and it seemed to reach far beyond the cluster of people around her. *Something else is happening,* Sophia realized, dread suddenly filling her chest like a bitter breath.

She was abruptly aware that she could not see the statue clearly, even though it stood only a dozen feet away. Something was making it hard to see—a cloud, a fog, a reddened mist. It swirled all around the base of the statue, obscuring it and the agents, who seemed suddenly diminished in numbers. She stared at the fog, perplexed. Where did it come from? There was a smell on the air that collided unpleasantly with the smoky scent of bacon sandwiches: sweet, luxuriant, and degraded, like a dying flower.

"Take my hand, Sophia." It was Errol, and he seized her hand firmly in his own, pulling her toward him. Someone screamed. Sophia looked up at Wren, who had been just to her left, and found that he was gone. *Did I lose track of time?* Sophia wondered, confused. Her thoughts were moving slowly. She was frightened by the scream, but other fears began to crowd her mind.

She looked down at the floor of the station and realized that the red fog was so thick that she could not even see her feet. The air felt heavy—incredibly heavy, as if it wished to pin her to the ground. Sophia realized that things were happening around her and she was not perceiving them fully. The single scream had become many, and they had been echoing now for quite a while. She could not say for how long.

Suddenly, Errol dropped her hand. Sophia glanced up in surprise, but she could hardly see him. He had already stepped away; then he was gone. She heard the metallic ring of his sword being drawn. "Errol?" She put her hands out in front of her. *"Errol!"*

There was a whistle as his sword cut through the air. Sophia felt a wave of terror. She dropped to the ground and covered her head. "Errol!" she cried. "What are you doing?"

The air above her moved. She looked up, hoping to see Errol's hand reaching down toward her. But it was not Errol's hand. Instead she saw giant talons, set in iridescent green skin, grasping at the thick air. Sophia gasped and tried to get her bearings. She dimly recalled open doors perhaps twenty paces ahead—and she stumbled. A shape moved above her. She caught a glimpse of a massive wing cutting through the fog: brilliant with red and orange scales. Then, as she crawled forward unsteadily, the beast's face suddenly appeared beside her. It was blue-skinned, with a long snout, golden eyes, and a set of massive jaws.

Its long teeth like knives bared, the dragon spoke: *"Sophia."*

Sophia choked on a scream. She pushed herself to her feet, rushing blindly into the fog. Disordered thoughts ran through her mind. The story of Tree-Eater flashed before her: the monster conjured by imagination. *But why would I imagine a dragon?* she asked herself, panicking. *I didn't! I didn't imagine a dragon, I promise!* She wanted to cry out to Errol, but she feared drawing the terrifying dragon-creature toward her. Unexpectedly, she heard Errol's sword ring as it hit stone—the marble floor of the station?

She hurried toward the sound, hands out in front of her. It was not far. She heard the ring again, and a grunt of effort. She had reached him. Sophia dove in a final burst toward the sound. Then she looked up in horror. She had not found Errol. This was something else: a giant; a massive statue made of iron. He leaned toward her, his helmeted head with its closed visor emerging from the fog. The iron giant lifted his sword—*Errol's sword*, Sophia realized—into the crimson mist, preparing to strike. Sophia froze for a moment, mesmerized.

Then she bolted.

As she stumbled in what she hoped was the direction of the doorway, the din around her suddenly flooded her ears: roaring and clanging, screaming and wailing, the echoing report of pistol shots. Sophia felt a sob rising in her chest. She ran as far as she could before her foot caught on some person or thing hidden by the mist and she fell, sprawling forward onto the ground.

17

NOSH'S EYE

—1892, August 9: 4-Hour 22—

The Eerie have a reputation as healers, and it is true that some of their skills lie in healing. But I have found that their talents are not adequately described thus. Perhaps the best way of putting it is that the Eerie have a talent for perception—they perceive many things that others do not. And we might consider how some of their habits encourage this talent for perception. They almost always live alone—Elodeans shun big cities—and they often live in the company of animals. I suspect any of us might develop a greater talent for perception if we lived alone in the woods with a family of raccoons!

—From Sophia Tims's Reflections on a Journey to the Eerie Sea

SOPHIA LAY ON the ground, her senses battered by the horrible sounds that echoed through the station. Now that she could hear them, they overwhelmed her, like a wave that filled her mind and pushed out every other thought. Dimly, she understood that Goldenrod, Errol, the pirates, and Wren were somewhere in the confusion, but although the realization made her anxious, she could not think what to do with it. She could not even comprehend what it meant that they were there, in the midst of the fog, with the dragon and the knight.

The two creatures she had seen loomed in her mind, coming into focus. From somewhere that felt terribly remote, as if it had happened long, long ago, she suddenly remembered words of significance: *When you see the knight and the dragon, you must think only of your own safety. Your instinct is to stay. You must flee.*

Who had spoken these words? Were they from the Ausentinian map? No—Sophia did not think they were. But then where did they come from?

Maxine. The name came like a breath of clean air. *Maxine said the words to me, only a few days ago.*

Sophia clung to this thought; it seemed the only thing she could trust, for she could not trust what was happening around her, and she could not trust her own senses. *Safety.* She opened her eyes. She was on the marble floor, curled around her satchel. The red fog was beginning to settle, leaving a thin scum on her fingers and clothes. Around her, the screams and terrible sounds continued.

Sophia urged herself up onto her hands and knees. Directly ahead, she realized, there was silence. The sounds were behind her. Moving inch by inch, she crawled away from them and toward the silence. Her palms struck the floor of the station blindly, and she dragged her knees along behind her. She kept her head tucked down—there was nothing to see if she raised it. The sounds behind her, although they continued to echo, seemed to grow a fraction more remote.

Then there was a sound ahead of her—a footstep and a low laugh. Sophia looked up slowly, dreading what she would see.

There was nothing—only red mist. And then the mist parted briefly, and a white figure appeared: tall and regal, wearing a full-length dress and a long veil that obscured her features. Her hands were gloved; her delicate fingers moved gracefully, parting the red mist as if brushing aside a branch. She nodded gently, and her movements were terribly familiar. As she reached to lift the veil, the fog consumed her once more. But that momentary glimpse had been enough. *Blanca,* Sophia thought, horrified. *She survived. She's here. She's* here.

Sophia scrabbled blindly away. She heard the footsteps following her, easy and assured, unhurried. *I have to get away from her. I have to get away from her. I have to get away from her.*

The single thought pushed her forward, through the red mist and into the unknown, still crawling on hands and knees. Suddenly her hand touched something firm and somehow rubbery. Sophia recoiled in horror. *What is it? What is it? A hand? A foot?* She stared down at the object, and the nature of it slowly, slowly dawned on her. *A potato,* she said to herself, as if assuring herself that it really was. *A potato.* She touched it experimentally. It did not change. The red fog swirled and parted: an overturned vegetable cart appeared. A large crate of potatoes had fallen from the lower shelf, half its contents scattered. Sophia crawled toward it desperately, even as the fog again descended.

Safety, she repeated to herself. *Your own safety.* Reaching the cart, she poured out the remaining potatoes and overturned the crate, fitting herself beneath it.

Huddled there, Sophia waited. Blanca's footsteps were

no longer audible. She peered anxiously through the cracks, trying to catch a glimpse of her old foe, but there was nothing to see beyond the red fog. She could not track the passing time. It seemed to her that over the course of many hours she heard the din of the station: running footsteps, screams and cries, the abrupt clatter of collapsing wood. At one point, in her silent corner, someone—a stranger—ran past toward one of the nearby train platforms. Sophia realized, watching his retreating back through the slats of the crate, that he was visible because the fog had begun to clear.

She could see things as far as twelve or even twenty feet away: terrible things. She saw people slumped on the floor. She saw a man holding a chair like a shield, trembling, his eyes closed tightly. One arm held the chair while the other hung at his side uselessly, bleeding onto his clothes and the ground. A red sediment covered every surface. Even the potatoes, strewn all around her, were dusted with crimson.

While one part of her watched the station, frantically observing the same few details over and over again, another part of her was wrestling with the visions that flashed through her mind: Blanca, the knight, and the dragon. *How is Blanca here?* Sophia asked herself silently. *How can she be here? How could she have survived in Nochtland? How would she know that we would be here—today, at this time?* The image of the scarred Lachrima lifting her veil appeared in her mind, the red mist swirling around her. Then the dragon appeared and turned its head, nostrils flaring, and great claws flexed open. A pair of great, strong wings with blue veins unfurled, and a long tail cut through the air like a falling tower. Then the knight's sword shone brightly, catching some shaft of light that pierced the fog, and with a rattle of armor the sword swooped toward her.

Sophia began to realize, with slow perplexity, that she remembered more of them than she had seen. The thought made her uneasy and even more greatly confused. *Did I see more and not remember? Did I lose track of time? If I didn't see more, where do these visions come from? Am I imagining more than I saw?* She could not settle her mind—she could not even bring herself to see the frantic circle of her thoughts as something useless. Now that she had found relative safety in the potato crate, her thoughts seemed to run wild, beating about inside the crate like a trapped thing.

More time passed, and the station grew quiet. The fog slowly dispersed. The great statue of the veiled woman came into view, and she was now no longer white—she was red. But she was solid and immobile—a monument, not a person. Sophia realized she could see the entire station; the air had cleared completely. And her thoughts had started to clear as well. The desperate cycle of panicked images began to slow. It seemed fruitless to whirl through them again and again, seeing first the dragon, then the knight, then Blanca, and then the dragon once more. She began to wonder, in a confused and uncertain way, what she had actually seen.

Suddenly a thought burst onto her mind. *There are no dragons.* She seized upon it with relief and surprise. Using the thought as a handhold, she inched forward. *There could not have been a dragon in the station,* she thought to herself tentatively, *could there?*

Then what did I see? Who was the knight holding Errol's sword? And Blanca . . . Could it be that, after seeing Blanca's statue, I imagined seeing Blanca herself? As her mind stumbled through these questions, another suddenly occurred to her: What had happened to her friends?

With a flood of awareness, Sophia became conscious of how utterly confused she had been. While hiding in the potato crate she had not even wondered about them.

She was on the verge of throwing off the crate and going to look when she heard a sudden echoing sound in the silence. It was heavy clop of footsteps—more hoofbeats than footsteps, and very different from Blanca's light tread. Sophia looked through the slats, but could see nothing. The sound approached her from the side; she could not shift inside the crate, and so she waited, unmoving, for the creature to pass. Suddenly a great brown face appeared, inches from her own, and a great brown eye gazed at her through the slats. Sophia startled, shifting the crate. It was lifted into the air, exposing her. Sophia curled up, covering her head with her arms and bracing herself for a sudden blow.

None came. There was a brief silence. "We're not going to hurt you," a voice said. "I'm sorry Nosh startled you. Only he knew where you were. I would never have found your hiding place."

Sophia slowly lowered her arms and looked up. Standing above her was the boy she had seen in the antler's memories, and behind him, looking concerned and faintly apologetic, was the creature himself: a great brown moose with heavy antlers. "Nosh," Sophia whispered, "and Bittersweet."

The boy raised his eyebrows. "You know my name." He held out a hand as green as Goldenrod's. "We must leave. In a city of this size, there is sometimes looting after the fog has passed, and it can be just as bad as the fog."

Sophia felt dazed. She knew that her mind had still not fully cleared, and she still did not trust her own thoughts. But she understood that the boy and the moose were offering to help her. "But my friends," she said weakly.

"I know," Bittersweet said, glancing over his shoulder, into the station. "We must leave without them. They are already gone."

There was a sharp whistle, keen and high, from somewhere outside the building. Bittersweet grasped Sophia's hand. "That's the looters," he said. "I'll explain more later, I promise. But we have to go."

He cupped his hands by Nosh's round belly. "Step up on my hands," he said. Sophia put her raider's boot onto Bittersweet's palms and heaved herself up onto Nosh's back. Bittersweet climbed up behind her. "Take us the safest way you can, Nosh," he said, patting the moose's side, "and the sooner we get out of Salt Lick, the better."

18
THE BACKWOODS

—*1892, August 9: 16-Hour 43*—

The raiders of the Baldlands have no fixed capital, no center. They do not even have towns. Rather, they form groups based not on kin but friendship, and those groups have settlements throughout the middle Baldlands. Some half dozen raiders always remain at the settlement, or fort, as they are wont to call it, while the others head out on raiding parties. Usually raiding parties travel at most two or three days' distance from the main fort, but ambitious raiding groups are known to embark on longer journeys for greater gains.

—From Shadrack Elli's History of the New World

CASANOVA TRIED TO stay awake. It was his third day on the road and his third night without sleep. The night before he had driven the wagon through the night, through an inch of fallen ash that made the ground white and eerily warm. Squinting down at the strange substance, he worried most about whether it would make them easier to track. That morning, in a farm north of Fort Pitt, he had left the surviving mule—exhausted from fear and overwork—in the hands of a farmer, and exchanged half the contents of the wagon for a draft horse. Fortunately, his northeasterly route had prevented him from encountering any New Occident troops. He had chosen the less trafficked path to the state of New York, cutting across the northwest corner of Pennsylvania, on purpose. But for the same reason his journey proceeded slowly; the narrower road made for difficult travel. The draft horse was strong and needed less rest than he had feared. And yet, he knew they could not arrive soon enough.

Theo had woken on the previous afternoon, probably at the sound of Casanova's rifle when he was forced to shoot the injured mule. When he heard the boy's groan of protest, Casanova hurried to the rear of the wagon. Theo had not improved since then. He had a high fever. Sometimes he drank water, but most of the time he pushed it away, battling Casanova with his good arm as if fending off a poison draught.

Casanova urged and cajoled him, doing everything he could to bring him to consciousness. "Theo—hey, Theo," he said desperately. "Wake up. Just for a few seconds." There was no response. "Theo. Please. You have to drink water." He felt a moment's panic when he could not feel the boy's pulse, and then he saw Theo's eyelids flutter. "I'll make it worth your while. You know what? If you just open your eyes and take this drink of water, I'll tell you the story of the scar. Don't you want to hear the story of the scar?" he pleaded. Theo's head lolled to the side.

Casanova took a long, shaky breath. When he inspected Theo's wound, he found it terrifyingly red and swollen. He knew then that, whether because of a substance on the arrowhead or simply because the injury could not heal properly with the embedded pieces of flint, the wound had become infected.

After that, Casanova redoubled his efforts. As he continued on their route, driving through the evening and night, his weariness grew and he began to drift into that state of exhaustion in which doubts hover like specters and nothing seems certain. He wondered whether he should have sought a doctor in Fort Pitt. But, he argued with himself, the moment the wagon had fled the battle—no, the moment *he had driven on*, away from the battle—they had become deserters. He could not count on the goodwill of the commanding officers in Fort Pitt. Most likely they would enforce the law against sedition to the fullest extent, because he and Theo were convict-soldiers. Before the boy even had a chance to heal, he would find himself at the end of a hangman's rope.

So Casanova rode on, though he knew another day and a half on the road lay ahead.

The sun had not yet set, but on the narrow path through the woods, dusk had already fallen. Casanova let his chin drop, the reins slack in his hands. His eyes closed. Before he could drift into sleep, the sudden halting of the horse jolted him upright.

He blinked into the gathering darkness and saw, only twenty feet ahead on the path, a cluster of torchlights. They moved toward him. The men carrying them were at least six in number; they had long hair and heavy boots. If he had not been lulled by the sound of the horse's hooves and the creaking wagon, he surely would have heard the men, for every inch of their hair and clothes rang with silver. Raiders.

Casanova sat motionlessly, the reins now tight in his hands.

There was no place to go. The track was too narrow for him to turn around, and the woods on either side too thick. There was no opportunity for flight. *Then it will have to be bargaining,* he thought.

"Evening, gentlemen," he said casually, as the raiders approached the wagon. He noted that two of the men wore goggles loosely around their necks, as if in readiness. Casanova waited.

One of the raiders with goggles came up to the side of the wagon and amicably slapped the horse's haunches. He gave Casanova a wide grin, and his metal teeth shone in the light of the torch he held. "Well, friend. What have we here?"

"I might ask the same. You boys are rather more east than you usually are, am I right?" Casanova asked.

The raider's grin widened farther. "That we are. War makes for good hunting."

"Maybe in some places."

Another raider, this one unsmiling, stared at Casanova. "Bloody Fates, man, you have one ugly face."

Casanova looked back at him. In the long pause that followed, Casanova heard all the tinkling bells the raiders wore go silent as the men fell still. He waited, letting the firelight of the torches play over his scarred features, knowing well how it would look. Then he smiled wryly. "Seems to me the pot's calling the kettle black," Casanova said.

There was a moment more of silence, and then the raiders burst into laughter. Casanova shook his head good-naturedly and took up the reins. "Well, my handsome friends, I know what you're here for, and I know there's six of you and one of me. However, what you don't know," he added, and the raiders' laughter died away, "is how much damage one of me can do. I make it a point of aiming for the face, just so you have a little something to remember me by. So I recommend you keep your good looks. Help yourself to anything you like, excepting enough food and water for the boy."

The raiders gazed at him warily, and he could see that they were deciding whether to take offense. Casanova put up his hands in mock surrender. "You've got me. I won't say fair and square, but nonetheless. All I want is to get that sick boy in the back of the wagon to safety, and I need enough food and water for one day and a night. If you'll do that for me, I'll be much obliged. By way of thanks, I'll tell you what I know of the nearest troops, and I'll throw in a pair of goggles. Looks to me like you might need them."

The raider who had first spoken stared at Casanova through narrowed eyes, and he turned to the man next to him. "Check the back of the wagon," he said curtly.

The man ambled off with a sound like a purse full of coins falling down a set of stairs. Casanova waited. There was silence as the raider peered into the back of the wagon, and then the same metallic cacophony as he returned. "Yeah. Full of loot. Very sick kid," he muttered. Then he said something to the leader that Casanova could not make out. It sounded like "lucky."

"All right," the first man replied gruffly. "Leave them food for two days and clear out the rest." He turned to Casanova. "That should tide you over."

Casanova nodded. "I'm grateful to you."

The raiders emptied the remaining contents of the wagon, taking all of the major's linens, wine, and costly preserves. Casanova watched with some regret as pickled vegetables, bags of fine flour, coffee and chocolate from the Indies, and jars of summer fruit jams vanished in the raiders' arms. He told their leader about where he had seen troops, and about what had happened to his own company under the leadership of Major Merret. The man listened in silence, and nodded gravely when Casanova described the archers who sprang from the side of the road. "Their masks covered their mouths," Casanova commented, "not their eyes."

"Did they, now?" the raider said, intrigued. "Might be they know more than we do. Haven't had the good fortune to see any red cloud myself," the raider said dryly.

"A red cloud? Is that what the goggles are for?"

The raider gave a curt nod. "I take it you haven't seen it, either."

"No."

"Red clouds that turn the mind. Make your own flesh and blood appear as monsters, they say. Hard to know the truth of it, since I've only heard secondhand, but a man two days south told me he met a boy who speared his sister with a pickax. He thought she was a bear."

Casanova scoffed. "Sounds improbable."

"Maybe. Maybe not." The raider turned away, and Casanova heard him climb into the back of the wagon. After some silence, he got out and walked some distance into the woods, where his own horse was presumably tied up. He returned with a small cloth pouch, which he tossed up to Casanova. It was light, its contents like pieces of frayed rope under the cotton cloth.

"What's this?" Casanova asked.

"Dried beef," the raider replied. He gave Casanova a keen look. "The boy needs food with iron in it."

Casanova blinked in surprise. "Is that right?"

"He's Mark of Iron," the raider said. "Won't survive without it."

Casanova looked down at the pouch and back up at the raider, whose teeth, glinting in the flickering torchlight, seemed less forbidding now. "Thank you. Can I ask your name? To tell the boy who helped him, when he wakes."

"You can tell Lucky Theo that Skinny Jim and the gang passed by. He'll remember me from old times."

Wordless, astonished, Casanova watched Skinny Jim follow the other raiders back up the path. They led their heavily laden horses into the woods, and soon the light of their torches flickered out among the trees.

He sprang to his feet, his energy renewed. He tied the reins and hurried to the back of the wagon, where he found that the raiders had left them more than enough food. A lighted gas lamp was standing on a barrel of water. They had even left Theo's bedding, propping him up between the major's fine cotton quilts. Casanova felt a spasm of relief. They had gotten off easy. He knelt down and reluctantly shook Theo awake.

"Theo—Theo, you have to wake up."

Theo's eyes opened, and he looked up at Casanova uncomprehendingly.

"You're going to have some water and food," Casanova said, putting his arm under Theo's head. Theo did not even react when Casanova accidentally brushed his injured shoulder—a bad sign. He gazed blankly ahead, and Casanova tipped the water canteen into his mouth. Theo choked, coughed, and then swallowed. Casanova gave him the smallest piece of dried beef he could find. "Chew that over, Theo," he said quietly. "Skinny Jim says you need iron. So chew on that, and get better, would you?"

Theo chewed obediently and swallowed, but his eyes remained glazed over, and when Casanova lay him back against the bedding, he turned and closed his eyes without uttering a sound.

19
THREE HINTS

—1892, August 9: 11-Hour 14—

There is no upward mobility for bureaucrats at the State House, however. The parliamentary posts are invariably purchased from the outside by industrialists or legacy politicians. Necessarily, anyone with the wealth to procure such a seat would not seek out a lowly position as office assistant or messenger or timekeeper. And so, for all those who work in the State House, there is a clear ceiling: they might progress from one office to the next, and they might well make a respectable career in the august offices of the capital, but they will never rise to become part of the lawmaking body itself.

—From Shadrack Elli's History of New Occident

EXTRAORDINARY EVENTS RARELY remain extraordinary. Even if they continue unexplained, their very strangeness gradually becomes less and less strange. So it had been with the sinkholes, which at first were described in alarmed tones as localized subterranean eruptions or—by the city's more fantastically minded—as an army of giant worms. Then the alarm faded, and soon enough the people of Boston began to think of them as nothing more remarkable than bad Boston weather. They calmly went about their days, giving the sinkholes wide berth.

And so it was with the falling ash, which left a good inch of powder on the city that turned to paste with the first dewy morning. Those who did not clear their streets and walkways found that a thin crust of cement, baked by the sun, had hardened on every surface. Boston took on the unlikely appearance of a crusty, gray mummy. The morning newspapers made alarmed noises about the consequences of "The Anvil," but for the most part, all of New Occident seemed to be treating the ash as if it was simply another kind of precipitation.

Shadrack looked about him in amusement as he walked to the State House. He saw more than one workman chipping ash crust from windows, and he passed a pair of children flinging the hardened ash into the river. No one seemed particularly disturbed by the sediment, despite its unknown origins. The notable exception was the Nihilismian prognosticator, a self-styled street prophet who always stood at a corner of the Common, haranguing passersby about the evils of the Age of Delusion. On this morning, he had drawn a small crowd and was energetically accusing his listeners of having ignorantly led the Age toward certain apocalypse. "It is no longer a mere expression," he shouted, his beard trembling with excitement, "to say that the sky rains fire. The rain of fire and brimstone, so feared in the Age of Verity, has actually come to pass!" His voice rose to a shriek. "One might even say that the Age of Verity is reaching into this deluded Age to destroy it!"

"Except that there's been no fire," a man called back from the sidewalk.

"Or brimstone," a woman chimed in.

Shadrack chuckled to himself at the Nihilismian's consternated expression and walked on, heading up the State House steps.

He had already written several letters that morning to diverse correspondents across the region with the intention of discovering what he could about the strange phenomenon, and he planned to spend the morning investigating the matter further. But when he arrived at his office, he found a young woman with short black hair and a trim suit standing at his closed door. The prime minister's assistant was waiting.

"Minister Elli," she said, with a brief smile. "Unusual weather, isn't it?"

"Good morning, Cassandra," he replied. "To say the very least. Any theories?" He opened the door and ushered her in.

"I have some ideas." Her expression was mischievous. "But I'd like to have some evidence before I speculate out loud."

"Very wise," Shadrack said with a smile. "My housekeeper suggested the Fates were having their chimney swept."

Cassandra laughed.

"I am not entirely sure she was joking," Shadrack said, with a shake of his head.

"Surely every theory is worth testing when there is no clear explanation," she said.

Gamaliel Shore had been sorely disappointed to lose

Cassandra Pierce, and the Prime Minister was quite proud of having lured her away. Both parties recognized her as the best assistant in the State House. She was known to be discreet, punctual, tireless, and incredibly resourceful. Moreover, she was friendly without being unctuous, professional without being cold, and informative without being a gossip. She bore very little resemblance to the Nihilismian archivist called "Remorse," who had, it was thought, departed on a mission to another Age. Even her appearance was different—brighter and cleaner, somehow. Those few people in Boston who had business in the Nihilismian archive *and* the State House would have had difficulty realizing that Remorse and Cassandra were one and the same.

And Shadrack, having never visited the archive, was himself no wiser. He had assumed that anyone who chose voluntarily to work with Broadgirdle was bound to be either wildly deluded or perilously dim-witted, so he paid little attention to the new assistant whenever he had contact with her. But Cassandra would not be ignored. Because he would not hire an assistant, much preferring to work alone, Shadrack had to deflect her insistent visits himself. She began making a habit of stopping by Shadrack's office, at first with messages from Broadgirdle (that could easily have been delivered by the messenger boy) or papers to sign (that were far from urgent), and later with questions that, to his surprise, piqued Shadrack's interest.

Usually, these questions were about maps. Were there new

maps showing the position of Princess Justa in the western Baldlands, and how far did her rule there extend? Did the maps of the Indian Territories show exact or only approximate positions for the westernmost towns? How did the maps of the Territories and Baldlands account for migratory populations that traveled north and south over the course of the year?

Shadrack had begun to feel less dread when he saw Cassandra at his door, but this morning proved to be different almost from the start. "May I close the door?" Cassandra asked once Shadrack was seated at his desk.

"Certainly," he said with some surprise.

Taking a seat across from the desk, Cassandra held up a bundle of papers. "I was wondering if you could help me with something."

"I would be glad to try."

"I have found that the key to being a good assistant is to anticipate what the prime minister needs before he knows he needs it."

"That is certainly an admirable goal, though it sounds impossible to me."

Cassandra smiled. "Usually, it just means thinking ahead a little bit."

"Very well—if you say so."

"In this case, it has to do with the terrible fog attacks that have struck in the Indian Territories."

"Fog attacks . . ." Shadrack echoed. "Is that how we are describing them?"

Cassandra blinked. "Is my description inaccurate?"

"No." He paused. "But 'attack' suggests intention and deliberate action. I was not aware that we knew as much."

Cassandra pursed her lips. "You are probably right. The prime minister does not call them attacks. But I just cannot help seeing them that way." She gave a sheepish smile. "Perhaps it is in my nature to see malicious people doing bad things where there are none. Surely not a good quality!"

"Well," Shadrack conceded, "they could be attacks. We do not know."

"Precisely," Cassandra continued. "Which is why I think it is best to be prepared." She placed the bundle of papers on the edge of Shadrack's desk. The top sheet, Shadrack could see clearly, was a list of addresses.

"You mean to be prepared for an attack here?"

Cassandra nodded.

"I . . ." Shadrack leaned back in his chair. "I confess it had not occurred to me. It seems a very remote possibility. To date, all of the occurrences have been in the Indian Territories."

"Nevertheless," Cassandra said, raising her forefinger, "a good assistant thinks ahead."

Shadrack gave a slight smile. "Right. You've made your point. And what is it you would like to do in anticipation of a possible attack here?"

"My first thought was to ensure the safety of all the prime minister's properties." Casually she handed the top sheet of paper across the desk to Shadrack. "Other precautions must also be taken, of course, but surely it would help to somehow secure them."

Shadrack took the paper without a word and attempted to school his face into an expression of helpful rumination. He could not believe what Cassandra had just given him. For weeks, he had searched for this information without success, for Broadgirdle kept his personal matters carefully concealed. If it truly listed all of Broadgirdle's properties, what he was now holding could very well point to the location of the kidnapped Eerie. "Hm," he said, scanning it quickly. "That sounds challenging," he commented. There were five addresses. One was the mansion on Beacon Hill, which he and all of Boston already knew about. Another was an address in western Cambridge. Two were warehouses near the water. And the last was a farm in Lexington. "How would you secure these properties?"

"I asked myself the same question. Without knowing what this fog *is*, we cannot begin to protect ourselves from it."

"I could not agree more," Shadrack said mechanically. He repeated the addresses silently to himself, committing each one to memory.

"So I thought it might help to consult a botanist," Cassandra said brightly, looking pleased with herself.

Shadrack felt a sudden tremor of warning. Putting the list of addresses carefully aside, he clasped his hands and looked at Broadgirdle's assistant. He felt immediately, undoubtedly certain that Cassandra Pierce knew much more than she was saying. Her expression, so cheerfully self-satisfied, looked no different from usual. But her eyes were grave—deeply, meaningfully grave.

"Why a botanist?" Shadrack asked quietly. "I should have thought you would look for a chemist if you think the fog storms are deliberate attacks."

"Ah," Cassandra said, without changing her tone, "but everyone who has reported on the attacks says the fog smells like flowers."

"Many substances smell like flowers."

Cassandra frowned. "So you think it's a bad idea to consult a botanist?"

"Not necessarily. I was only trying to understand how you had come to your conclusion."

She sighed. "I suppose, to be thorough, I should also consult with chemists. You are right—we cannot know the nature of this substance. Nevertheless," she went on, handing him the second sheet of paper, "these are the botanists I was able to identify in Boston who have enough expertise to consider the problem."

Shadrack glanced at the list of names. None of them was familiar. "How did you determine their expertise?"

"I looked at their scholarly work. Though I am by no means an expert in botany, it is a small field, and there are only three scientists in Boston who publish their research with any regularity. These are the three.

"And finally we come to my request for assistance," Cassandra said, leaning forward. "You will see that one is circled.

I could locate the other two, but not this one. Then I realized that he teaches at the university—I believe you hold an appointment there as well, do you not?"

Shadrack looked at the circled name. *Gerard Sorensen.* "I do," he said slowly.

"I thought perhaps, with your connections there, you might be able to locate him."

Shadrack looked up at Cassandra and realized that he had misunderstood. His first impression had been that she was in Broadgirdle's confidence and that her knowledge came from him.

But no—she was not in his confidence. Cassandra Pierce was working behind Broadgirdle's back.

She said the words just as they were meant to sound: hopeful, light, and without particular significance. Shadrack heard their significance nonetheless. As he looked in her eyes, he understood the words she really intended: *This man knows what the crimson fog is. I am giving you his name. Go find him.*

He could not fathom how or why Cassandra Pierce had come to this knowledge, or how she had come to a point where she was betraying Broadgirdle's secrets. Perhaps, he considered, this had been her intention from the start. After all, she was relatively new to the prime minister's office. But however she had arrived and however she had decided to betray her employer, one thing was clear: Cassandra Pierce was trying to help Shadrack. She had already given several indications of what to do, and he could not ignore them. The woman sitting before him suddenly looked entirely different than she had when she knocked on his office door, even though nothing about her had changed.

"I think it's very likely that I could locate him at the university," Shadrack said. "Would it be helpful if I tried to speak with him?"

Cassandra's face lit up. "That would be *so* helpful."

"Then I'd be glad to help."

"Thank you so much."

"No, Cassandra," he said, handing the paper back to her. "Thank you."

—*August 10, 16-Hour 10*—

THE PLOTTERS HAD been reduced to four when Miles left for the Indian Territories. But they continued to meet, of course, their goal being more urgent than ever, and on August tenth Winnie and Nettie were happily devouring a blackberry tart made by Mrs. Clay while they waited for Shadrack to join them. Speculation as to the meaning of Cassandra's clues—reported by the housekeeper to the junior plotters—flew around the table.

"She must hate Broadsy as much as we do!" Winnie declared triumphantly.

"She might not hate him," Nettie said thoughtfully, taking a forkful of tart. "Perhaps she has some long-term plan of her own that involves the crimson fog."

"I just want to point out," Mrs. Clay sniffed, "that I might have been wrong about the origin of the fog, but I am very right about its dangers. If anything, this means it is even worse than we thought."

"But the problem is that we don't really *know* anything," said Nettie. "Until we find this Sorensen—and even then . . . he might know something, or not."

The knob on the side door rattled, and the door flew open. "Well, my friends," Shadrack announced. He brought the outside air, dank as an extinguished fire, into the room with him. "I have good news and bad news."

"And we have blackberry tart!" Winnie announced, holding up his laden fork.

Shadrack smiled. He sat and gladly accepted the plate Mrs. Clay handed him. "The good news," he said, diving into the tart without delay, "is that I located Sorensen's office at the university. He is, indeed, a member of the botany department, and he has been working there for nearly thirty years."

"Oh, he must be *old*," Nettie said.

"Rather. The bad news," Shadrack swallowed the tart, "is that Sorensen has not been seen in his office for months. He is missing."

"Missing?" the plotters echoed.

"Yes. And Sorensen, while his wife passed away some years ago—the departmental assistant informed me—does have two grown children and several grandchildren in Boston. He has reason to stay in the area, and it is unlikely that he would willingly disappear without a word of explanation, as he has."

"Broadgirdle," Nettie said grimly.

"Very possibly. So our answers are not as near as I hoped. But," he said, pausing briefly for another bite of tart, "we do have another lead as to the location of the missing Weatherers, thanks to Cassandra. We have the addresses. The two warehouses and the farm in Lexington are the most likely prospects. That is where we shall start our search."

"I can go," Winnie said quickly.

"You *can*, no doubt," Shadrack replied just as quickly, "but it would be both dangerous and foolish."

"Why isn't Cassandra doing this herself?" Nettie asked. "I'm not ungrateful, of course, but I am trying to understand what her part is in all of this."

"You ask a good question," Shadrack said, "which I have wondered myself. She is playing a deep game here, and I cannot pretend to understand the objectives fully. The best I can say is that she is also working against Broadgirdle but perhaps believes that pursuing these leads openly while working as his assistant would put her in jeopardy."

"So she gets us to help," Nettie said.

"Yes—in some ways, we are helping her as much as she is helping us. She's suggesting a division of labor, perhaps. While she infiltrates his office and learns what she can, we take action to pursue the leads."

"It seems dangerous to me," Mrs. Clay said unhappily.

"But we *have* to do it," Winnie insisted.

"We already are," Shadrack put in. "Winnie and his colleagues at the State House have been following every lead." Winnie nodded gravely. "Nettie has been tactfully observing Inspector Grey's progress on the investigation."

Winnie scowled. "Or lack of progress."

"He is not entirely to blame," Shadrack said. Then he addressed Nettie. "Perhaps we should tell your father about this most recent development. When Broadgirdle is apprehended, it must be official. I think it is time for Inspector Grey to investigate anew."

Nettie shook her head. "My father is persuaded that by arresting Mr. Peel he arrested the right man, Mr. Elli. He believes Broadgirdle is innocent. And I don't think these hints from Cassandra are going to change his mind. In fact—we can't even tell him where the hints come from. Think about what it will cost Cassandra if we can convince him to look at these addresses and it turns out that nothing is there."

Shadrack hesitated.

"Nettie and I can go!" Winnie repeated. "Broadgirdle doesn't know us, and we look perfectly innocent." He adopted an expression of beatific gentleness that made him appear disturbingly empty-headed.

Nettie smiled. "I agree with Winnie. Just as a first step. If there's anything to see, we bring the matter to my father."

Again, Shadrack hesitated. "Very well. I can see the difficulty of persuading Inspector Grey with so little tangible evidence. But I can't see the sense in sending the two of you to explore alone. We shall go together."

Winnie beamed. "Fizzing. Where to first?"

"I think the warehouses. We can go tomorrow afternoon, when I return from the ministry."

He looked at the two eager faces before him and felt a pang of guilt. The deception he had set in motion was for their own safety, he reminded himself. Broadgirdle was far too dangerous for two children to reckon with. The next steps he would have to take alone.

20

BITTERSWEET

—1892, August 9: 5-Hour 31—

The Elodeans (Eerie) do come together frequently, contrary to popular rumor. But those who would wish to see many together in a single place should know, it is almost impossible to predict when and where the gatherings will occur. Several times a year, I have been told, messengers are sent to all the Elodeans within a ten days' journey of the Eerie Sea. Then they come together to discuss whatever matter has called them forth. From what I know, these are singular occasions, entirely unlike the gatherings of other peoples. There are no celebrations, no songs or ritual performances. The conversations take place over several days, in small clusters rather than large gatherings. At some point, the issue is considered resolved or unresolvable, and they all go their separate ways.

—From Sophia Tims's Reflections on a Journey to the Eerie Sea

SOPHIA, RIDING ON Nosh in front of Bittersweet, had a clear view of Salt Lick. Wide streets of pounded dirt were lined by log-frame buildings. Each building resembled a large box stacked atop a smaller one; narrow passageways ran between them. Down a passage to her left, Sophia saw the fleeing hindquarters of a panicked horse, trailing a saddle and what looked like a blue blanket. Smoke plumed out into the street through the buildings' narrow windows. A woman leaned out of one near them and screamed, "Ivan! Ivan!" before abruptly collapsing inward and disappearing from sight.

It was evident that the crimson fog had struck everywhere. Having never seen Salt Lick before, Sophia could hardly compare, but it seemed to her that the city had been shattered. Fires burned in open doorways, charring the buildings, and in the middle distance, smoke filled the horizon. The street outside the station was almost empty. A lone man sat in the dirt, weeping quietly into his hands. Sophia shuddered.

"The cruelest thing about the fog striking at dawn," Bittersweet said behind her, "is that people are often at home with their families. They turn on each other."

Sophia could hardly comprehend his words. "Then the fog is a poison," she said, trying to reason it through.

Bittersweet did not speak for a moment as Nosh circumvented an overturned cart and clopped quickly down a side street. "A poison, yes. In small doses it only distracts and confuses, but here . . . the quantities are almost lethal."

The red sediment that covered Salt Lick gave it an unearthly aspect: it coated every building, every street, every motionless figure that lay strewn in their way. Salt Lick had no public clocks, as Boston did. Instead, there were thick logs standing on every corner: gradual sculptures carved away carelessly or lovingly, inexpertly or skillfully, by passersby and residents. They were not time markers; they made strange, ornate sentinels that watched the city impassively. The carvings' ridges, intricate and rune-like, were dusted with red. Here and there,

Sophia could see footprints tracking through the red dust, winding through the silent streets. "Small doses?" she asked.

"Yes. The fog comes from a flower."

It made no sense. "This was done by a flower?"

"No," Bittersweet said firmly. "This was not done by a flower. This was done by men."

Sophia did not understand, but she put aside her questions for a more pressing concern: "Where are we going?"

"Out of the city—to safety."

"My friends will not know how to find us."

Bittersweet hesitated. "I hope they will. I am trusting Nosh. He said we were to find you, and that's what we've done. I hope Goldenrod can help the others."

Sophia realized that she had not mentioned Goldenrod. "How did you know she was with me?" she wondered, turning to look at him over her shoulder.

"Nosh knew," Bittersweet said. He set his mouth in a line. "Nosh is the only one who knows anything these days. The old one will not speak to me." He frowned. "What is it, Nosh?" He stared over Sophia's head at the packed dirt road before them. Here the footprints were many, and the red dust had already been worn away, leaving a muddy track in its place. "Very well," he said, to some silent comment made by the lumbering moose. "Do what you can."

"What's wrong?" Sophia asked.

Before he could reply, there was a whooping sound in the narrow passage between the buildings to their left. Sophia turned to see a cluster of young men hurrying toward them and recoiled instinctively. She saw before her, suddenly, a flock of guards from the palace in Nochtland, swooping toward her with their obsidian spears. Then they changed, appearing as hooded figures with beaked masks: the Order of the Golden Cross that had pursued her through the Papal States. Sophia squeezed her eyes shut, trying to steady herself. She was beginning to understand how the red fog worked, combining sight with imagination and imagination with memory. But understanding it did not stop the sight from making her heart pound. *There are no Nochtland guards,* she said to herself steadily. *There are no clerics of the Golden Cross here.*

Nevertheless, the whooping sound continued. Sophia opened her eyes and looked back. The intruders had turned out of the passageway and were following them down the street. Now she could see them clearly: seven of them, all but one barefoot. They were hardly more than children, and yet they carried heavy sticks; one wielded an ax.

"Looters," Bittersweet said in Sophia's ear.

Already, they were burdened by their strange spoils. One wore a tall silk hat and a velvet cape and carried a silver-tipped cane. Another wore a glittering array of necklaces. Yet another hauled a finely made saddle on his shoulder; it made keeping up a challenge.

"Hey!" one of the boys called after them. Nosh picked up his pace and Sophia heard the boy's footsteps patter. "Hey!" he called again. In a moment, they were all running in pursuit. The others took up the cry, shouting as their feet pounded in the dirt.

What do they want from us? Sophia thought, panicked. "We don't have anything," she shouted over her shoulder.

"They won't listen," Bittersweet said grimly. "They're just in it for the chase now."

Sophia leaned down toward Nosh's neck as the moose ran faster.

Bittersweet let out a breath that sounded strained. Glancing down, Sophia saw his hand just beside her. He held it palm up, as if waiting for raindrops. Suddenly a thin, green tendril appeared above his palm. Sophia gasped. Bittersweet turned his palm outward, toward the passing buildings, tossing the tiny plant aside.

"How far, Nosh?" Bittersweet asked over the sound of the moose's hoofbeats and the cries of the gang. There was a stone building on the corner with wooden eagles affixed to the beam over the doorway. Their open wings, dusted red, were held high, and their open beaks seemed to cry in silent victory.

Nosh turned at the corner, and Sophia's eyes widened. Thick, fronded vines were covering the log buildings on either side, making them into lumped mounds that were hardly recognizable. The vines were reaching and growing, interlacing with one another like serpents, ducking into the narrow windows and burrowing into the chimneys. Unbidden memories folded into the present once more, and she remembered standing deep underground below the city of Nochtland, watching as trees with luminous leaves sprang from the earth. It was the same lithe movement, the same surprisingly silent opening of sprout and leaf. She remembered vines that crawled before her in the dark, illuminating the way upward to an unseen opening, and she felt again the panic of knowing there was someone behind her, in pursuit. Her feet would not move quickly enough. The way was too long; there was no knowing where it ended.

Sophia closed her eyes and opened them with a deep breath: there was a clear path ahead of them, bordered by green vines. And more—here there was no trace of red sediment, other than in the road below their feet. The vines had overwhelmed it.

At the next corner, Nosh turned again, and Sophia saw that they had reached the edge of Salt Lick. A lone building, still powdered crimson, stood untouched by the vines. A blue flag attached to one of the strange, carved posts of Salt Lick fluttered uncertainly beside it, marking the town entrance. Nosh galloped past it and down the long dirt road that stretched ahead, toward a cluster of wooded hills. Gradually he slowed his pace. Sophia could feel the great breaths filling the moose's lungs. She realized that she could no longer hear the looters. "Won't they follow us?" she asked Bittersweet.

In response, Nosh stopped and turned. Sophia saw that the road they had taken out of the city was gone. Entirely consumed by vines, the entrance to Salt Lick was nothing but a verdant wall, as if the place had been abandoned and overgrown ages earlier. The fluttering blue flag alone remained visible, the only movement in the green stillness.

"They won't follow us," Bittersweet said. "But we should keep moving nonetheless."

PART III
Rain

21

THE LONG HOUSE

—*1892, August 10: 12-Hour 00*—

Beyond Salt Lick and Six Nations City, many homes in the region preserve the pre-Disruption style: long houses built of logs, which serve many purposes at once. Over the course of the century the bermed house has become more common, perhaps due to the Eerie influence. Other practices in the region have unknown origins. For example, there appears to be no traceable origin (and no useful purpose) for the birch wind wheels that sprout on every bermed rooftop like mushrooms. As light as paper, the whirling wheels—also called "pinned wheels"—are like miniature windmills, and yet they mill nothing. It can only be concluded that the inhabitants find them visually appealing.

—From Shadrack Elli's History of New Occident

THEO WAS HAVING a nightmare; he was bound to a railway line. He could not move. In the distance, inexplicably, he could hear the conversations of the people aboard the approaching passenger train. They sounded content, their tone calm and conversational. As he came to, the railway ties hovered before him, and he realized that he was looking up at a ceiling made of dark beams and white plaster. Theo turned his head and saw clusters of dried herbs hanging from one of the beams. Along the wall, wooden shelves stacked with innumerable bottles and jars surrounded a stone fireplace. Sunlight streamed in through two mullioned windows on the opposite side of the room. The windows flanked a green door. The door stood open. Theo could see grass and clumps of flowers beyond the open doorway.

"He's awake," a woman's voice said.

Theo tried to lift himself up, and pain knifed down his left arm, running all the way from his shoulder to his fingers.

"There now, one step at a time." Casanova's scarred face came into view. Beside him was a woman of some fifty years. Her dark hair was laced with gray and drawn into a long braid; she tossed it over her shoulder as she bent over Theo with a look of concentration. He lifted his right hand to fend her off. Casanova took it reassuringly. "Don't worry. This is Smokey. It's thanks to her you're awake. She is an excellent medic."

"I need to look at your shoulder, Theo," Smokey said.

Theo found that when he opened his mouth, he could barely croak a reply. He nodded. Smokey lifted the cloth that covered his shoulder. "The infection is contained," she said, her voice firm. "I think the worst has passed." She gave Theo an appraising look. "If you can sit up, we could get some food in you, and that would help."

Theo swallowed. "Yes, please," he managed.

Smokey smiled, altering her face entirely. Her dark eyes shone, making fans of fine wrinkles at her temples. "That's good," she said approvingly. "Lift him up, Grant," she said to Casanova, and turned away.

Casanova gently lifted Theo's head with one hand and slipped his other arm under his back. Theo felt the pain in his shoulder again as he tried to shift upward, and he gritted his teeth until he was propped up against the wooden headboard with pillows stuffed under him. "How's that?" asked Casanova.

"Good," Theo gasped. Now that he was sitting up, he took in the room around him. Smokey stood by a wood stove. There was a large table covered with herbs, knives, bowls, and jars. At the back, a darkened corridor led to the rest of the house. The bed he lay on had clearly been temporarily pulled into this kitchen-workroom. Casanova sat down in a wooden chair beside him with a pleased expression. Theo wasn't sure what to ask first. "Where are we?" he finally croaked.

"This is Smokey's house. We're in southwest New York."

"How did we get here?"

Casanova raised his unscarred eyebrow. "You don't remember any of the journey?"

Theo shook his head. "I remember . . ." He winced. "I remember the attack."

Smokey approached the bed with a wooden platter. It held a cup of water, a bowl of steaming soup filled with mushrooms and green onions, and a bowl of late-summer berries. "Go slowly," she said, "and see how it lands in your stomach. You haven't had much to eat for days now." She pulled a chair up to the other side of the bed, near the window, and drew a bunch of hand-sewn linen pouches toward her. She began stuffing them with dried herbs from a tray.

Theo lifted the spoon with his right hand and sipped. He sighed; he had never tasted anything so delicious in his life. The green onions smelled of grass, and the mushrooms smelled of earth. "Thank you," he said to Smokey. "This is amazing."

Smokey smiled at him. "I'm glad."

"Can you tell me what happened?" he asked Casanova after another spoonful of soup.

"Do you remember how your shoulder was injured?"

"I only remember seeing the bowmen come out of the woods, and then the mule beside me was struck. I tried to run to keep up with the wagon."

"Well," Casanova said. "Let's see. The bowmen came out of the woods, and everyone started running every which way. I didn't see the mule get struck, but it and the other one must have panicked, because they bolted, dragging you with them. You couldn't run fast enough with that harness attached, so you fell." He shook his head. "I think the yoke protected you some as you were pulled along the ground. But I had trouble catching up. And trouble getting the harness off." He gave Theo a grimace. "By the time I finally got you free of it and into the back of the wagon, the mules had carried us away. I thought about going back to the company, Theo. I did." He shook his head again. "But I wondered whether we'd have any troops to return to. And your wound was pretty bad. I cleaned it and bandaged it with the major's best napkins, but you had scrapes all over you from being dragged. When you woke up, you seemed poorly. And I realized there might have been something poisonous in the arrowhead. Those are the kind that break on impact, and I hadn't pulled all the pieces out most likely. I decided then and there we'd head here to Smokey's. Luckily, we were just on the western side of the border, so all I had to do was ride northeast. Soon enough we were in Pennsylvania and then New York. We got here at dawn yesterday. You'd had a fever for more than twenty hours. Smokey opened up the wound right away and took out all the rest of the pieces. She sewed you up and put you right."

"So we're deserters," he said when Casanova had finished.

Casanova looked into his lap. "Afraid so. I'm sorry."

Theo tried to smile. "Nothing to be sorry for. Well, maybe. If you regret saving my life." He felt the blood pulsing in his temple. Casanova had brought him to safety, but at what cost? Would it be impossible to return to Boston now?

"He's getting tired, Grant," Smokey said.

"I'm fine," replied Theo. He looked out through the doorway at the green grass. "Where are we, exactly?"

"This is Oakring," Smokey said, following his gaze. "We're in New York, just south of the Eerie Sea."

"Is this where you're from?" Theo asked Casanova.

Casanova shook his head. "No. But I spent some time here before moving east." He and Smokey exchanged a glance. "Smokey took care of me once. Just as she's taking care of you now."

"Ah," Theo said. "She knows about the burns."

"I do," Smokey said, without looking up from her task, "but if Grant won't talk about them, it's not my place to."

"What if he gave you special permission?"

Casanova gave a short sigh. "It just so happens that when you were sick, I made a promise."

Theo looked at him hopefully.

"I promised that if you got better, I'd tell you the story."

"Finally!"

"Maybe when you're a little better. The story's not one to lift your spirits. For now, you need food and sleep, not tales of misery."

Theo felt his eyes closing. "I like tales of misery," he mumbled.

"I can see that," Casanova replied lightly.

"When I wake up." He smiled tiredly. "Tell me the story when I wake up."

He woke again in the evening, when the setting summer sun made the kitchen a jumble of purpled shadows. Casanova and Smokey were sitting outside, just beyond the door; Theo could hear their murmuring conversation and the occasional crack of a wood fire. For a few minutes, he lay still in the growing darkness, letting his senses waken fully. The pain in his shoulder was no better and no worse, but the overwhelming lethargy he had felt earlier was passing. He smelled the herbs hanging above him from the rafters, and his stomach grumbled.

Pushing the blanket off carefully with his good arm, he swiveled slowly on the bed and lowered his feet to the floor. The packed dirt felt good, solid beneath them. He levered himself upright. As he tried to take a step forward, the room tipped precariously. Theo grabbed ahold of the bed with his right hand.

"Theo?" Casanova stood in the doorway. He hurried over. "Sure you want to get up?"

"I'm sure."

"Walk slowly," Casanova admonished, walking him the short distance to the door.

It was a warm night, but Smokey had lit a fire in a small pit surrounded by stones. She sat on a wooden bench, and Casanova lowered Theo down beside her. He sighed with pleasure, stretching his bare feet toward the fire.

"We have cornbread and beans, Theo, if your stomach finds that agreeable." Smokey held out a plate.

"Very agreeable," he said happily. "Thank you."

Smokey waited to see that he was eating before she said, "Grant has told me of your connection with Shadrack Elli."

"You know him?" Theo asked, his mouth full.

She nodded. "Most everyone knows him. But I know him perhaps a bit better than most. We've been corresponding during the war. There's a trader named Entwhistle who travels through here and other places. He gathers news and then goes to Boston. When he makes the return trip, we hear from Shadrack, too. Perhaps you'd like to have him take Shadrack a note?"

"Yes, thank you—I've met him. When will he be here next?"

"He is due any day now." Smokey watched Theo with satisfaction as he ate. "You are healing well."

"It's no wonder," Casanova said with a smile. He sat on a tree stump a few feet away, the scarred side of his face in shadow. "He's in the hands of Sarah Smoke Longfellow, the most skillful medic in New Occident and the Territories combined."

Smokey laughed. "Grant likes to exaggerate my talents," she said to Theo.

"It's no exaggeration," Casanova said firmly.

"Speaking of Smokey's talents, you promised you'd tell me the miserable story," Theo reminded him.

"This story is not one that is likely to make you feel better."

"Come on," Theo said, his mouth full of cornbread. "I went and got myself shot just so you would tell me the story, and now you refuse?"

Casanova smiled ruefully, then fell silent. "The truth is," he said at last, staring into the fire, "that usually I don't think of that time at all, but lately I have thought of it often."

"Because of the war?" Smokey asked.

"Yes. No doubt. And because of the ash."

Casanova leaned forward, resting his arms on his knees. He held one of Smokey's cups in his hand, and he swirled the liquid in it slowly, as if pondering its contents. "You will have heard everyone call me a coward," he said to Theo.

"Once," Theo acknowledged. "After that, no one said it in front of me."

"Thank you, but there was no need for you to defend me. There is no doubt that I am a coward. I have always been."

Theo waited for Smokey to contradict him, but she only watched Casanova with a closed expression, as if braced for pain.

"I was born west of here," Casanova began, "in a village near the border. When I was seven, my parents and my brother were killed by settlers from New Occident. I only survived because they thought I was dead. The blood of my little brother, which covered my head and shoulders, protected me. Passing over us like vultures, the settlers did not notice my breathing. They saw only two bloody boys, lying still in the dirt."

Theo stared at Casanova. He felt the food turning in his stomach.

"The few of us who lived were taken in by another village, and I grew up among them. It was one of the warring villages. Over decades—centuries, most likely—they nurtured an enmity with another people on the shores of the Eerie Sea. Sometimes the villages made war on each other every few months. And sometimes there would be peace for years at a time—perhaps a decade, when we were lucky. I grew to manhood during one of these periods of peace. The village did well. When I was old enough, I married and had a child. Though I was always an outsider because I had been adopted into the village, I began to feel that my place was there, among them.

"And then the peace we had was broken. It was unclear how. But the warring began again, and I refused to take part. No one could believe my refusal. Every grown man—every boy, even—was eager to prove his valor, his loyalty to the village. They called me a coward." Casanova threw the contents of the cup onto the fire, and it flared angrily. "Of course, they were right. But I had seen my family killed by settlers, and I had no grudge against the people with whom we warred. When I imagined going with them, my thoughts conjured a vision of what would surely happen in the end: I saw myself hovering like a vulture over the body of some bloodstained boy, just as someone had stood over me. I much preferred to be a coward.

"Then the man who led us—everyone called him Four-fingers, for as a child he had lost one finger to a dog bite—Four-fingers said that if I did not fight, then my family would be exiled. Set to drift, alone, without anyone to offer aid in the hard winters." He shook his head slowly. "I should have said, 'Yes, give us exile.' But I did not.

"My wife, Talise, had been raised in the village. Her entire family was there. I could not ask her to leave them forever, and to wander with me and Ossa—only four years old—in search of a new place. Where would we go? How would we eat? We could not take up with the settlers to the east; they would kill us. And all the people near the Eerie Sea would know the reason for our exile. They would not take us in: a coward and his family.

"So I went. It was a night in April—clear, moonless. We approached the village silently—forty-six of us, all as quiet as snow in late spring. Four-fingers gave the sign, and we sent arrows into the village as a first warning. Then their men came out to meet us. I could not see the battlefield. My vision was filled with a red mist that I thought at the time was blood. But it was not blood. It was a memory.

"My mind flew back to the past. Instead of seeing the place around me, I saw myself in the bright sunlight fifteen years earlier. I felt the earth shake under the horses' hooves. The house was only a short run away. I saw my brother taking uncertain steps backward, and I reached out for him, too late. The horse charged past, and my brother, broken in half, soared toward me like a crushed bird. I felt his weight upon me, and I went still.

"I struggled to plant myself in the present: in the dark April night, in the battle that surrounded us. And then, as clearly as if she had been standing beside me, I heard my daughter, Ossa, call out for me.

"Now all visions of the past vanished. I saw where I was. I heard Ossa's cry, repeated—she was calling out in pain. Without even considering how it was possible, knowing she was more than three miles away, I knew that her cry was real. I fled from the battle. I ran as fast as I could. Believe me . . ." Casanova paused. He swallowed. "I used every fragment of strength in my body. But still, I arrived too late. I could smell the burning wood from half a mile away. At that point, my daughter's cries faded. I could no longer hear them.

"When I arrived, the long house was charred black. The door had been barred from the outside. I lifted the bar, and the people who were yet alive spilled forth. I went in and carried out those who lay on the dirt floor, felled by the smoke. Still I did not see them—Talise and Ossa. At last I found them— toward the back, surrounded by flames. My wife held Ossa in her arms, wrapped around her as if her body would somehow stop the fire.

"But it did not. I carried them out of the long house and extinguished the flames. They were already gone. They held one another so tightly, even in death, that I could not pry them apart. We had to bury them together."

Casanova turned his face so that the scars were visible. He smiled grimly, the scar twisting with the effort. "Afterward, they called me a coward for having left the battle."

"You saved more than thirty people in the long house, Grant," Smokey said quietly.

"Yes." Casanova looked back at the fire. "But you and I do not reckon lives the way warriors do. It is another method of calculation that I do not understand. To them, the loss of so many people was only greater reason to make war again. And again.

"We learned that the long house had been burned by settlers. Allied with our enemies. Making use of our absence. With all of the grown men gone, it was easy enough to herd the women, children, and old people into the long house. Terribly easy."

He took a small stone and dropped it into the fire. "I was glad to leave them, then. Glad to be exiled. I would have gone anywhere, but I knew of Oakring. Everyone knows it as a place of tolerance. A place that takes in exiles. So I came here."

"Grant does not mention that half his body suffered from burns," Smokey said. "It is a wonder he made it here at all. The recovery was slow—many months."

"But in anyone else's hands I would have died." He looked at her solemnly. "And I would have welcomed it, then. Perhaps I chose too skillful a healer."

"I'm sorry," Theo finally said. He was ashamed now of having prodded Casanova so many times, of having made his friend unearth a thing of such pain. "This war must seem disgusting to you," he added.

"It seems pointless," Casanova replied. "Mindless. Destructive without reason."

Theo felt a sudden chill. He shivered. Casanova, he realized, had always planned to desert Major Merret's company. The only question was when.

22

DATURA

—*1892, August 9: 6-Hour 11*—

I have heard some of the Elodeans (Eerie) call it cloud-reading. It is more an art than a science, as far as I can tell. Looking at a cloud formation for a length of time—several seconds at least, though several minutes yields more—one can see in the pattern, shape, and texture traces of where the clouds have been.

—From Sophia Tims's Reflections on a Journey to the Eerie Sea

AS THE TRAVELER from Boston and the Elodean from the shores of the Eerie Sea rode northwest out of Salt Lick, thousands of men to the south and east of them continued their slow swarm westward, to the Indian Territories.

In some places, they collided with enemies from the Territories, leaving a trail of human debris along the path and at its edges—coiled around the trunk of a tree, submerged in a creek, clutching the side of a boulder that had offered no defense. But in most places there was slow, steady movement: a tramping of boots marching north out of Kentucky behind New Occident's General Griggs; a similar tramping of boots north and west out of Virginia behind General June. From the west, trickling south toward where the Territories met New

Occident, smaller clumps of men journeyed by day and night; lone messengers ran and rode between them, drawing them toward a single purpose, toward a single place.

A map of their movements would have shown Sophia that she was joining them: that carried along by Nosh's steady pace, she was following another path to the same point. But there was no such map that she could see, and the suspense in the air around her—the trees listening to the rumbling of distant footsteps, the winds carrying the scent of so many human currents—seemed not like suspense but like ordinary silence.

Even if such a map had existed, Sophia would have been too distracted to read it. Nosh ambled along at a moderate pace, and Bittersweet murmured a few words to him now and then—one half of an inexplicable conversation. Sophia was only half-aware of the path before them. Usually, in moments of shock, she felt the time around her slow down: it gave her space to think about what was happening and to find her place in it. Not this time. The onset of the red fog, the strange visions in the station, the terror of hiding and waiting, the appearance of Bittersweet and Nosh—she could not figure out how to begin making sense of it. She could not even figure out the right questions to ask. The images sat in her head like fragments that had nothing to do with one another.

Then, finally, she found a piece that made sense. The words of the Ausentinian map, so engraved in her mind that she could not believe they had only occurred to her now: *In the City of Stolen Senses, you will lose your companions. Remember that though in your brief life you have met Grief, confronting it alone, you have not yet met Fear. It dwells in the west, a companion on every path, a presence in every doorway. You will meet the wanderer who is sweet and bitter, and you will travel together, your fates bound on each step of the journey.*

"It finally happened," she said aloud, her voice hushed with wonder. "Just as the map said."

"What happened? What map?" Bittersweet asked behind her.

"I have a map that foretold this. That said I would lose my companions. I thought somehow we could avoid it. But we didn't."

"You cannot avoid the crimson fog once it appears. To survive is difficult enough."

"What *is* it?" Sophia tried to turn to see his face. "You said it was a flower. How can that possibly be?"

Bittersweet gave a slow sigh. "Can we stop for a little while, Nosh?"

In response, the moose slowed his steps. He made his way off the path to a cluster of apple trees and slowly sank to the ground. The moment Sophia and Bittersweet climbed off, he began eating the fallen apples with a look of supreme contentment. Bittersweet sat next to him, reclining against Nosh's side.

Sophia propped herself against the trunk of the nearest tree. She took a deep breath, inhaling the scent of apples and grass and damp dirt. It cleared her head. Salt Lick was not yet lost from sight, but the countryside around them seemed peaceful, as if the crimson fog had never struck. The road they were on led northeast, and all around she could see fields of corn and clover.

"How much did Goldenrod tell you about me?" Bittersweet asked.

Sophia opened her satchel and removed the wheel of wood and the piece of antler. "I was given these," she said. "And the antler had memories of you."

Nosh looked up and Bittersweet took hold of the two items with interest. "I see. Then you know how to read them?"

"Only a little. I was learning from Goldenrod. When I told her what I had seen—your house in the woods and the moose—she said that it must be you. Then she said that it was your family she had gone to find in Boston."

"She did not find them," Bittersweet said, "as I learned far too late. But I don't know what happened to her beyond that."

"She never had a chance, for she was attacked when she arrived. Then she was asleep for months. And then . . ." Sophia took another deep breath. "It's a long story. We've been across the ocean and only returned to New Occident a few days ago."

Bittersweet nodded as if this was not at all surprising. "It has been a long and fruitless search. No one has found them. Though I have come close once or twice." He put his head back against Nosh's side. "My sister, Datura. My mother, Solandra, and my grandfather, Lycium. They vanished traveling east last winter, and no one has had word of them since. This is strange, since it is usually possible for us to hear news of one another at long distances."

Sophia nodded. "Goldenrod has told me of the Climes."

"Ah," Bittersweet said. This did surprise him. He considered

Sophia in silence for a moment. "And did she notice that ours no longer speaks?"

"Yes—she noticed when we left New Orleans. What does it mean?"

"It has been this way for some time. And I do not know what it means. Though I have suspicions. The Clime has been out of balance—in the last month, it has been much worse. The debris clouds . . ."

"Debris clouds?"

"The heavy yellow clouds that rain ash and other debris."

Sophia nodded. "We saw the clouds—they are everywhere in New Occident. People call them 'the Anvil.' And then we saw falling ash on the train to Salt Lick. But no debris."

Bittersweet sat up and leaned forward, encircling his bent legs with his arms. His pants were worn through at the knees, Sophia noticed, and his shoes had been mended more than once. His black hair was cut so short that she could see a birthmark in the shape of a loose question mark over his right ear. Bittersweet pressed the green fingers of his right hand into the palm of his left. "You have seen Goldenrod's gift?"

"You mean the flowers that come out of her hands?"

Bittersweet smiled, as if amused by the clumsiness of her description. "Yes—that. Mine is a vine, as you saw in Salt Lick. My sister, Datura, has a gift of red flowers shaped like fluted trumpets. At the base they are pale—almost white. Then they darken until they reach a brilliant crimson at the mouth. They are very beautiful." Bittersweet's hands tightened their grip on each other. "And very poisonous. They can be fatal if ingested, but even their scent affects the brain. It causes delirium, so that one cannot tell fantasy from reality."

Sophia caught her breath. "The crimson fog."

Bittersweet stared at his clasped hands and frowned. "But my sister learned very young—from the time she could walk, practically—to keep the flowers from causing harm. I know she caused the crimson fog, and I also know that she would only do something like this if she were compelled." He had spoken matter-of-factly, and Sophia was surprised to see tears suddenly fill his eyes. "I dread to think of what has been used to force her hand. She must be terrified," he said quietly.

"Nosh and I have been following the fog," he continued. "It has been appearing all this last month—the very length of time that the Clime has been out of balance. Almost always, we arrive too late. Sometimes, like today, we arrive soon after the fog begins, and I search for her. Salt Lick is a larger city than most, and I knew from the start it would be almost impossible. And besides, Nosh had it in his head to find you." He reached out absently and patted the moose's vast head. "Nosh always knows best," he said, a little regretfully.

Sophia watched him. The fog caused pain and terror in many ways, but for Bittersweet it caused a different kind of anguish. She remembered what Goldenrod told her in the Papal States about the power of the Eerie, and how there were some who would use such power for evil ends. *This is what she meant,* Sophia thought, with dawning horror.

"The fog is greatly damaging to people, but to plant life it is nourishing," continued Bittersweet. "You saw how the bitter-sweet vines grew so quickly."

Sophia considered this. "If the fog helped your vines to grow, would it do the same for Goldenrod's flowers?"

"Almost certainly. Goldenrod is not immune to the effect of Datura's vapors, but her gift will be greatly enhanced by them all the same."

Sophia knew from the Ausentinian map that her path led onward, alongside Bittersweet. Yet now that her head had fully cleared, and she understood that the fog came from the hands of a terrified girl, she felt the impulse to return to Salt Lick.

"You are thinking about going back to look for Goldenrod," Bittersweet said, observing her thoughtfully.

"I am," Sophia said, startled.

Bittersweet smiled. "I cannot read minds. You were wearing the thought on your face."

"Oh. Yes. I don't like the feeling of going off without knowing what happened to my friends."

Bittersweet frowned. "The old one no longer speaks to me, but Nosh can still read its thoughts, much as I just read yours. What Nosh tells me is that Goldenrod and the others are safe."

"Then we should go back and try to find them." She stood up and walked out from the shelter of the apple tree. Salt Lick was still visible in the distance: a dark cluster of buildings on the plain. Above, the sky was cloudy, but without the oppressiveness of the previous days. Ordinary white clouds, thin and broken, trailed one another slowly. She looked at the city, wondering what was happening in Salt Lick Station. Had the agents of the League fled? Had they taken all her friends captive? What if they had all scattered and now were unable to find one another?

A dark speck in the sky made her heart stop, and a panicked thought flashed through her mind: *Dragon.* She shook her head as if to dislodge the thought. *There is no dragon,* she told herself. The speck grew larger. It was flying fast and straight at her. Sophia looked up with new attention. The soaring shape came into view as it dove toward her.

"Seneca!" Sophia cried.

The falcon screeched, releasing something from his beak as he wheeled in the air above her. Then he turned back the way he had come. The stem of goldenrod he had carried fell at Sophia's feet, and she stooped quickly to take it up. "It's from Goldenrod," she said with relief to Bittersweet, who had come to stand beside her. "This is what we agreed on. If we were separated, as the map said we would be. She said she would send me goldenrod to assure me of her safety."

Bittersweet looked up at the small, retreating shape that was Seneca. "I'm glad she was able to send you word. Then it is just as Nosh says."

"It still doesn't feel right." Sophia considered the cluster of goldenrod and then pulled her notebook from her satchel, placing the flowers carefully between the pages.

"Nothing feels right in the wake of the fog."

"But leaving without them . . ."

Bittersweet considered her sympathetically. "We should continue."

Sophia sighed. *"You will travel to where the silent bell rings and the dormant seed grows,"* she said. "That is what my map tells me."

Bittersweet's eyebrows rose with understanding. "Ah— I see."

"You do?"

Nosh raised his head and grunted impatiently.

"Yes, you did say so, Nosh, but sometimes you can be a little vague," Bittersweet replied. He reached out to help Sophia onto Nosh's back.

"You know where this place is?"

Bittersweet climbed on behind her, and Nosh rose to his knees, then heaved himself upright. "I do. We're headed to a place called Oakring, on the edges of the Eerie Sea."

"Is that far away?"

"Four days or so, if the weather is not too disruptive."

Nosh grunted again as he made his way back to the path.

Bittersweet chuckled. "Sorry, sorry. I didn't mean to question your speed. Three days, then."

23

WEATHERING

—1892, August 9: # Hour—

In the Indian Territories it is called a "weather glass," and in
New Akan it is called a "storm glass." Though they serve much
the same purpose, they look quite different from the storm barom-
eters used in Boston. The storm glass resembles a rounded pot
with a long, curving spout. The weather glass is a tear-shaped
glass that appears to clear, cloud over, or grow gray with the
changing weather. I have even seen one fill with condensation
before a rainfall.

—From Sophia Tims's Reflections on a Journey to the Eerie Sea

THEIR ROUTE TOOK them away from the farms surrounding
Salt Lick, northwest into the hillier country. Fields of clover,
corn, wheat, and oats gave way to uncut fields of wildflowers
and sparse forest. The white clouds overhead thickened. Nosh
moved at a steady pace, his antlered head nodding gently. For
all of the long morning, they saw no one else on the road.

Sophia could not entirely forget her concern for Goldenrod
and the other travelers, but she tried to put the worry aside.
*Goldenrod has sent me a sign, and they are perfectly capable of taking
care of themselves,* she told herself. *It is absurd to think that they would*

need my help. Whenever this did not entirely quiet her doubts, she told herself to trust the guidance of Maxine and Ausentinia. The prophetic map had steered her to safety all the way across the ocean; it had shown her the way to save Ausentinia itself; surely it would not lead her in the wrong direction now.

She found traveling with Nosh and Bittersweet surprisingly comfortable, despite the fact that they carried almost nothing. In part this was due to Nosh's knowledge of the route, but it was also due to Bittersweet's close attention. Though he claimed not to read her thoughts, he seemed effortlessly aware of them, sometimes before she was herself. He handed her water and she realized she was thirsty; he asked Nosh to stop and she realized she was tired. "This is the right path," he said at one point, as they entered a darkened tunnel of overhanging branches. "I've been along it many times."

"That's good to know," she said. *Perhaps he felt me recoil,* she thought, *for how else could he know I doubted the path?* She wondered if his ability had something to do with how he listened to Nosh and how, when it spoke, he listened to the Clime. It could be that Bittersweet had an instinct for even the most subtle signs of the beings around him, she reflected. *Perhaps it has to do with being without time,* Sophia realized.

"Goldenrod said that you are a Weatherer," Sophia said, glancing back at Bittersweet over her shoulder.

"Yes—all my family are."

"And that means you have no sense of time," she said.

Bittersweet gave a slight smile. "That isn't how we think of it, but I suppose it is one way of describing it. We call it 'weathering' time—that's why among Elodeans we are known as Weatherers. As I see it, I can bend something that for other people remains rigid. Imagine what it would be like to be unable to bend your knees. Difficult to walk, don't you think? Being a Weatherer means you can bend time—much easier to walk through it."

Sophia, looking ahead, smiled at this description. "So you're saying being a Weatherer is like having extra knees?"

Bittersweet laughed. "Why not?"

"You're right—I never thought of it that way." She paused. "You see—I have that, too. I grew up thinking of it as having a broken clock. But lately I've come to see it a little differently. Goldenrod told me it's a quality I share with you—the Weatherers."

"I thought you might," Bittersweet replied thoughtfully. "I could see from the moment we found you in the station."

He had anticipated her yet again. "How could you tell?"

"It's hard to explain—I could see in your eyes when you first looked at us that you were moving through many thoughts, many possibilities. You were stretching the time. Datura's fog makes it very difficult to order one's thoughts at all, and if you were able to do this under its influence—well, I suspected you could weather time."

Sophia pondered for a moment. "Is that how you are able to notice so many things? Are you stretching the time?"

Bittersweet was silent. Sophia glanced over her shoulder to

see his expression and found him pondering, too. "In a way, yes," he said slowly. "And no. Yes, but there's more to it." He laughed quietly. "It's funny, I've never had to explain it, because all of us just *know*. But let me try." Sophia waited. "Stretching the time is the first step. It allows you to have the space you need. The next step is to use that space in a particular way."

Nosh came to a stop. They had reached a shallow stream, its bed full of mossy rocks. "Nosh wants us to fix this footbridge," Bittersweet said, dismounting. He held his hand up to Sophia, but she swiveled as he had done and slid down the moose's side. "We can just put these logs back." Bittersweet pointed to several narrow birches, arranged by some previous traveler, that had slipped into the water. He reached into the cool stream and lifted one out. Sophia stepped forward to help him.

"Imagine," Bittersweet continued as they worked, "that you have an hour to study someone. All you have to do during that hour is watch them and observe and think about what they are doing. You would learn a great deal, wouldn't you? Even if you were not a terribly observant person."

"Yes, I guess so."

"Or, if you had a year to simply listen to the trees and the wind and the rain—hearing the patterns they make and how the sounds overlap. You would learn a great deal about their workings."

"I see what you mean." Sophia placed the last narrow log tightly against the others and straightened up, wiping her hands on her travel-worn skirt.

"So the Weatherer," Bittersweet said, splashing his face quickly with water from the stream, "makes that space I was describing. You make an hour, and with that hour you watch someone. You learn a great deal about them. Or you make a year to listen and learn about the trees and the wind. But, to others, only a few moments have passed—so it would seem to them that somehow, in an uncanny way, you see and know so much. But really you have been using the time in an ordinary and deliberate way—making the space and then concentrating, inside that stillness, on your observations."

He held his fingers interlaced for Sophia to climb up again, and she swung herself onto Nosh's back. "There you have your bridge, Nosh," he said, climbing up behind her. Nosh grunted happily and stepped into the cool water, glancing with satisfaction at the repaired bridge.

"He is incurably altruistic," Bittersweet muttered to Sophia. "I have fixed more bridges in the last month than I care to think about."

Sophia smiled and patted Nosh's neck. "You are very kind, Nosh."

"You mean I am kind," Bittersweet protested. "Nosh never does a thing to help me." Nosh turned his heavy head and gave Bittersweet a cold stare. Sophia laughed. "But I thought you already knew something of how to do this," the Eerie went on, "since you were able to read the maps you showed me."

Sophia shook her head, embarrassed. "It just happened. I fell asleep holding the antler and I saw the memories as I was sleeping. It took no skill."

"Ah, that explains it," Bittersweet said. "Nothing to be embarrassed about," he added, noticing Sophia's reaction, though her face was turned away. "I'll show you how to practice when you're awake."

"I saw something in one of Nosh's memories," Sophia said, hesitating. "A grove of trees in a valley. And two people walking toward it. You called them 'Wailings.'"

Bittersweet fell silent once more. "You've reached the very heart of the matter," he finally said, his voice grave. "When we stop tonight, may I look at the maps so I know what else they contain?"

"Of course." A mourning dove cried in the branches overhead, and then a flutter of wings announced its departure. The trees were still and silent in the humid air.

"The grove you saw is the great mystery I have been trying to understand these last two years." He sighed. "It lies in Turtleback Valley, which I have known since I was small—but the grove did not exist then. I first saw it in May of 1890, and it was smaller then: a cluster of a dozen gigantic trees. They seemed out of place—a species I had never seen but that reminded me of tales told among the Eerie of giant trees near the Pacific. I don't know how much you saw, but Nosh and I have returned many times. Not so much as of late, with our search for Datura, but in the past, we would go often. Almost always, we saw Wailings find their way into the grove, only to go silent and never emerge. But we cannot approach. The old one pushes us away, powerfully, so that neither of us can come any closer than the ledge from which we watch.

"There is something happening there that I do not understand. This summer, as the old one has stopped speaking to me, Turtleback is the only place where I still perceive its sentiments. And I can tell that great fear surrounds this grove."

Sophia felt her pulse quicken. "Yes—Goldenrod learned from Seneca, the falcon who travels with us, that the Clime was afraid of something. He said that its fear revolved around a place in the north."

"This is it. But afraid of what? And why?" He made a noise of frustration. "I don't understand it."

"These Wailings," Sophia asked. "Are they . . . Lachrima? The people who are faceless?"

"Yes—we call them 'Wailings' here, but I have also heard them called 'Lachrima.'"

Sophia caught her breath. Her pulse raced even faster, and she dug a hand into Nosh's solid back. She thought about the long search that had started in Boston: her journey to the Papal States, her passage through the Dark Age to Ausentinia, and her return with the Ausentinian map in hand. All of this was leading her to two people: Bronson and Minna Tims, her parents, who had vanished long ago and transformed into Lachrima. Wailings.

"What is it?" Bittersweet asked gently.

"Goldenrod told me once that Weatherers can heal Lachrima. She said she had seen it done. Is it true?"

"It's true. Assuming they are still more flesh and blood than phantom. They fade with their travels, as you may know. The Wailings are lost in the flood of memories visited upon them during the moment of disruption. When they have not yet faded, the Weatherer can wade into all those memories, letting the time in which they took place expand, considering each memory in turn until he finds the ones belonging to the Wailing. Then those memories are pulled out of the great mass of others around them, and the Wailing comes into focus. It is like looking at a field of mustard flower: a yellow blur taken all at once, but if a single flower is pulled from the rest, it becomes a particular thing with stem and petals. So, yes—it can be done."

"Can we go see this grove?" Sophia replied, her voice trembling.

"It is on our way—not far from Oakring. Though I expect things will be as they have been, and we will be unable to approach it." He put his hand on her arm reassuringly. "You've had a shock. What is it?"

"It is the whole reason I am here," Sophia told him, her voice barely audible. "Just as you search for your sister, I search for my parents. They were transformed into Lachrima when I was a child, and I have reason to know they traveled toward the Eerie Sea. I think this place, this grove in the valley, might be where I will finally find them."

THE ASH CAUGHT up with them in the afternoon. First the sky grew heavy, and then the familiar yellow clouds rolled in. As Sophia watched apprehensively, they grew dense and low, until they seemed to touch the very treetops.

"You see"—Bittersweet signaled unnecessarily—"the debris clouds."

They rode on in silence. Moments later, the first flakes of ash began to fall: powdery and gray. They disintegrated, almost like snow, in Sophia's hand.

"It's warm," she said.

"Yes," Bittersweet replied. "And notice the smell."

Sophia sniffed at her palm. "It smells like ash from a wood fire."

"The clouds must carry the ash from distant fires here. But to what purpose, I cannot imagine."

Nosh plodded on, his antlers dusted with ash, and soon the path before him and the trees on either side were coated with the gray powder. He let out a hoarse noise that Sophia realized was a cough, and then he shook his antlered head.

"There's water up ahead," Bittersweet said to him reassuringly.

The woods seemed to grow more still with every step, as if the ash were sedimenting into place. Even the thin stream where Nosh drank to clear his throat carried gray ribbons in the swirling water. Nosh gave a low, appreciative bellow, and Bittersweet laughed wryly in reply.

"What does Nosh say?" Sophia asked as they moved on.

"He says he misses winter and that the old one is kind to send us this summer snow." Bittersweet shook his head ruefully. "I wish I could agree with him."

24

ONE HUNDRED CRATES

—1892, August 10: 8-Hour 41—

Pockets of the manufacturing industry had already appeared by the time of the Disruption—in Lowell, in Boston itself, and in Rhode Island. But after the Disruption these pockets expanded, and in the vicinity of Boston several areas became dedicated exclusively to the manufacturing of dyes, textiles, Goodyears, Goodyear boots, and so on. Because the harbor provided an easy method for the deposit of waste, many such manufactories developed along the wharf, occupying space in a manner that soon drove out other businesses.

—From Shadrack Elli's History of New Occident

THE WAREHOUSES STOOD side by side near the water, and the open door of one gave Shadrack hope. An open door indicated less concealment, and less concealment meant less danger. The warehouses were brick, four stories high, with dusty windows. No sign or nameplate indicated their purpose. When a man in a checked vest stepped outside to pack a pipe, Shadrack decided to make his move.

He approached the man directly and raised a hand in greeting. To his surprise, the man recognized him. "Minister Elli!"

he said amiably. A heavy mustache and sallow cheeks greeted him beneath a brimmed hat.

Shadrack searched his memory, but he could not place the man's face. "Good morning. How are you?" he asked noncommittally.

"Very well, Mr. Elli. Always glad to see the Minister of Relations with Foreign Ages. Excuse me"—he corrected himself—"and War Cartologer. You won't know me, sir, but I certainly know you. Ben Ferguson, at your service. All of us here are very proud to work for you."

A confused Shadrack shook the man's offered hand.

Ben had tucked his unsmoked pipe into the pocket of his vest when he saw Shadrack approaching. Now he gestured to the open door of the warehouse with a wide smile that showed a row of tobacco-stained teeth. "Would you like to see how the work is proceeding, Mr. Elli?"

"Please call me Shadrack, Ben. As for the work—that's the reason I've come," Shadrack said as he struggled to make sense of the unexpected reception.

"Excellent!" Ben said, with genuine excitement. "Come in. Everyone will be delighted to meet you."

Shadrack followed Ben into a vast room that ran the length of the building. Wooden crates were stacked high, making tidy aisles. They stretched from one wall to another. "Here's the storeroom," Ben said, gesturing expansively to the crates. "Everything packed and ready to go. We keep an inventory here on a peg by the door, so every crate is accounted for. We have one hundred awaiting distribution at this very moment.

Not a one has gone missing, you'll be glad to know."

"Very impressive," Shadrack said, a sense of unease simmering in his stomach.

"Through here we connect to the other building," Ben said, winding his way through the crates. At the far end of the aisle was an open door that led to a narrow alley, and Shadrack followed Ben across the alley into the neighboring warehouse. Here there was more activity. On benches beside long tables, arranged all through the room, men and women sat hunched over their work. They seemed to be sewing. At a table near the front entrance, four women were minutely inspecting what looked to Shadrack like leather pouches. *Canteens?* he wondered. "We know how important it is to make these well," Ben said. "You'll find we have very high standards, Mr. Elli. Very high. No need to worry for New Occident troops on our account."

"I'm glad to hear it," Shadrack said, latching on to this clue. *Equipment for the troops,* he thought. *Of course—the masks Broadgirdle ordered.*

"Over here we inspect the finished gear," Ben said, guiding him to the table where the four women worked. "Would you like to try one on?"

"Why not?"

Ben grinned toothily. "This is Minister Shadrack Elli," he said to the women, who all stood to nod and shake hands with Shadrack, seeming pleased and a little bashful in his presence. "He's going to try one on himself."

"Try this one, sir," one of the women said, handing him the

leather mask. "I just looked it over, and it's in fine shape."

"Thank you." Shadrack took the mask in hand. It was untanned leather with a strap at the neck. He pulled it on, fumbling more than he wished to with the awkward opening. Finally, it rested snugly on his head. He looked out at Ben through green glass eyepieces. A patch of cloth at his mouth and nose made every breath taste of starched cotton and charcoal. Ben and the four women eagerly awaited his verdict. "Very effective," Shadrack said, with what he hoped was enthusiasm. *And unbearably warm,* he thought, pulling it off. He handed it back to Ben.

"So glad to hear it, Mr. Elli," Ben said, beaming. The women looked delighted. "So glad," he repeated. "It's a relief to know that all these months of work have been worthwhile."

Something in Shadrack's unsettled mind fell into place, and the sense of unease blew open, filling him with sudden panic. "All these months?" he echoed, before he could check his words.

"Certainly, sir. We began in March, didn't we?" Ben looked at the women for confirmation.

"That's right, March," they agreed.

"As you ordered, sir, correct?" Ben added, searching Shadrack's face. "The instructions came directly from your office."

Shadrack looked at their anxious expressions in silence, his mind working quickly with an anxiety of its own. *From my office? Broadgirdle started this in March? But that means he had these masks made before he was prime minister. Before the war started. Before Bligh was murdered! Before any of it.*

It could only mean that Broadgirdle had planned everything in advance: not only the murder and the war, but the crimson fog itself and the means to protect New Occident troops from its effects. *This has been months in the making,* he said to himself, aghast.

Abruptly, too late, he realized that he'd made a mistake. He should never have pretended to know what was happening at the warehouses. Now it would seem to Ben and everyone he had met that he was, in fact, complicit in the making of these masks. And whoever was complicit in making the masks was complicit in planning the war. Without intending to, he had made it seem as if he, Shadrack Elli, had indeed been planning this all along.

It's exactly what Broadgirdle intended, Shadrack realized, stunned. *And it's exactly why I am still the Minister of Relations with Foreign Ages. So that I can be made accountable for all of it.*

25

LICHEN'S QUARRY

—1892, August 9 to 11—

The most curious thing about an Elodean (Eerie) dwelling is how it appears that everything within it was not made, but found. Of course some things are made, but a chair might actually be a fallen tree, or a curtain might be a piece of torn sail. The effect is curious, as if a weirwind piled a hundred pieces of debris into one room and then some patient hand went about putting all the debris tidily into place, and to use.

—From Sophia Tims's Reflections on a Journey to the Eerie Sea

NOSH KNEW EVERY inch of the terrain, and he had a stopping point in mind for every rest, every meal, and every overnight stay. Sophia learned why the Eerie were so impossible to find: they all lived hidden in plain sight.

On the first night they stayed with an Eerie named Lupine, whose burrow of a home was carved into a mounded hill. Lupine asked them nothing about their journey, learning everything quickly from Nosh, but she told them what she had seen of the war, she showed them how the ash had nearly ruined her hives, and she gave them enough food to last for days: blackberry cake and apple bread and hard cheese and honey.

On the second night they rested with Pruce, whose tree house overlooked a clearing surrounded by conifers that he said had reminded his forebears of the Red Woods left behind on the western shores. As they finished their meal, it began to rain, and they watched with relief from Pruce's windows as the water washed away the gray ash that had coated the trees. Sophia was glad for the moss-covered roof that absorbed the rainfall like a sponge. The air turned unseasonably cool, and Pruce lit his wood stove and sat in silence with them, listening as the wind and rain tussled with the trees.

On the third night they stayed with Lichen, who made his home in a deserted quarry. They arrived late, just as the sun was setting, and Sophia was beginning to droop over Nosh's neck. They passed through a narrow opening between two boulders, and suddenly a hooded figure appeared in their path. Sophia started. "Nosh, Bittersweet," a man's voice said cordially, and she relaxed. The man reached up to stroke Nosh's nose.

"Good evening, Lichen. This is Sophia. Thank you for meeting us," Bittersweet said.

"Not at all," Lichen replied. "The path can be difficult in the darkness." He led them in silence along the edge of the quarry, until at the far end they reached an opening in the earth—a dark tunnel. He lit a torch that illuminated a clean stone passageway. "Nosh can rest here," he said, patting the moose's neck. He helped Sophia down from Nosh's back, and she caught a glimpse of a quiet face and long black hair beneath the hood.

Sophia and Bittersweet followed Lichen down the short

tunnel to where a stone stairway wound upward. At the top, a house of stone with wide windows overlooked the quarry. Sophia walked toward the glass, awed. "It's filled with water!" she exclaimed. The dark pool was just visible in the faint moonlight.

Lichen had removed his hood, and he joined her at the window. "Yes—it fills with rain. It has a strange hue now, thanks to the ashfall we had." He turned toward the room behind them. "Please make yourselves at home."

Mismatched chairs stood around a woolen rug. Sophia sank into a nest-like chair padded with pillows. Her legs ached from riding; she wanted to curl up and sleep for a week. At the windowless back of the room, a long worktable was covered with the elements of a half-cooked meal. Lichen picked up where he had left off, cutting vegetables and dropping them into an iron pot.

"No luck yet, then?" Lichen asked Bittersweet.

Sophia was beginning to grow used to the Eerie style of conversation, where most of what transpired took place in silence. "No luck," Bittersweet replied. He sat down on the floor and threw himself back against a heavy pillow.

"Nosh seems less discouraged."

"Nosh is an optimist," Bittersweet said dryly, "for reasons I cannot fathom."

Lichen gave a slight chuckle. He finished what he was doing and carried the pot to the woodstove, covering it tightly before joining them on the woolen rug.

"And what about you, Sophia?" Lichen asked, his eyes bright. "You are also on a search." His face was worn from age, but his expression was youthful, even mischievous, and he moved with the agility of a much younger man. Sophia noticed that his hands were callused from heavy work, and she wondered how much of the house had been hewn by hand.

"Yes, I am also searching—I have been for some time."

"And your search takes you to Oakring."

"We follow Nosh's orders," Bittersweet said wearily, closing his eyes. "Why he wants to go to Oakring now is beyond my understanding."

Lichen smiled. "I suspect Nosh knows best, as he always does." He rose to check the contents of his pot, which was beginning to fill the room with the scent of stewing vegetables, and when he returned he asked Sophia, "Has Bittersweet told you how Oakring came to be?"

Sophia shook her head. "I know nothing about it, other than the location, which I have seen on my map."

"Ah!" Lichen said, pleased. "Then I can tell you the story."

Bittersweet, his eyes still closed, commented, "Sophia likes stories."

Though Sophia understood in principle how Bittersweet could know things about her so easily, she still found it unnerving. That very morning, as they rode through a patch of forest, Bittersweet had pointed to a stone stained with moss and water: "It looks like a map, doesn't it?" he had asked, voicing her thought.

"I do like stories," agreed Sophia.

"So do I." Lichen smiled. "And this is a good one. It is about two people who fell in love many decades ago. The woman, Orli, had the Mark of the Vine, and the man, Baer, had the Mark of Iron. Their families were horrified at the affection between them, and forbade them to be together. So they planned to run away. But on the very first day of their journey, they were stopped on the road by an old woman, who claimed to be a diviner. She warned them that if they stayed on their intended path, they would come to ruin. Orli and Baer asked what they could do, for they had no wish to return to their families and be divided from one another forever.

"'The trouble,' the old woman said, 'is that one of you is rooted and one of you is rootless, and if you do not reckon with the difference, you will never be at peace. Those with the Mark of Vine are rooted—their great power is that they draw upon the earth, but their great weakness is that they have difficulty uprooting. Those with the Mark of Iron are rootless—their great power is that the iron in their bones guides them like a compass, but their great weakness is that they have difficulty staying in one place. If you travel together now, Orli will always want to stay, however dangerous or inhospitable the place may be, and Baer will always want to go, however ideal it may be.'

"'Then what are we to do?' Orli asked.

"'You must part ways and reach your destination by different paths.' Orli and Baer looked at one another, dismayed, but they recognized themselves in the old woman's descriptions, and they nodded their assent. 'Take this bell,' the diviner said to Orli, 'and take this acorn,' she said to Baer. 'When the bell rings in your hand, Orli, you will have arrived. And when the acorn sprouts, Baer, you will have arrived.'

"So the two went their separate ways. Baer, though he missed Orli greatly, was happy to wander, and he almost forgot about the acorn that sat in his pocket. As he traveled wherever his iron bones led him, he told his tale to everyone he encountered. 'Orli and I will found a new place,' he said to them, 'where those who are outcast elsewhere are welcome.' And so earnestly and warmly did he describe his destination that people of all kinds began to follow him.

"Orli suffered greatly, for she had no wish to wander. But the bell the diviner had given her urged her onward, for whenever she rang it, she seemed to hear a distant ring—not in her hand, but just on the other side of the hill, or just beyond that patch of trees. She went on in search of the sound, hoping with each step that the bell would ring in her hand. And when she encountered people along the way, she told them of her quest, and she described with longing the place where they would finally arrive to find safety and quiet and rootedness. Many who heard her were moved, and they chose to go with her, so that by the seventeenth month of her journey she traveled with almost thirty people.

"It was summer, and Orli had journeyed far north—almost to the Eerie Sea. She had arrived at the edge of a forest where a great oak tree threw its branches outward, and beneath the oak a busy group of strangers labored, clearing small trees and building foundations and gathering stones for walls. Orli rang the bell, and this time it rang in her hand: a high, pure voice announcing that her journey had ended. Then one of the group beneath the oak tree stepped forward. It was Baer. The great oak tree was the tree that had sprung from the acorn he carried, and the bell announced to them both that they were home.

"And that was the founding of Oakring," Lichen said, rising to his feet. "It has always been a haven for outsiders: people who find themselves unsuited to life anywhere else. But it is also known for being a place where people of great differences— the Mark of Iron, the Mark of the Vine—can be reconciled. You may not know that the man who brokered peace after New Akan's rebellion was from Oakring."

"Was he?" Sophia exclaimed. "No, I didn't."

"A place for peacemakers, they say." Lichen ladled the stew he had made into wooden bowls and brought them over to the rug.

"Thank you," Sophia said. The stew smelled of sweet corn and squash.

Bittersweet sat up and took his bowl eagerly. "Thank you, Lichen."

"There are even some Elodeans who live there," Lichen went on, watching his guests eat for a moment before picking up his own spoon. "Most of us avoid such crowded places—much too loud—but even among Elodeans there are outcasts."

Bittersweet raised his eyebrows. "Even among Elodeans? I would have said we are all outcasts. And some among us . . ." He looked at Lichen meaningly.

Lichen nodded.

Sophia followed their exchange of glances. "What? Some among you what?"

"Some outcasts are too far beyond the pale, even for Oakring."

"What does that mean?" Sophia persisted.

Lichen and Bittersweet ate in silence for a moment, both staring into their bowls. Finally Bittersweet raised his head. "No one likes to speak of it. But there were three Elodean sisters, some years ago, who took refuge in Oakring. We had cast them out." He shook his head. "You should tell the story, Lichen. I was not even alive then."

Lichen had grown somber. "I'm afraid there is little I can tell. The people in Oakring may tell you more. We cast them out for wanting to use their gifts in destructive ways. You understand—to cast out an Elodean does not mean to remove them from a place, since we all lived scattered."

"Then how are they cast out?"

"They can no longer call themselves Elodean."

Sophia put down her spoon. "How terrible."

A flash of grief crossed Lichen's face. "Yes. We did not make the decision lightly. The sisters took refuge in Oakring. But, not long after—and not entirely to our surprise—the people of Oakring also cast them out. In fact, the three sisters are the only people ever to be cast out of Oakring."

"They must have done something dreadful," Sophia said.

Lichen did not answer. He swallowed another mouthful of his stew and then ate on until he had scraped the bottom of the bowl. "They fled to the Eerie Sea," he said finally, breaking the silence. "And as far as I know, they make their home there still."

The stone house had several rooms, and Lichen led Sophia to a small bedroom with a square window that overlooked the quarry. All was black beyond the glass. Lichen opened it, saying that the night was warm. A scent of piney soil drifted in through the open window. He gave her an extra pillow and a cotton blanket before saying good night, and Sophia wearily removed her boots and prepared herself for bed. Washing her face in a bowl set above the bureau, she wiped away the many miles they had covered that day. *So tomorrow we reach Oakring,* she thought. *And we will see the grove where the Lachrima disappear.* She felt a tremor of nervousness, wondering what the new day would bring. Shaking out the blanket, which smelled faintly of wood smoke, she climbed into the bed. As she rested her head on the pillow, the words of her Ausentinian map came to her with a flash: *"You will travel to the Forest of Truces, where the silent bell rings and the dormant seed grows. From then on, the map you follow must be your own."*

26
WAILING GROVE

—1892, August 12: 8-Hour 12—

And there are species that I have not seen elsewhere, even apart from the Red Woods. A gray-white flower with four petals grows there upon a creeping vine. The leaves, heart-shaped, end in a curled point. At night, the flowers open, revealing four purple petals within the four white. The scent is strong, like concentrated honeysuckle, and it draws to it what I call the night bee, another creature I have seen nowhere else. Black with white dots along its back, the night bee looks in other respects like an ordinary honeybee. We do not yet know if it also makes honey and, if so, what kind.

—From Sophia Tims's Reflections on a Journey to the Eerie Sea

THE DAY DAWNED overcast, but the clouds were dark gray, not yellow, and Lichen told them he expected rain to move east in their wake, catching them by midafternoon. Bittersweet replied that, with luck, they would arrive in Oakring before then.

"Turtleback Valley," Sophia reminded him urgently.

He nodded. "Don't worry. It's on our way."

Lichen gave them apples, walnuts, and sandwiches of dark bread with blackberry jam. After walking them back along the narrow path beside the quarry, he stood by the boulder where he had met them the night before and waved them on their journey.

Nosh traveled quickly, the prospect of either a heavy rain or a dry bed pushing him onward, and Sophia felt a growing nervousness in her stomach. She sensed Bittersweet restraining himself from interrupting her thoughts, and she was grateful; her mind was in turmoil.

To settle herself, she practiced the approach to map-reading that Bittersweet had begun to teach her. Instead of falling entirely into sleep, she tried drifting into a frame of mind that he called "discernment": a state in which her active senses fell asleep, in a way, so that her sense of perception could fully waken. She hardly understood it, and as yet she'd had no luck finding her way into such a state, but she practiced it nonetheless. Bittersweet said that she had to "stop seeing and begin perceiving," a suggestion that did not, unfortunately, make things easier.

The air was damp with condensation, and Sophia felt the clouds amassing overhead. Every step Nosh took seemed to add to the suspense. Sophia took a deep breath.

"Use your dream eye, not your outer eyes," Bittersweet murmured.

"I'm *trying*," Sophia replied.

"It's very hard to do when you're so tense."

Sophia shot him a look over her shoulder.

"Sorry." He looked genuinely sympathetic. "We're almost there. Please don't hope for too much," he said earnestly.

"I know."

Sophia gave up on using her dream eye and instead looked closely at everything around them. The path was crumbly and dry, stony on the incline. A few wildflowers grew sparsely amid the maples. Nosh had been climbing steadily all morning, and the forest was thinning. Now he stepped off the path, heading right, toward a slow rise.

Suddenly, between the trees, a great valley came into view. The hills below were dark green. The flattened mound that gave the valley its name lay to the north: a hill shaped like a crawling turtle, its arms, legs, and head just visible. At the valley's base, the ground was rocky. A gray river wound along it, flat and colorless beneath the heavy clouds.

"There's the grove," Bittersweet said, pointing. But Sophia had already felt its presence. A tight cluster of dark trees interrupted the stream, surprisingly tall, their trunks dark red. They seemed misplaced, as if they had been dropped there, whole and intact in their incongruity, by a stranger with no knowledge of the valley. *Tree-Eater's red trees*, Sophia thought.

Looking at the grove, she felt a storm of feelings that she knew with certainty were not her own. They belonged to the Clime, the old one. And the sense of intention behind them seemed so familiar that she wondered how she had never observed its source before, for surely this was the wellspring of the pressure, reassurance, suggestion, and guidance that she had known all her life. She recognized its influence in a hundred minute decisions that had seemed on the surface to be hers: an unspecified suspicion of another person; a trenchant unwillingness to make the choice that seemed by all other signs obvious; a desire to look farther into a deserted place. She remembered vividly hearing this voice-that-was-not-a-voice only two months ago, when she searched for the Nihilismian ship known as the *Verity*: it formed as a sense of excitement, urging her onward. The old one had been speaking to her all along.

In that moment, she understood what Bittersweet meant by *perceiving rather than seeing*: it meant to know something without questioning how one knows; to accept the intuitive sense one has of what is right; to bypass the slow steps of seeing, judging, and deciding. She perceived what lay before her as clearly as if the old one had spoken it in her ear: This grove was secret. It was too dear, too fragile, too dangerous. They were not to come near.

This was why the old one had fallen silent. Everything for miles and miles and miles had gone quiet and still for the sake of this place. The fear was not *about* the grove; it was *for* the grove. It had to be protected at all costs.

"Bittersweet," Sophia whispered. She found that she was standing next to him, and she did not remember having dismounted.

"What is it?"

"The Clime is guarding this place."

Bittersweet looked out toward the grove, and a sudden flash of lightning shuddered across the valley. Several seconds later, the thunder echoed, low and muted. "Yes," he said. "You're right. The sense of it is sharper now. Things have changed. I wonder what has happened."

"It is so palpable here," Sophia said, still whispering.

Bittersweet glanced at her. "It is. Perhaps because the old one has drawn all its attention here, to this place, its presence is very strong. Had you never sensed it before?"

Sophia shook her head. She continued staring as splinters of lightning cracked the dark sky. *Move on, move on, move on,* they seemed to say. *This is not the time.* The grove stood, dark and impenetrable, still untouched by the coming storm. At such a distance, it seemed a slight and frail thing: tiny in the vastness of the valley.

The rain reached them before it reached the valley floor, and it began to fall in cold, hard pellets. The droplets pattered on the leaves overhead, and then they began in earnest, falling with a roar. Almost immediately, the valley was obscured from view, but Sophia still saw it clearly in her mind's eye: the secret grove of Red Woods; the great valley that drew the wailing Lachrima to its center; the place so vital, so cherished, that the burden of protecting it had awoken fear in the heart of the old one.

"We can go now," Sophia said loudly, over the crashing rain.

"Really?" Bittersweet asked, surprised.

"The Clime doesn't want us to go near. Maybe later, but not now." She turned to him, feeling elated, so clear was her sense of what to do. Then she realized that the falling rain had grown sharp and leaden. Looking up, eyes half-closed, she felt the hail pelting against her skin.

When she turned back to Bittersweet, he was standing motionless, staring at his outstretched hand.

She at first did not understand what she was seeing. Bittersweet's palm was filled with black pellets. His face was streaked black, as if with paint.

"What is it?" Sophia asked, horrified.

They looked up at the trees around them and saw the green leaves smeared with black. The trail before them was already flooded; the hail made a black path leading into darkness.

"Char. It is raining char upon us."

27

OAKRING

—1892, August 12: 14-Hour 22—

Every story tradition is different, I have found, but there are noticeable similarities among them. Elodean (Eerie) stories all have endings with morals, but these morals tend to be enigmatic and open to interpretation. Stories from the Closed Empire dwell upon the fantastical, relying upon it to explain things that seemed inexplicable in ordinary life. Stories from the Eerie Sea come in light or dark—light with comic characters who seem to find favor with the world despite many mishaps, or dark with tragic characters who fall deep into grief, no matter what they do.

—From Sophia Tims's Born of the Disruption: Tales Told by Travelers

THEY HAD MOVED Theo's bed out of Smokey's kitchen into a separate room as soon as he could get up and walk about on his own. Most of the day he spent resting, staring up at the ceiling and trying to ignore the throbbing in his left shoulder. But now he stood by the window, watching the charcoal hail pelt the flowers and herbs of the garden until they lay crumpled and beaten.

It was after fourteen-hour when he saw Smokey coming up the slow incline across the field. She was draped in a thin rubber tarp that made her look like a shapeless shadow drifting steadily uphill. Theo left his room and joined Casanova, who was waiting by the front door.

Smokey threw off the rubber tarp, hanging it on a peg. "No one knows what it is," she said at once. The black pellets rolled off her clothes like tiny marbles.

"Any idea how far it reaches?" Casanova asked.

She nodded. "Hardly anyone out, as you can imagine, but a pair of travelers came in this afternoon, and they said they saw the hail start in Turtleback Valley. About three miles southwest of here." She moved over to the cold hearth and began to light a fire. "If this ever clears, we can go down to the ring. The travelers will be there, I'm sure, and we can hear the rest. No sign of Entwhistle, though he's due to come in tonight. If the storm hasn't stopped him."

"What's the ring?" Theo asked.

"We have a circle of stepped stones near the great oak—not unlike a little theater. Whenever travelers come, they give us news there at sunset. You would be surprised how hard it is to stay connected with the world in a place like this. It's not Boston," she said, smiling. She had stacked the wood and now she lit the fire; she knelt before the hearth until the flames caught. "I don't know the girl," Smokey continued, "but Bittersweet travels through here often. He is the only remaining Weatherer in these parts, since the other three disappeared."

Theo felt Smokey's words come into sharp focus. "A Weatherer?" he said.

The other two looked at him, noticing his change of tone. "Yes."

"I must speak to him," Theo said. His heart was suddenly pounding. It threw him off balance.

"Easy," Casanova said, reaching out and taking his arm. "Have a seat here by the fire." He steered Theo into a chair and looked at him closely.

"I have information about the other Weatherers," Theo said. He felt dizzy, and his breath came with difficulty, as if he had just been running.

"He'll want to hear that," Smokey said, now hovering over Theo, too. "You can tell him when we gather at the ring."

As Theo nodded and made an effort to calm his breathing, the other two exchanged a look. "Maybe we could ask this Bittersweet to come here," Casanova suggested.

"That's a good idea," agreed Smokey. "As soon as this hail stops, I'll go find him. For now, Theo, you just rest. Don't worry—he's not going anywhere in this storm."

"Okay," Theo said. "Thanks." He sat by the fire, feeling his heartbeat slow. Casanova began helping Smokey with the cooking, and their conversation drifted to people in Oakring that Theo did not know. He listened to the steady pattering on the roof and stared at the fire, hoping it would calm him, but fire these days did not seem peaceful. He still had Casanova's story ringing in his ears, and he remembered too clearly the memories from the wooden ruler-map: a girl tied to a chair; a bright fire too close to her singed skirts.

AT SIXTEEN-HOUR, the hail finally stopped, turning to a thin drizzle of ordinary, clear water. Smokey was ready. "I'll be back with Bittersweet before long," she told him.

"Thank you," Theo said. He had not moved from the chair. Now he watched the doorway, where the fading light tinted the passing storm clouds a bright purple. The discoveries he had made in Boston seemed somehow to have taken place years earlier. Thoughts of Winnie and Nettie made him smile, but his memories of them seemed distant and unclear. Even Broadgirdle, the man he knew as Wilkie Graves, had faded somewhat; the fury Theo had felt realizing Graves would go free had diminished to a rumble of discontent. And yet the memories from the wooden map were still clear and bright: perhaps it was the nature of maps to make them so.

He heard Smokey's voice as she climbed the hill back toward the house, and he realized that a good half hour had passed. Casanova rose to his feet. "Do you want to stand up?"

"Yes." Theo got up on his own and stood by the chair, ready to sit when he needed to.

Smokey arrived with the travelers: not one, but two. Talking to her was a tall young man Theo's own age with a calm face and a steady gaze; he had the aspect of a man much wiser than his years would allow. On her other side was a young woman with braided hair and a tanned face; she wore a raider's cape strung with silver bells. She was smiling at something Smokey had said, and her eyes were lit with laughter.

"Sophia?" Theo breathed.

They all stopped. Sophia looked up at him, frozen for a moment in shock. In the next instant she had crossed the room and thrown her arms around him. Theo held her tightly, certain that if she pulled away, he would fall back, for he could hardly stand. With her familiar face so close to his own, everything about his past life in Boston that had seemed so remote suddenly rushed back to meet him, proximate and full of life. He realized, with faint surprise, that there were tears running down his cheeks. "Ow," Theo said finally.

Sophia drew back, her own face damp with tears. "Oh, Theo! What happened to you? You look terrible."

He laughed shakily. He sank back onto the chair but held Sophia's hand tightly. "A lot has happened. A lot. You have no idea."

It TOOK SOME time for Sophia and Theo to recount the passage of the last two months. They had much to tell each other and even more to explain for the benefit of their friends. At times giddy and incoherent, at times sober and slow, they related all that had transpired since the fateful day in June when they failed to meet at Boston Harbor. Theo began by explaining why he did not arrive, and then he had to tell them about finding the body of Prime Minister Bligh, Shadrack and Miles's imprisonment, the involvement of Gordon Broadgirdle and the Sandmen, his own knowledge of Broadgirdle as Wilkie Graves, and the long route that led to his capture and conscription, even as Miles and Shadrack were finally freed. Then he told Sophia about his time in the army, about Major Merret and Casanova, and how he and Cas had found their way to Oakring and to safety with Smokey.

Sophia described her journey with the Nihilismians, and her meeting with Errol Forsyth, and her encounter with Goldenrod. She answered many questions about the plague and the Dark Age and Ausentinia. She showed them the Ausentinian maps and the purse full of garnets. She explained the significance of meeting Richard Wren and discovering her mother's journal. And she related how all of them, including Calixta and Burr, had come to find themselves once more in New Occident.

Theo, Casanova, and Smokey listened in rapt silence as she described Burr's capture, Goldenrod's revelations aboard the train, the crimson fog in Salt Lick Station, and the arrival of Bittersweet and Nosh. Finally, she told them what they had seen that very day in Turtleback Valley: a grove of trees that held a secret, a place she hoped might hold the answer to her parents' disappearance.

It was hard for Theo to believe that circumstances had carried them both to this place, the safety of Smokey's home, in a small town by the Eerie Sea—a place neither of them had ever heard of before. "It's no coincidence," Bittersweet said. "I am sure it is the old one guiding us all here. This is always the way with circumstances that seem coincidental. Sarah knows Shadrack, Sophia's uncle; she knows Casanova; she knows me. The old one guided each of you to people who would find their way here."

"But what does it have to gain?" Theo wondered.

Bittersweet smiled. "We are all pieces of a complex puzzle. Who knows? Perhaps something we do is of use to the old one, however small we might be."

Theo looked at him appraisingly, somewhat surprised by how likable the Weatherer was, despite his earnestness. "And I have a piece of the puzzle to give you," he said. "It is the reason Smokey asked you to come here."

"Yes. She said you had something to tell me."

"It has to do with the other Weatherers." Bittersweet tensed. "In the course of trying to find how Broadgirdle was responsible for Bligh's murder, I found a wooden ruler. It was among Bligh's possessions. He said in a letter that he had gotten it from the Weatherers themselves, and when I looked at the ruler closely, I found that it was a memory map. The memories showed a girl and an old man—but those memories belonged to a third person."

"My mother," Bittersweet said eagerly. "They must be hers. My sister and my grandfather are the two people you saw. What was in the map?"

Theo hesitated.

Bittersweet leaned toward him. "Are my grandfather and sister alive?"

"Yes. In these memories, they were alive. All three were

captives. They were kept in a closed room. It seemed to be underground. One of the memories showed your sister being . . . threatened with fire. As the fire came closer, flowers bloomed in her hands. In the last memory, I saw the Sandmen making boxes. I think to keep them in winter sleep."

Bittersweet looked down at his hands, his face creased with worry. "That explains it." He looked up.

"What does it mean?" Sophia asked softly.

"Mother and Grandfather in winter sleep . . ." He swallowed. "Winter sleep can offer renewal and rest. But when it continues too long, it can lead to death."

Sophia gasped.

"No plant can live underground forever. This Broadgirdle is keeping their lives hostage. I knew only something terrible would drive my sister to such desperate lengths."

28
PIP'S DELIVERY

—*1892, August 13: 7-Hour 23*—

Stories from the Baldlands, perhaps predictably, are difficult to characterize. Some are ominous; some are humorous; some seem simply to recount the past and offer no conclusion or argument. There is one I did not include here about an old woman who trades a penny for a pie, then a pie for a ham, then a ham for a saddle, then a saddle for a cart, then a cart for a horse, then a horse for a house. Apart from describing the old woman's impressive bartering abilities, I cannot tell what the purpose of it is!

—From Sophia Tims's Born of the Disruption: Tales Told by Travelers

SMOKEY TRIED TO order Theo to his room, seeing the exhaustion on his face, but he would not move from Sophia's side. Even after everyone else had gone to bed, Sophia and Theo sat comfortably together on a pile of blankets before the cooling fire in the kitchen, unwilling to part. They had too much to talk about.

Finally, past twenty-hour, Theo fell asleep with his head on Sophia's shoulder. She moved out of the way carefully, lowering him onto the bundled blankets. Beside him, she tried to sleep, but her weary mind ran in circles. She tried to make sense of all that had taken place in Boston without her:

Bligh's murder, Shadrack's arrest, and, especially, Theo's long confrontation with Gordon Broadgirdle. She wondered what it was about Broadgirdle that unsettled him so deeply, for she had seen it in his eyes. He had said only that he knew the man as Wilkie Graves, a scoundrel and villain from the Baldlands who had no right to be Prime Minister in Boston. But she could sense that there was more, and it worried her to see Theo keeping secrets once again. *He'll tell me the truth when we're talking alone,* she thought.

Sophia rested a gentle, protective hand on his good shoulder. She could feel his chest rising and falling with each breath, and it reassured her to know that Theo was there, sleeping safely and soundly. It was well past one-hour when she finally fell asleep herself, and then she slept so heavily that it seemed only a moment had passed before Smokey was quietly stacking logs to light the fire. Sophia burrowed deeper into the blankets and squeezed her eyes shut to block out the light. Some time later she heard Smokey, Casanova, and Bittersweet talking near the door of the house. A fourth voice joined them, one she did not recognize. Then, quite unmistakably, the unknown voice said, "Shadrack Elli."

Sophia's eyes flew open. Theo was nowhere to be seen. She sat up and pulled her hair quickly into a braid. Padding up to the doorway, she saw Smokey, Casanova, and Bittersweet sitting around the ashes of a fire with a stranger. He had a gap-toothed smile, a bulbous nose, and a square-cut white beard. His head was entirely bald, and he was fanning himself with a canvas hat.

"Good morning!" he said merrily to Sophia. "You must be Sophia Tims! I have heard such a great deal about you. Not from these good-for-nothings, who are worthless as gossips, but from Miles Countryman, my friend and associate in Boston."

Smiling at this peculiar greeting, Sophia extended her hand. "I am glad to know you."

The stranger winked. "Well, you don't know me yet." He stood up and gave a little bow. "Pip Entwhistle, at your service. Trader, merchant, purveyor of fine goods and curiosities."

"Do you also know my uncle, Shadrack Elli? I heard his name just now."

"I do!" declared Pip. "The finest cartologer of our Age, and a man of discerning taste, I might add. He and I share an interest in pennies."

"Pennies?" Sophia said, surprised. "He's never mentioned that."

"Oh, yes, indeed. Pennies." Pip grinned. "Would you like to see one?"

Sophia, perplexed, glanced at Smokey and saw there a look of knowing amusement. She gave Sophia a small nod. "Why not?" Sophia replied.

With a flourish, Pip produced a penny from an inside coat pocket. He held it up but did not hand it over. "Did you know that the first copper pennies were made in 1793, before the Disruption?" Sophia shook her head. "They were not a great success. In execution, not conception. Everyone liked the idea. After the Disruption, New Occident began the manufacture of what we know as the clock penny." He held up the familiar wheel of copper, as large as a chestnut. "And yet this special penny, which your uncle and I have a keen interest in, is a little different than most. Why do you think that is?"

He handed it over to Sophia, who examined it curiously, still wondering why they were discussing pennies, of all things. The penny had the twenty-hour New Occident clock on one side and a tiny map of the states on the other. "There's something here on Upper Massachusetts," she said, noticing a different texture.

"You got it! Right on the nose!" Pip exclaimed triumphantly, tapping the side of his own. "You would find, if you were to consult a jeweler, that it is rose quartz. Mined in Upper Massachusetts. And, we think quite suitably, embedded in the portion of map that depicts the region." He beamed.

"Why rose quartz?" Sophia asked when it appeared Pip would not be explaining the obvious.

Pip winked. "Because precious stones are the stickiest things in the world."

She was entirely baffled. "Stickiest?"

"Sticky for memories, that is. Precious stones seem to absorb memories at the lightest touch—it is simply remarkable."

"Oh!" Sophia exclaimed, with sudden understanding. She turned the penny over to look at Upper Massachusetts again. "This is a memory map?"

Pip laughed with delight. "Yes! Shadrack and I had three hundred made in total. I put the pennies into circulation, and everyone who touches them leaves a few memories in the rose quartz. The pennies work their way around and around, from one hand to another. Eventually, some of them work their way back to me, and I pass them along to Shadrack. They are each a treasure chest of information. They have given us invaluable insights into what is happening here and in the Territories, and all without having to actually *go* there."

"How do you read them?"

"Thumb on the quartz, forefinger on the map, and your other hand on the edges. Otherwise, everyone would be reading the map by accident, you understand."

Sophia followed his instructions and held the penny in both hands. Brief but vivid memories flitted through her mind: Pip, laughing and waving good-bye at the entrance of a tavern; a messy kitchen with broken crockery; a country fair where cows wore blue ribbons and pies sat on a long, checkered cloth; a watch shop in which the proprietor bent over his work, examining minute gears to the music of chiming clocks; and Pip again, holding up a contraption that looked like a telescope. "How wonderful," Sophia said, smiling, as she handed it back.

"Entirely devised by your uncle Shadrack," Pip said, taking the penny in his palm. "He is shockingly ingenious, if I do say so myself. Shockingly ingenious."

"We were speaking of your uncle, Sophia," Smokey put in, "because Pip has brought me a new map."

Sophia raised her eyebrows. She saw now that a map lay unfurled on Smokey's lap, and, on either side of her, Casanova and Bittersweet had been studying it. "A map of what?"

"Shadrack has been sending us maps of the troops' movements. It is part of his effort to avoid bloodshed in this war." Smokey smiled. "You should be very proud of him—he has done a great deal in a short amount of time."

Sophia sank down beside Bittersweet, and Smokey passed her the map. "He sends them to you?" she echoed.

"Here's how it works," Pip said, drawing himself up importantly. "I take my goods to Boston, as I have done from time immemorial, and of late I always make a point of stopping by Shadrack Elli's house, in case he has any interesting maps to sell, which I pay for with copper pennies." He winked broadly and tapped the side of his nose.

"Oh, I see!" Sophia exclaimed.

"I usually find at least a few interesting maps, you may not be surprised to hear. Then I travel back to my usual circuit, here on the border of New Occident and the Territories, and I stop in on half a dozen acquaintances, and since I excel at trade and barter, I am usually able to persuade them to take one of these peculiar maps off my hands. In exchange, they give me some scribbles that I tuck away and carry back to Boston next time I go. It works very well," he said, pleased with himself.

"Every week Shadrack sends us updates," Smokey said, rather more directly, "and we keep him informed of things here. This map shows the troop movements since the start of the war and, as far as he knows, where they are headed."

Sophia considered the map. It was the first new map of her uncle's that she had seen in months, and the familiar hand made her ache. It was clear that he had rushed, but as usual, he had not compromised on precision. A line of arrows, annotated with dates, showed the progress of the troops since July. She found Oakring, just south of the Eerie Sea, and to the south-west of it was a shaded cloud marked *August 20 or thereabouts.* All of the lines with arrows pointed to it. Sophia frowned. "And they are all meeting up there?"

"We were discussing this as you came out," Smokey said. "It seems Broadgirdle plans a large-scale confrontation. He is amassing almost all the New Occident forces there later this month. General Griggs will lead the armies, which almost certainly means that Fen Carver will be bringing the Territories' troops to the same place. "

"It's not far from here," Sophia murmured. "Is it even in the Territories?"

"You've hit upon the problem," Bittersweet said, his voice heavy. "This place is not in the Territories at all—it is Turtle-back Valley."

Sophia looked up at him, horrified. "No!"

"I'm afraid so."

"But the grove . . . We can't let them harm it—we must stop them!"

"I know," he agreed. "I fear that with a force so large, the old one's influence will be useless. The grove would be destroyed. And there is more. Pip, do you have a pen or pencil in that massive pack of yours?"

Entwhistle, who had listened to this exchange with some

bewilderment, reached into his jacket and withdrew a blue pen with a silver nib. "Here you are. Manufactured in Charleston. Flawless construction. Never leaks."

Bittersweet took the pen without comment and began marking the map with small Xs, dating each one. "There," he said, holding it up. "It's just as I thought."

"What is?" Sophia asked.

He handed her the map. "Each *X* is where Datura has been. It didn't make sense to me before, because I didn't know all the troop movements, but look. In every single case, the crimson fog precedes New Occident forces. They send in Datura first, and then they come afterward with fire. Destroy what little survives."

Sophia caught her breath and Pip gave a low whistle. Casanova shook his head grimly. "I am sorry to say that it does not surprise me."

"That must be why this war has moved so quickly," Smokey said.

"No doubt," Bittersweet agreed, his expression aggrieved. "They are using her as a weapon, clearing the way for New Occident troops."

Sophia gazed at the map, appalled by all that it contained. "What is the *purpose* of destroying these places so completely? Not just the crimson fog, but gunfire, and—fire? Why?"

"It ruins crops, and it ruins morale," Casanova told her.

"I cannot believe that Broadgirdle would do this," she declared.

"He is capable of anything," said a voice from the doorway.

Theo stood there, looking tousled but better than he had the previous evening.

"Theodore Constantine Thackary!" Pip cried, standing up once more. "How good to see you again, though I would prefer to see you with fewer bandages."

"How are you, Pip?" Theo greeted him, putting his arm carefully around the older man.

"I am perfectly well. You, on the other hand, were in better condition last time I saw you," Pip said disapprovingly.

"We stayed with Pip when Miles and I traveled west in the winter," Theo explained to Sophia. "A lot has happened since then," he told Entwhistle.

"Yes, yes—I know," he replied gravely, stroking his beard. "Sit down, sit down. This Broadgirdle has wreaked havoc on New Occident, but I know he has been devilish to you in more particular ways."

"What has he done now?" Theo asked.

Sophia handed Theo the map. "He plans to amass the New Occident army in Turtleback Valley. Where the grove is. And Bittersweet says that the troops have followed in the wake of the fog."

Theo studied the map in silence. "Well, we needed no proof that Graves is a monster."

"Graves?" Pip asked, eyebrows raised.

"I know him from the Baldlands," Theo explained. "He's not even from New Occident. When I knew him, he went by Wilkie Graves."

Pip's eyes lit with understanding. "Oh, ho, *ho!*" he said,

slapping his knee. "Wilkie Graves. Wilkie Graves!" he said again.

"You know him?"

"Pip knows everyone," Smokey said, looking at him thoughtfully.

"I do indeed, I do indeed," Pip declared. "And it doesn't surprise me at all, now, to find he is at the root of this disastrous war. Not at all. He has a very violent past. Did you know him as a slave trader?"

Sophia caught her breath. "A slave trader?"

"I did," Theo assented, his tone guarded.

"Well, I knew him from even before that, and his earlier past is even more colorful, shall we say. And now we find him at the head of government and leading an army." He shook his head and rose to his feet. "My friends, I know you have much to discuss and much to do here. But I have work of my own to take care of, and this very helpful bit of information will speed me along." He looked at Theo meaningly. "I may not return for longer than usual," he told Smokey. "So I'll send word to you somehow—I hope before August twentieth, our day of reckoning."

The group rose to bid good-bye to Entwhistle, who shook hands all around, pulled on his canvas hat, and lifted the leather pack that sat beside him. He waved as he walked off down the hill toward Oakring, his boots squelching in the mud.

Sophia watched him go, but the moment he was out of sight she turned her attention back to the map. "What are we going to do?" she asked, looking in turn at Bittersweet, Casa-nova, Smokey, and Theo. "We have to stop them marching into Turtleback Valley." She was grateful that none of them tried to argue that it was impossible or unnecessary. Their faces told her how seriously they considered the question of what to do.

"A distraction somewhere else?" suggested Theo.

"What kind of distraction?" asked Casanova. "It would have to be dramatic."

"A weirwind would be distracting. A weirwind as long as the valley."

"The old one isn't even listening to me these days," Bitter-sweet said, shaking his head. "Persuading it to make a weir-wind is out of the question."

"Perhaps they could be led in the wrong direction some-how," Sophia offered tentatively.

As she spoke, Nosh ambled up to them and rested his head lightly on Bittersweet's shoulder. He exhaled noisily. "That's a nice idea, Nosh, but it's impossible," said Bittersweet.

"What?" Sophia asked.

"He said we could show them the valley from the old one's perspective, and then they would not want to harm it." He rubbed the moose's chin. "Nosh is such an idealist."

Sophia frowned. "But wait a moment. It's not such a bad idea..." she said. As she considered Nosh's suggestion, she spoke her thoughts aloud. "If you put it that way, then yes, it sounds unlikely. But if they somehow saw—really *saw* the Clime for what it was . . ." She trailed off pensively. "*The old one remembers more than anyone*, is what my map from Ausentinia says. I wonder. When I arrived at the edge of Ausentinia, I saw the Clime's past—its memories of how it had been. I was—" She shook her head. "They were overwhelming. What if we could somehow make that visible to others? Yes," she said eagerly, the notion taking shape in her mind. "Through a memory map. A map that shows the memories of the Clime. Wouldn't that have the power to change someone's mind, to show them something they cannot ignore?" She looked around at the others.

"It could work," Smokey said slowly. "From the little I've seen of Elodean memory maps, they do have incredible power. To be immersed in the Clime's memories . . . If we gave it to someone in the right position, General Griggs or General June, it might just be impressive enough to make one of them pause."

"But how would you make such a map?" Casanova asked.

Smokey clearly did not like having to give the answer. "I only know one person who has made such a map—a memory map of an old one." She looked meaningly at Bittersweet.

Bittersweet looked back at her. "It is much too dangerous, Sarah."

"If there were any time to court danger, this would be it," she replied.

"We could not go, you and I. It would have to be the three of them, and they are ill-equipped to reckon with her." Bittersweet pressed his lips together. "But perhaps you are right. Perhaps this is the time."

"Who are you talking about?" Theo asked.

Bittersweet addressed Smokey. "You tell them."

"Borage," Smokey said solemnly. "She lives north of here, in the Eerie Sea, in an Age of her own making. Only two other people live with her. Sage and Ash. They are the three sisters—cast out by the Elodeans and banished from Oakring."

29
The Exiles

—1892, August 13: 7-Hour 57—

I have also noticed interesting tendencies in how the various traditions imagine good and evil. In some traditions, notably in the Closed Empire and the Papal States, evil is external and unalloyed—what is evil has always been and will always be evil. What is good is in peril, threatened by the potential corruption of evil. In contrast, the Elodeans (Eerie) almost always characterize evil as something that comes from within, and it can coexist with good. That is, a person is not entirely good or bad—she can be both. And it is not just a matter of changing over a lifetime— good falling into disgrace, evil redeeming itself—but actually preserving the two in oneself at the same time.

—From Sophia Tims's Born of the Disruption: Tales Told by Travelers

"WHAT DOES THAT mean?" Sophia asked, in disbelief. "An Age of her own making?"

Nosh shuddered and turned away, as if avoiding her question. Bittersweet and Smokey stared at the cold ashes of the fire. "You said Goldenrod told you that one of the Elodeans had tried to practice the Ars, did she not?" Bittersweet asked.

"Yes, but she didn't say what that meant," Sophia pressed.

Smokey cleared her throat. "Well, let us be frank," she said. "Neither one of us has been there, so much of what we know is secondhand. What we know is this: Borage, Ash, and Sage were—are—Weatherers like Bittersweet. Wildly talented, so that even to the Elodeans their feats sometimes seemed like magic."

"I never knew them," Bittersweet put in, "but my mother is full of stories. Some are good stories." He smiled. "Once, my mother said, the three sisters helped lead a pair of lost children out of the wood by sending them a cloud of fireflies."

"Not everything they did was so charming," Smokey continued. "Borage, in particular, the most talented of the three, grew vengeful as she grew older. She hated the way people of the Territories treated the old one, and once, in her fury, she brought a weirwind that left more than a dozen settlers dead. The Elodeans cast her out for it, and she came here. For a time, we accepted her. There were some who called her a murderer and would not look her in the face, but we pride ourselves on taking in outcasts here, and most tried to countenance the three sisters. Until Borage revealed her plan for Oakring." Smokey shook her head. "She decided that it was not enough to speak with the old one and influence its actions. She wanted more. She wanted to *be* an old one herself."

Sophia caught her breath.

"But what would that even look like?" Theo asked skeptically.

"That is the part we do not know, for we forbade it. Borage wanted to claim Oakring and the land all around it, making it her own. We banished her. She went north, with her sisters, to the Eerie Sea, and it is there that she attempted to create and inhabit an Age of her own."

"What we hear," Bittersweet said, "is that every tree and rock and blade of grass there is an animated expression of her consciousness. Even the animals—and there are also creatures of her own making. But it is hard to say, for few have ventured there. Ash and Sage spend all their energies attempting to contain her."

Although Sophia found the portrait Bittersweet and Smokey had painted unsettling, she could imagine worse. She thought about other ways the armies of New Occident might be stopped, and all of them seemed more outlandish and more dangerous: surrounding the grove to protect it; provoking the army to march elsewhere; persuading the commanding officers on the strength of her conviction alone. Traveling into the Eerie Sea still seemed the better option.

"It sounds strange but not dangerous," Casanova said, voicing Sophia's own conclusion. "I will go."

"The three of us can go," Theo said. "Her grudge is against the Eerie and all of you from Oakring, right? So we should be fine."

"You, Theo, are not ready to travel," Casanova objected.

"He may not be," Bittersweet said, "but Theo is likely the only way you will find them. It is quite difficult to find the shores of the Eerie Sea. We have no maps, and none of you is Eerie."

"What do you mean, I'm the only way?" Theo asked.

Bittersweet and Smokey exchanged a glance. "You have the Mark of Iron, do you not?" asked Bittersweet.

Theo held up his hand. "Yes."

"Well, what did you think it was for?"

"For?" Theo echoed.

Nosh let out a breath that sounded uncannily like a laugh. "That's unkind, Nosh," Bittersweet remarked, but he was trying to control his smile. "Many people in the Baldlands don't know its meaning."

"What did he say?" Theo asked indignantly.

Bittersweet hesitated. "He finds it amusing that you don't use the Mark," he said, clearly editing Nosh's comment.

"The Mark is a compass, Theo," Smokey said, reaching out to press his scarred right hand. "People in Oakring with the Mark of Iron use it for way-finding. That's what it's for."

THEO WAS INCREDULOUS, then furious, and finally, after a time, elated. Though it seemed a disgraceful waste to have lived almost seventeen years without knowledge of the Mark's power, he decided that the most important thing was to waste not a minute more. The lethargy brought on by the strain of recovery vanished. Insisting that time was short, he persuaded Smokey to take him into Oakring.

True to the story Lichen had told them, there were both people with the Mark of Iron and people with the Mark of the Vine in Oakring. Sarah Smoke Longfellow, as the town's medic, knew them all. She decided that they would ask a man named Everett, a renowned tracker, to teach Theo how to use his hand. Theo could hardly contain his excitement. As he headed off with Smokey and Casanova, leaving Bittersweet and Sophia behind, he seemed to have forgotten his injured shoulder entirely.

"You and I have our own work to do," Bittersweet said as he joined Sophia at Smokey's kitchen table. "Do you have the tree ring?"

Sophia took it from her satchel and put it on the table. "Here it is."

"Have you been able to read it yet while waking?"

"Not yet."

"Try again. You may find a new purpose in doing so." He touched the wheel of wood. "When I looked at it the other night, I saw something interesting. This tree has memories of the three sisters."

Sophia's eyes widened. "It does?"

"It would be an advantage to you, I think, to see them in this way before you venture north into the Eerie Sea."

Sophia regarded him. "What will you do while we head north? Will you stay here with Smokey?"

Bittersweet shook his head. "Thanks to your uncle's map, I have a fair idea of where Datura will be next. I aim to get there ahead of her this time." He stood up. "I will leave later today, and I have plans to make with Nosh. Good luck with the reading," he said with a smile. "I'll be back to say good-bye."

Sophia turned her attention to the disc of pinewood before

her. Every time she had tried to read the map while awake, it had remained silent. *Maybe now it will be different,* she said to herself, trying not to struggle against a sense of frustration. *Maybe now that I have seen the grove and understood what it means to perceive rather than see.*

She rested her fingertips on the wooden surface. Closing her eyes, she focused on the texture of the pine. It felt the way it always did. She willed herself to lose track of time, so that the moment expanded loosely, making a protective room all around her. Her arm felt heavy, then surprisingly light. The pine was smooth and slightly warm, but the warmth did not register as temperature; the warmth was something else.

Sophia paused in her observations, realizing that something important had happened. Warmth was not warmth; wood was not wood. Her fingertips no longer seemed to rest against a solid surface. In a way that Sophia did not understand, in a way she urgently, deliberately did not question, her fingertips were touching memories. She could feel them brushing up against her skin like filaments of fine thread. It was the memories that made the heat.

The memories lay before her. She could see them just as she would in a memory map made by human hands: snowfall, spring mornings, summer storms, autumn evenings, another snowfall. People came and went. A girl climbed the trunk and clambered up the branches, laughing. An old man rested against the exposed roots, tired and aching, catching his breath. A furtive boy dug and dug in the ground, making a deep hole and dropping a sack into it before covering it again with dirt. The wind howled; the moon waxed and waned.

Then three women of middle age sat on the ground side by side, looking out over a town, which Sophia now recognized as Oakring. She could see only their backs. They were laughing. The bright colors of sunset were spread across the horizon, and the air smelled of clover. One of them reached out to cup a firefly, and the action sparked Sophia's memory. *The three sisters,* she thought. "Don't let it go to your head, Borage," one said to the woman holding the firefly.

"And why not?" came the light reply. Her voice was low and rich, with a pleasing musicality. "It's true. We can see thoughts as they take shape. We can call on the wind and the rain. The old ones love us. Through our guiding hand, they shape the future. It's not just that we seem like the Fates. We *are* the three Fates, sisters."

30

FOUR PAWNS

—1892, August 10: 9-Hour 50—

As it is with the study of the earth, so it is with the study of flora and fauna. Both had made significant progress before the Disruption, but the event itself has changed the nature of the pursuit. Now, the preexisting assumptions no longer hold. It is not just the proliferation of other species and other land masses. As explorers have demonstrated, the very categories we once considered stable are now unstable. James Hutton's groundbreaking geological work just prior to the Disruption has been largely questioned—or rendered elementary, at the very least—by geologists in Nochtland, just as Carl Linnaeus's excellent work, however influential, seems less and less adequate to describe our New World.

—From Shadrack Elli's History of the New World

SHADRACK DID NOT wait to digest the significance of his discovery, nor did he wait to discuss it with the other plotters. Leaving the warehouse as soon as he could graciously extract himself, he took the trolley into town and hired a carriage that would take him to Lexington. The trip took a good hour, and it was close to midday when he arrived at the town's center. There, he paid the driver for his time and his lunch, asking him to wait until he returned. "If I don't return by thirteen-hour, go to this address," he said, writing Mrs. Clay's name beside the East Ending Street address. "Tell the housekeeper where you brought me, and she will do the rest."

He was grateful for the clear skies and for his sturdy shoes as he trekked across Lexington Green in the direction of the farm he had seen listed as one of Broadgirdle's properties. As he did, he mulled over the consequences of his discovery at the warehouse. Broadgirdle had arranged matters so that he could not be blamed for anticipating a war. That blame would fall to Shadrack. What else would he be implicated in? If Broadgirdle was capable of planning such a thing so far in advance, what other plans lay unseen, waiting to reveal their results? Which of them involved the missing Eerie?

Shadrack arrived at the farm at half past ten-hour, and he approached it with caution. He did not know what he would do if he found himself confronted by Sandmen with grappling hooks. A long avenue lined by oaks led to a farmhouse at the top of a slight hill. The fields on either side seemed untended, as if they had not been mown for many summers, and they were coated with a layer of ash. But the fence all around the property was in good repair, and the latch on the gate was well-oiled. Shadrack opened it and stepped onto the avenue.

The farmhouse was silent as he drew near. Most of the windows were open, and pale yellow curtains fluttered in one of the rooms. Shadrack took a deep breath. He walked up to the blue door and knocked. Almost immediately, he heard a quiet shuffle inside. A minute passed, and then another. Shadrack looked around him and noticed that while the fields grew wild, the gardens in the immediate vicinity of the farmhouse were well tended. A blueberry bush by the door was starting to bear fruit, and a gnarled apple tree showed signs of being well picked over. Herbs grew against the house in tall clumps: verbena, mint, and lavender. Shadrack knocked again. He leaned toward the open window nearest him, where a box of creeping thyme was in full bloom. "Hello? This is Shadrack Elli. Is anyone home?"

The shuffling sound came again, and this time he heard footsteps. A latch was thrown, and the blue door creaked slowly open. Shadrack found himself looking down at an old man with wispy, white hair and a pointed beard. His eyes were filled with tension. The furrows of his brow seemed engraved by the sharp point of some vexing burden. "Shadrack Elli, the cartologer?" the old man whispered.

"Yes. I am Shadrack. Are you Gerard Sorensen, doctor of botany, by any chance?"

Fear flashed in the man's eyes, but he nodded.

"I mean you no harm. I have been looking for you. May I come in?"

Sorensen hesitated. "I do not think you should," he said quietly.

"I want to help, Dr. Sorensen. Can't you tell me what has happened?"

"Will you ensure my family's safety?" Sorensen asked, his voice pleading.

Shadrack swallowed. "Are they in danger?"

"I am here against my will, Mr. Elli," Sorensen said, with

rather more firmness in his tone. "If my children and grand-children were not under threat, I would not be here at all. And if speaking to you imperils them in any way, everything I have done will be for naught."

"Dr. Sorensen, I am only beginning to understand this puzzle, which your predicament is part of. I know that Gordon Broadgirdle is somehow to blame, and I know that unless we stop him, the lives of many more people will be forfeit. If you will only explain to me your part in this, I will do everything in my power to make sure your family is safe."

The indecision was plain in Sorensen's face. Finally, he opened the door with a little sigh. "We are lucky it is a Wednesday," he said. "Come in. Perhaps we can do this without anyone being the wiser."

Shadrack stepped into the farmhouse kitchen and found himself in a room that reminded him immediately of Martin Metl's laboratory in Nochtland. Soil lay everywhere. Empty pots were piled high on a worktable, where a watering can and a pair of gloves had been hastily put aside. Plants covered almost every surface and much of the floor. Among those that Shadrack recognized were potted orange trees, papyrus, a miniature willow, and ferns: more ferns than he had ever seen in a single space. There was nowhere to sit.

"I will tell you quickly," Sorensen said, "and then you must go."

"That is all I could ask," Shadrack agreed. "Thank you."

"It began in late winter of this year. I was approached by a man named Gordon Broadgirdle who said he would pay me handsomely to examine a plant specimen he had acquired from the Eerie Sea. I am interested in the plants of that region, so I accepted. He invited me here, to this farmhouse. To my dismay, I found . . ." Sorensen touched the orange tree nearest him with a distracted air. "I found that the specimens he had were not plants. They were people."

Shadrack nodded as the pieces came together. "Three people: an old man, a woman, and a girl. Three Weatherers of the Eerie."

"Yes!" Sorensen said. "How could you know this?"

"One of them managed to send a message, despite her captivity."

"I see," Sorensen said, relieved. "I am glad to hear it. But apparently it was not enough. The one of most interest to Broadgirdle was the girl, for her hands bloom with flowers known as datura—a flower that is toxic. Once the flowers are loosed from her hands, their vapors cause terrifying delusions. They are dreadfully poisonous."

"The crimson fog," Shadrack said, shaking his head. "Now I see."

"I did not," Sorensen said quietly, "until it was too late. I demanded that the Eerie be set free, and I refused to participate in what Broadgirdle had planned. He said, in reply, that he would send his men after my family." Sorensen put a hand over his eyes. "From then on, I did everything he asked. I confirmed what the flower was capable of, and, once I did, Broadgirdle ordered me to place the other two Eerie in winter sleep. I know very little of the Eerie, and I have only read about such sleep in written accounts—but Broadgirdle said that if I did not, he would end their lives. So I did my best. The girl was taken away, I dread to think for what purpose, and the other two remained here."

Shadrack was galvanized. "They are still here?"

By way of answer, Sorensen turned and left the room, leaving Shadrack to follow him. In the adjoining chamber, dark curtains were drawn to block the sunlight, and Shadrack had to wait in the doorway while his eyes adjusted. Once they did, he could see that the room was empty except for a stack of wood beside the open fireplace and two long crates that looked like coffins. They were closed. Sorensen shuffled over to them and gently removed their lids, tucking them back behind the crates. "See for yourself," he said.

Shadrack drew closer, a sense of dread creeping upon him as he did so. It was still difficult to see in the darkened room. As if hearing his thought, Sorensen rose and walked to the fireplace, where he took a candle in its holder from the mantel. He struck a match and lit the wick, then knelt by the nearest crate with the candle in his hand.

Shadrack peered down into the crate and saw that Sorensen had told him the truth. It was filled with dirt. A pair of white hands, one folded over the other, interrupted the soil near the middle. Three white flowers, delicate trumpets upon a dark vine, were entwined between the limp fingers. And at the top end of the crate a woman's pale face—eyes closed, her expression tranquil—lay waxy and still in the black soil.

PART IV
Storm

31
HALF A LIE

—1892, August 11: 12-Hour 22—

On balance, it is clear that other Ages love their gardens more. Nochtland, the capital of the Baldlands, would be aptly dubbed "a city of gardens." Even the Papal States, asphyxiated as it is by the plague, pays more consistent care to the fountain gardens of its cities. Travelers to New Occident often remark that the rural areas are lovely enough, but the cities are choked with bad construction, cobbled streets, and too few trees. Boston has its Public Garden, but apart from that, the largest parks are cemeteries. As one illustrious visitor remarked, "Wouldn't it be better to have more gardens for the living and fewer for the dead?"

—From Shadrack Elli's *History of the New World*

SHADRACK HAD RACED back to Inspector Grey's office; he had persuaded the inspector and twenty of his men to follow him to Lexington; he had compelled Grey to guarantee Sorensen and his family police protection; he had convinced Sorensen to wake the two Weatherers; and he had taken charge of the Weatherers himself, placing them with a friend in Concord so they could recover fully from their long winter sleep. Then he returned to East Ending Street, exhausted, and reported to the plotters what had happened. Winnie and Nettie were furious, but they forgave him when he explained what was likely to happen next. At last, his tasks completed, satisfied that he had done all he could, he waited.

He half expected that Broadgirdle would knock on his door that very evening. But the confrontation occurred the next afternoon, several hours into the workday. Shadrack had spent the morning gathering his papers, and now he stood at the window of his office, looking out at the Public Garden. He was remembering how, as a child, he would walk there with his parents on Saturday mornings. The roses seemed as tall as trees, and the air was filled with the quiet conversations of other people walking past. Boston had seemed like a winking jewel to him then, full of brilliant light and unexpected treasures.

Broadgirdle did not knock. He burst through the door and slammed it closed behind him. Shadrack took in one last lingering view of the garden and turned, somewhat reluctantly. He could see the man making an effort to rein in his anger, and it struck him as interesting that the prime minister had accosted him in a fury instead of waiting to bring himself in check. "This will cost you," Broadgirdle finally said, his voice strangled.

Shadrack paused, reminding himself that there was nothing to gain by provoking the man further. "I've done only what seemed necessary," he said. "The Weatherers and Dr. Sorensen had suffered enough at your hands, it seemed to me."

Broadgirdle sneered. "You imagine yourself a man of the world, with your maps and your exploring friends—but you are as narrow-minded as the most provincial man in Boston. You cannot see the forest for the trees."

"And what is the forest that I cannot see?"

"The *purpose*. The purpose of it all." He waved his hand around the room, ending at the windows and all of Boston beyond them. "The purpose of our Age. Of what we do in it. Of the Disruption."

Shadrack clasped his hands before him patiently. "You see your plans as part of a larger purpose," he said.

"Of *course* they are," Broadgirdle said, planting his fists on Shadrack's desk and leaning forward. "It's not just about fulfilling our Age's destiny and expanding westward. It's about who wins and who loses. Who will triumph and who will be extinguished. Would you want this hemisphere overrun by *raiders*? Or *Indians*?"

Shadrack raised his eyebrows. "I was not aware that either was interested in overrunning the hemisphere."

"You are a fool," Broadgirdle said dismissively. "You know quite well that its fate hangs in the balance. We can follow the path we are on, into greater and greater disintegration, or we can follow the path set out for us in the Age of Verity: Unity. Cohesion. Progress."

"I do know that there are several possible directions for our Age," Shadrack replied in a measured tone. "But I do not see them as you do."

Something in Broadgirdle seemed to crest and fall. He stepped back from the desk, and his tone now was cold, almost indifferent, as if he had abandoned the prospect of persuading someone so dim. "This Age of Delusion is so misguided. The extent of the derailment is"—he shook his head—"tragic. Hopeless. And yet . . . and yet. This is the only Age we *have*. We will save this Age or we will not. Do you see?" He smiled grimly. "There is no other possible solution. I lament that you have failed so utterly to understand this."

Shadrack heard the Nihilismian logic in Broadgirdle's words, and he realized, as if he had ever doubted, that reasoning with him would be impossible. "Well," he said, "then you are right—I do not see the forest. Or perhaps it is more accurate to say that I see a different forest."

"The cost of your failure will be high," Broadgirdle said. His voice was ice. "I warned you, and I am true to my word. Those threats were not made idly. Sissal Clay and Theodore, if he survives this war, will be deported. And when she returns to Boston, Sophia will be arrested for fraud. I hear juvenile prisons are no better than adult prisons—lack of funds, no doubt. And that's where you will be, of course," he finished triumphantly, "for having planned this war under Bligh's nose. The evidence is at a warehouse near the wharf." He grinned, his white teeth gleaming.

"I am aware of it," Shadrack said calmly.

To Broadgirdle's credit, he did not seem in the least surprised. "Then you are even more of a fool than I thought."

Shadrack turned back to the window. "I hear that in the Age of Verity, Boston is not this nation's capital."

Broadgirdle took a moment to reply. "That is correct."

"I can imagine such a world. In which Boston is not the

center, but a place on the edges. How I love this city," he said quietly. "Its crooked streets and absurdly cold winters and absurdly hot summers. Its face of brick, its heart of green grass. But it has changed. With the border closure, it has become a pale ghost of itself. I have the sense that it is already gone. Even living here, I already miss it." He turned back to the other man. "Perhaps this will make it a little easier to leave. Not so much an exile as a journey to find a city like the one Boston once was." He smiled sadly. "Nochtland perhaps, or the distant cities of the Pacific. I have never seen them."

Shadrack had placed all his effort into planning that journey, and the destination seemed strangely secondary. He had not allowed himself to imagine what it would look like when they were all safely reunited somewhere: Mrs. Clay, Theo, Sophia, and himself. There were too many things yet to plan and too many things that might yet go wrong before tomorrow, when he closed the door of the house on East Ending Street behind himself for the last time.

Broadgirdle's gaze was heavy with disdain. "You put safety above principle, do you? You have a small mind, Shadrack."

Shadrack still smiled. "I believe it is principle that has urged me to take this course, Gordon. Had I been more concerned for my safety, I would have left the Eerie where they lay, in their coffins filled with earth. But I am glad I did not. When we are all together, my family and I, somewhere far from here, I will have nothing on my conscience as I explain my actions."

32
SMOKE MAPS

—1892, August 14: 6-Hour 22—

The chapter by Sarah Smoke Longfellow (Smokey) concerns the origin of smoke maps, which are worth knowing about. They are widely misunderstood. Many people believe that "smoke maps" are impressions made by smoke on paper—that is, a kind of drawing or painting done in smoke. These are interesting to look at, no doubt, but they have no mapping properties in and of themselves. If anything, a more interesting map might be made by drawing with smoke on cloth, which is the standard medium for mapping weather.

—From Sophia Tims's Born of the Disruption: Tales Told by Travelers

NOSH AND BITTERSWEET left on the afternoon of the thirteenth, setting out to find Datura. Sophia found it difficult to say good-bye. From the moment Nosh's gentle face had appeared so close to hers in the Salt Lick train station, the moose and the boy had surrounded her with a sense of considered protectiveness. She had traveled with only two Eerie in her short life, but both of them had a kind of measured stillness that was reassuring in difficult circumstances. She felt worried, uncertain, and suddenly less safe. *First Goldenrod, then Bittersweet; I've been traveling with an Eerie by my side for a month and a half,* she thought as she stood outside Smokey's front door, watching moose and Weatherer depart. *Now I'll have to get used to traveling without one again. When will I see them next?*

Theo was mending well, and the excitement of learning the Art of Iron, as Everett called it, infused him with energy. Nevertheless, Smokey said she would feel more confident about her patient if he slept one more full night in quiet and safety.

"That is," she added with a smile, "when you're finished telling us about it." They were all standing in the kitchen after dinner.

"It's like listening," he said, extending his scarred right hand, "but with your bones."

"That sounds impossible!" said Sophia.

"It's not easy," Theo admitted, with the air of someone who is a little embarrassed at the greatness of his own gifts. "At first, I had no idea what he meant. But he said to stop thinking about it and just focus on hearing what my hand had to say."

Sophia reflected that it was not unlike what Bittersweet had taught her: to observe and interpret without considering *how.* "What are you trying to find now? Your boots?" she teased. "I'm pretty sure I saw them under the cot."

Theo laughed good-naturedly. "I was trying to sense the Eerie Sea. I know which way it is, because I know it's north, but I was trying to see if I could *feel* the way."

"Can you?" Casanova asked, watching with interest.

"A little. It's like I *want* to go that way"—he pointed—"and I can't explain why."

"Is it pulling you to bed?" Smokey asked. "Because that's where you ought to be right now." Theo laughingly accepted her reprimand, and they all retired for the evening.

ON THE MORNING of the fourteenth, Sophia woke to the sound of Smokey's quiet preparations in the kitchen. She was wrapping bundles of food, setting them aside in tidy piles. "Bread, dried meat, and fruit," she said, seeing that Sophia was awake. "There is water along the way. Casanova has one pack, and you'll borrow one of mine."

Sophia rubbed the sleep out of her eyes. "Thank you, Smokey."

"I've set out some clothes for you to wear that are better than that raider garb. Everyone will hear you for a mile around." She held up a pair of buckskin pants, buckskin boots, long woolen socks, a linen shirt, and a wool cloak. "Pants are better for travel anyhow. I'm only a little taller than you, so I hope they will fit."

"They look wonderful, Smokey—thank you." Sophia changed rapidly into the clothes, finding them only slightly too large—but comfortably so. The boots were a perfect fit, and she looked down at them admiringly, happy to find that everything was so warm and light.

"You'll find the weather cooler than here, because of the ice."

Sophia folded the cloak carefully and tied it onto the borrowed pack. "I wonder how far away the sisters are."

"There's no telling." Smokey finished wrapping another bundle. "But you must turn around and start back when you are halfway through this food, regardless of where you are. You'll find nothing to sustain you there."

"The three of them must eat somehow."

Smokey shook her head. "I wouldn't eat what they eat," she said darkly.

Casanova and Theo joined them in the kitchen. Casanova carried a large pack that seemed already stuffed to the brim, but he set it on the table and opened it, stowing all the food Smokey had prepared.

"Wool blankets and rubber tarps for the ice," Smokey said, handing them to Casanova. "Theo, these are for you." She held up a linen packet. "Clean bandages and a small flask of medicine. Take no more than a sip or two if your shoulder begins to hurt again. It will numb the pain. And choose a good walking stick—your balance will be off with your arm in a sling.

"There's enough food for four days, no more. If you aren't back by the eighteenth, we'll have to head in after you, and I can't promise it will end well. So turn around in two days," she said, "regardless of where you are. Besides, if you aren't back by then, it will be too late to save the grove anyway," she added matter-of-factly. "And one more thing." She held up three short candles.

"Ah," Casanova said, smiling and taking them in one large hand. He handed one to Theo and one to Sophia. "Carry these on your person. You don't want to lose them."

"But we already have enough candles," Theo said.

"Not candles made by Smokey."

"They are smoke maps," she said, a trifle apologetic. "You'll forgive me for worrying. But I just want to be sure you can find your way back, should anything go wrong. Light the candle, and the smoke will guide you here, to me."

"Oh!" Sophia exclaimed. "Thank you. A smoke map," she murmured. The short candle looked quite ordinary and smelled pleasantly of beeswax. She tucked it into her satchel and then placed her satchel inside the pack, making room between the wool blankets.

"Do you have to take your satchel, Sophia?" Casanova asked. "All that paper. It's a lot to carry."

She nodded. "It has my maps. And my notebook. And the garnets they gave me in Ausentinia. I have to bring it."

"Sophia never goes anywhere without her satchel," said Theo, smiling. "It is as well traveled as she is."

"Very well," Casanova said with amusement as Sophia blushed. "Let's head off, then. Smokey," he said, turning to embrace her, "thank you. We'll be back on the eighteenth or sooner, I promise. I'll take good care of them."

"I know you will, Grant." She hugged Sophia and Theo in turn. "One more thing," she added as she stood in the doorway. "The Eerie Sea carries its name for a reason. Do not be troubled by what you might see or hear there. It is an uninhabited Age, and it cannot harm you. Until you reach the realm of the three sisters, at least." The three started down the path. "Be safe," she called after them.

THEY WALKED NORTHWARD, away from Oakring. For the first part of their journey, they had no need of Theo's guiding hand, for Casanova knew the way toward the Eerie Sea. Elodeans traveled there periodically to spend time in the ice caverns, and their trails were visible, though overgrown.

Sophia felt deeply grateful, as they proceeded, that Theo had been so fortunate as to meet Casanova in the Boston jail. At Smokey's house, she had already seen the gentleness with which he cared for her friend. Now she could see that he was a thoughtful companion on the road, as well. Clearly he had taken his promise seriously. He held the branches up out of their way to let them pass; he warned them of loose rocks underfoot; and he seemed to know the name of every plant and the meaning of every sign around them.

"Owl pellets," he said, holding up a tufted bundle of what appeared to be lint and bones. "The owls cannot chew, so they swallow their food whole and regurgitate some of it. You see," he said, pulling it apart, "the remains of a little mouse."

"Seems messy," Theo commented.

"You try eating a mouse whole," said Casanova.

The land they traveled through was mostly flat and sparsely forested. The trees seemed to droop overhead, their foliage battered by the charcoal hail. The path was covered with fallen twigs and torn leaves.

As they walked, Sophia periodically looked up at the skies.

She had not seen Seneca since he had dropped Goldenrod's token, and some part of her was always waiting for the falcon to appear. Every flutter of wings drew her eye. "That's a duck hawk," Casanova said, following her gaze when a swooping figure made her stop.

"Very beautiful," Sophia commented.

"Also known as a peregrine falcon. They are fairly common in these parts."

"Casanova," she said, "Theo was lucky to meet you in the Boston jail."

He smiled. "Lucky Theo."

Theo stopped in his tracks. "Why did you call me that?"

Casanova smacked his forehead with the palm of his hand. "How could I have forgotten? So much has happened, it entirely passed me by. When you were ill on the way to Oakring, we were stopped by raiders. They knew you. They even gave me dried meat, saying it had iron you needed. And one of them, named Skinny Jim, called you 'Lucky Theo.'"

Theo's strained expression relaxed into a smile. "Skinny Jim," he repeated. "Well, well." He turned back to the path, still smiling.

"Who is he?" asked Casanova.

"A raider I used to know." Theo laughed, tapping his walking stick against a tree trunk. "He made his name as a knife thrower, actually, before he turned to raiding. He was one of the few I met who seemed to think there were rules to raiding. He never stole from women or from old people or from people who had children."

"That rather shrinks the pool, doesn't it?" Sophia remarked.

"Considerably. I never said he was a successful raider. But a few times, it worked out for him. He robbed a rancher in the southern Baldlands once and made off with enough money to live for two years. Of course, he spent it all in six months, but it was good while it lasted. Skinny Jim. A thief with scruples."

"Like the pirates," Sophia said.

"Like Casanova," Theo suggested.

Sophia eyed Casanova cautiously. "Is that true?"

Casanova shook his head, a smile twisting his face. "I've never told Theo why I landed in the Boston jail. He's fishing." He ducked beneath a tree trunk that had fallen across the path. "Could be I was in jail for embezzlement. Or murder." He turned and gave them a menacing look.

Theo laughed. "Sure. Very likely."

"Or treason," said Casanova, with less mirth in his voice.

"Treason," Sophia repeated.

"'Course it was treason." Theo scowled. "With Broadgirdle as prime minister. Cough too close to him and it's treason. No doubt he was trying to stuff the Boston prisons so he'd have enough foot soldiers."

Casanova pointed up the path. "There's a clearing up ahead, and we'll take a rest." Theo and Sophia waited, hoping he would say something more. He did.

"I was arrested for protesting the border closure and New Occident's policy toward the Indian Territories. I was part of a crowd on the State House steps. The police took us in. At first, it didn't seem serious. But I had trouble getting a lawyer, and the days passed. And then Broadgirdle—who wasn't prime minister yet, but still in parliament—got a law through that made certain forms of protest count as treason. The law applied even to people who had already been arrested on lesser charges. So there I was—in prison for treason." He paused, holding a branch aside so that Theo and Sophia could pass. "No doubt if I hadn't been conscripted," he said matter-of-factly, "I would have been hanged."

BY MIDAFTERNOON, THEY had reached the limits of the territory Casanova could navigate. He paused in a clearing where a rotting lean-to stood decomposing beside a cold fire. "This is a stopping point travelers use to travel east–west. We're as far north as I know to go."

Theo raised his right hand. "Time to use the Art of Iron. Stand aside."

"Please do," Casanova said, with a mock bow. "Just keep your other hand on the walking stick, would you?"

Theo scowled at him. Then he closed his eyes and held the scarred hand out, palm down, as if waiting for something to float up into it.

Sophia watched him with anticipation. Minutes passed. Surreptitiously, she pulled her watch from her pants pocket and checked the time. She and Casanova exchanged a look.

"I can actually feel it pulling me," Theo said finally, his eyes still closed.

"What's pulling you?" Sophia asked.

"I don't know. It's just this tug. Not so strong that I can't ignore it, but it's noticeable when I pay attention."

"Which way is it going?"

Theo opened his eyes. "But I can't do it if I have to look around. How am I going to walk with my eyes closed?" he wondered aloud.

The other two looked at him blankly. "Maybe you can stop every few steps," Sophia suggested.

Theo frowned. He closed his eyes and held his hand out once more. Then he took a hesitant step forward, opening his eyes as he did so. A few more steps took him to the edge of the clearing, and another carried him onto a boulder. He scrambled up it with some difficulty, leaning on the walking stick. Sophia and Casanova, glancing at each other, followed. "That way," Theo said when they had joined him. "Where the trees are more yellow."

"I don't see anything," Sophia admitted.

"Neither do I," said Casanova. "But if you see it, then it must be there. I can take us that way."

He helped Theo down off the boulder and guided them through the trees. Once, Theo stopped him, tapping his shoulder and pointing to the right. Another time, he pulled Casanova to a halt before a piney trail that wound uphill. "That's a dead end. We should stay to the west of the pines."

Casanova eyed him, impressed. "Expert at the Art of Iron, I see."

Theo smiled, but Sophia noticed his weariness. She could tell that his injury was bothering him. He had been struggling ever since they left the clearing, and was trying to hide it—badly. More than once he had tripped, and only Casanova's quick hand had prevented him from falling. She was on the verge of claiming that she needed to rest, thus sparing Theo's feelings, when something made her shiver: a cold wind cutting through the dank air like a draft in a warm house.

"Do you feel that?" she asked.

Casanova nodded. "The breeze off the ice. We are very close."

Soon after thirteen-hour, they stepped out of the forest and found themselves at the edge of the Eerie Sea.

The first thing they saw was a glacier. Cold air drifted off it in visible waves, and its surface gleamed in the afternoon sun. The sea itself was a sheet of silver, bounded on either side by mountains. The three travelers stood on the pebbled ground, amid a network of streams: some thin as ribbons, some that looked much deeper. "You found the way, Theo," Casanova said, putting a hand on his good shoulder. "Well done. The Eerie Sea."

"Doesn't look so bad."

"Glad you think so," Casanova said dryly. "Personally, I did not come prepared for ice-climbing."

Theo shook his head. He held his right hand out loosely, palm down, and then pointed. "There. We're not going over the ice, we're going under it. An opening to the caves."

As he spoke, something moved from the direction he had indicated. The three of them stood silently, watching. It drifted smoothly, like a leaf on the wind. Sophia realized that it was an object floating on one of the many streams that wound toward them, most of which disappeared into the woods they had just left behind. "It's on the water," she said.

"That stream comes from the cave," Theo added.

Casanova took a more considered look. "Yet it is moving in the wrong direction—*away* from the sea." They continued to watch as the object drew closer: brown and white, like the feathers of a falcon or the wood of a birch tree. "A canoe."

"It's empty," Sophia realized when it was close enough to see clearly. The canoe drifted easily along in the shallow stream, now one hundred feet, now fifty feet, now ten feet away from them. And then, when it reached them, it stopped. Sophia caught her breath and stepped back. The water continued to move, but the canoe did not, as if stopped by some unseen obstacle in its path.

"I think we are meant to climb in," Casanova said.

33

OARLESS

—1892, August 14: 14-Hour 00—

The story of the first expedition into the Prehistoric Snows is well known. Rumors of the endless ice had already come down to Boston from trappers and traders. There were rumors, too, of great ice caves so vast that whole ships could be seen trapped within them. The expedition of 1808 found no such caves and no such spectacles. What they did find were frostbite, and avalanches, and in at least one case snow blindness from the glare. The expedition members who survived quickly became unreliable sources about their own journey. They spoke of woolly beasts and strange sounds, of echoes that returned their own words back to them, distorted. It was assumed that the snow had caused some madness in addition to the blindness.

—From Shadrack Elli's History of the New World

"IS THAT A good idea?" Sophia asked. The canoe waited patiently for them in the running water, as if held in place by a phantom hand.

"I don't know." Casanova looked up toward the Eerie Sea, as if the answer to his doubts might lie there.

"I say we try it," said Theo.

Sophia looked at him sharply, and she realized that his face was drawn and he was leaning on the walking stick with both hands. He was even more exhausted than she had realized. From the look on Casanova's face, he had clearly come to the same conclusion.

"There are no oars, which is a problem," Casanova said, studying the canoe. "This current goes south. We need to paddle against it."

"Look!" Sophia exclaimed, crouching down beside the canoe. A bundle of blue flowers lay in the hull. The blooms were like two five-pointed stars set atop each other, blue petals alternating with narrow dark green leaves. The bouquet was tied together with a length of white string.

"Starflower," said Casanova.

Something about the string reverberated in Sophia's mind. She realized that it reminded her of the length of string tied around the Ausentinian maps. And, with that, her sense of unease began to fade. Someone had placed these flowers here. Someone had *sent* the canoe. How could such a gentle gesture possibly bear ill will? "I've never seen starflowers before," she said, reaching for them. "They are so beautiful." She pressed them into her face and found that they smelled faintly of honey.

"They aren't very common here, unless they are planted in gardens. Smokey has some—they have medicinal properties. Starflower is another name for borage," Casanova added.

Sophia's hand tightened on the bouquet. "The canoe comes from her. From Borage."

"It would seem that way."

Theo had not moved; he was so tired that he had not even commented on the flowers. She wondered how much the Art of Iron had drained him.

She looked at the flowers in her hand and then the waiting canoe. "I think we should get in. Perhaps her sending us the canoe means something we do not understand. Perhaps it is not as kindly as it seems. But I believe it is a way for us to travel north, toward their realm. And that is what we want, right?"

Casanova nodded. "Yes. Your reasoning is sound." He looked around. "Well, I will need to make paddles. Give me some time."

"And since this friendly canoe is so obliging, instead of making paddles, I am going to wait for you in it," Theo said.

Casanova put down his pack and appraised the nearest trees. "When I packed, I omitted an ax," he said wryly.

"Can I help?" Sophia asked, and began to remove her pack.

"Hey!" Theo exclaimed.

Sophia and Casanova turned as one to see the canoe, with Theo in it, beginning to drift northward, whence it came.

"It's moving on its own! I'm not doing anything."

Casanova scooped up his pack; Sophia re-shouldered hers. He hurried after the canoe, dropping the pack in the hull, behind Theo. The canoe had already drifted several feet.

"Take the bow." Casanova walked beside the canoe, waiting to make sure that Sophia climbed aboard before doing so himself. "I'll try to be our rudder."

Placing her pack in front of Theo, Sophia scrambled in awkwardly, the canoe tipping slightly as she settled onto the front seat. She turned and saw Casanova climbing in after her. "Give me your stick, Theo," he said.

But before Casanova could use it, the craft began to gather speed, moving steadily forward.

"How is it propelling itself?" Theo asked.

Casanova peered over the edge into the shallow stream. "It's not the canoe. It's the water. The water's moving upstream now."

"What?" Sophia rose slightly from her seat to get a better view, and she saw that he was right. The water had changed direction and was taking them toward the cave, not away from it. "How is it possible?" she breathed.

"Well," Theo said comfortably, seeming no longer bothered by the problem. "Smokey *did* say the Eerie Sea was eerie. If this canoe wants to carry us northward, I'm all for it."

Sophia had to laugh. Then she looked at him appraisingly. "Are you all right?"

"I'm fine. But I'm glad to be sitting."

"Eat," Casanova said, handing him one of Smokey's packets of food. "We have yet to see how long this unexpected assistance lasts. Better take advantage while we can."

Sophia turned to face forward as the canoe approached the cave opening. She felt a flutter of apprehension. The cluster of starflowers was still in her hand, and she clutched it more tightly for reassurance. *I hope these waters have our best interests at heart,* she said to herself.

The cave entrance was dark, and as soon as the canoe passed under the overhanging rock, it turned a sharp corner: right, toward the ice. The waters had yanked them into sudden, overwhelming darkness. Sophia could only tell that they were still moving by the quiet sound of the rippling water beneath them. Then, as they drifted farther, shimmering threads of light appeared overhead and on either side. "What are those?" she whispered in the darkness.

"I am not sure," came Casanova's quiet reply. "Perhaps veins of mica."

Sophia thought her eyes were adjusting, for the craggy walls grew slowly visible, but then she realized that a greater source of light lay ahead. The tunnel turned left, and suddenly the rock around them was replaced by ice. Illuminated by unseen sunlight beyond, the ice shone pale blue. The walls and ceiling around them had shallow bowls and sharp points, as if they had been carved away in pieces by a giant spoon. Here the stream was deep and wide, its bottom no longer visible. The canoe moved serenely along, the mysterious waters maneuvering the vessel through the ice cave with uncanny ease.

"This is magnificent," Sophia said to Theo and Casanova. Like her, they were both staring about them, awed. It was hard to believe that the massive glacier they had seen from the shore was actually hollow.

The ceiling rose higher and higher as they moved forward, and the space opened into a vast cavern. It reminded Sophia of an earlier adventure—navigating the labyrinth of the lost

Age beneath Nochtland. The blue ice, the waves of chill air, the echoing sounds recalled the monumental pyramid of the Glacine Age that had met her when she finally emerged from the subterranean passages.

In the canoe, surrounded by unearthly ice, Sophia hardly felt the cold. She came unloosed from time. Of course Elodeans would want to come here, to experience the majesty of such a place. It had a sense of perfect stillness, and she almost longed to step out of the canoe so that she could stand in the great cavern, within the quiet of the ice.

Or was it quiet? The sound she was hearing, Sophia realized, was not only the rippling water around the canoe. There was something else intermingled with it—a kind of whispering. She cocked her head, trying to hear past the gurgling stream. Yes, now that she listened for it, the sound was clearer: a susurration, as if somewhere in the great ice cavern, people were talking to one another in hushed voices.

"Do you hear that?" Sophia asked, turning back to look at Theo and Casanova. Theo had fallen asleep. He was curled up around Sophia's pack, resting his head on a folded blanket.

"I hear it," said Casanova. "The whispering?"

Sophia nodded. "What is it?"

"I don't know. It sounds like human voices, but I cannot make out the words." He reached into his pack and took out a napkin-wrapped bundle. "Try to ignore it," he told her. "And Sophia—remember what Smokey said. You should eat, too—you haven't had anything since midday."

Sophia took the packet Casanova passed across to her and

unfolded the napkin on her lap. Slowly chewing on the dried meat and fruit, she tried to discern whether the cavern had entrances that might lead to other caves. "There," she said to Casanova, pointing off to the right. "Another opening."

"I see it."

The more she looked, the more Sophia realized that there were innumerable passageways leading off the great cavern. It was a network of waterways and ice tunnels, but the water beneath them guided them past every one. *Perhaps,* she thought, *there are people in those other passageways.* There was no telling how sound would travel through such an unusual space. The thought was disquieting. Elodeans traveled in solitude. Who else would be wandering the ice tunnels of the Eerie Sea?

Finishing her meal, Sophia shook the napkin out, folded it, and stowed it in her pack. She turned all her attention to the canoe's route. *I should be mapping this,* she realized, reaching for the notebook in her satchel. She hurriedly reconstructed the route they had taken so far, doing her best to capture the contours of their own meandering path beneath the glacier. Then she began making note of where the tunnels branched on either side, marking them with half circles.

They had almost reached the far end of the cavern when the canoe began turning to the left, toward one of the arched openings in the ice wall. Sophia quickly marked the location on her map and then looked up, eager to see where they were headed.

The canoe entered a narrow passageway with a low ceiling. It seemed smaller than the others she had observed—so narrow that it was only just wide enough for the canoe. And the space overhead was shrinking. With a flash of unease, Sophia realized that Casanova would not have been able to stand had he tried. Perhaps the unseen hand that steered them was not so benign, after all.

Little by little, the ceiling dropped. Her unease bloomed into panic. "What if the ceiling meets the water? Casanova, we'll freeze! There's no way to climb out!"

His face was grim. "I don't know." He had to lean back to look up. "I should have made that paddle." Jabbing at the ceiling experimentally with Theo's walking stick, he said, "If it comes to it, I can keep us in place with this. We won't be dragged underwater."

This did not make Sophia feel much better. She turned forward once more, trying to see if the ceiling would rise again, but, if anything, it seemed to dip lower. She ducked her head. *"Casanova!"*

"What's happening?" Theo mumbled.

"Stay down." Casanova had slid down from his seat and was holding the walking stick at the ready, preparing to use it as a brake against the ice.

"Wait!" Sophia cried. "Wait! Don't stop us. I see a different kind of light ahead. Not blue—yellow."

She huddled down. The low ceiling continued for another ten feet, twenty feet, fifty feet, and then the canoe turned a corner. Without altering its speed, it drifted through the low archway and out into the open air, leaving the ice tunnels behind.

"Thank the Fates," Casanova murmured, climbing back onto his seat.

Sophia took a deep, relieved breath.

The canoe had emerged beyond the glacier, drifting into a stony landscape that seemed limitless. The air seemed brighter and cleaner than she had seen in days—the sky was a cloudless blue. Behind them, the glacier wedged between the mountains was like a cork in a funnel: a barrier from the world of upper New York. Before them, granite outcrops with surprising shapes—leaning mounds and tall cones and bulging humps that looked like faces—made a prospect of sculpted stone. The canoe seemed to move with renewed energy along the narrow stream that cut through the rock.

The sun was low on the horizon, and Sophia estimated that they had perhaps an hour or so of light left. She checked her pocket watch; they had been inside the glacier for more than two hours.

"Is this still the Eerie Sea?" asked Theo.

"You know as much as I do," Casanova replied. "What does your hand tell you?"

Sophia looked back to see Theo with his hand outstretched, concentrating once more.

The landscape drifted past. A few minutes later, he told them, "We are going the right way. But I have no idea if this is the Eerie Sea."

"There's someone watching us," Casanova said abruptly.

Sophia whirled. "Where?"

He pointed toward the west, to a distant rock ridge. Sure enough, a figure stood there, with the sun behind it. "It's been there since we came out of the glacier—always a little ahead of us, as if it knows where we're going."

"Doesn't surprise me," Theo said, yawning. "Even the canoe knows where we're going. We're the only ones who don't, apparently."

Sophia watched the figure and found that what Casanova had said was true. It remained always at the same distance, always to the west and a little ahead of them. She shook her head and turned back to her notebook, intent on continuing the map she was making. "Maybe it is one of the sisters," she said, sketching the route through the stone.

"Could be," Casanova replied. "It seems agile to me. More than I would have expected for an eighty-year-old woman."

"Is that how old they are?"

"Around that. From what Bittersweet said about how long his mother and grandfather knew them."

The sun began sinking into the horizon. All around them, the stone was bathed in orange light. Here and there, cliffs jutted up into the darkening sky, bright red and shaded purple. "Oh!" Sophia exclaimed. She pointed ahead. A cluster of fireflies had appeared in the air above the stream, and as the canoe approached they danced toward them, their lights glancing on and off.

Casanova observed them warily. "The three sisters must have sent them."

To Sophia they seemed anything but ominous, and she

smiled as the fireflies heralded them onward. "A retinue of fire-flies," she said. "I think it's very welcoming."

As the sun sank lower and the sky above them made a dome of fading indigo, the canoe began to slow down. The stony outcrops disappeared, leaving only a flat stone table stretching east and west. Abruptly, the stream widened. Sophia realized, as they floated forward, that it had opened into a lake: a wide body of water bordered entirely by stone. And now, as the fireflies flickered toward it, she saw the island that rose in the middle of the lake. Steep and thickly forested, it jutted from the still water like a craggy horn. At the hill's peak was a great stone edifice that seemed carved from the island itself. Lights shone in the windows—amber lights that flickered like candle flames, or fireflies.

34

THE ISLAND

—*August 1892: # Day, # Hour*—

For the Elodeans (Eerie), fireflies have particular significance.
They are also called "lightning fliers," and they are admired for
the blinking patterns made by their lights. The Elodeans contend
that these patterns are not arbitrary but intentional, and that the
blinking is a manner of communicating. I have not seen the lightning fliers talk in this way, but I believe it might be possible.

—From *Sophia Tims's* Reflections on a Journey to the Eerie Sea

THE CANOE DRIFTED across the lake until it reached the island's
rocky shore. Casanova jumped out and pulled the canoe to
ground, raking the birchbark against the stones, then helped
Theo out of his seat. Sophia shouldered her pack.

The fireflies had moved and were waiting at the base of a
trail that wound steeply upward. As Sophia watched, her eyes
widened with surprise. "Look," she whispered.

Theo and Casanova turned. The fireflies flickered and stead-
ied. Their lights were no longer a meaningless cluster; they
were *letters*.

"Up," Sophia read aloud.

"Let us hope they are honest as well as literate," Casanova

said. "Do you have it in you to climb this hill, Theo?"

Theo planted his walking stick firmly in the ground. "Definitely."

They followed the fireflies' winking lights. Ash trees grew densely on either side of the uphill trail. Sage and borage filled the air with a scent that was both earthy and sweet.

After leading them up and around the island twice, going higher and higher still, the fireflies turned a sharp corner, and Sophia realized they had arrived at a stone archway. It opened onto a square courtyard. Theo stopped, leaning on his walking stick to catch his breath.

The granite castle loomed darkly above them. It was more fortress than castle, with high, solid walls and gated windows. Burning torches flanked its massive wooden door, which stood open.

And, in the doorway, someone was waiting for them.

A long laugh that ended in a cackle echoed through the courtyard. "I was right! I was right!"

The three travelers waited, poised, as the strange figure approached.

"I told Ash and Sage that you would never make it if you had to walk. And I was right. You'd be floating in the icy waters of the glacier by now, or lost in one of the tunnels." It was an old woman's voice, as surprisingly strong and nimble as her gait. She stood before them in the flickering torchlight. Her grin seemed genuine, but her eyes flashed with something sharp and malicious.

Casanova spoke first. "The canoe made our journey here much easier. Did you send it?"

"Of course we did," she replied, suddenly serious. "How else would it have arrived?"

"Thank you," Theo said. "You're right. I would never have made it otherwise."

The old woman grinned again, her eyes gleaming. "Well, come in, come in! I know why you've come, and we must get started. You've lost too much time already." She turned toward the open doors and beckoned for them to follow. "I am Borage, in case you had not solved that puzzle."

Glancing at one another, the travelers followed Borage toward the darkened doorway. They found themselves in a small anteroom, facing a spiral staircase made of stone. "More steps," Borage announced. "Fifty-three of them," she added cheerily. "And then you can rest, Lucky Theo. And you can ask me about the old one, Sophia. And you can get a poultice from Sage for the complaint you are hiding, Grant."

Sophia and Theo turned to stare at Casanova. "It's nothing," he said. When they did not reply, he added, "I brushed up against a poisonous plant."

"Ah!" Borage said, already climbing. "But it will grow worse if you do not get the poultice. And the scarring will add to your already impressive collection." Her voice became muffled as she wound upward. "He was holding back the plant so it would not touch either of you, of course."

"Cas," Theo admonished.

"Come on," said Sophia. "The sooner Sage attends to him, the better."

At the top of the narrow staircase, they reached a room made entirely of stone, with pillars and a vaulted ceiling. A fire roared in a great fireplace, and the windowless walls on either side of it were hung with tapestries. Both the tapestries were maps: woven maps that showed every detail of the Eerie Sea and the region south of it. Before the fire was a long wooden table, where two other elderly women sat, waiting for them.

"Good evening," one of them said as she stood. She had short white hair, cut unevenly in wayward tufts, and a broad smile that was unexpectedly warm. "I am Sage. Please forgive Borage her peculiar welcome. She insisted on meeting you alone."

"Because they came to see *me*," Borage pointed out.

"Yes, Borage, but we are *all* glad to see them. And they would not have arrived without Ash's canoe, as you so rightly pointed out."

The third woman, Ash, nodded with a timid smile. "I'm glad Birke carried you here safely," she said, her voice barely audible.

Now that they stood together in the firelight, Sophia could see the resemblance among the three sisters. They all had rather pointed features, with sharp noses and wide mouths, and they carried themselves like women half their age. In contrast to Sage's tufts of short hair, Ash had a long white braid that reached nearly to her waist, and Borage's hair was an untidy cluster of pins and starflowers. The sisters wore long, simple tunics sashed at the waist, and Sophia suspected, having caught a glance of a loom in the corner, that they wove their own clothes—and perhaps their tapestries as well.

"Sit down, please," Sage said. Theo sank at once into one of the wooden chairs. Taking a small basket, filled with what looked like moss, from the table, Sage turned to Casanova. "Shall I tend to your arm, Grant?"

"Thank you," Casanova said. He put down his pack and approached the table, folding back his sleeve to reveal his red, blistered forearm. Sophia winced.

"I'm afraid you will need to take that off so we can wash it," Sage said. "The poison will have soaked into the fabric."

After a moment's hesitation, Casanova pulled off his cotton shirt. Sophia realized at once that he was not embarrassed to be shirtless, but rather reluctant to bare his scars. They covered most of his chest and much of his back. She stopped herself from gasping and turned away.

Borage met her horrified gaze with a smile. "Yes," she said. "Grant wears it on his skin, the cost of war. Would that every man were forced to wear the cost so visibly."

"Borage," Ash said, her tone reprimanding.

"What?" Borage scowled. "If everyone were so marked by the idiocy of war, perhaps it would provoke greater prudence."

"I agree with you," Casanova said quietly, holding out his arm while Sage spread the green poultice over his forearm.

"I know you do," said Borage. "That's why I'm not biting my tongue. My sisters seem to think there is a place for delicacy where war is concerned." She made a derisive noise. "Utter nonsense. There is nothing delicate about it." She turned to Sophia. "You are here to stop a war, and I intend to help you. And though I know you are probably hungry, and Ash has promised to set out a banquet, we should begin. Time is very short."

"Will what we have to do take so long?" Sophia asked apprehensively.

Borage gave another one of her piercing laughs. "I suppose you are under the impression that you left Oakring this morning."

Sophia felt a sudden stab of dread. *Have I lost track of time even more than I realized?* But Theo and Casanova looked as perplexed as she felt. "Yes—we left this morning."

Borage chuckled, and again her laughter made Sophia unsure. "Today is the nineteenth of August. You left Oakring five days ago."

Sophia gasped. "No! How is that possible?"

"You are mistaken," Casanova said at the same time.

"No mistake. It took you five days to reach us." Borage seemed very pleased, as if observing the workings of a convincing magic trick.

"It is the glacier," Ash told them in her quiet voice. "You are right that the distance is a day's journey, but the glacier changes things. Time is unruly there. Unsteady and unpredictable. We have seen some travelers spend years in the tunnels, unawares."

Sophia realized with sudden panic that the day of reckoning, the day upon which the armies would descend into Turtleback Valley, was only hours away. The time she'd counted on to make the Clime's memory map was already gone. "But then we must leave right now!" she exclaimed.

"Why do you think I told you that time was short?" Borage asked, exasperated.

Sophia shook her head in despair. "I didn't know. I didn't understand."

"Borage is alarming you unnecessarily," Sage said, giving her sister a sharp look. "There is *plenty* of time. There," she said, looking at Casanova's arm, which she had wrapped in clean cloth. "You should leave that for two days, and the rash will slowly subside. Now," she said, replacing her materials in the little basket, "Theo will rest by the fire; Ash and I will finish preparing the meal; and Sophia will make the map with Borage. Then we will eat together, for though it feels like only a day has passed, your bodies will soon start to realize that they are exhausted and hungry."

Sophia felt calmer when Sage had finished speaking. She could see that Casanova and Theo, too, were ready to take her advice.

"Thank you," Casanova said. "You have prepared for every circumstance."

Sage smiled. "The consequence and benefit of knowing too much."

"Fine. Good. Come along, then," Borage said to Sophia unceremoniously, pointing toward a door at the back of the room. "We go to the workroom."

BORAGE'S WORKROOM WAS in a turret. The walls were curved, lined with ash-wood shelves that were overloaded with books. Narrow windows looked out into the starry sky.

Disorder reigned. A round table in the center of the room formed an island, and the island was crowded with every manner of tool and implement. Sophia recognized tongs and a hammer, bellows and an awl, scissors and paintbrushes. The confusion reminded her of Shadrack's work spaces—it was a disorder born of activity and enthusiasm, not neglect.

"I've already made my part of the map," Borage announced, skirting piles of books, an empty cage, and what appeared to be a wasp's nest.

"How did you know?" Sophia ventured, while Borage rummaged through the assorted contents of her workroom.

"Know what?"

"That we were coming. That we needed a map."

Borage stopped to look at her with incredulity, as if astonished to hear so inane a question. "The same way we know anything. Through the old one. The one you call 'New Occident.'"

"But my friends Goldenrod and Bittersweet also speak to the old one—and still they do not know everything everywhere."

"We don't know everything everywhere, either." Borage scowled.

"But . . ."

Borage put her hands on her hips and let out a huff of

impatience. "When you talk to Iron Theo, do you know everything *he* knows?"

"Iron Theo?" Sophia asked, confused.

Borage waved away the question. "That's a joke of ours. Don't get distracted—Theodore. Do you know everything he knows?"

"Of course not."

"But can you ask him questions about things he knows that you don't? Such as how Casanova got his scars, or what Theo did to Major Merret, or how he knows Wilkie Graves?"

Sophia blinked rapidly. "Yes," she said. "I can ask him questions. And most of the time, he'll tell me. Not always."

"Exactly!" Borage exclaimed. "We ask the old one, and most of the time it tells us. Not always." She turned away as if this concluded the matter, and reinvigorated her search. "Where is it, now?" she muttered, pushing aside the objects on the table. "Ah!" She triumphantly held up a long cylinder. "Here it is." She handed it to Sophia. "See if you can figure it out," she said, mischief in her voice.

Sophia took the cylinder in her hands. It was a metal tube covered with leather. One end had a removable lid made of glass. The other end had an eyepiece. "Is it a telescope?"

Borage rubbed her hands together and grinned. "Guess again."

Sophia took off the lid. There was something inside—a roll of paper. She pulled it out carefully. A very crude map labeled "The Stone Age" showed a riverine route from a mound identified as "The Glacier." The route ran directly north until it reached a pear-shaped body of water: "Moat," and, within it, a small island: "Home."

Mystified, Sophia rolled up the paper once more, returned it to the cylinder, and replaced the lid. She looked through the eyepiece. For a moment, she saw nothing. Then the cylinder shifted in her hand, and light moved through the tube, creating a sudden constellation of shapes. The route she had just taken to the island appeared before her: the misshapen stones, the slender river through the rock, the still pond, the towering island. As the cylinder turned slightly, the light winked and the angle of her passage changed. She caught her breath. "I don't know what it is, but it is beautiful." She put the instrument down. "Is it a map reader? It seems to show what the map describes."

Borage was unexpectedly abashed by the compliment. She took her creation back and looked at it fondly. "Thank you. I call it a 'mirrorscope.' There are mirrors inside, and they combine with the light and the map to show its contents."

The images were still behind Sophia's eyes. "Can I put *any* map inside it?"

"Of course. That is the idea."

She fumbled in her satchel for her worn pocket map of upper New York. Rolling it carefully, she tucked it into the empty scope that Borage handed her and replaced the glass lid.

Falling leaves, a path through the woods, a bridge over a rushing river, a cluster of houses nestled in a valley at dusk, a mountain pass in the snow: as she turned the cylinder, one image after another appeared. These were not memories, for the map was not a memory map. It carried no sounds or smells, no sentiments; but it nonetheless conveyed a crystalline sense of how the paths rendered on the map would look to a traveler.

"So wonderful!" Sophia exclaimed, smiling with delight as she lowered the scope. Then she paused. "But how can we use it to make a memory map of the Clime?"

"I don't know," Borage said matter-of-factly. "That is your part."

Sophia stared at her, aghast. "What do you mean?"

"Just that. I know my scope is the receptacle for the map, but the map itself has to be made by you."

"*From then on, the map you follow must be your own,*" murmured Sophia. She felt a sinking sensation.

For the first time, Borage looked puzzled. "I thought you would have the map that goes inside."

"I don't! I have no idea what it even looks like."

The old woman was silent for a moment, and Sophia wondered if she would fly into a sudden rage. But instead she burst into laughter. "Well, well," she said, grinning widely. "You'll have to find the answer before tomorrow, then, won't you?"

35

BIRKE'S VOYAGE

—*1892, August 19: 18-Hour 01*—

Most often the characters in Elodean (Eerie) stories are named after animals or plants that supposedly reflect the character's qualities. But sometimes the associations with that plant or animal are surprising. For example, one story related to me about someone named Rose cast the character as a cunning and indefatigable warrior—not, perhaps, what we would imagine for such a name. But the Elodean explained to me that the wild rosebush is tenacious and tough, with a protective armor of tiny spines.

—From Sophia Tims's Reflections on a Journey to the Eerie Sea

THE MEAL SAGE and Ash had prepared was waiting on the table. Sophia recalled Smokey's warning as she looked at the food and wondered where it had come from: corn porridge with mushrooms, bread and butter, summer apples baked with honey. Still, she was very hungry, as Sage had predicted. Casanova had already served himself a full plate; he seemed to have accepted the three sisters' hospitality entirely. She took his cue, gratefully, and joined them.

"Sophia does not know what goes in the mirrorscope," Borage announced, helping herself to bread.

"What does that mean?" Theo asked, his mouth already full.

Sophia held up the mirrorscope and explained its purpose. "I suppose I am meant to create a map of the Clime, but I have no idea yet how to do it." She shook her head, dejected. "Shadrack never got to that part in our lessons. I've only ever learned to read memory maps, not make them."

"Well, you'll have to learn yourself," Borage snapped.

Sage gave her a look. "Yes, Borage, she knows that."

"Perhaps we are to help her," Ash suggested quietly. "After all, it is the three of us who converse most with the old ones. We know their thoughts quite well."

"We *did* help," said Borage. "Sophia would never have known to make the mirrorscope, would you?"

"That's certainly true. I wouldn't even recognize this as a map reader if you hadn't told me."

"Knowing their thoughts is not the same as mapping their memories," Sage reflected. "I am sure Sophia will discover the way." She held the basket of bread out toward Theo, whose plate was already empty.

"But there's no time!" Sophia's stomach was in knots, and she was having difficulty eating, though the food was delicious.

"Here's what we will do," Sage said, pushing back her chair. "Sophia?" She went to the tapestry that hung at the left side of the fireplace. "This map shows where we are—here." She took up the poker and pointed to a gray circle in a tear-shaped blue lake. Narrow blue passageways fanned out from the lake in every direction, including south. "These are the streams that wind through the Stone Age," Sage said, tapping some of the blue ribbons. "And here is the glacier, to the southeast. Birke will carry you this way, southwest, to avoid it altogether." She trailed the poker along a riverine route that cut through the gray Stone Age and into the green lands south of them. "This stream runs quite far, look. All the way here, through upper New York, and into..." She pointed at a green shape that looked vaguely familiar to Sophia.

"Turtleback Valley!" she exclaimed.

"Precisely."

"Birke can carry us all the way there?" Sophia wondered.

"What she means is: Does our sorcery extend into New Occident?" Borage commented from the table.

"I—" Sophia began. "Well, I didn't mean sorcery, but I do not even know where your realm begins and ends."

"It is a little grand to call it our 'realm,'" Sage said with a smile. "I don't know what you heard in Oakring, but I suspect they remember things rather differently than we do."

"They said you were banished here," Theo put in bluntly, "for attempting to remake New Occident."

"And," Sophia added, "that you came here to make your own Age."

The three sisters exchanged glances, and Sophia saw in their eyes many years of disagreements. "That is true, in a manner of speaking," Sage said.

Borage frowned and stared at the table with an embarrassed air.

"It took many years for the Stone Age to become what you see now," Sage added gently.

"It was a disaster," Borage said curtly, not looking up. "Or, rather, many disasters, one after the other."

Sophia waited, hoping for more explanation.

"It is more true to say that we have exiled ourselves here," Ash said. She reached out and tenderly covered Borage's hand with her own. "The fewer people who come here, the better. Apart from the three of you, no one has come to the Stone Age for more than two years."

"We did see someone," Casanova commented. "In what you call the Stone Age—following us along as the canoe carried us northward."

Borage chuckled. "One of Ash's tree-children snuck out after all," she said, squeezing her sister's hand. "Sage has tried to keep all this as decorous as possible, but truth will out." She grinned.

"What do you mean?" asked Sophia.

"We did not wish you to be alarmed as you traveled here," Sage explained. "Let us say that you are only seeing one side of our world. Not all of it."

"My tree-children are not alarming," Ash whispered.

"Not to you, my dear," Borage commented, pushing her plate aside. "But that is the point. Most people *do* find animated bundles of roots disconcerting, especially when they are bound up with string in that way. And their voices are a bit odd, you have to admit. Like creaking floorboards." She sighed. "But I admit some of my experiments had even worse results."

"But then the people of the Indian Territories have it wrong," Sophia said, surprised. "Even the Eerie."

"Of course they have it wrong." Borage scowled. "They are ignorant. What they know about the workings of our Age would not fill this cup," she said bitterly, holding up her cup of water. There was a long silence as Sage and Ash looked at their sister, waiting.

Finally, when Borage seemed unwilling to say more, Sage spoke. "What Borage does not say," she put in gently, "is that we were ignorant as well—at first. We shared the assumptions of our fellow Elodeans, and those assumptions turned out to be wrong."

"What assumptions?" Sophia asked, intensely curious.

"The easiest way to think of it is as a room," Sage said, gesturing to the space around them. "If someone from your city of Boston were to imagine the relationship between a people and their Age, they might think of it as a person inside a room. What the Eerie know is that this 'room' is sentient. The Eerie imagine a living, waking room that can hear you when you laugh and shout inside it."

Sophia nodded. "Yes—that fits what Goldenrod has told me."

"And this is why we hoped to make an Age," Ash put in quietly. "For cannot the occupant change rooms, and even create a better, more beautiful room?"

"This was the mistaken assumption," Sage continued. "For, as we learned, it is not accurate to imagine the Age as the room. It is more accurate to imagine the Age as *another person* in the room." She paused and looked at them for acknowledgment.

Sophia, Theo, and Casanova looked back at her in silence,

dumbfounded. "I don't understand," Theo said frankly.

Borage let out a low, bitter laugh. "Imagine how annoying it is to be in a room with someone who ignores you completely. You talk to them and they seem not to hear you. You try to persuade them not to light a fire on the floor, and they do it anyway, and then when you stamp the fire out, they look around shocked, trying to figure out what happened to their fire. Or," she said, growing more animated, "they start swinging an ax in every direction, smashing the furniture and the walls, and finally hitting you in the shoulder. *More* than annoying!" she fumed.

"You mean," Casanova said slowly, "that the actions we take have consequences for the Clime. They upset the Clime."

"And that what you see happening in the Age around you are responses," Sage said.

"The rain of ash," Sophia said, with dawning realization. "The char."

Borage stormed to her feet. "Among other things. This war is wreaking havoc on every Age it touches," she raged, stamping over to the tapestry map. "Sinkholes, storms, weirwinds, and more, I'm sure, to come." She jabbed at the map with a broom. "There is a crack in the earth—*here*—that runs a mile long, and no one seems to wonder where it came from!"

"So the war is causing all of this?" Theo asked, perplexed.

Borage whirled to glare at him. "You can't keep firing a pistol in a closed room without consequences. Keep firing that pistol and you're going to hit someone. And make them very, *very* angry."

THE THREE SISTERS walked with them all the way down to the island's shore, where the canoe waited under the starry sky. "Sleep as much as you can," Sage advised. "You can trust Birke to carry you safely."

"I hope you find the solution, Sophia," Borage said, her voice unexpectedly earnest. "We have mostly left your Age behind, but some part of me still grieves for the destruction I have seen in it—past and future."

"Certainly you will find it," Ash said. "This is for you," she added, handing Sophia a roll of paper. "For the map you are making of the way through the glacier and the Stone Age. It will preserve the memories more clearly."

Sophia realized that it was a roll of birch bark. "Oh, thank you!"

She had packed the mirrorscope in her satchel, close to hand, and as she said good-bye to the feared, disowned, and outcast sisters who had given them such an unexpected welcome, half of her mind was still turning over the problem of the memory map, as it had been ever since she and Borage had left the turreted workroom.

She intended to ponder the question more fully as they traveled.

Casanova pushed them off, stepping quickly into the canoe and taking his seat at the stern. Theo had already curled up against the hull. Sophia settled herself so that her head was at the bow and her feet lay parallel to Theo's. Facing northward, she saw Casanova's silhouette and, behind it, the larger shape of the island castle. Only one light shone in it now, pale yellow but steady. As they began to move, she glanced upward at the clear sky, almost aglow with starlight. There was no moon. The constellations appeared motionless, despite the speed of the canoe.

The murmuring sound of the water beneath them shifted as Birke left the lake and entered the stream that led southwest. It was a low murmur, quiet and calm, and Sophia imagined it was how the three sisters would sound now, sitting around their fire, talking of the travelers who had visited their realm.

Without meaning to, Sophia fell asleep. Her dreams were strange and vivid. She heard high-pitched laughter that sounded almost like birds chirping. A forest came into view, and among the trunks, children were running, chasing one another. It was their laughter that rose and fell, giddy and gleeful. One of the children ran toward her and threw his arms around her. Only then did she see that he was not a child, but only moved like one. Every part of his body was a tangled cluster of roots, and he was clothed in a fine film of thread like a cobweb. His eyes were little brown nuts, and his laughing mouth had no teeth, only a green leaf of a tongue. He pressed his head against her side and cried, "Hiding, hiding!"

The dream shifted, and now Sophia looked out onto a flat plateau of stone, where a giant made of rock tipped his head back and raised his arms high. He seemed about to summon the sky, but instead he suddenly swung down and smashed his head against the ground, as if intent on breaking himself to pieces. The ground trembled, and the giant raised his head again and brought it down once more, and again and again and again, until his great forehead shattered and the splintered fragments cascaded outward like the shards of a broken vessel. Then Sophia heard the voice that had been calling uselessly to him all along, wailing now with anguish, "No, Rore, no! How could you? How could you?" The words trailed off into weeping, and Sophia felt a deep pang of grief, for the stone giant and for the woman whose wordless lament went on and on.

In the last dream, there was a storm. Sophia felt the ground beneath her rumbling. The sky was heavy with rain, and the clouds seemed to press down upon her. They were there, just beside her: great angry clouds of fury, in which the lightning shuddered like a spasm of violence. Sophia felt herself pushed back, and back. The clouds would pin her to the ground, they would eat her alive, they would destroy her. Her mouth was filled with water. She could not breathe. All the air was gone, and the lightning flashed now through water, a cruel stabbing of light that was meant to end her, end her completely.

Sophia woke with a start, sitting up so suddenly that the canoe rocked. The first thing she saw was Casanova's scarred face watching her. She realized that she could see him because the sky was light; a gray dawn was upon them. Dark clouds overhead recalled her dream, and for a moment she imagined that it would begin again: the clouds would enclose and then suffocate her. Her breath came hard and ragged; her heart was still pounding. She shook her head sharply.

"Nightmares," Casanova said quietly. "I have them, too." He motioned with his head at the way before them. "But don't worry. You've left them behind now, and things are going well here in the waking world. We've made good progress."

They were deep in the woods, floating rapidly along a stream that gurgled over mossy stones, past pines and maples. The air was moist and heavy with threatening rain. Birds cried out urgently, as they do before a storm, and only then did it occur to Sophia that it was the first time she had heard birdsong since entering the glacier.

She looked down and saw that she was still clutching the roll of birch bark that Ash had given her, and slowly her thoughts ordered themselves. Her eyes drifted upward to the trees around them. *Dreams,* she thought, *dreams that are memories. Just like the wheel of wood and the piece of antler. I was remembering what this birch has seen.*

Theo woke up then. He looked around sleepily and adjusted his sling, wincing slightly. "What?" he said, in response to Sophia's stare.

"I was thinking," she said slowly. "About memory maps. What makes them. Not who—what. How they are made. Especially when they are memories that aren't human. Is it a person who makes them, or are they made by the memories themselves? Do the memories gather on the substance from which the map is then chosen?"

Theo scrunched up his face. "What?"

Sophia's eyes opened wide. "Sticky," she said with a burst of awareness. "Casanova, he said they were sticky."

Casanova nodded and then winked, tapping his nose, in imitation of Pip Entwhistle. "So he did, so he did."

"What are you two talking about?" Theo asked.

"Precious stones are sticky," she said excitedly. "They gather memories more easily than anything." It occurred to her then that mapmaking, great mapmaking of the kind she admired, was as much about inspiration as it was about skill. What had inspired Shadrack to make memory maps out of pennies? Was it the long years he had spent devising maps that revealed the hidden past, or was it a momentary insight when a shopkeeper handed him a palmful of change? Was it a beggar on the corner with hands outstretched, asking for coins? Was it the feel of the metal clinking in Shadrack's pocket, sounding out a subtle melody that told a story about where each piece had been? Perhaps, Sophia thought, great mapmaking began with noticing such moments and really listening to them.

"Maybe I don't have to make the memory map! Maybe it is already made!" She dove into her pack and pulled out her satchel, wrestling with the contents until she had drawn out the mirrorscope and then a small leather purse tied with blue string. "Garnets!" she exclaimed triumphantly. "The memories are in the garnets!"

"But you got those in Ausentinia," Theo said, confused.

"I did. But somehow—*somehow*—I am sure that when we see them through this mirrorscope, we will find that they are not from Ausentinia at all. They are from here. And they hold the memories of the old one that lives and breathes around us."

As she opened the mirrorscope, Sophia thought about her

last few days in Ausentinia. She remembered when Alba had handed her the purse of garnets—they had seemed so much less important than the map accompanying them. Sophia had thought of them as currency of some kind: pretty pieces of red stone whose value lay in how they could be traded and what they might procure in exchange. She realized now that she was wrong. The garnets were not to be traded; they were precious stones in a different way altogether—and yet the way she had gotten it wrong allowed her to connect the pennies with the garnets and make the leap. She carefully poured the garnets into the mirrorscope's compartment, then fastened the lid. For a moment she paused, looking at the instrument apprehensively.

"Well, what are you waiting for?" Theo prompted. "Try it."

"What if it doesn't work?"

He grinned. "Then you'll figure out what does. Try it."

Sophia took a deep breath and put the mirrorscope to her eye, pointing the glass end toward the growing sunlight. Her vision was flooded with crimson. For a moment she saw a beautiful constellation of red and white, and then it was gone. The memories of the old one filled her mind. She had expected something like her encounter with Ausentinia—an immersion into some unrecognizable landscape. But this was nothing like that. The memories contained in the garnets were recent and recognizable, if not familiar. They were one kind of memory, over and over again, recurring with terrible variety and ingenuity and yet repetitive in their horrors. There were people in all of them. And what the people felt, the old one felt. Sophia had not understood until then that the old one not only watched and listened, but *sensed*. A brief pang of heartache echoed in the old one like a sharp cry in a cavern: filling every dark chamber, vibrating into the deep darkness. This was how it could know so much in so many places—every twitch of gladness and grief was amplified a thousandfold. The question was not how the old one could know and see so much; the question was how the old one could hope to ignore any of it: the dull ache of a doctor dressing one wound after another; the anguish of a mother burying her son; the terrible uncertainty of waiting for a soldiering father to return; the bitterness of hunger in the aftermath of razing fire; the sense of futility, hearing the war cries once more; the emptiness at the sight of a buried town; the fevered desire to be done with life, to be gone from the world, when everyone who mattered in it was gone.

There was too much: too much misery, too much agony, too much despair.

Sophia dropped the mirrorscope into her lap. Her hands were trembling. She did not know how much time had passed; every moment had seemed to unfold an entire lifetime of pain.

"It didn't work?" Theo asked. Then he saw her expression. "What happened?"

Sophia could not speak. She squeezed her eyes shut, trying to forget what she had seen. It was impossible. Red filled her vision; cries filled her ears; she felt a tearing at her chest that seemed both cruelly fresh and achingly old. Her breath moved through her with difficulty, as if something inside of her, now crushed, was blocking the way. When she opened her eyes, Theo and Casanova were staring at her, worried and perplexed.

"The old one remembers war," she said, her voice faltering. "Wars of the past and wars of the future. They are never-ending."

36
SEVEN WITNESSES

—1892, August 17: 10-Hour 11—

In particular circumstances, individuals from other Ages may be granted temporary endorsement, a short-term passage that permits them entry to New Occident. The sponsoring party in New Occident must apply directly to the Minister of Relations with Foreign Ages, who will grant the endorsements on a case-by-case basis. Justification for these endorsements will be made at the end of each parliament session by the Minister. It should be noted that this temporary endorsement will not be granted for commercial purposes, only for extraordinary circumstances of diplomatic necessity, such as the visit of a foreign dignitary for the purpose of establishing a treaty.

—Parliament decree, June 14, 1891

SHADRACK KNOCKED ON the door of Broadgirdle's inner office, which adjoined the War Room. "Yes, Cassandra," came the reply. "It's unlocked. As always," he added, a trifle sourly. Shadrack opened the door and stood waiting for the figure behind the desk to look up from the neat pile of papers before him. "What is it?" the prime minister asked, without raising his head.

"There are some people here waiting to see you," Shadrack said.

Broadgirdle looked up at the sound of Shadrack's voice, and surprise flashed across his face. "What are you doing here?" He half smiled. "I thought you would be on the road to Nochtland by now," he said, his voice edged with malice.

"I found that, after all, it made more sense to stay."

"Excellent," Broadgirdle said, rubbing his hands together, his smile widening. "I do love a good fight."

"So I hear," Shadrack replied. He turned and left the office deliberately, heading toward the War Room.

"What do you mean by that?" Broadgirdle called after him.

"If you would follow me, you'll see."

Shadrack walked down the corridor, and after a moment Broadgirdle followed him into the War Room. There, Inspector Grey stood holding a piece of paper, and he motioned to the two officers who stood beside him. Without a word, they moved to stand on either side of Broadgirdle.

"What is this?" Broadgirdle asked with a scornful smile.

"Prime Minister Gordon Broadgirdle," Inspector Grey said, reading from the paper in his hands, "I have been ordered by the parliament judges to conduct you from your office to a parliament hearing, which in this instance will be held in the State House parliament chamber. Due to the nature of your responsibilities as prime minister, there can be no ordinary arrest and trial at this time. The parliament judges ask you to answer immediately to the accusations."

Broadgirdle frowned, the levity of his expression giving way to hostility. "What accusations?"

"Allow me to continue," Grey said, without looking up. "You will be conducted by my officers to the hearing chambers, where a legal representative appointed by parliament will inform you of the accusations. I have been urged by the judges to add that this hearing must be conducted with the utmost discretion and speed, with the hope that the affairs of state will suffer minimal disruption." He raised his eyes from the paper. "Please follow me."

For a moment Broadgirdle stared impassively at Grey, and Shadrack thought that the man would burst into rage—or worse. But then the hard expression shifted, as if with awareness of some new perspective, and the supercilious smile that was so characteristic of him returned. "Of course, Inspector," Broadgirdle said, his rich voice edged with mirth. "Let us by all means conduct this quickly and discreetly, so I can get back to the business of governing this nation."

Unfazed, Inspector Grey nodded to his officers, who led Broadgirdle out of the War Room. Shadrack walked behind them, nodding reassuringly to the assistants who leaned out of their offices and peered into the hallway. "Please return to your work," he told them. "The prime minister is assisting the police with official business."

The winding trip through the building brought them finally to the great hall where parliament met. The ninety members, previously summoned, were seated in their chairs. Nine judges, selected by parliament from the district courts of New Occident, sat on a raised bench across from them. At a table to the left of the dais was a middle-aged man in a black suit and barrister's robes. To the right of the dais was another table, this one with an older man in a similar costume, accompanied by seven people.

The seven people made a strange sight. Even to Shadrack, who knew them all by name, they were something of an odd assortment: Pip Entwhistle, with his white, square-cut beard and bulbous nose; Gerard Sorensen, with his perennial air of surprised disarray, who would not take his eyes from the table; the Eerie named Solandra, whose green hands were clasped before her and who regarded Broadgirdle with undisguised contempt; her father Lycium, whose green complexion seemed to darken at the sight of the prime minister; Susan Eby, a slight woman with black hair braided into two neat buns behind her ears; Victor Manse, a tall man with a tired expression and a worn hat, which he handled nervously; and Hannah Selvidge, an elderly woman in a floral dress with puffed sleeves, who looked hard at Broadgirdle through her spectacles. None of them seemed to belong in the State House.

In fact, the only person who appeared entirely at ease in the silent, austere room was Cassandra Pierce, who sat apart from the rest in the area ordinarily reserved for the public. She and Shadrack were the two-person audience to the strange hearing that began as Broadgirdle was led forward. "Prime Minister," one of the judges said, rising to her feet. Her round, impassive face considered Broadgirdle without expression. "Mr. Appleby has been appointed as your counsel. He will apprise you of the accusations and discuss your recommended response. As of this moment, there will be no recesses, and no one will leave the room until this hearing is concluded. You may confer."

The judge sat down. The members of parliament and the attorney for the state, who had also been standing, sat down. In the considerable rustle made by their movements, Broadgirdle and Appleby began a furtive conversation. From his seat beside Cassandra, Shadrack could hear nothing, but he could see the shape of the conversation reflected in Broadgirdle's face as Appleby apprised him of the accusations and suggested a course of action. For the most part, Broadgirdle was silent and unmoved. No doubt the presence of these particular witnesses led him to guess the nature of the accusations. Broadgirdle listened with eyebrows raised, unimpressed, for several minutes. He seemed to answer Appleby's questions with a dismissive wave of the hand. Appleby launched into an earnest appeal, leaning toward the prime minister and gesturing to the judges. After nearly a minute of silence, Broadgirdle nodded his assent.

Appleby rose to his feet, seemingly relieved. "We are ready to proceed, Your Honor."

"Thank you," the judge said. She took the top sheet of the pile of papers before her and read aloud. "Prime Minister Gordon Broadgirdle, we are here today to inquire into the potential criminality of several actions taken by you, both before and during your tenure as prime minister of New Occident. If these inquiries suggest that criminal activities did occur, you will be immediately removed from office. You will then be formally arrested and charged, and a trial will take place through the proper channels. Allow me to reiterate," she said, putting the paper down, "this is not a trial to determine your innocence or guilt. This is merely a hearing to establish the likelihood of criminal acts, and based on the outcome of this hearing, charges relating to those criminal acts may or may not be brought against you. Is this understood, counsel?"

"Understood," Appleby said.

The judge nodded and returned to her paper. "We are here to inquire into the following: Did you or did you not remain in New Occident without proper documentation after the border closure? Did you or did you not present false credentials when seeking political office? Did you or did you not engage in the illegal traffic of human beings, banned as part of the treaty negotiations with New Akan in 1810? Did you or did you not forcibly detain four people in the winter and spring of 1892, keeping them against their will at your property in Lexington, Massachusetts?" The judge turned from Broadgirdle to the table with the odd assortment of people. "Is the attorney for the state prepared to call witnesses?"

The older gentleman rose to his feet. "I am, Your Honor."

"Thank you, Mr. Fenton. You may proceed."

Mr. Fenton was the kind of man who was easy to overlook. Everything about him was nondescript. His voice was quiet and unassuming; his clothes beneath the open robes were plain and unassuming; and the features of his face, fleshy and soft beneath a neat haircut and a neat gray beard, were bland and unassuming. Only his eyes gave him away. As he strode to the dais, he gave Shadrack a quick glance, and a sudden current seemed to pass between them. "I would like to call Phillip Entwhistle, also known as Pip, to give testimony."

Pip rose to his feet.

"There is no witness box here, Mr. Entwhistle, so you may remain where you are."

Pip nodded.

"Would you please identify the man sitting beside my colleague, Mr. Appleby?"

"Happy to. He is Gordon Broadgirdle, current prime minister of New Occident."

"And do you know him personally?"

"I do, but not as Gordon Broadgirdle."

There was a murmur of surprise from the gallery of parliament members.

"I knew him years ago as Wilkie Graves. And before that, I knew him by the nickname 'Terrier.'"

The murmur from Parliament grew more consternated. "Silence, please," the judge called.

"Thank you, Mr. Entwhistle. Would you please, in your own words, tell us how you came to know this man?"

"I will, Mr. Fenton, though I must admit it takes me back to a time I would rather not recall. I first met Terrier when I was a young man, and, frankly, not a very good man. I was young and stupid and much too taken with gambling. I would bet on anything. I would bet on whether there would be rain in the afternoon. Horse and dog races were as intoxicating as wine to me. Rather bad wine that always left me the worse for wear.

"I say that not to excuse what I did, but to explain how it is that I traveled to a dusty patch in the middle of the Baldlands, on the rumor of a gambling game that many of my dissolute fellows had warmly recommended. I arrived, and I found that it was much as they had described. A man named Herrick was running dog fights."

Pip paused, and the members of parliament seemed to pause with him, waiting for the significance of this strange circumstance. "I stayed at the dog fights longer than I should have. The town nearby had its own unsavory appeal, and it was easy enough to spend a day at the dog fight, an evening at the tavern, and a night passed out under the stars." He shook his head. "Thinking back on it, I wonder how my stomach could take it." He sighed. "And the dog fights drew such crowds. My, they were nasty. Horrible spectacles, in retrospect. Blood sport. Can't imagine how I ever watched. The dogs tore each other limb for limb. At the time, I'm ashamed to say, I found it exciting. People would bring their dogs, and you always hoped they would somehow surprise you and win the day, but Herrick's dogs were beasts, and they always won. There was something that pulled you back—wanting to see those beasts of Herrick's finally beaten, but somehow always knowing it wouldn't happen. Until the man with the kerchief arrived."

Pip looked up at Broadgirdle, and a flash of something unexpected—sympathy, perhaps—brightened his eyes. "I never learned his name. He wore a red kerchief around his neck, and his boots were so worn there was no tongue on either one of them. You could see at a glance that he was down on his luck, and that he'd come to the ring to gamble with Herrick because he was desperate. He proposed something crazy, and to everyone's surprise, Herrick agreed. The man with the kerchief proposed putting not a dog in the ring, but his own son."

There was a moment's silence, and then a rumble of dismay from the parliament members.

"Oh, I know," Pip said, with a forlorn air. "It was reprehensible. It gives you a sense of what we were all like, the men standing around, that we didn't stop this deranged experiment but instead looked forward to it eagerly as another good gamble." He shook his head, appalled at himself. "He could not have been more than eight or nine. The first fight was a big one. It had drawn quite a crowd—people had come from miles around to see the boy who would fight dogs. He wore ordinary clothes. His only protection was in the form of boxing gloves and a leather helmet." Pip's voice faltered. "And he was terrified."

"Speak up please, Mr. Entwhistle."

"He was shaking when he stepped into the ring," Pip said, only a trifle more loudly. "But like the brutes we were, we didn't do anything about it. We cheered. I am glad to say we cheered *for* him, but that is not much comfort, is it?" He paused and took a deep breath. "Well, I have no wish to tell you the details of that fight. I will mention only that when the dog first bit him on the leg, the boy ran to the corner and begged his father to take him out. He was weeping so hard and scrambling to escape, and his father pushed him back in. I remember clearly what he said to the boy: 'Get in there, Terrier. Get in there. Are you no better than a *dog*?' I suppose he meant it as some kind of encouragement, but it sounded instead like an insult. The question stayed with me. At the time, I was madly cheering along with the rest of them, but later that question began to strike me differently. You could even say that the cruel words spoken to Terrier were responsible for ending my gambling, for when I stood at the racetracks or stood at the dice table, I would hear that question in my ears: 'Are you no better than a *dog*?' No, frankly, no," Pip said, shaking his head. "I was not."

He took another deep breath. "Terrier won that first fight, and I suppose he made his father some money. I stayed for a few more, and then, as I said, something in me seemed to turn. Wish I could say it was righteous disgust or another noble impulse, but it was not. It was more like boredom. If I'd had my senses about me, I would have gone back to those fights and taken Terrier out of the ring and found him some place of safety. Instead, I left that filthy patch of desert and made my way elsewhere. And the words of Terrier's father, as I have said, gradually curbed my excesses.

"I did not see him again for more than a decade. It's a wonder I recognized him at all, frankly, since he had changed in more ways than one. He was a man, not a boy. He was no longer in the ring, of course. And the air of terror that he had had in the ring was replaced by a kind of swagger. How did I recognize him? Well!" Pip exclaimed, tapping the side of his nose. "You may be surprised. He looked exactly like his father. Indeed, he was a younger and less-impoverished version of that man with the kerchief, but he was the spitting image. There was no denying it.

"I came upon him at an inn in the southern Baldlands. In those days I was already a merchant, though I mostly sold worthless dreck. Terrier was sitting by himself at a booth, and I approached him. Perhaps I hoped to give him something like an apology for having stood by when he was thrown into the ring. Or perhaps I was merely looking to sell some dreck. Who can say? I cannot pretend that even then, after I had stopped gambling, I was always guided by better instincts.

"I approached him and said, 'You look familiar. Can it be I am standing before the great fighter known as Terrier?' I said this with an admiring air, you understand. For a moment something like suspicion passed across his face, and then he gave a broad grin. 'Certainly, though it's been many years since anyone called me that.'

"I tell you—he was entirely changed. He had a great, booming voice filled with confidence—a man used to getting his way. We had a meal and a drink together, and I had a chance to know him better. Terrier told me that his name was Wilkie Graves. His father, he said, had passed away some years earlier—I did not ask how. Throughout the entire conversation, what he did for a living did not come up. I suppose I dreaded asking, thinking that he might still be caught up in the world of fighting and gambling, and that world had little allure for me now. Instead, we talked about dreck. I showed him the books and pamphlets and other little scraps that I had with me, and he expressed great interest and told me about other pieces of dreck that he had come across. I remember he bought a page of newspaper from me—I was glad to have made a sale that day.

"Then we each repaired to our beds, and only the next morning when I saw him outside the inn, hitching his wagon, did I learn by accident what his new profession was." Pip looked across at Broadgirdle, whose expression throughout the entire testimony had been a mask of scornful indifference. "He was holding a crate of food, with jugs of water and a couple of loaves of bread and a handful of apples. As we talked, he opened the locked wagon and put the crate inside, on the floor. There were three women and two men shackled there. Graves saw my expression, and he gave me a quizzical look. I struggled for words. 'Transporting criminals, I see?' I asked hopefully.

"'Criminals?' He smiled wryly. 'I'm no sheriff, Pip.' No doubt he could see the consternation written on my face. Graves considered me for a moment, and then he gave a great, deep laugh. 'You don't mind seeing a boy torn to pieces by dogs, but the sight of a few slaves in shackles makes you itchy?' He shook his head. 'You've got a strange sense of right and wrong, Entwhistle.'"

The members of parliament erupted with murmurs of horror and disbelief, and Pip waited, shaking his head sadly. "What could I say? He was right. Entirely right. I was left speechless, and Graves, with a cheerful wave, locked the wagon, climbed aboard, and made his way out of town."

MR. FENTON THANKED Pip for his testimony. In the pause between witnesses, the murmuring among the members of parliament grew louder. Shadrack caught a phrase or two and smiled. ". . . simply outrageous." "The temerity . . ." ". . . nothing more vile."

He glanced at Cassandra, who nodded slightly. "Very effective testimony," she said.

The judges had to quiet the room before Mr. Fenton could call his next witness. "Miss Susan Eby, your honors," he said, gesturing to the slight woman with the braided hair, who rose silently at the sound of her name.

She was nervous. Her hands clutched a yellow handkerchief, which she worked through her fingers as if attempting to wring every last drop of moisture from the faded fabric.

"Please take your time, Miss Eby," Mr. Fenton said reassuringly. "I am aware of the difficulties you face in being here today. The judges and I are grateful for your testimony."

Slowly, the woman raised her eyes to Fenton's face. She kept her gaze pinned upon him all throughout her testimony, seemingly afraid of what she might see if her eyes wandered. "Would you please identify the man sitting beside Mr. Appleby?"

"His name is Wilkie Graves," Miss Eby said quietly.

"Thank you. Could you please tell us, in your own words, Miss Eby, how you know him."

For several long seconds she looked into Fenton's eyes, agonized. He gave her a slight smile, and Susan Eby took a deep breath. "I met him fifteen years ago, when I was eleven. My mother and father passed away, and my sister and I were put in the home of a neighbor who ran a home for children. Only there was no one to pay for our stay, and we were not yet old enough to earn our keep. Three months and four days after we went to the home, Graves took us away. At the time I did not know he had bought us. Carol and I thought we were being adopted." Susan had rushed through her words as fast as she could, and she stopped now to take another deep breath. "We learned we were wrong when Carol was sold to a farmer near Mud Flats and I was sold to a factory six hours away. I lost touch with my sister for seven years, but after that time I ran away and found her, thank the Fates, and we were reunited."

"Do you know for certain that you and Carol were sold?" Mr. Fenton asked, as kindly as he could.

"I do," Susan said, with more firmness than she had used yet. "I saw the money change hands both times."

"And did you ever encounter Graves again?"

"I did not. After Carol and I found one another, we moved to New Akan, where there is no slaving, and we have lived there by ourselves ever since. I have not seen Graves again, thank the Fates, until this day."

"Thank you very much, Miss Eby."

Shadrack watched with some curiosity as Broadgirdle, his face unchanging, kept his eye fixed upon the balcony. He seemed entirely uninterested in the witnesses and their testimony. The members of parliament, on the other hand, grew more agitated with each one. They no longer made any attempt to conceal their disgust and disapproval, and the rapid conversations that followed Miss Eby's account were unequivocal in tone.

"Is that confidence or capitulation on the prime minister's part, I wonder," Shadrack murmured to Cassandra.

She smiled. "Of course it is confidence. Though he alone knows why."

"I would next like to call Victor Manse," Mr. Fenton declared when the judges had finally quieted the room.

Victor Manse lumbered to his feet and put his hat carefully down on the table. In response to Mr. Fenton's questions, he said in a slow, deliberate voice that he knew the man sitting beside Mr. Appleby as Wilkie Graves. "Though we always called him 'Early Graves,' those of us who knew him," he said with a wry smile, "as he had a reputation for sending those he sold to an early grave. I was bought and sold by Graves three times," he continued somberly, "because I always caused some trouble to those who bought me. I believe I even caused Graves some trouble," he added with satisfaction, "since thanks to me he had more than one unhappy customer." He gave Mr. Fenton the names and locations of those places where he had been traded, and concluded by saying that his last master had died, leaving him and the other slaves he owned free.

"Thank you, Mr. Manse. Let me call Mrs. Hannah Selvidge."

The old lady in the puffed sleeves and spectacles did not even wait for the attorney's first question. "That's Wilkie Graves, all right," she said, pointing accusingly at the indifferent Broadgirdle. 'Early' Graves, just as Vic said—we all called him that.

He had a reputation, for sure. We even joked about how many days we'd survived with him, since any amount of time with Graves between purchase and sale was perilous. You'd think he had no care for his merchandise!" she scoffed. "I imagine it would be hard to sell a dead slave, but Early Graves seemed not to worry about that, giving us just the barest crumbs to eat on the way to wherever we were going.

"Time I spent with Graves was eighteen days, and I tell you, by the end of them I was practically asking to be put on the auction block. It couldn't be worse than Graves, I figured. There was a boy working with him then—a young boy, and I'm guessing it wasn't by choice. Fates above, he was scrawny. I urged him to run away—he wasn't chained, was he? But he looked at me terrified, as if I'd suggested he jump off a cliff. That's how Graves was—he made everyone afraid of him. And the more time you spent, the more afraid you were."

Hannah Selvidge concluded her testimony with several vehemently stated facts about when and where Wilkie Graves had circulated as a slaver. And then Mr. Fenton turned his attention to Sorensen and the two Eerie.

He began with Solandra, who rose and stood with a stately air, gazing coolly across at the prime minister. It was clear that many in parliament had never seen the Eerie's distinctive green skin. She waited patiently for the whispered comments to stop before speaking.

"My name is Solandra, and I am one of the Elodeans living south of the Eerie Sea. In New Occident, I believe you call us 'Eerie.' I had no knowledge of Gordon Broadgirdle before this past year, when we came to Boston in response to a letter sent our way by Shadrack Elli, the cartologer." She nodded to Shadrack, who gave her a brief, regretful smile. He was well aware of how his request for aid had unwittingly plunged the Eerie into their nightmarish misadventure.

Solandra, her green arms crossed across her chest, turned deliberately to face the parliament judges. "We never had the chance to speak with Shadrack, for we were captured by seven men. I did not know them at the time, but I have since heard them refer to each other as 'Sandmen.' They share several qualities, among them scarred faces, a curious choice of weaponry, and an unquestioning loyalty to Gordon Broadgirdle, who soon made himself known as the architect of our capture. The purpose of our capture was quite clear. Broadgirdle had heard rumors of the Elodean gifts, and he desired to use them for his own ends in the course of the war against the west."

"And remind us when this planning for the war took place?" Mr. Fenton prompted her.

"Late autumn of 1891."

A murmur from the parliament seats reflected their collective surprise.

"Well before Broadgirdle was prime minister," Mr. Fenton clarified, in case the judges were in any doubt. "And what is this gift you speak of?"

Solandra uncrossed her arms and held out her hands, palms up. She took a breath like a long sigh, and suddenly clusters of white blooms appeared in her hands.

The members of parliament burst into urgent exclamation.

Their comments reflected awe and wonder and not a little wariness.

"Please," Mr. Fenton urged them. "Let us allow the witness to continue her explanation."

Solandra smiled. "There is little to explain. All the Elodeans have similar gifts. I believe in the Baldlands they say that people like us have the 'Mark of the Vine.' In us, the Mark is especially strong. Elodeans vary in their gift, though gifts are familial. And my daughter . . ." she said, and paused. For the first time, she seemed upset, and she swallowed hard before speaking. "My daughter," she continued, with visible effort, "has a gift that is most dangerous. The flowers she brings forth hold poison, and it is this poison that Gordon Broadgirdle has been using to fight his war."

—11-Hour 01—

INSPECTOR GREY, STANDING outside the closed doors of the parliament chamber, heard the running footfalls with apprehension. "Inspector Grey," the officer panted, rushing toward him.

"What is it, Ives?"

"Twenty men. On the State House steps."

"What do they want?"

"You'd better come yourself, Inspector."

Inspector Grey kept his pace steady as he accompanied Ives

back along the corridor to the entrance of the State House. There twenty men waited, just as his officer had reported. All of them were scarred, with long, uneven lines that ran from cheek to ear. They carried weapons: pistols and long, curved grappling hooks on ropes. "How did they know to come?" Grey asked Ives quietly.

"We don't know, sir. It must be that someone in the State House who saw us escorting the prime minister conveyed the news."

Grey nodded curtly, suddenly furious at himself for not taking greater precautions.

The man nearest to Inspector Grey stepped forward and rested his hand loosely on the grappling hook that hung at his waist. "We're here for the prime minister," the man said flatly.

"What is your interest in him?" Grey asked coolly.

"Our interest is not your concern," said the man. "We're here to take him away, and we're not leaving without him. I'm not asking."

37

THE IRON CAGE

—1892, August 20: 5-Hour 32—

The Elodean (Eerie) story-explanation for the weirwind describes a creature known as the Ording, a kind of giant magpie. It gathers trinkets of no value to anyone but itself, hoarding them as treasure. The weirwind is the Ording's manner of gathering the precious pieces of the world, blowing through to collect wonders great and small.

—From Sophia Tims's Born of the Disruption: Tales Told by Travelers

BIRKE'S PASSENGERS WERE mute as the southward-running streams took them through the woods of New Occident. They had all looked through the mirrorscope, each for only seconds, but the visions had stayed in their minds, leaving them shaken.

Overhead, the sky darkened. Beneath them, the rippling water had become inaudible—it seemed to rise and fall and splash without so much as a murmur. The birds had fallen silent. Then a high, distant keening sound began. At first Sophia could not place it, and then she knew: it was the mounting of a weirwind.

The tree branches murmured uneasily in the gathering wind. Sophia felt fear in her stomach: tense and coiled and trembling. She was afraid of what she had seen, and she was afraid of what the gathering storm might mean, and she was afraid that they would arrive too late. What if they reached the grove only to find the kind of horrors she had seen in the mirrorscope actually happening?

The fear made her mind turn in panicked circles, racing from one thought to the next, until they all ran together: memories from the birch bark; visions from the garnets; sights and sounds from the woods around her; and scenes of what might already be happening in the grove. Sophia could not open her eyes. As the howling wind grew sharper, she thought she heard voices. Who was crying out in the distance? Were they human? Where were they?

Birke plummeted down a short waterfall, and the icy spray made them all gasp. Sophia's eyes flew open. A flash of lightning cut through the dark clouds. Thunder crashed, drowning out the keening wind. Rain began to fall in heavy sheets, and the forward motion of the canoe made the droplets bite.

"Here!" Casanova shouted, holding out one of the rubber tarps that Smokey had packed. "Get down into the hull and cover yourselves."

Thunder crashed around them once more. Sophia and Theo huddled down, pulling the tarp over them and peering out uselessly into the driving rain. They could not see where they were going—yet Birke shuttled onward as steadily as ever, coursing along the turbulent waters, circling boulders that appeared suddenly out of the gray, wavering storm. The howling weirwind seemed more remote now, but now there was something else—an uneven sound more like a whistle than a howl.

"Do you hear that?" she said loudly in Theo's ear.

He nodded. "It's Fen Carver's men. It's the call."

Sophia shook her head under the tarp, signaling that she did not understand.

"They whistle before they attack," Theo said.

Sophia listened again, and now she heard the difference between the howl of the weirwind and the piercing call of the troops: a haunting rise and fall like the whistle of a dying fire.

THE RAIN DROVE down, and they drove forward. Finally, the tree canopy diminished, and as the rain drew back from downpour to shower, Turtleback Valley came into view. Sophia and Theo pushed the tarp aside. It was difficult to see what lay below them on the floor of the valley. The grove appeared to stand intact, the tall trees swaying with the force of the winds. Beyond the grove, two great patches discolored the slopes on either side of the river: to the east, Fen Carver's troops, a meandering brown stain punctuated by patches of blue and green and yellow; and to the west, the New Occident troops, a rectangle of red and white. In a flash of lightning, Sophia saw the river that ran between them, a long, uneasy serpent of gray.

Just as she had standing at the edge of the valley with Bittersweet days earlier, Sophia perceived clearly the old one's fear, concentrated around the grove. The Clime's intentions had hardened. There was desperation in the howling wind and the crashing thunder, but the desperation was controlled. Now there was also determination in the relentless wail of the weirwind that waited at the crest of the western hills, ready at a moment's notice to raze the ground before it. Sophia looked toward it apprehensively, and as the hilltop crackled with light, she realized that this was no ordinary weirwind. So tall that it merged with the clouds overhead, the weirwind carried lightning inside it. It was just as Borage had said: *Keep firing that pistol and you're going to hit someone. And make them very, very angry.*

With horror, Sophia saw what would happen. When the troops moved forward and launched into battle, the weirwind would descend to protect the grove, and the men would be obliterated, destroyed—killed. She half stood in the canoe, and it rocked dangerously. *How can they not see it?* she asked herself. *How can they not see what will happen?*

The whistling of Fen Carver's troops and the howling of the weirwind were interrupted by a long roll of thunder, and when it rumbled into silence, the whistling had stopped.

"Are we too late?" Sophia cried.

"They are negotiating," shouted Casanova. "Look!"

Halfway between the two armies, on the western bank of the river, was a small cluster of men on horseback. "Negotiating what? Surrender?"

"The terms of battle," Casanova replied. He gestured to the east and west. "Fen Carver's troops are in a defensive position. They would gladly walk away from this if they could.

It is General Griggs who will attack. Carver is likely trying to ensure the safety of any troops who survive. We still have time," he decided, "but not much."

As if in response, Birke picked up speed, taking the short waterfalls with greater abandon. Water splashed into the canoe. Sophia stared so hard at the dark cluster between the two armies that her eyes hurt, and her hands ached from clinging to the sides of the craft.

Finally, Birke reached the base of the valley. As they surged along the winding river, Sophia lost sight of the negotiators, only to spot them again at the next bend.

The grove was before them now, on the right bank, so much larger than Sophia had imagined. Red trunks towered overhead, and the long branches tossed this way and that like frantic arms. Sophia thought of Tree-Eater, and for a moment it seemed she could see the great monster, standing at the edge of the grove in anticipation of the destruction he would cause. His great jaws and antlers were made of men, and his golden eyes were made of fire. In the dense clouds of the storm, the figure wavered, and then it was gone.

Birke moved onward. The grove was behind them, and the axis of the battlefield came into view. A group of boulders formed a natural bridge across the river, and water stormed through its crooked archway. Caught at the mouth of the funnel it rose rapidly, swamping the banks. Theo clutched Sophia's hand.

But before they reached it, the waters governed by the three sisters launched Birke onto the eastern bank. Theo and Sophia stumbled out into the mud. Casanova dragged the canoe away from the river, along the stony ground.

Sophia rushed forward with the mirrorscope; then she slowed her steps, confused. Several hundred feet away, the armies were waiting on the slopes to either side. The front lines of each stood in apparent stillness, the individual faces obscured by the rain. But there were no negotiators. The horses and men she had seen from the hilltop were gone. In their place was something else: a large square frame—as tall and wide as a man.

As she walked on toward it, Sophia squinted. What was it? A *house*? A *wagon*? She moved closer.

"Sophia! Stop," Casanova shouted as he caught up to her, seizing her arm.

"What is it?" she asked, looking at the strange box.

"I am not sure." He frowned. "Let me go first."

Theo joined them. "I know what it is," he said, with faint surprise. "It's harmless."

After a moment, Casanova continued onward, with Theo and Sophia close on his heels. Only when she had nearly reached the motionless object did Sophia realize what it was: an iron cage with long carrying poles, like a palanquin, rested on the ground by the banks of the river.

There was someone inside. As they drew closer, Sophia realized that it was a girl. She could not have been more than ten or eleven. Her long, black hair hung loose and wild, and she was weeping. The sobs were inaudible in the thunderstorm, but they were visible in how they wracked her body. The girl clenched the iron bars and leaned slowly forward against them, as if exhausted, sinking into a pile of her own skirts.

Their hems were charred.

In a moment, Casanova was at the cage, working upon the lock. Theo watched his futile efforts. "It's the Weatherer," he said in Sophia's ear. "The one I saw in the memory map."

And then, in a rush, she understood. It was Datura—the sister Bittersweet had sought so desperately for so long. *She is just a child,* Sophia thought, shocked. She found it hard to believe that the small, wretched creature before her was the cause of so much catastrophe. "Datura," she called out over the rainstorm, reaching to touch the small fingers that gripped the iron bars.

The girl's sobs stopped abruptly, and she looked up. Her face, green at the edges where it met her dark hair, was white and strained. She looked half-starved, her cheeks gaunt and her green fingers bony. Her lips were scabbed from old cracks and red from new ones. With eyes wild and despairing, she looked from Sophia, to Theo, to Casanova, and back again.

Sophia leaned in close to make herself heard without shouting. She covered the girl's fingers with her own. "Datura," she said gently. "I'm a friend of your brother's. Bittersweet is looking for you, searching everywhere. He will be so glad to know we've found you."

Tears filled Datura's eyes once more, and she pulled her fingers away. "He will not be glad. I have done terrible things." Her trembling voice was not the voice of a child; she sounded to Sophia like a woman who had lived long enough to regret decades of her life—a woman who had lived enough to grow bitter and weary. She dropped her head again, covering her face and renewing her sobs. "Terrible things," she cried.

Sophia reached through the bars and took Datura's bright green hands in her own, drawing them away from her face. They were small and terribly cold. "You had no choice."

"I did have a choice," the girl said, looking up, her expression agonized. "I *do*. And every time, I choose my gift. Every time, I choose Mother and Grandfather over everyone else. It is *unforgivable*," she whispered. *"But I love them too much."* Her words were almost inaudible.

Sophia felt tears in her eyes as she pressed the girl's hands. Suddenly, a muffled bugle call sounded from the direction of the New Occident troops. Datura started. She scrambled to her feet and stood in the center of the cage, her arms rigid. "That means I have to begin," she said, her voice trembling. "You must run as far as you can. The vapors will spread in seconds."

Sophia glanced at Theo, who looked tired and wet, and Casanova, who looked stricken and uncertain. He had given up on the lock. Sophia could see him calculating the weight of the palanquin, wondering if he could lift the front while Theo and Sophia raised the poles at the rear. She had briefly considered the same thing, but with Theo's injury it was out of the question. Looking meaningly at Casanova, she shook her head. "Go," she said. "I will stay with Datura."

"*All* of you must go," Datura insisted. The bugle sounded again, and she jumped. "Please, please, I beg you!"

Theo and Casanova had not moved, but Sophia could see, taking in every sight and sound around them, how the circumstances of the present would unfold. The roaring of the storm seemed to recede, and she felt time slow around her. The New Occident troops in the distance were a blur of red and white. Behind them, the weirwind waited, enraged and hungry. Casanova was shielding his eyes from the rain, and the water ran down over the bandages of Sage's poultice. Both his arms were trembling. Sophia realized that he had overexerted himself yet again—had he tried to lift the palanquin alone? No—it must have been earlier, while steering the canoe. She noticed that Theo's boots had sunk into the mud, and he was frowning fiercely, squinting at Sophia with a look that was one part exasperation and two parts agony. He would not leave her with Datura. He would not leave her here, the way he had in the driving rain outside of Nochtland the year before, because if he could help it, he would never leave her again.

That was when she knew: Theo had changed. He was no longer happy to save only his own skin; he no longer counted himself lucky when he slipped away unnoticed. He was tied to people and places now, and he wanted to be. He was tied to *her*—to Sophia. It was in every line of his furious, loving scowl. Sophia wondered how she could have missed it. *I'm weathering,* she realized. *I'm making space so that I can see everything. This is what Bittersweet described to me, what seemed so hard to imagine when he did.*

And a chain of events unreeled before her. The terrified child in the cage would open her hands, and red flowers would bloom from her palms—Datura's gift would blossom once more. The scent of the flowers would drift, carried by the powerful winds, and the tension of the waiting armies would collapse in the chaos, confusion, and carnage of the crimson fog. The weirwind would descend the slope, and the troops from both sides would be battered into death. When the storm passed, there would be little more than the wreckage of an iron cage.

Sophia could see no way to prevent these things from happening that did not begin and end with persuasion. She had to persuade Datura to wait. She had to persuade the commanders to wait. She had to convince the armies to wait.

But though it was Sophia's gift to have all the time in the world, she had run out of time.

THERE WAS A crashing sound, and Sophia felt the ground shaking under her feet, as if from the impact of a horse's hooves. The space she had created around herself collapsed; time ran on as usual. She looked desperately to either side of the valley. Had the weirwind descended? Had the troops begun their charge?

"*Da-tu-ra!*" came a distant shout. Sophia turned. She could see only a dark blur, racing toward them along the riverbank, but she knew that voice. Even though she had never heard it shout, she recognized it. The dark blur became a moose, charging toward them with its antlers lowered, moving at an incredible speed. "*Datura!*" came the cry once more.

"It is Bittersweet!" Sophia exclaimed, reaching through the bars once more to take Datura's hands. "You see, he has come to find you."

Datura stood staring, wide-eyed and wondering, as Nosh bulleted toward them. The bugle sounded again, but she ignored it.

Sophia saw, out of the corner of her eye, an uneasy stirring at the front line of the New Occident troops. She imagined how this would appear to General Griggs, who had now ordered Datura three times to release a fog that did not come: first, three figures in a canoe had appeared, and now another who knew the girl by name. Clearly, he was only waiting because he expected the fog to begin at any moment. How long would he wait? She willed Nosh to run faster.

He closed the distance, now fifty feet away, now twenty, and finally Bittersweet slid from Nosh's back and ran to them, soaked to the skin, his face bright with exertion. He threw himself against the bars and pulled Datura toward him. They held each other close. "Little sister," Bittersweet murmured, his hand on her head.

With effort, she pulled back, and her face was strained with grief. "You must go," she said, trying to push him away.

Bittersweet was unmoved. "I am not going anywhere."

"But Mother and Grandfather," Datura said, dissolving into tears. "If I don't—"

"They will understand," Bittersweet reassured her.

"They will be dead! They are in winter sleep and will never wake unless I do everything the men ask!"

As Bittersweet and Datura spoke, Sophia felt a tremor of warning course through her. Perhaps, in the past, she would have pushed it aside as her own baseless anxiety. Or, if by chance she listened to it, she would have ascribed it to some mysterious better instinct. Now she knew that it was neither baseless anxiety nor sound instinct; the warning came from the old one, and she raised her head abruptly.

It was not the New Occident troops advancing toward them, as she had feared. It was the muddy river water, rising and falling in mutinous currents. A section of grassy earth disappeared beneath a swell of water; the riverbank was being eaten before their eyes. Sophia looked down, aghast, at the widening fissures in the soft ground underfoot.

"We must move!" she shouted, seizing one of the poles of the palanquin. The others looked at her, startled. "The riverbank!"

Bittersweet was the first to understand. He took up the pole beside Sophia and began straining to lift it.

Casanova followed suit, pushing Theo aside and attempting to lift both poles at the rear of the palanquin. Sophia could feel his exertion through the wood in her hands, but the iron cage did not move.

"It is too heavy," Datura cried. "They use eight men—you will not be able to lift it!"

Sophia looked at Bittersweet in anguish. She could see in his face the same desperate, fruitless unreeling of what lay before them: the rush of the river, the muddy soil, the crumbling ground, and the heavy iron cage. Before long, the ground underfoot would give way, and Datura's prison would fall into the water. Datura, trapped inside, would drown.

Sophia's mind worked rapidly through one possibility, and then another, and another; she could see only one way forward, and it was precarious.

"*Go!*" she shouted to Casanova, pushing him away from Datura's cage. "Get Fen Carver! Tell him Griggs has agreed to negotiate a truce!"

Casanova did not protest that this was a lie. He did not ask how the lie would be made true. Without a word, he ran toward the boulders that served as a bridge to the western riverbank.

Sophia turned to Bittersweet and Theo. "Keep her alive," she said. Then she ran uphill, toward the soldiers who stood, unmoving, like rows upon rows of black teeth, preparing to devour the valley whole.

38

ONE TERRIER

—1892, August 17: 10-Hour 56—

In addition to the above measures prohibiting the sale and traffic of human beings, New Occident hereby agrees that any person in this Age known to engage in such sale and traffic after the passage of this treaty, even if such sale or traffic occur beyond the boundaries of the nation, shall be tried for his or her crimes. The penalties in this case will be identical to those described above for the sale or traffic within the boundaries of New Occident.

—1810 Treaty of New Orleans

SORENSEN AND THE Elodeans had given their testimony, and Mr. Fenton had summarized the narratives offered by the seven witnesses, explaining to the judges what evidence was laid before them.

Gordon Broadgirdle, he asserted, was Wilkie Graves, a known and notorious slaver. Graves had made his way into New Occident and pursued a political career, shedding his old identity and taking on a gang of armed men to dissuade the intervention of any who might get in his way. Though there was not yet evidence to prove it, Broadgirdle had likely begun his plot to kill Prime Minister Bligh months in advance—all with the intention of starting the war he had effectively begun in the summer of 1892. What had been proven beyond doubt, Fenton argued, was his treatment of Gerard Sorensen and the Eerie, who had been most cruelly used in pursuit of his agenda.

The judges heard this summary solemnly. "You may be seated, Mr. Fenton," the chief judge with the impassive face instructed. All of Mr. Fenton's witnesses shifted slightly, their attention turning to the defense.

"Mr. Appleby?" said the judge. "Please present your evidence."

"I certainly will, Your Honor," Mr. Appleby said, rising. "I have counseled the prime minister to tell you the truth, and I hope you will take this into consideration as you determine the next steps. Prime Minister," he said, nodding to Broadgirdle.

Broadgirdle rose, and with the confident air that always hung about his person like an ornate cloak, he strode to the dais instead of remaining by the table. Shadrack considered him with reluctant admiration. There was nothing in the man's expression to suggest that he was the target of multiple devastating accusations—that he was on the very verge of losing not only his high position, but his freedom. He seemed, rather, the same self-assured politician he always was, primed to deliver a momentous speech that he knew already his audience would applaud.

"Your Honor and members of parliament," he began, looking at them all with a slight smile. "I will heed Mr. Appleby's wise counsel, and tell you the truth about my past, thereby filling in the considerable holes left by the testimony of these . . . ahem, unusual witnesses." He cast his eye over them wryly. "What these seven don't know would fill a chamber much greater than this one, Your Honor. In fact"—he shook his head with a low chuckle—"what they don't know might fill an entire Age. For you see, honorable judges, members of parliament, you are right—I am not a native of New Occident. Nor am I from the Baldlands. In fact, I am not of this Age at all." There were murmurs of considerable surprise.

Shadrack frowned. He had expected a well-crafted response from Broadgirdle, but he had not expected this. He noticed out of the corner of his eye that Cassandra was looking sharply at Broadgirdle with something like concern. "I," Broadgirdle said, waiting for the suspense to climax, "am from the Age of Verity."

The murmurs from parliament shifted to become something more disbelieving—more ridiculing. "My father was a criminal," Broadgirdle said, cutting into the murmurs. There was instant silence. "He came from another part of this Age of Delusion—Australia. As the testimony from Pip Entwhistle has intimated, he was a desperate man prone to dramatic and excessive measures. One of those excessive measures was to flee his native Australia when threatened with life in prison for a crime he had committed. He escaped to this hemisphere, where he landed on the western coast of the Baldlands and met my mother. My mother died at my birth." He covered his eyes briefly with his hand, and Shadrack recognized the falsity in the gesture—but he doubted any of the judges would. "With a motherless infant and a criminal past, he made his way east, toward the middle Baldlands.

"You can imagine the kind of life I led," Broadgirdle continued, his voice low and strained, "with such a man as a father. It was a difficult life. And it was made more difficult by a discovery I made when I was fifteen. Due to the circumstances, of course, my father had brought very little with him from Australia. He had a small wallet with him, however, that contained all of his identification papers, and I had occasion to examine the contents when my father was taken ill. I found in the wallet a surprising piece of dreck—dreck that described me *by name*. I lived in Australia, a grown man—an important man. A man of influence and power. The fact that my father had kept this piece of dreck spoke to me clearly: coming to the Baldlands had not only been an act of desperation, it had been an act of selfishness. He had stolen from me the future I ought to have had.

"I left my father on that very day, and I have not heard of him since. I will leave aside the intervening years, as I tried—without success—to recover the fate my father had stolen from me. And then the course of my life was changed again—by Pip Entwhistle." He looked at Pip with what seemed a smile of genuine warmth. "Yes, indeed. You did not know it, but the piece of dreck you sold me set me on a new course. For it mentioned me by name as a great political leader in a great war, uniting the western continent."

"But . . ." Pip protested, entirely out of turn. "But that newspaper made no mention of a Wilkie Graves."

"Wilkie Graves is not my true name," Broadgirdle said with a gleaming, assured smile. "I recognized at once the meaning of the paper in my hands. Now there were *two* pieces of dreck, both of which described my illustrious future. It was clear that I was destined for such a path regardless of which Age I inhabited. Within the year, I had joined the Nihilismian sect. Of all the misguided people in our world, I understood that they, and they alone, were attempting to restore the Age of Verity that we had all lost. With their guidance, I began to see more and more the true nature of the world around me. I realized that there are certain people, certain paths, that will transcend even disruptions of the kind that occurred ninety-three years ago. And I was one such person.

"I have tried," he said, leaving his explanation and past behind, his voice rising to a crescendo, "to bring this misguided Age of Delusion closer to its true path—closer to the Age of Verity that is irrevocably lost to us. We *must*," he said, pounding his fist on the podium, "correct the mistakes of this deluded Age. We *must* do everything we can to align ourselves with the events that transpired in the Age of Verity. That Age is beyond saving, I know." He looked at the parliament judges with reproach. "But to sit here idle while Verity runs away from us—it is inexcusable. Every one of my actions," he said, with an air of great self-righteousness, "has been an effort to keep us on track. An effort to recover the world we have lost. An effort to save what little can still be saved."

INSPECTOR GREY, GLANCING around him, understood at once that he was outmanned. He had only eight officers, and half of them looked terrified. Grey turned back to the scarred face before him and wondered if it would be better to lie about Broadgirdle's whereabouts. On principle, Grey never lied, but in this instance, he reasoned, such a course might be the only way to prevent his officers from being killed.

"The prime minister is not in the State House," Grey said firmly.

The man before him slowly took the grappling hook from his belt and held it with a casual air. The others around him followed suit. "You can tell us where he is, then."

"I don't know where he is. The prime minister fled the State House as we were taking him to chambers."

The man with the grappling hook frowned, and suddenly the hook was whirling in the air like a lasso. "You are lying," he said.

The officers drew their pistols. The nineteen men before them began whirling their grappling hooks. Grey, his hands at his sides, sought desperately in his mind for a way to avoid the confrontation. He could think of nothing. As the man before him drew the circling hook over his head, preparing to launch it, a sudden whoop sounded, piercing and clear, from the colonnade behind him. A chorus of shrill, exuberant cries echoed the first, and Grey watched in amazement as a fist-sized rock flew past him, hitting the man with the grappling hook soundly on the ear.

He fell back, stunned, and a volley of smaller stones followed, pounding down on the twenty men like a hailstorm. Grey turned his head in astonishment and looked up at the gallery of the State House.

The inspector was of strong constitution, but he nearly fainted when he saw his own daughter, grinning from the gallery. She gave him a cheerful wave before launching another missile. Grey stared at her, aghast. Beside her were some twenty-five or thirty street urchins, all of them enthusiastically pitching rocks at the men on the steps. The stones were small, but many hit their mark, and as they continued without pause, they made it impossible for the men to throw their grappling hooks.

The anxious parent in Grey wanted to run up to the colonnade and drag Nettie home. The inspector in Grey reasoned that he and his men were getting the very help they needed. He agonized for several seconds, watching as several of their attackers fled the steps and two others huddled down, covering their heads with their hands. There would be no other chance, Grey realized. The inspector prevailed over the parent.

"Cuff them," he shouted to his men. "I want to see them all in the station within the hour."

39
RED GARNETS

—August 20, 7-Hour 41—

In contrast, the story from Oakring about the origins of weirwinds describes a man who lost everything—his home, his family, his livelihood—in a storm. Others with similar losses sat bereaved, broken and hopeless, until they hardened and turned to stone. But this man grew with his anger, until his great, desperate sobs became gales and his tears became storms. It is striking to imagine the weirwind this way—animated loss, taking back from the world what can never really be recovered.

—From Sophia Tims's Born of the Disruption: Tales Told by Travelers

SOPHIA HAD RUN only a few feet when she heard a snort behind her. She turned, and Nosh was there, barring her way. "Thank you, Nosh," she said gratefully as he sank down so she could mount. He grunted in reply as he rose, clearly offended that she had tried to run off without him. "You're right," Sophia conceded, patting his neck. "It was not the best part of my plan. Your legs are much stronger than mine."

Nosh galloped uphill through the muddy grass, toward the center line of the New Occident forces. As they neared the troops, Sophia saw a cluster of three riders who waited before the rest. She swallowed her nervousness. Nosh slowed his pace and stopped ten feet away. The riders did not approach her. They did not move at all.

Two of the men wore goggled masks. The third, who wore a hat and carried his mask in the crook of his arm, was clearly General Griggs. Although his uniform sagged with the weight of the rain, he held himself erectly in the saddle, and his eyes considered Sophia with dispassion. The eyes were hard without being cold. Griggs seemed, in his upright posture and stern bearing, a man more guided by principle and obligation than by bloodlust, cruelty, or ambition. It was evident, from the white knuckles and slow breaths, that he was weary.

"The Eerie girl is caged for a reason," Griggs said.

"And she is about to drown," Sophia said. "I am here to speak for Fen Carver and the troops of the Indian Territories," she declared in a clear voice.

Griggs did not respond. He leaned toward the soldier to his right and asked a question. The man removed his mask, revealing a round face with a red beard. Then he drew a telescope from the inside of his jacket pocket, wiped it with a handkerchief, and held it up to his eye. After a moment, he pocketed the telescope and said something to his commander.

Griggs sat back. "Go down, then, and pull it back twenty-five feet."

The bearded soldier assented and waved to the soldiers behind him. Seven of them followed, plodding downhill at a measured pace. Sophia felt relief like a breath of dry air. Datura would be safe for a little while longer. *On to the next step,* she told herself.

"Now," Griggs said to Sophia. "Explain. I've already agreed to terms with Carver. You've violated those terms by meddling with the girl. Does Carver want me to ignore my side of the agreement as well?" Rivulets of water dripped over his white eyebrows as if over an awning. His mustache was a sodden broom.

"Yes," Sophia said. "He was waiting for us to arrive with this." She held up the mirrorscope. "And we arrived too late for your initial negotiations."

Griggs took in the mirrorscope, and the white mustache twitched with his wry smile. "What is this? Some magical Indian weapon?"

"No," Sophia replied. "No magic. It is a telescope. Carver is certain that if you look at his troops with this telescope, you will want to change the terms of battle." She was relieved that her voice did not sound pleading. It sounded surprisingly confident. In fact, she realized, she felt confident.

General Griggs pondered her in silence. Then he urged his horse forward and held his hand out—not with curiosity, but with the unhurried air of a man who would conclude his business regardless of the trivial obstacles placed in his path. Taking the mirrorscope, he nudged his horse back a few paces. He examined the instrument briefly, turning it in his hand.

For a moment Sophia thought he would decline to look through it. But then he held it up to his right eye. He rotated it slightly. Sophia held her breath. The rain fell against his hat in a constant patter. Behind him, the troops stood still and anonymous, faceless in their dark hoods. The weirwind howled; the storm crashed around them like waves. Sophia had the momentary impression that she and Griggs were floating in a tiny vessel, large enough for only the two of them, while an ocean raged around them.

There was no change in Griggs's expression, and he remained perfectly still—one arm around the goggled mask, the other raised with the mirrorscope, sitting astride his horse in the rain. But the effect of the mirrorscope was nonetheless evident—upon his horse. Sensing the invisible change in its rider, the animal raised its head in sudden terror, eyes wide, every muscle suddenly rigid. There was a long pause, in which Sophia imagined the horse bolting, throwing Griggs and the mirrorscope into the mud.

Then Nosh stepped forward and nudged the horse's neck. It startled, shuddered, and turned to consider the moose. Nosh held its gaze for several long seconds, until Griggs finally took the mirrorscope from his eye. Sophia watched his expressionless face for some sign of what he would do.

"How does this work?" Griggs finally asked.

Sophia looked at him, unsure of how to answer. "It is an Eerie device."

"But how does it *work*?" Griggs insisted, lifting his hat so that his blue eyes were looking steadily into hers. When Sophia did not answer, he put his mask down on the horn of his saddle and clasped the mirrorscope with both hands. He held it reverently, as if considering a sacred object. "I saw my father here," he said. "And my brother. I saw things I thought no one else in the world had seen but me. How is that possible? How does it work?" He had not raised his voice, but the words had quickened, and as he finished his question he raised the mirrorscope before him.

"I don't know," Sophia admitted. "I don't understand how it works. But if you saw things you remember, surely you must realize that the memories in the scope are true."

"Someone else has seen what I have seen," Griggs said, looking past Sophia, into the middle distance. His words were slow and considered, as if he was attempting to pinpoint the nature of his question. "Not just seen, but also *felt*. For I remember feeling nothing when I realized the horses had drowned, and the eye that remembers this"—he gestured to the mirrorscope—"felt grief. When I did not. It was many years before I felt grief." He stopped abruptly and lifted the mirrorscope to his eye once more.

This time he truly studied the garnet map of New Occident. Sophia watched him, astonished, as the minutes passed. She found it hard to believe that he could stomach such horror for so long. As he lowered the mirrorscope a second time, she saw that it had indeed taken its toll. His hand trembled slightly. He turned to look back at the slope where his troops were assembled. "As if I needed reminding," he said, his voice unsteady. His shoulders sagged. "Which one of us is not weary of war?" he asked. He seemed to be speaking to himself rather than to

Sophia or to his troops, who were out of earshot. "Which one of us does not wish to go home? To a home untouched by all that we have seen. A home now vanished, from days when our eyes were young. It is impossible to return to that place—that childhood, when the world was not a landscape of blood. A red place. And for some, even that childhood is no escape. All they remember, all they ever remember, is pain. There are children who fall like the rest of us. Who see what we do. Who fight." He clenched the mirrorscope in his hand.

Sophia watched Griggs's grave face in suspense. She had seen many things in the mirrorscope, in the brief glimpse into New Occident's memories, and she could not be certain that he had seen any of the same. But she understood his words. The sound that had stayed with her from her glimpse into the mirrorscope was the wail of a child—high and terrified and unabated—a sound that even now rang in her ears. It was like nothing she had ever heard, yet it reminded her of another wailing: the Lachrima's long ebb and flow of grief, the cry that had echoed in her mind from the moment she learned that her parents had transformed.

Griggs straightened in his saddle and took a deep breath. He interrupted the silence. "It is compelling, what you have shown me," he said, "but it cannot change my purpose in being here. I have no choice. I answer to the prime minister of New Occident. Carver knows this is no personal venture of mine."

"But you said—"

"I know what I said. But look around you." He gave a broad gesture that took in the entire valley. "This was not brought about by my hand. I did not wish this or make this. I cannot stop it, either."

"You *can* stop it!" Sophia insisted.

"Child, you will soon learn the most humbling lesson to be learned here, on this battlefield. We like to think that a single person can change the world. But there are times when one person counts for very little. There are times when he or she counts for nothing at all." Griggs held the mirrorscope out to her, his face hard.

It failed, Sophia realized, aghast. *He is going to attack despite what he has seen.* As Sophia struggled for words, taking the mirrorscope in her hand, the men Griggs had sent downhill returned.

The soldiers melted back into their places, and the officer with the red beard stopped before Griggs. "She is in position," he said. "Carver has come back to this side of the river."

Griggs shook his head very slightly. He lifted his horse's reins and said to Sophia, "Tell Carver I will honor the original terms. You and he have ten minutes to get across the river. Tell him I cannot disobey my orders."

"But what about the weirwind?" Sophia asked. "Look at it!" She gestured at the crest of the hill, where the wall of wind remained poised. "It will descend at any moment. The weirwind will destroy this valley and anyone in it."

"Eventually it will pass," Griggs said. "The weather is no obstacle to me."

Sophia did not know what to do. She had been so sure that the mirrorscope would change the general's mind, and though it had clearly shaken him, it had not altered his course. All it had done was delay him.

Wait, something said in Sophia's mind. It was not her own inner voice, but the other voice—that familiar instinct that she was beginning to recognize as the old one, as the Clime: as New Occident. *Wait,* it said again.

"Wait!" Sophia cried aloud.

Griggs paused, and she stared at him desperately, waiting herself for the old one to explain itself so she would know what to do next.

And then she saw them. Battling the rain, dipping and wavering and faltering, a flock of pigeons was flying through the storm. Above the pigeons flew larger birds—falcons and ravens—whose broader wings served as a canopy, protecting them from the worst of the rain. "Look!" she cried. "Iron pigeons!"

Griggs and his officers looked up. The mass of birds descended, arriving in a burst of cawing and screeching that seemed to explode around them. The falcons wheeled dizzily, circling and swooping before driving upward once more, while the ravens landed on the ground around them. The iron pigeons fluttered to a stop on Nosh's antlers—more than a dozen of them, cooing and shaking their feathers.

"Marcel!" Sophia exclaimed, recognizing at once the pigeon who had flown from Maxine's house in New Orleans with her message to Shadrack.

With trembling fingers, wet and clumsy, Sophia opened the compartment on Marcel's leg. She read the words on the tiny slip of paper, protecting it with her hand. Then she read the next pigeon's message, and the next. All of the pigeons carried papers with the same words.

Then, her hand shaking, she reached out to General Griggs and handed him the papers. He read a few in silence, his drooping mustache twitching once. With a short exhalation, he tucked the papers inside his jacket, protecting them from the rain. "Is Carver still below?" he asked his officer.

The man with the red beard consulted his telescope. "He is."

"Hold the troops here. I will return in a moment. Come along," he said to Sophia.

Griggs led his horse downhill, with Nosh and Sophia behind him. They came quickly upon Datura's cage, where Bittersweet clung resolutely to the bars. Theo and Casanova stood beside him, their faces expectant. Beside them, a hatless Fen Carver stood in a dripping buckskin coat, a worn rifle slung across his shoulder. A handkerchief covered the lower half of his face, and he reached to pull it downward as Griggs and Sophia approached. He was frowning, but under his furrowed brow, his eyes held something light and fragile, like hope. "Well?" he asked, after Griggs had reined his horse and dismounted.

Griggs removed his hat. He reached into his coat and handed the slip of paper to Fen Carver. "Prime Minister Gordon Broadgirdle has been removed from office," he announced. "By emergency vote, parliament has ended aggressions with the Indian Territories and New Akan." He paused. "My orders from the Minister of Relations with Foreign Ages are to return to Boston."

There was a pause, and then an explosive cheer from Theo,

echoed by Casanova. Carver, who had read the messages with a grave face, handed them back to Griggs and gave a slight bow. Then he took the white scarf from his neck and tied it around the muzzle of his rifle. Lifting it over his head, he waved the rifle, and a slow eruption of shouts, muffled by the storm, sounded from across the valley.

Griggs walked to Datura's cage. Taking a key from his pocket, he unlocked the door. "It would be an insult to offer you my hand," he said, "after what you have seen and I have done. You would be right not to take it."

She stood, dazed and disbelieving. "I can go?"

"You are entirely free." Griggs stepped back from the cage. "I had my orders," he said to her, "but there was no dignity fighting in your wake." He gave her a brief nod and turned to ride uphill, where the troops of New Occident waited.

Still, Datura did not move until Bittersweet ran up and pulled her from the cage. She stepped down with trembling legs, and her brother embraced her. "It's over, little sister," he said, holding her close. "It's over."

40

RED WOODS

—1892, August 20: 7-Hour 02—

But what has yet to be thoroughly understood is how some places can so effectively make time pass in different ways. What is it about a place that changes the texture of time within it? I would like to see a considered study of how time passes in different places, similar to the one conducted in Boston last year. (For those who have not read the work, it was found that a majority of Bostonians experienced a slowing down in time between ten-hour and ten-seventeen.) Is this about some property of the Age, or is it some manner of living that has created synchronous experience? We do not yet know.

—From Sophia Tims's Reflections on a Journey to the Eerie Sea

THE RAIN STOPPED abruptly, and the valley was suddenly quiet. The only sound was the river, which churned on, sending its swollen waters south. Fen Carver stood on the flooded banks, watching the currents with a pensive air. His troops waited for him, the groups of warriors from every corner of the Territories coming into focus as the clouds retreated.

Sophia looked up at the crest of the hill. The weirwind had gone—retreated or disintegrated. There was nothing left now but a scorched line where the contained lightning had held itself in check. The New Occident troops were already with-drawing, marching steadily toward the path leading out of the valley. Theo and Casanova watched them depart, and Theo leaned heavily on his friend's arm, suddenly overcome.

As the air warmed, a gray mist began to form. It blanketed the valley, enveloping Datura's cage and hiding the muddy ground from view.

Sophia could sense the change all around her—a deep breath exhaled, a tension unwound. The old one knew that the danger had passed. Turtleback Valley was calm and still.

Casanova, Sophia, and Theo stood at a slight distance, wit-nesses to Bittersweet and Datura's reunion. Datura leaned against her brother's shoulder, and, his arm around her, Bitter-sweet spoke steadily, telling her how they would leave the val-ley and go spend some time with Smokey, and how they would write to Boston for news of Mother and Grandfather.

Sophia watched them with a mixture of gladness and reluc-tance. On the one hand, she could almost feel the relief that was evident in each of their faces. On the other hand, their reunion reminded her painfully of the unavoidable possibilities that had finally arrived. When it ended, she would have to venture into the grove, where Minna and Bronson either would be or would not be. All the signs had led there; there was no place else to go. *If I don't find them there,* she thought, *I won't find them at all.*

Sophia looked away from Bittersweet and Datura and con-sidered the mirrorscope in her hand. She packed it carefully in her satchel. "The scope gave him pause," she said to Theo and

Casanova, "but without the messages from Boston, it would not have been enough."

"Yes," Casanova said, "but if Griggs is anything like me, those glimpses of what war can do will linger for much longer—they may never go away—and change how he thinks and acts in the future." He gestured uphill, where the New Occident troops had begun to withdraw. "What you see now is only the first step. But those images are lasting ones, and they will have a lasting effect."

Theo took Sophia's hand and pressed it. He gave her a crooked smile. "Borage will be very impressed. Shadrack, too, when we tell him."

Sophia smiled back. "Perhaps. It is really Shadrack who stopped this war." She took one of the slips of crumpled paper from her pocket and showed them the blue stamp—the official seal of the Ministry of Relations with Foreign Ages. "He sent a dozen pigeons. To be sure the news arrived."

"Let us go," Bittersweet announced, walking over, his arm still around his sister's shoulders. Nosh plodded after them, the pigeons still perched on his antlers. "We are ready to venture into the grove. And you should go first, Sophia."

Without realizing it, she had turned her back on the grove of Red Woods. With a deep breath, she faced it. "Very well," she said, her voice determined. "If you are ready, I am ready."

They headed toward it, quiet descending upon them. As they approached, Sophia deliberately chose to observe what was around them, rather than anticipate what was to come.

The trees were unlike any she had ever seen. They reminded

her of the red trees described by Goldenrod in her story. Their bark was the color of old bricks, and they seemed as tall as the surrounding hills. Standing at the very entrance of the grove, Sophia peered up and found that the treetops were lost from view, blurring as they reached for the sun. A narrow dirt path cut between rolling mounds of clover, and the base of each tree was almost hidden by ferns. The bright green of the clover, the dark red of the tree trunks, the vivid blue of the morning sky: the grove seemed entirely composed of shining parts, making a brilliant whole.

Theo gave her a slight nudge, and Sophia stepped onto the path. She walked along it slowly, entranced by the stillness of the grove. The silence seemed intentional and aware, as if the grove itself were watching them with bated breath. Following the winding path, she skirted a mighty tree with a trunk so wide, ten pairs of arms would not have encircled it. "Have you ever seen trees so large?" she whispered over her shoulder.

Theo shook his head.

"Never," Bittersweet replied.

Casanova and Datura were lost in wonder, gazing up at the massive trunks. Nosh ambled happily in their wake, bending his head to nuzzle the ferns.

The path turned, opening onto a clearing. The fallen needles of the Red Woods made a carpet in the center, and at the far side of the clearing were two great trees that had grown toward each other, meeting several feet in the air, their trunks becoming one that stretched upward toward the sky. The space between them was a natural shelter, cool and shady—

almost like a room made by the trees themselves. Sophia walked toward it with delight, stepped into the dark chamber and smiled; something here struck her as safe and welcoming. She felt at home.

And then she froze. Inside the shelter, between the two trees, hung a watch on a chain. The trunks had grown through and around it, swallowing parts of the chain whole, and yet Sophia could see the watch face well enough to recognize it immediately. She had seen it before, in a memory map made of beads. She had seen, through the eyes of a faithless sheriff, two condemned prisoners wrap it around their wrists to join hands. It was the watch Richard Wren had given to Minna and Bronson Tims.

A sob caught in her throat. She reached up to take the watch with both hands, but it was too high up, and her palms fell against the brick-red trunks on either side of her.

The grove fell away, and memories flooded her mind. She had never before seen memories so vivid, and even as she felt bewildered at their clarity, some part of her paused and understood what had been working below the surface of her mind for some time. The disc of wood, the antler, the birch bark scroll, and the garnets: they had suggested to her the possibility that *all* such remnants had the potential to be memory maps. And now she was proven right.

She saw the memories in disordered flashes—meaningless bursts of light, faces, darkness, groans, crashes, piercing silence—before she realized that her own frantic touch was creating the turmoil. She was skipping feverishly through the memories, glancing at them too quickly, searching for something without knowing what it was she sought. She took a deep breath and stilled her hands. The memories slowed. She could see them now with greater clarity: the long years spent as Lachrima and the preceding ones spent as living, thinking, loving people. There was not yet a sense of order, of linear time, but Sophia dwelt in the memories with intention now, with enough restraint to see coherent moments.

A young Minna remembered making a castle out of sticks as a child, patiently breaking and building over and over until she was rewarded with a fantastic porcupine of an edifice. An older Bronson remembered meeting Shadrack, a young man with untidy hair and ink all over his hands. Minna, now grown, made a pie in midsummer out of stone fruit, and she sat on the porch with her feet on the railing, letting the smell of the baking waft out through the open door. Bronson sat as a child in school, staring out the window, daydreaming about exploration. Minna remembered squeezing Shadrack's hand tight as a doctor stitched the aching gash on her knee. Bronson remembered seeing Minna throwing snowballs in the Public Garden; she laughed, her hair disordered and her cheeks pink from the cold, and he felt a stab of something both terrifying and comforting—he had loved her at once. Minna remembered falling asleep on Bronson's shoulder; they had meant to stay awake to watch the sunrise, but she felt such exhaustion and relief that she could not keep her eyes open. Bronson remembered holding a smiling Sophia, who had new-grown front teeth, and as he leaned forward to bump noses with her he felt an overwhelming joy that left him breathless. Minna remembered cradling Sophia as she fell asleep in her arms.

Standing between the red trees with her hands upon their trunks, Sophia felt overpowered, not at the sight of her own face, but at the resounding happiness that filled Minna and Bronson when they saw it. It slowed her progress, and suddenly the memories flashed forward and took on a clear order.

She recalled with abrupt and shocking vividness the events Minna had described in her diary: conversations with Captain Gibbons, long evenings spent on the deck, the gentle rocking of the ship, the explosive storm that passed so quickly it seemed to swell and burst like a bubble. She saw Wren's familiar face, and she felt her heart pounding with relief as she clutched Bronson aboard the *Roost*. Wren moved through the memories like a bright and sturdy cable, anchoring them in the possibility of safety. He vanished as Seville appeared, wrecked and desolate, still plague-ridden. The kindness of the innkeeper, the terror of discovering the plague in Murtea, the slow and building desperation of imprisonment, all finally led to the moment before the bridge. She saw the moment now not from the vantage point of Murtea's sheriff, who had looked on with such reluctance, but from the eyes of both Minna and Bronson. Both appeared calm to the other, and both burned with terror. It was as palpable as the watch chain that linked their wrists together. It astonished her to feel the texture of this terror, for it was not about what they would find when they crossed the bridge; it was fixed on a distant point on the other side of the ocean—a smiling face that could not be lost, that must be remembered at all costs.

Her own—Sophia's—face.

Minna and Bronson crossed the bridge, and the piercing light of the shifting Age moved through them. The world became blurred—not blurred by sight, but blurred by grief. What would have appeared to an untouched mind like hills and paths around them seemed, rather, like a flat canvas. It was visible, but it meant nothing. Even when it changed, giving way to towns and then cities as they fled across the Ages, it seemed to have no meaning. The only intelligible thing was the despair, which filled every corner of their minds with its terrible, inescapable language. The words spoken by people near them, the expressions of horror, the landscapes of ice or hills or desert were all there, but it was impossible to understand them, for grief weighed down upon Bronson and Minna's minds like a visor. Even the rising and setting of the sun seemed incomprehensible, a predictable cycle that remained senseless in its repetition. Through this, they moved with heavy hearts toward a single point of clarity: a place. The place had meaning—as yet unknown meaning, but a meaning nonetheless; the unseen place promised them an end to the grief; it shone on the horizon like a dawning star. And so they followed it.

The desert pathways grew hot and cool with the passing days. Rain fell in sudden bursts, and then cleared. Bands of traders rode past, galloping away from them with shouts as if fleeing a plague. The deserts gave way to mountains, and strange animals became their companions. Silent and tall, covered with gray-white fur, they radiated a gentle and stubborn intention that made its way past the grief. At first the creatures walked beside them. Then they carried Minna and Bronson in their arms. The two were passed from one pack of creatures to another, and the creatures spoke to one another in silence, tapping their feet against the earth. Their kindness slowly made itself evident, even to Minna's and Bronson's dulled minds: warmth and shelter, wrappings of fur for clothing and shoes, a low and penetrating hum at night that lulled them into uneasy sleep.

Years passed in this way, with the mountains flattening into hilly plains, and the plains giving way to long expanses of ice. The creatures left them, reluctantly, when the ice ended.

For a time yet, Minna and Bronson sensed the heavy trembling in the ground that came from the creatures' footsteps, and though the meaning of those messages was obscured, the reassurance of their continued presence in the distance carried the weary wanderers a way farther. Then the footsteps faded, and the world was a green tunnel. The place they had sought was close. It had a sound. That sound was a voice—a constant, quiet call that spoke their names.

"Sophia," someone said.

She resisted. She did not want to be drawn away from these memories. She wanted to see them all—every one of them— and then she wanted to see them again.

"You *will* see them all," someone else said. "There will be time."

Sophia felt a moment's confusion. She had not spoken. Had she? She realized that her eyes were squeezed shut. After a slight hesitation, she opened them. She had fallen back against the wall of the shelter; her hands rested on the gnarled trunks of the trees.

Standing before her were Minna and Bronson Tims.

Sophia could not find her voice. "Is it really you?" she finally whispered.

Minna smiled, her eyes shining as she gazed at Sophia's face. She reached out impulsively and then checked herself. Slowly, she drew back her arm. As she did, Sophia realized that the brick-red trunks behind her were still visible. Minna and Bronson were fading.

"It is really us," Minna said quietly.

"We have waited as long as we could," Bronson said. His voice caught. "And it was enough."

Sophia could not stop looking at them. This was no feat of the imagination, for she could not have imagined the way their faces were lined with age and long exhaustion. Minna's hair was streaked with gray. Bronson's beard was gray around his mouth, and a long scar ran along his neck. They wore strange clothing—soft leather molded and tucked around their bodies. It seemed alien: a fragment of another world. She felt a sudden, inexplicable sense of betrayal. *They changed,* Sophia thought. *They changed without me.*

"How?" she asked out loud. "How are you here?"

"We traveled here," Bronson replied. "All the way from the Papal States. Through the Middle Roads, into the Russias, across the land bridge into the Prehistoric Snows. And finally into New Occident. To here."

"You saw some of it," Minna added. "It was a dark time, and our memories are no clearer than what you yourself saw."

"But why here?" Sophia pressed, unable to fully voice her true question.

"We were called here," said Bronson.

"Our hearts did call us to Boston," Minna acknowledged. "I believe every movement for years carried us in that direction. Toward Boston—toward you. But then the call began."

"It promised us wholeness. An end to the life, if you can call it that, we were attempting to survive."

"But who called you?" Sophia asked. And then she realized: "The old one."

"Yes," Minna said. "We came here, to this grove, because we were called." She gestured at the two trees above and around them. "This grove, this place you stand in, is the start of a new world." She smiled gently. "We are making it. Not just us—all of us who were effaced."

Effaced. "The old one is healing the Lachrima?" Sophia breathed.

"It is more than that," her mother told her. "Yes, it is healing the Lachrima, but in so doing, it is creating an answer to the kind of grief that burdens the Lachrima. An answer to the war that almost destroyed this valley."

"This grove," Bronson said, his eyes shining, "is even an answer to the Disruption."

"The Disruption?" Sophia did not understand.

"The great conflict that erupted as the Climes faced their own extinction. An extinction they might understand, but we as yet do not. The cause is obscured. The 'old ones,' as you call them, could not agree on how to prevent their own annihilation. The Disruption was the result of their disagreement—instead of one solution, many solutions. From the Disruption emerged a world with old ones in different times, different Ages. But we hope that this disagreement has ended. We hope that this place will prevent such a thing from ever happening again."

"How?" Sophia wondered.

"By bringing to the surface what is hidden. By making the past always visible in the present. With the surfeit of memories we—the effaced—carry, a place *made* of memories can come into being. For now it is just this grove, but the Ages will slowly be remade so that they are entirely made of memories."

"What do you mean, 'made of memories'?"

"Just that," Bronson said. "Every blade of grass, every stone, every drop of water—they will contain the memories of what they have been part of."

It was as Sophia had imagined, considering the wheel of wood, the antler, and the birch bark. Here, in the grove, the old one had rendered memory in a way that everyone and anyone could see. It required no expert knowledge, no skill of discernment, no elaborate device. The old one wished these memories to be attainable at a single, thoughtless, touch. "Everyone will know what the past is made of," she murmured, comprehending at last.

Her mother nodded. "And though there are many who are misguided in this world, we believe, as does the old one, that knowing the past so entirely will offer guidance."

"But to make such a place," Bronson continued, "to begin, the grove had to emerge from memory itself. And that is what Lachrima are. What we are."

"Then these two trees . . ." Sophia began.

"The two of us are everywhere in the grove, but mostly we are here. When we came to the valley, we wished to make a space that you would find one day, and this is it."

"We knew you would come," Minna whispered.

"But I can see you—your faces. Can you not leave now, as you are?" Sophia heard the desperation in her own voice.

For the first time, Minna and Bronson took their eyes from Sophia's face and glanced at one another. "No, we cannot. We are hardly here at all," her father said, with a sad smile. "Everything that we are has gone into the making of this place. But it is right," he added gently. "This is how it should be."

Sophia's vision blurred, and she felt the tears begin. "But I just found you," she whispered.

"It is more than we ever hoped," her mother said, her face softening. "And it is better to see one another briefly than not at all. Isn't it?"

Sophia could not speak. She nodded wordlessly.

When she looked up, she saw that they were both kneeling

before her, their insubstantial figures as close as they could be without touching her. "Won't you tell us about the young woman you have become, dearest?" Minna asked. "You have our memories here," she gestured to the trees, "but we have only you. Tell us." She tried to smile. "Tell us everything."

At first, Sophia could not bring herself to tell her parents about her own past—it seemed impossible when there was so much else to think about in their presence. And she could not imagine where to begin. But slowly, with her mother's gentle questioning, she found herself talking about what had happened beyond the grove, with the discovery of Datura and the two armies, and then she found herself explaining the realm of the three sisters, and the long journey that had led to the Eerie Sea. She described the wonder of Ausentinia, and the terror of perceiving its memories; she recounted the Atlantic voyage with the Nihilismians and the earlier journey to Nochtland; she told them about Blanca, and the anguish she had felt hearing her cry. All the people she had met on her voyages, all the sadness and disappointment she had felt with Shadrack, all the changes that had brought her to the present began to fall into place.

What had seemed impossible became easy. She found herself describing who she was, recounting things great and small: memories from growing up with Shadrack, early days at school, the discovery of favorite books and favorite places, her anxiety losing track of time, and the notebooks she had drawn to mark the days. Minna and Bronson wondered and asked and exclaimed. When her mother laughingly told her own tales of how she lost track of time, and when her father spoke of his own drawing notebook, she marveled at how things that had once made her feel so strange and solitary now made her feel secure and rooted. To her surprise, there were even moments when the three of them found themselves laughing, and she saw, then, brief glimpses of what a life with them might have been like.

She was astonished when the light around her began to fade; night was approaching, and she had spent the entire day between the two Red Woods, in her parents' company. "I don't want to go," she said, looking out at the clearing in the growing darkness.

"You can stay, of course," Minna said.

"Will *you* stay?"

"We will stay as long as we can," Bronson replied softly.

Sophia gazed at them. Already, it was difficult to see their features. She could not tell if it was the fading light or their figures slowly fading from the grove. Abruptly, she realized that she was exhausted, and she fought to keep her eyes open. "It is beautiful, this place you have brought into the world," Sophia told them. "It is going to change everything. It is the most remarkable thing I've ever seen."

"But not the most beautiful or remarkable thing your father and I have brought into the world," Minna whispered, leaning over her.

Sophia closed her eyes without meaning to. She heard

a hummed melody that was familiar, though she could not remember how she came to know it. It reminded her of something: a time and feeling she had lost sight of for years. There was an unshakable sense in her very center that all was safe and well, that she was encompassed and known, and that everything was as it should be.

41

REUNION

—1892, August 21: 5-Hour 20—

Now the markers appear as far as New Orleans and Charleston: RED WOOD GROVE, they say, noting the miles one must walk along the paths of New Occident to reach the valley. Even as the grove remains a distant destination to many, it is, quite literally, growing closer. Other travelers have reported to me—and I have seen for myself—that the number of Red Wood trees has increased, taking the pathways out of Turtleback Valley as their guides. Reader, you will find contained herein the map to Red Wood Grove, drawn as it existed in the summer of 1892.

—From Sophia Tims's Reflections on a Journey to the Eerie Sea

WHEN SOPHIA WOKE, Minna and Bronson were gone. At first, it struck her like a blow, and she wanted to return to sleep to forget how irrevocable was their departure. But then she realized, to her surprise, that the sense of comfort and security she had fallen asleep with was still there. Yes, Minna and Bronson were gone, but they had left her with that unshakable stillness that was the heart of the grove.

She stepped tentatively out of the Red Wood shelter and found Theo sleeping outside it, curled up among the ferns. She smiled. Instead of waking him, she sat beside him and waited, letting the morning light filter in through the trees. In the east, the sun rose over the hills and reached them in the clearing, slowly igniting the red trunks with orange light. The grove itself was awake. Sophia could feel its watchfulness, its steady purpose. She listened to it with all her senses, awed and profoundly glad that she had been so fortunate to find her way to such a place.

When Theo woke, he sat bolt upright. Then he groaned. He eased his arm out of the sling and stretched it gingerly. "Are you okay?" he asked anxiously, searching her face.

She smiled. "I'm fine."

"Are they gone?"

Sophia nodded. She glanced at the two trees. "Yes. Though not entirely. Their memories are there. And they will be—always. I will get to spend more time with them that way, at least." She turned back at him. "Thanks for waiting with me."

Theo drew one of Smokey's food packets out from under him and unfolded it, revealing a flattened piece of bread, a squashed apple, and crumbled nuts. "I saved you this delicious meal," he announced.

Sophia laughed. "Thank you." She took it, grateful for anything to put in her rumbling stomach. As she ate hungrily, she asked, "Where are the others?"

"They camped out by the river last night." He smiled at her sideways. "We have company."

"Company?"

"When you're done, we'll go join them."

She glared at him. "I can walk and eat!"

Theo put his arm back in the sling, pulled himself to his feet, and took up his stick. Sophia followed him along the path, eating hurriedly. The luxuriant ferns were still, and the clover seemed damp with dew. Sophia gazed at the foliage and the fibrous trunks of the trees with new eyes, imagining how all of it contained the memories of people like her parents. They had, indeed, created a perfect place.

When the trees parted and the valley came into view, Sophia saw an astonishing ship on the riverbank: a ship built around the roots of a living tree, its broad sails, made of leaves, tightly furled. It was out of place here, far from Nochtland: a boldevela. At the base of the boldevela's steps, Nosh was happily eating grass. The pigeons were pecking at the ground nearby, keeping their safe distance from the larger bird that now perched on his antlers. Sophia squinted. *Not a pigeon,* she thought.

A falcon! Seneca!

Goldenrod, Errol, Bittersweet, and Datura sat nearby, talking quietly.

Sophia raced toward them. "Goldenrod! Errol!"

They rose and hurried forward, both of them embracing her so tightly that she had to fight for breath. She drew back, a little laugh of happiness escaping her. "I am so glad to see you well!" Then she realized that Errol's shoulder was wrapped in bandages.

"We are well now," Goldenrod reassured her, taking Sophia's hand. "Though there were some difficult moments. And we have heard a great deal from Bittersweet about all the difficulties you have overcome."

"Did you find them, Sophia?" Errol asked, with intensity.

"Yes. I was even able to talk with them before they had to go."

"We have been speaking of this grove, and how it was made," Goldenrod said, looking up at it wonderingly. "Though I know it cannot amend their loss, to have been a part of making such a place . . ."

Sophia nodded. "I know."

Datura, Bittersweet, and Theo had joined them. Theo yawned. "Where do all the memories in the grove come from? In the trees, even the ferns. I still don't totally get what the grove *is*."

"A living memory map," Sophia told him.

"But there are lots of memory maps."

"Yes. But they are difficult, if not impossible, for most people to read," added Goldenrod. "These are fully manifest. Anyone can experience these memories."

"It's like the difference between talking to someone in person and reading about them," Sophia continued. "To read about them, you have to know how to read. But when you actually *talk* to them . . . they are there—right in front of you, obvious and alive. The grove is like that, but with memories."

"It will change everything," Goldenrod said gravely. "Imagine the power of the garnet map that you brought here—but everywhere, in everything. When the past is so visible, so present, it counsels our actions—it makes us considered and aware."

A sound aboard the boldevela drew Sophia's attention.

"How did that boldevela come to be here? And what has happened to Calixta? And Burr?"

Errol smiled wryly. "Oh, you will find them quite well. In fact, I advise you to speak to the others before the pirates wake, or else you will not get a word in edgewise."

"Others?"

As if in reply, a figure appeared at the tree-ship's railing. "Hello!" the old man cried, cheerfully waving a cane.

"*Martin?*" Sophia exclaimed. She took a step forward.

"And Veressa," Theo said. "Oh, and Miles."

"And Wren," Errol added.

Sophia shook her head in wonder, hurrying to meet Martin at the base of the stairs. "My dear Sophia," he said, embracing her warmly. "How good it is to find you—older and wiser, I can see, but safe and sound."

She smiled up at the familiar bright eyes and wrinkled cheeks, feeling a surge of affection. "Martin, I cannot believe you are here."

Martin Metl laughed happily. "Nor can I! Here with you! At the foot of the greatest botanical wonder of the world!" He raised his cane triumphantly. "We have a great deal of catching up to do."

AND CATCH UP they did. All of Sophia's fellow travelers—with the exception of Casanova, who had left the day before to assure Smokey of their safe return from the Eerie Sea—were in one place. She could not stop being astonished, as the happy day wore on, to see her beloved fellow travelers together in one place: Miles and Theo, Calixta and Burr, Martin and Veressa, Goldenrod and Errol, Bittersweet and Datura, and Richard Wren, who was looking more like himself now that the Indies tattoos had faded.

It touched Sophia deeply to see so many people of diverse Ages, many of whom had never met, folding into one another's company as if they had known one another forever. The only person who was missing, she reflected, was Shadrack. As she looked around at her gathered friends, she committed the sight to memory—so that she could record it in her notebook and describe it to Shadrack when she returned home. They filled the deck of the boldevela: Miles standing at the mast, gesticulating wildly as he argued with Theo, who looked quite content with the argument; Calixta in her linen skirts, eating blueberries with her feet propped up on a chair; Burr snoozing under his hat; Martin, with his pant legs rolled up, engaging in enthusiastic conversation with Goldenrod, who examined his leg of wood and leg of silver with interest; Veressa, her thorned arms relaxed as she leaned out over the deck, describing to Errol the route they had taken from Nochtland; and Richard Wren, creating a sculpture out of paper for Datura's entertainment. She and Bittersweet watched the Australian captain as he folded and unfolded, cut and clipped, until a miniature moose appeared in his palm. Datura laughed, enchanted, and Wren smiled in satisfaction. Sophia realized that despite their disparate origins, varied dress, and oft-incompatible senses of humor, they also had a great deal in common. They acted on principle; they were courageous; and they helped fellow travelers. *With such friends behind me,* she thought, *it is no wonder we did not fail.*

When Burr finally awoke from his nap, Goldenrod and Errol began the story of what had happened to them in Salt Lick Station. They were interrupted by Calixta, who insisted that they were telling it wrong. "I saw a giant troll come out of the mist," she said. "And he was holding Errol's sword."

Errol rolled his eyes. "A troll," he scoffed.

"Naturally, I shot him," she continued.

"And what a good thing that you are such a lousy shot, or we would all be attending my funeral in Salt Lick."

"I was aiming to disable you," Calixta said defensively. "Not that *your* aim was any better." She raised her injured leg. Being Calixta, she had managed to find new linen skirts that complemented her bandages.

Sophia had already come to the conclusion that the knight she had seen was Errol and the dragon was Calixta, but she had very deliberately failed to mention the illusion to the pirate captain. She leaned forward. "But then what?"

"Then," Errol said grimly, "we all fought for our lives."

"And when the fog finally cleared, all the Encephalon agents were gone," Wren put in.

"Gone?" Theo asked. "Or dead?"

Burr was blunt. "Quite dead. And no one"—his voice was a trifle peevish—"has mentioned the fact that I managed to emerge—unscathed—with my hands still tied. Which I believe deserves notice."

"Well done, my dear brother," Calixta said dryly. "We have taken notice. There must be a prize of some sort, awarded to the valiant soul who emerges unscathed from the fog in the most unlikely way, and you would no doubt be the happy recipient."

"Actually, I believe I would," said Wren as everyone laughed. "If that fog hadn't struck, I would be aboard a vessel to Australia right now, on my way to serve a life sentence."

"Do you see?" Calixta said, patting Datura on the knee and beaming at her. "Your fog did us a great service."

Datura looked scandalized. "But it also ruined and ended many lives!"

"And it's exactly what Broadgirdle intended," Miles growled, frowning at no one in particular. "He knew the moment he found you that he would be ruining and ending *many* lives, all in the name of his dream for westward expansion. That was exactly what he wanted. You never had a chance against him, my girl."

Datura considered this in silence. "Consider that he also got the best of Mother and Grandfather," Bittersweet reminded her gently.

"Not to mention me," Goldenrod said.

"And me," Theo added quietly.

"*We* had the best of *him* in the end!" Miles exclaimed, pounding his fist against the mast.

"But did you know all this about Datura already when you left Boston?" Sophia asked.

Miles shook his head. "Not a bit of it. Well—we knew

about the existence of the fog, and we knew, of course, that Broadgirdle was pressing westward. That's all. We had no idea what the fog was. Shadrack wrote to Martin and Veressa, urging them to come north to investigate it, and I headed west to meet them. We had just found one another in the Indian Territories when Shadrack sent us a message by iron pigeon to say that you were here, in New Occident, and headed to Salt Lick."

"But we arrived in Salt Lick too late," Veressa said, speaking for the first time. "We found not only the destruction wrought by the fog, but also the second wave of destruction brought about by the New Occident troops. They had burned much of the city."

"And where were you by this point?" Sophia turned to Goldenrod, Errol, and the pirates.

"We," Burr said grimly, "were nursing our wounds. Or rather, I should say I was nursing Calixta's wounds and Goldenrod was nursing Errol's. You can imagine who had the better bargain there. I heard not a word of complaint pass Errol's lips. Meanwhile, Calixta . . ." He made a flourish with his arm, as if his sister's complaints were too many to enumerate.

"I don't know what you're talking about," Calixta said indignantly. "I have a great tolerance for pain, and I did not even wince when you sewed my stitches."

"Oh, naturally. You did not wince. But you complained something terrible about how crooked the stitches were, and how they were going to leave the wrong kind of scar instead of a scar you could boast about, and how your new raider dress was stained with blood, and on and on."

"Every one of those things is true!" Calixta cried, to general laughter. Even Datura had to smile.

"We," Errol said, "were camped outside of Salt Lick. We had seen the wall of bittersweet, and Goldenrod assured us it meant that you, Sophia, were safe. Then we had confirmation of it from Seneca, who flew ahead." Sophia thought of the sprig of goldenrod, pressed in the pages of her notebook. "It would have been impossible to catch up with you, because of our injuries. Several days went by, and we managed to avoid the troops only because Seneca warned us that they were coming."

"And then *we* arrived!" Miles said, throwing out his arms.

Calixta picked up the thread. "Miles, Veressa, and Martin arrived in the boldevela, and not a moment too late, for I was running out of clean clothes."

"Will Shadrack know that we are all safe?" asked Sophia.

"Iron pigeon," Miles said matter-of-factly. "He will know." He smiled at Sophia and put his arm around her, pulling her into a rough hug. "Of course, he will be much happier when he sees you in person, little explorer."

Sophia pulled herself free of Miles with difficulty, laughing. "I will be happier when I see him, too," she agreed.

42

THE TERMS

—1892, August 23—

All other policies enacted during the tenure of Prime Minister Gordon Broadgirdle will be subjected to review by committee. The parliament judges recognize the contributions of Cassandra Pierce in bringing the prime minister to justice and hereby appoint her the official steward of the review committee. Miss Pierce's knowledge of the prime minister's official business, along with her understanding of executive process, will prove invaluable for the committee's operations.

—Orders given by the New Occident parliament judges, August 18, 1892

THEY STAYED ANOTHER whole day, and Sophia spent much of it within the grove, with memories of Minna and Bronson. As much as she longed to stay—with her friends, and with the remembered presence of her parents—she also longed to return to Boston and Shadrack.

And so on August 23 the boldevela, somewhat overstuffed with its occupants, traveled onward to Oakring. Sophia leaned over the railing, watching the hills rise and fall behind them. Even when the valley was long lost from sight, the sense of quiet from the grove remained with her, and she began to wonder if that stillness would always be a part of her now, lodged there by the Red Woods.

Bittersweet and Datura rode Nosh, taking the narrow paths that cut through the woods more directly, and they stayed two miles from Oakring with an Eerie friend. The boldevela arrived in town in the afternoon, anchoring at the outskirts.

While Goldenrod, with Errol in tow, sought out an Elodean friend in the village, the pirates and Wren hastened to the tavern. Veressa and Martin remained with the boldevela, and Sophia, Theo, and Miles headed across the fields to Smokey's house. She was waiting for them in the doorway. Stepping out to meet them, she smiled broadly and threw her arms around Theo and Sophia at the same time. "I'm so glad to see you back safely," she said.

"We felt so terrible that we could not get back sooner," Sophia said. "I hope you did not send people to look for us."

"I did not, as it happens," the woman said, with amusement, "because on the eighteenth I was visited by some surprisingly communicative fireflies. They spelled out the word 'safe,' and I made a guess as to where they came from."

Sophia smiled at the thoughtfulness of the three sisters. "Oh! That was clever."

"How's your arm?" Smokey asked Theo.

"Very well." He grinned. "It held up. I slept through about three-quarters of the journey."

Smokey laughed. "Good. Very good—I'm glad you did. Miles," she said, reaching out a hand to be engulfed in Miles's massive palm. "Lovely to see you again."

Miles pulled her into a bear hug. "Thank you for saving our

Theo," he said gruffly. "Casanova told me how poorly he was. You brought him back."

"I only gave him the final push," Smokey said, extracting herself. "Casanova is the one who pulled him from the battle and brought him all the way here." She glanced over her shoulder at Casanova, who was leaning in the doorway.

"Yes, well." Miles scowled. "I already tried to thank him, and he said it was entirely due to you. It seems neither of you is willing to take the credit."

With a smile of his own, Casanova came forward to usher the travelers into the house. "Is it wise to take credit for saving such a scoundrel?" he asked, putting his arm around Theo's shoulders.

"I'm certainly not giving you any credit," Theo replied, looking up at him. "Way I see it, I was the one who got you out of Merret's company. You were just looking for a good excuse."

"Speaking of which," Casanova said, dropping his arm. He looked at Smokey. "Should we tell them now?"

Sophia had perched on a bench by the cold fireplace, and Theo sat beside her. Miles hovered, too restless to sit. "Tell us what?"

"It is official," Smokey said, smiling. "We have a new prime minister."

"Who?" Miles exclaimed.

"There was an emergency election within parliament," Smokey explained, "where so many people defected from Broadgirdle's Western Party that the New States Party gained a majority. New States appointed Gamaliel Shore the interim prime minister, until official elections can be held, but it is likely Shore will stay on."

"Finally!" Miles shouted, raising his hands dramatically to the ceiling. "A man with sense in the State House."

"Yes," Smokey agreed. "His first act was to extend the emergency act of parliament and officially end the war. His second was to forgive all deserters."

Theo gasped. Sophia threw her arms around him and squeezed him tightly. "Ow," he whispered.

"Sorry." She grinned. "But I am so, so, *so* relieved."

"Me, too. Obviously."

"And that's not all," Casanova said. "The war was ended on terms that will allow the Indian Territories and New Akan to remain a part of New Occident. His third act was to overrule the border closure."

There was stunned silence.

"I love that man," declared Miles.

"We can all go back to Boston!" Sophia exclaimed.

"And we can leave it again. And go back again. And leave once more." Miles sighed happily. "The Age of Exploration will be reborn."

ON THEIR SECOND evening in Oakring, Sophia and Theo gathered their fellow travelers at the round amphitheater by the giant oak. The good news from parliament, that New Occident was once again a peaceful place with open borders, was gladly received. Veressa and Martin were eager to visit Shadrack in a city they had never seen, and the pirates planned to contact the *Swan* by paquebot from Boston Harbor. But with open borders came more choices, and not every road led to Boston.

Casanova had already broken the news to Theo, and now he announced his decision to the group. "I've made up my mind to stay on here with Smokey," he said with a smile in her direction. He gestured at the great oak above them and then at the nearby town, its houses glowing with yellow lights. "Oakring could have no better medic, but if I train with her for a time, I might make myself useful somewhere else."

There were sounds of approval. "Perhaps you could look at my leg sometime," Calixta said. "The medic who cared for it was quite incompetent, and I am sure it would do better in your capable hands." She gave him a radiant smile.

Casanova blushed.

"Offensive *and* shameless," Burr said, shaking his head, appalled. "If it weren't for me, you would be limping around on a peg leg. No offense, Martin," he added to the white-haired botanist.

"None taken, my boy. Peg legs among pirates are a very different matter."

Smokey smiled back at Casanova, clearly happy with the plan, but Sophia looked at Theo, sitting beside her on one of the split-log benches, with concern. She knew how much he had grown to rely on Cas. "We'll just have to visit Oakring more often," Sophia said to Casanova and Smokey.

"Of course we will," Miles exclaimed. "Once a season, at least."

"Bittersweet, Datura," Goldenrod said. "Will you journey to Boston to join your mother and grandfather?"

Bittersweet shook his head. "We've already sent them word with the pigeons. We will wait for them here, near Oakring."

"I've seen enough of Boston," Datura said quietly. "Limited though my view was."

Sophia looked at Datura with sympathy. Privately, Bittersweet had reassured Sophia that with time Datura would heal. She would have three Weatherers with her, and she would, he said with confidence, one day be herself again. Sophia was not so sure; she had seen the garnet map, and she imagined that Datura's eyes had most likely seen even worse.

"Once Mother and Grandfather join us," Bittersweet told the other travelers, "we will retreat for a time. What we want most now is time together."

"Of course," Goldenrod said. "I regret that Errol and I will not be nearby, but you can always reach us through the old one."

Errol put his hand over Goldenrod's green one. "My fairy here has kindly agreed to travel with me on my fool's errand." He smiled at her.

"You are following the Ausentinian map to find your brother!" Sophia exclaimed.

"We are," Errol said. "I was persuaded when I read the map two days ago and found that a good portion of it had already taken place. So the hunt is on." Seneca screeched happily at this proclamation.

Sophia leaned forward. "What is the next part?"

Errol furrowed his brow. "I think our next puzzle to solve is this one: *Four islands spell h-o-m-e.*"

"Oh!" Burr exclaimed, with mock illumination. "Of course! So obvious!"

"Is it 'spell' as in letters or 'spell' as in magic?" Smokey asked.

Errol shook his head. "I have no idea."

"What islands begin with those letters?" Wren asked, seizing eagerly on the riddle.

"Or perhaps the *shapes* of the islands themselves spell 'home,'" suggested Veressa.

As the travelers debated the possible meanings of the map, Sophia considered what it would mean to part ways with Errol and Goldenrod. It pained her to think of traveling on without them, but she understood all too well the compulsion to search for lost family.

Wren, too, was taking his leave of them all. It was most likely that the League would conclude that Agent Richard Wren had met his end in Salt Lick, and Wren wished to do everything he could to maintain the illusion. Goldenrod had promised him safety with an Elodean recluse who would keep him hidden until the Australians forgot about him.

The prospect of parting from such dear friends was not easy. When the time arrived on the following day, Sophia found it most difficult to say good-bye to Goldenrod. But the Eerie promised that, with the new border policy, things would be different. Travel would be easier and more frequent, as it had been in the past. "I hope our quest for Errol's brother is quickly concluded and that we will see you in Boston before too long," she said reassuringly.

Sophia stood by the steps of the boldevela. Theo, Miles, the pirates, and the Metls were already aboard. Before she said her last good-byes, she wished aloud: "Could we all agree to meet sometime, somewhere?"

"I have an idea!" Miles cried from the deck. "Once a year, every year, in Oakring. We meet at Smokey's house."

"I'll have some rooms added," she said, smiling up at him.

"Let's meet on this day," Casanova suggested, looking around at them all. "August twenty-fifth. To celebrate the finding of friendship, and the finding of peace."

"Peace," Burr qualified, leaning over the edge of the deck, "but perhaps not peace of mind, if Calixta is invited."

Calixta cuffed him lightly. "An excellent suggestion. We will be here."

"As will we," Goldenrod assented, clasping Errol's hand, who gave a little bow of agreement. Seneca fluttered his wings in approval.

"As will I," Wren agreed.

"We'll come, too, of course," Bittersweet said. Nosh, standing beside him, snorted indignantly. "With Nosh."

Sophia looked forward to the year ahead, now, knowing she would see her friends again at the end of it, and it made the sight of them, waving and diminishing and finally disappearing as the boldevela sailed away, easier to bear.

Epilogue
New Maps

—1893, January 18: 14-Hour 11—

Some of the stories collected here come from travelers I met in Boston, and some come from travelers I met elsewhere over the course of my own travels. What they have in common is how they shed light on their Age of origin, describing a way of thinking or a custom or an explanation for how something came into being. These stories demonstrate differences across the Ages, it is true; but they also demonstrate that in every Age, storytelling is vital to comprehending, interpreting, and appreciating the world around us.

—From Sophia Tims's Travelers from the Disruption: Collected Stories

"YES, YES, YES!" Shadrack exclaimed, looking over Sophia's shoulder. "That's it! You've done it!"

Sophia beamed. "It worked."

"Of course it worked," her uncle said affectionately. "You've been practicing for two months."

Miles, sitting in the armchair of the map room in the basement, raised his teacup to toast the accomplishment. "Well done, Sophia." He did not lift his eyes from the book he was reading.

"You could at least pretend to be impressed," Shadrack said dryly.

"Give me exploration maps over memory maps every time. You know my thoughts on the subject." He wet his thumb and turned the page.

"Well, *I'm* impressed," Theo said with a grin, getting up from his seat across from Miles. "Can I read it now?"

Sophia looked shocked. "I only just started. It's nowhere near done."

"But it's an excellent foundation, Sophia," Shadrack said with pride. "Your memories are crystal clear."

"Theo's . . ." Sophia considered. "Are not."

"I was wounded. I was asleep half the time," Theo protested.

"It will help when Casanova visits and we can add what he remembers," she said diplomatically.

Her memory map of the journey to the Stone Age, the realm of the three sisters, was coming along well. She had, as Shadrack reminded her, spent months perfecting the techniques that he had taught her in the fall. Having gratefully abandoned his post at the ministry and resumed his work at the university, Shadrack had much more time for mapmaking and map-teaching. And Sophia, of course, jumped at the chance. Every day when she returned from school, she read the manuscripts Shadrack left for her and practiced the exercises he laid out. Each night before bed, she practiced the map-reading that she had learned with Goldenrod and Bittersweet, studying the remnants of the world around her: leaves and stones, bark and soil.

Sophia settled into these routines, but there was a difference. With map-reading, it seemed that every day brought with it a new discovery. Finally, in January, she had begun to create her own map.

She was pleased with the process. It was an act of recollection, for it drew on all the sights and sounds and emotions she had experienced; and so making the map became a way of reliving them. At the same time, it was an act of creation; she felt herself infusing each sight, sound, and emotion with meaning and fullness. She loved it.

"Well, Shadrack," Miles said, finishing his tea and putting his book down with an impatient air. "I came here because you said you'd found a map, not because I wanted to watch Sophia practice mapmaking."

"Fine, yes, my rude friend," Shadrack said, walking around the table, opening a tin box and removing a folded packet of worn paper. "I bought it at the dreck market."

"Aha!" Miles exclaimed, eyes widening. He took the folded paper eagerly in hand. "And what does it show?"

"A city—a city on an island, in the far western Baldlands."

"Where the Eerie are from?" Sophia asked.

"A bit farther south."

Miles spread the map out on the table, and the four of them gathered around it, scrutinizing its contents. It was drawn by someone with a talented but untrained hand. The streets were tight and narrow, and a network of dots fell over the city like a constellation of stars. Sophia pointed at them. "What are these?"

"The legend is torn, as you can see," Shadrack said. "They could be anything. Since they are enumerated, I would guess they are all places of one kind."

"Or they could be numbered, like steps," Sophia suggested.

"Here is what caught my eye." He indicated the notation in the corner, beside the compass rose.

Theo read aloud, "1842. Believed lost in 1799."

"So the map was drawn in 1842?" Sophia speculated.

"And was the map believed lost, or was the *city* believed lost?" Shadrack wondered.

"I recognize this shape!" Miles exclaimed, drawing his finger around the island. "I have never been there, but it is thought to be uninhabited."

"Exactly," Shadrack said triumphantly.

"And it might not be?" asked Sophia.

Before Shadrack could answer, Miles thumped his fist on the table. "Fantastic!" he cried. "I will plan an expedition at once."

"I thought you might want to," Shadrack said calmly. "But I would recommend we wait until the summer, or at least the late spring. Travel across the continent in this weather would be unpleasant, to say the least."

"Nonsense, man," Miles exclaimed. "The snow is no obstacle."

"What about the school year? Sophia will not want to miss her classes, Winnie will want to but *should* not, and Nettie's father certainly won't consider letting her leave before summer."

Sophia seized her uncle's arm. "You mean we're all going together?"

"Of course." Shadrack smiled.

"Yes, yes, yes!" She practically danced.

Theo laughed. "This is going to be a long winter of waiting."

"Can't she take her books with her?" demanded Miles, with an air of impatience.

Shadrack sighed. "You have no conception of the scholarly life, Miles. It depresses me. I can't understand how you have made it this far as my friend."

"I simply ignore everything about you that is irritating."

Sophia and Theo glanced at one another with knowing smiles, anticipating one of the two old friends' epic and long-winded squabbles. Quietly, they left the table and made their way to the stairs, climbing up to the first floor. Mrs. Clay was writing letters in the study, and she waved her pen at them briefly as they walked by. They climbed again, to the second floor, and ended in Sophia's room, where the window overlooked the rooftops of East Ending Street.

"Secret chocolate?" Sophia asked.

"Absolutely."

Sophia opened her wardrobe and drew out a box, sent to her by Mazapán, their friend in Nochtland, and delivered by the pirates. She pulled out two chocolate spoons and handed one to Theo.

Perching before the window in unspoken agreement, they looked out over the city of Boston and ate their chocolate spoons. A companionable silence fell over them. The snow that had been waiting all day in the clouds overhead began to fall, filling the air with white dust and an air of possibility.

ACKNOWLEDGMENTS

I am grateful to the librarians, booksellers, and readers who have followed Sophia and Theo so far on their adventures. You've made me reluctant to end the journey! A special thanks to bookseller extraordinaire Kenny Brechner, for indefatigable enthusiasm and erudition.

Viking and the Penguin Young Readers Group have carried this surprising voyage to its happy conclusion. I am grateful to Ken Wright, Jim Hoover, Eileen Savage, Dave A. Stevenson, Stephanie Hans, Janet Pascal, Abigail Powers, Krista Ahlberg, Eileen Kreit, Julia McCarthy, Jessica Shoffel, Tara Shanahan, Amanda Mustafic, Zarren Kuzma, and the sales team (especially Jackie Engel and Biff Donovan) for ensuring that these stories made their way from sketchy lines in my head to beautiful books in readers' hands.

Sharyn November, were it not for your passionately offbeat (and excellent) taste, this trilogy would never have made it onto paper. From that first conversation we had, in which the shared favorites tumbled out by the handfuls, I've felt fortunate to have found such a like-minded reader and thinker.

Dorian Karchmar, thank you for the impeccable sensibility you bring to writing and the wisdom you bring to everything else about the process.

And, as ever, I could not have finished this book without the judicious comments of early readers. To my parents, my brother, and Pablo—thank you for leaping into every stage of this story and cheering me all the way. Mamá and Papá, I've noticed that you always keep my books in view on the coffee table. Thanks for treating all my scribbles, even the abysmal ones from when I was ten, as if they deserve pride of place.

Alton, knowing you will read a manuscript the moment I hand it to you persuades me, all the time and every day, that I'm doing something worthwhile. These stories are always somehow at their best in your imagination—thank you.

This book is dedicated to Rowan, who may someday actually read it. In the meantime, you are filling the world with words far more lovely, fantastical, funny, and profound. Thank you for the constant inspiration.